THE
COMPLICATION

THE COMPLICATION

AMANDA DuBOIS

A CAMILLE DELANEY MYSTERY

GIRL FRIDAY BOOKS

 **GIRL FRIDAY BOOKS**

Published by Girl Friday Books™, Seattle
www.girlfridaybooks.com

Produced by Girl Friday Productions

Design: Paul Barrett
Production editorial: Jaye Whitney Debber
Project management: Sara Spees Addicott

Image credits: cover © Shutterstock/Hdc Photo, Shutterstock/NataLT

ISBN (hardcover): 978-1-954854-34-5
ISBN (e-book): 978-1-954854-35-2

Library of Congress Control Number: 2021920275

First edition

To my mother, Patricia

CHAPTER ONE

Everything unique about a person disappears once the blue surgical drapes are in place. Dallas Jackson was no exception; all that could be seen of him was a large orange rectangle of skin glowing under the harsh operating room lights. Digital readouts on the anesthesia equipment flashed and beeped as the surgeon whisked into the dingy, white-tiled operating room, holding his freshly scrubbed hands out in front of his chest.

Nurse Sally Berwyn snapped Dr. Willcox's gloves around the cuffs of his gown and jerked back her birdlike hands as if she had just been burned. She repeated the procedure with assistant surgeon Dr. Burton, her eyes avoiding both men.

The scraping of the stainless steel instrument stand across the floor was like brakes squealing just before a high-speed crash. The sound exaggerated the familiar chill of the operating room.

Vic Jones looked more like a pirate than a scrub tech in a small-town hospital. He wore a black-and-silver Raiders scarf fashioned into a surgical hat and a thick silver hoop earring in his left ear. "So, do you and the wife have big plans for the Fourth of July fireworks tonight, Dr. Willcox?" Vic asked as he organized the instruments on his stand.

"We sure do. You ready, Sally?" Willcox asked the tiny nurse who was struggling to open a valve connected to a canister under the table by a stretch of clear tubing.

"Just a sec. Okay, go ahead. It's on." The patient's chart clattered to the floor, and the nurse swore under her breath as she stooped down to retrieve it. She sat down, nearly missing the stool.

Willcox directed his attention to the patient and held out his hand, palm up, waiting for the familiar *slap* of the scalpel. "Skin incision."

"Two fifty-three." The slurping suction machine nearly drowned out Nurse Berwyn's voice.

Willcox watched the thin line behind the scalpel transform into an oozing incision. He held his palm out for the electric cautery. He said nothing. They had been through this drill thousands of times. Willcox felt his pulse quicken as the pungent smell of burning tissue permeated his nostrils. A fog of wispy smoke gathered over the patient as he zapped the small bleeders.

Dr. Burton held the trocar over the patient expectantly. "You ready?" His booming voice was a sharp contrast to his slight stature.

"Yep. Let's do it." Willcox took the stake-like instrument and grabbed a fold of the patient's yellow-stained skin, placing the tip of the stake into the small incision. He took a breath, stood up straight to get good leverage, and grunted as he threw his entire body weight against the instrument, shoving it forcefully into the patient's upper abdomen. He deftly removed the inner, pointed portion of the trocar, leaving just a stainless steel sleeve approximately an inch in diameter protruding from the skin.

"CO_2." Willcox waited while Vic connected a tube to the trocar. A cobra-like hissing pierced the silence for the several minutes it took to expand the patient's abdomen so that the instruments could be inserted though the sleeve.

"His pressure's dropping," Dick Stark, the anesthesiologist, reported. "His BP was one sixty over ninety before I put him to sleep. It's one twenty over sixty-four now."

"Thank you, Dr. Stark," Burton responded.

"BP one hundred over fifty-two; pulse one twenty. Is this guy bleeding?"

Willcox continued slowly threading tiny instruments and a fiber-optic camera into the patient's abdomen through the stainless steel sleeve.

The anesthesiologist twisted around toward Nurse Berwyn, who was flitting around the room, checking and rechecking the equipment. "What's the blood loss, Sally?"

She ran over to the table. The paper drapes rustled as she pulled them aside. "The suction canister's got about six hundred cc's of blood in it."

Willcox glanced down and noted the plastic canister gradually filling with thick red liquid.

Willcox and Burton locked eyes over their surgical masks.

"Pulse ox is dropping." Stark turned and tended to the dials on his anesthesia cart. "We got trouble," he said firmly. "BP's ninety over fifty-five. I've pushed volume expanders and ephedrine with no response. This guy's bleeding from somewhere."

Willcox looked at the TV monitor that transmitted an image from inside the patient's abdomen. It had been carefully angled so it was out of the line of vision of the anesthesiologist. "He's not bleeding. I have a perfect view of the operative field." He continued to manipulate the instruments through the stainless steel sleeve for several minutes as the nurse kept her eye on the clock. She hovered over the anesthesiologist, clearly concerned.

Stark swiveled on his stool, his long arms grabbing vials off his cart. He frantically drew up medicines in various syringes while keeping his attention on the digital readouts to see if any of the medications were producing results. "He's bleeding. Trust me." The anesthesiologist quickly slid another needle into the patient's IV. "You're taking way too long screwing around in there."

"No . . . he's not bleeding. Here, I'll stick another trocar in and get a better look around."

"I wouldn't," Stark snapped. "You'd better get him open. You got a bleeder."

Willcox looked at Burton. "Hand me another trocar, will ya, Carl?"

Burton stared directly at the anesthesiologist as he very slowly handed Willcox the instrument.

Stark's voice rose an octave. "You can't repair anything through that scope. You really need to get him open. Now!"

Willcox looked at the large institutional clock over the doorway. It read three fifteen.

"How much blood do we have in the canister, Sally?" Stark demanded.

She squatted next to the table. "Nine hundred cc's." Her shaky voice was muffled by the surgical drapes.

"Okay, Doctor, you got a pumper." Stark's face flushed as he started an IV in the patient's other arm.

"I'm looking right at the field, and there's no bleeding in sight. The patient's having a reaction to the anesthesia. That's your problem, not mine. Give him some drugs if you're so goddamned concerned about his pressure," Willcox said as he continued to operate, asking for instruments.

"Twelve hundred cc's!" Sally pleaded.

"His pressure's bottoming. For Christ's sake, he's lost a quarter of his blood volume! Get him open!" Stark demanded.

Willcox waited as Vic hooked up the carbon dioxide again. "It'll just take a while to get the operative field open so I can investigate the possibility of any internal bleeding."

"Fifteen hundred cc's." Sally's disembodied voice filled the OR.

"Keep the CO_2 going, Vic. I'm getting a better look at the field, and there's nothing out of the ordinary here."

Stark stood up. "Okay, no more fucking around. Let's get going."

Willcox glared at the anesthesiologist. "You sit down and shut up. I'm the surgeon here! You do your job, and I'll do mine."

Stark's long, slender fingers turned up the second IV so it was running wide open. "Sally, get me some more blood in here stat!" he said, looking directly at Willcox. "I'm telling you for the last time, Dr. Willcox. Your patient is in hypovolemic shock. Open him *now* and get the bleeding under control!"

Willcox stepped back from the patient and folded his arms across his chest. "So, you wanna be a surgeon? Be my guest!" He swept his arm in an arc.

Burton chuckled quietly.

"Get Dr. Gonzalez in here!" Stark directed the nurse. "Tell him it's an emergency."

"He's lost seventeen hundred cc's and counting." Sally's eyes darted from Willcox to Stark as she headed for the phone, narrowly avoiding tripping over the wires snaking across the floor.

"Okay! Fine! You want the patient open? How's this?" Willcox pushed past Vic's bulky shoulders and grabbed a scalpel off the instrument stand. He tore open the drape and petulantly slit the large orange globe from the pubic bone to the breastbone. "Is this open enough for you?"

Sally stretched the phone cord and craned her neck to see the clock. "Laparotomy, three twenty-five." She quickly scribbled on her baggy scrub pants.

Stark had the blood set up in the warmer among the plethora of IVs already hanging around the head of the table. "Get me more blood, Sally! And plasma expanders! And hurry!"

"They're on the way."

Willcox and Burton slowly prodded around the deep incision. "Okey doke," Willcox said slowly, "here it is . . . Just a little puncture in the aorta. Don't get so bent outta shape. I can repair this with one hand tied behind my back. Hang up the phone, Sally."

Sally trembled as she wrapped herself in the phone cord. "Hello, Dr. Gonzalez? It's Willcox. He hit the aorta. Please hurry."

"I told you not to call him! I'm the surgeon. You follow my orders."

"How soon will Gonzalez be here?" Stark asked Sally anxiously.

"It usually takes him about five minutes. His place is close—and he drives fast in an emergency."

"Get some fresh frozen plasma, and order more whole blood. This guy's oozing like a stuck pig." Stark looked like an octopus at the head of the table, his gangly arms twisting knobs, opening vials, and sticking syringes into the jumble of IV tubing. "Do you have the aorta clamped off yet, Dr. Willcox?"

Willcox watched the blood squirt violently from the aorta and slowly fill the patient's gaping abdomen. "What the hell else do you think I've been doing here?"

"Can you open up another pack of clamps when you have a sec, Sally?" Vic winked flirtatiously at the harried nurse as she popped a freshly sterilized pack onto the instrument tray.

On her way back, Sally pulled the suction canister out from under the table. Her eyes widened. "There's nineteen hundred cc's of blood in the suction now!"

The intercom crackled. "Dr. Gonzalez is here!"

"Shit! I can't get this guy's pressure up!" Stark screamed as he wiped the sweat from his forehead with the back of his hand.

A man in his late thirties backed into the room, his wet arms raised out in front of him. He shuffled through the multicolored wrappers strewn haphazardly across the floor of the operating room and grabbed a gown off the table. "Okay . . . What's going on, Willcox?" Dr. Max Gonzalez asked impatiently.

Willcox sighed. "The patient's aorta was slightly perforated when I advanced the trocar." He dropped his voice. "I *immediately* opened him up and clamped the aorta. Stark overreacted. I've got everything under control. You can leave."

Gonzalez gloved himself and roughly elbowed his way into the surgical field. "Blood loss?" He glanced at Sally.

"Twenty-two hundred cc's."

"Holy shit!" Gonzalez stared at Willcox and shook his head. He turned his full attention to the patient. "Sally, you scrub in! Get me more clamps! Stat! Let's move it! *Now!*" Gonzalez placed his entire hand over the aorta and stood on his tiptoes to stop the bleeding. He turned to Willcox. "Dr. Willcox, your services are no longer necessary. I'm officially taking over."

"The hell you are!"

Gonzalez stood firmly, holding his hand over the aorta. A thick pool of dark-red blood crept up to the cuff of his gown. "Look, this guy's got disseminated intravascular coagulopathy, and we both know that means he has a shitty chance of surviving the next few hours." Gonzalez grabbed a huge clamp. "Give me some room here." He slid the instrument around the backside of the aorta. "I need some suction! Let's hurry it up, Sally!"

Sally hooked her foot under the step stool and dragged it through the sticky puddle of blood and climbed up next to Gonzalez. The metallic smell of blood was everywhere.

The rapid clicking of surgical clamps filled the room. "Need I remind you, Willcox, I'm a board-certified vascular surgeon. And you're not," Gonzalez said without looking up. "You want to explain to the disciplinary board why you wouldn't relinquish care of this patient?"

Willcox stood close enough to Gonzalez to breathe down his neck. "You wouldn't dare."

"The hell I wouldn't." Gonzalez wiggled his shoulders irritably. "Now get out and leave me alone so I can try to undo this mess."

"He's right, Andy. Let's go." Burton grabbed Willcox by the elbow and pulled him firmly toward the thick double doors. "Good day, everyone. We'll give the family an update on the patient's status."

"Here we go again," Gonzalez said to no one in particular as the doors swung shut.

CHAPTER TWO

Camille Delaney leaned over her husband's shoulder, watching him clean and fillet the salmon he and their three daughters had caught that morning. Their annual Fourth of July salmon BBQ was scheduled to begin in less than an hour, and, as usual, they were running late.

Camille wrinkled her nose as Sam threw another handful of fish guts off the deck of their Seattle houseboat and into the water. "I don't know how you can do that."

Sam paused. "They're fish, Camille. They have tiny little brains. They don't know what hit them." He lined the fish up in a perfect row on the blood-soaked newspaper and, starting at one end, began to cut off the fins.

"Do you think the fish families swimming around out there miss these guys?" Camille asked only half-jokingly.

"Probably no more than some of your divorce clients miss their kids."

"That's a low blow, Dr. Taylor." Camille recalled with fondness the day she had met the handsome resident during her first career as head nurse in the emergency room at Boston General Hospital. With the exception of his silver-streaked hair, her husband hadn't changed much in the ensuing twenty-one years. She smiled.

"Well, at least the fish don't pretend to care about each other." Sam stacked the last fillet on a clean newspaper. "I don't know how you can sit there and watch families get chewed up and torn apart day in and day out. If you ask me, these fish are better off. At least we appreciate their sacrifice."

"You have a point. I don't imagine that there are many baby fish held hostage out there just so the mommy or daddy fish can get a better financial settlement," Camille agreed.

"Like I said, it's a heartless game you play, babe."

"Well, I don't see you complaining about the new Boston Whaler I bought you for your birthday." It had been such fun to see the look on his face that day as he came out on the deck of their houseboat to see their three daughters all bundled up and ready for a ride in their dad's new boat.

"Yeah, you've come a long way from the days when you barely got a paycheck." Sam methodically wrapped the fish in a clean piece of newspaper, tucking the corners to form a perfect package.

"You mean back when I felt like I was actually making a difference in the world, representing plaintiffs who were taking on big insurance companies in the name of truth and justice?" Camille grabbed Sam's hand and pulled him up from his position squatting on the deck. "You know, I never thought I'd miss scrapping around with those insurance assholes."

"As I recall, truth and justice didn't pay the girls' tuition."

"But it sure felt better than arguing about who's gonna get the condo at Lake Chelan and who gets the house in Vail."

Sam handed the neatly wrapped fish to Camille. "There you go. Now you can pretend that you got the fish from the market, and you won't have to admit that you're eating some poor salmon's father or brother." He kissed her on the cheek.

Camille turned around to see their oldest daughter, sixteen-year-old Angela, standing in the doorway, hollering at a group of her friends who were running down the wide cement dock that was lined with large elegant "floating homes." Angela shrieked as she ducked to avoid a water balloon that bounced off Sam's shoulder and hit the new leaded glass window in the blue houseboat next to the Delaney-Taylor's.

Sam grabbed a kayak paddle perched next to their front door and splashed the kids as they hopped onto the houseboat. One of the boys swore loudly as he dropped the end of his sleeping bag in the lake while fending off a surprise attack from another gang on an inflatable rubber raft. He saw Camille and quickly clamped his hand over his mouth.

"Okay, children." Camille glared jokingly at her husband. "Take the balloon fight up on the roof deck. And try not to hit any of the neighbors' windows." Camille tousled her husband's wavy salt-and-pepper hair. "And you are no help at all." She laughed.

Camille glanced at her watch and headed up to the large gourmet kitchen on the second floor of the two-thousand-square-foot floating home. Camille loved the reverse floor plan. The city view was so spectacular. "And by the way, I could use some help here." Camille looked at Angela, who was running up the stairs into the living area, and gestured with her head at the bag of corn on the butcher-block island in the middle of the kitchen. She unwrapped the fish and plopped it into the teriyaki marinade. Her friends had been to parties at her house often enough to know that party prep was simply part and parcel of the evening's entertainment. She was never ready on time. "Let's get moving," she shouted at Angela, whose perfectly round face was temporarily obliterated by a huge pink bubble as she grabbed the brown paper bag of corn and headed out to the deck to husk it.

As they began to husk the corn, Robin, Camille's surrogate sister, breezed into the kitchen carrying a heaping platter of gooey nachos. She dodged the parade of screaming teenagers racing by, their water balloons poised for attack. Robin balanced the heavy tray in one hand as she pushed away a tendril of frizzy brown hair that had escaped from a haphazardly placed ponytail. "I used low-fat ground beef, but that fat-free cheese wouldn't melt, so I went ahead with the Monterey Jack."

Camille cleared a place for the nachos by rearranging open containers of soy sauce and sesame oil. She brushed a pile of ginger remnants into her hand. "Here."

Robin put down the platter and started cleaning up after her friend. "God, you really know how to make a mess."

Camille grabbed the T-shirt of a six-foot-tall adolescent boy racing to catch up with his friends. "Hey, slow down, you guys. And please take the water balloons outside!" Camille ran her fingers through her short dark hair as she greeted the first group of adult partygoers ascending the stairway into her living room.

By nine thirty, the party was in full swing. Laughter filled the huge kitchen-living area. Smoke swirled around the Weber kettle grill, and the aroma of mesquite salmon floated in through the open french doors. Camille bopped around the kitchen in time with marimba music that pulsated through the ceiling from the rooftop deck. The ring of Robin's cell phone could barely be heard above the din. The name *Gloria* flashed on the phone.

"Robin, Gloria's calling!" Angela yelled up the stairs to the rooftop deck.

"Can you grab it? I'll be right down!"

"Happy Fourth of July!" Angela screamed. "Sure, she's right here." She handed the phone to Robin.

"Hello?" Robin plugged her free ear with her hand so she could hear. "Oh my God! When? Where are you? I'll be right there."

Robin fell into the nearest chair, her eyes unfocused.

Camille stopped arranging the huge tray of grilled veggies and wiped her hands on a green-and-white dish towel. She felt a twinge of butterflies as she dropped into the oversized chair next to Robin and gave her a hug. "What happened? What's the matter?"

Robin was clearly in shock. "I gotta go. It's my dad. He's in the hospital, something about a surgical complication. Oh my God." She hunched over and took a shallow breath.

"Surgery? When did your dad have surgery?" Camille asked. "I didn't know he was sick."

"It was some kind of an emergency."

Waves of nausea overcame Camille. As a former nurse, she knew that doctors rarely performed surgery on holidays. It must have been serious. Camille's heart sank as she pictured her friend and mentor lying on an operating room table. *One step at a time. Maybe it was just an appendectomy or something.*

"What hospital's he in?" Camille knew enough to be wary of hospitals in small towns like Friday Harbor in the San Juan Islands, where Robin's dad, Dallas, lived with his wife, Gloria, aboard the forty-two-foot wooden sailboat he had built himself.

"Friday Harbor General."

Camille drew a sharp breath. Robin and Dallas were much more than friends to Camille. They had met years ago when she had answered an ad in the *Daily*, offering free room and board at Dallas's drafty but charming old urban cabin on Portage Bay, across from the University of Washington. The deal was free rent in exchange for someone who would hang out with his ten-year-old daughter. It was family at first sight.

Camille told herself to stop jumping to conclusions. But the thought of Dallas undergoing emergency surgery in a small-town hospital on the Fourth of July bounced around inside her head like a pinball. Dallas had taught her long ago not to let negative thoughts overtake her and that she could always center herself by taking deep, slow Kundalini breaths. Camille stood up and tried to breathe away the fear that was currently washing through her body.

Robin's eyes slowly came back into focus. "He had to have emergency gallbladder surgery this afternoon, around three o'clock. There was some kind of complication, and he's in intensive care." Her voice cracked. "They're not sure he's going to make it. The doctor said something about an aneurysm. Cam, what does that mean?"

Emergency gallbladder surgery? Shit. As far as Camille could remember, there was no reason on earth why someone would need emergency gallbladder surgery on a holiday. The Kundalini breaths didn't seem to be working.

Sam danced through the deck door into the kitchen. He twirled around, gyrating his pelvis, and sang Elvis's "Hound Dog" into the BBQ tongs, then stopped abruptly and threw the tongs onto the countertop. "What's up?"

Robin spoke softly. "Dallas is in intensive care."

Sam pulled off his stained apron and sat on the footstool in front of Robin, holding her knees. "What happened?" he asked softly.

Camille watched her husband comfort their friend. He was a gentle man, with more yin than yang—or was it more yang than yin? At any rate, he had a way about him that set him distinctly apart from any other man Camille had ever known.

"It was an emergency," Robin whispered.

At times like this, Camille was grateful to have a doctor in the family, even though Sam was a research epidemiologist who hadn't practiced clinical medicine in twenty years.

Sam grabbed the phone. "I'll call and find out what's going on. What hospital's he in?"

"Friday Harbor General."

Camille caught Sam's gaze. His look spoke volumes. She knew he too was questioning the reason for doing so-called emergency gallbladder surgery on a holiday in a small-town hospital.

Smoke began to pour in off the deck. Camille jumped up and headed out to rescue the salmon while Sam rubbed Robin's back as he popped in his EarPods.

Camille hastily piled the salmon fillets on a platter and climbed up to the rooftop deck, where a sea of colorfully adorned bodies bounced and swayed to the beat of the live marimba band. Drinks seemed to be supernaturally suspended in outstretched hands. She scanned the party for her paralegal, Amy.

Camille handed her the fish. "Can you keep an eye on the food for me?" She hollered, "Dallas is in the hospital. I'll be back up in a bit."

"Don't worry. I've got everything under control." Amy shot Camille a worried look. "Go ahead."

Just as Camille opened the kitchen door, her middle daughter, thirteen-year-old Libby, and three of Libby's dripping-wet friends threaded past her, snaking their way up to the party. Libby's delicate appearance was in complete contradiction to her outspoken personality.

"What's going on with Dad and Robin?" Libby hung from her perch halfway up the ladder.

Camille tried to sound casual. "Dallas is in the hospital. He had some kind of complication in surgery."

Libby stopped. "I hope he didn't have to go to some Podunk hospital. Those places are full of quacks, aren't they, Mom?"

Camille looked down, searching for an explanation that would satisfy Libby's curiosity. But her pause was a dead giveaway.

"Mom! Oh my God. He's in some icky little hospital, isn't he?"

With Libby, Camille wasn't always sure who was the mother and who was the daughter. Ever since Angela and Libby had made their dramatic entrance into the lives of the Delaney-Taylor family on a 747 from Korea when they were four and seven years old, it had been obvious to Camille that Libby was a very old soul. As it turned out, Libby never had entirely fit in with her peers and was currently in the process of dragging the entire family through a long and tortuous childhood.

Libby ran past Camille and threw herself, wet bathing suit and all, onto their friend's lap. "Oh my God, Robin! Oh my God!"

Robin smoothed Libby's tangled hair. "Thanks, Libs. He's gonna be fine." Robin's voice was uncharacteristically soft.

Robin and Libby curled up together in the big cream-colored chair. Their eyes reflected their fervent prayer for Dallas's health, but from the looks on their faces, they feared the worst.

Sam put down his phone. "The nurse said Dallas had a congenital condition called an aortic aneurysm. Apparently, the doctor inadvertently hit the aneurysm with one of the instruments." He sounded stern. Like a doctor. "He's extremely critical. Robin, you'd better get up there." He turned to Camille. "Tony's upstairs. Can you go ask him to get Robin on a flight up to the Island ASAP?"

Camille rushed up to the deck and yelled into the ear of the lanky retired airline pilot who owned and operated the local floatplane service. "Hey, Tony!" She gently yanked his gray ponytail. "Can you get Robin up to Friday Harbor? Like right now?"

Tony was lost in the music. "Are you crazy? No one's flying out of Lake Union tonight. The place is completely closed to air traffic because of the fireworks!" The aloha shirt would have looked ridiculous on anyone else in Seattle, but it was so very Tony. He held a Full-Sail Amber Ale in one hand and a clove cigarette in the other. Both were still as the rest of his body gyrated like a Sufi dancer.

"How 'bout Lake Washington? Kenmore must be open."

"What's the rush? I can get her on a flight tomorrow." Eyes closed, he didn't miss a beat.

"It's Dallas. He's in intensive care."

Tony's head snapped around, and his body stiffened. "What do you mean? I just had dinner with them on their sailboat last night. He must've eaten three platefuls of enchiladas. With lots of Tabasco. He was fine." He pulled his phone out of his pocket. "I'll see if Steve can take her up." He held up his beer. "I can't exactly fly tonight. How's she gonna get to Kenmore? The traffic's a nightmare."

"She can take the Boston Whaler. It's not more than an hour to Kenmore from here by boat." Camille gave Tony a peck on the cheek and wound her way through the party to Sam, who was leaning on the rail, looking across the lake at Gas Works Park, where the Seattle Symphony would soon be accompanying the fireworks.

At exactly ten o'clock, a hush fell over the crowd. A helicopter flew around the lake with an enormous American flag hanging proudly from its underbelly while the symphony thundered the national anthem. A couple hundred thousand spectators stood at the perimeter of the lake with their hands over their hearts.

The fireworks had taken on special significance for Camille after her adopted daughters had been sworn in as citizens at an emotional ceremony on the Fourth of July several years earlier. It seemed beyond comprehension that this fateful day in Dallas's life would happen on the family's special holiday. Camille squeezed Sam's elbow and whispered into his ear. "I'm going with Robin. I can't just wait around here—besides, she's gonna flip out when she sees her dad on all that equipment in intensive care." Camille kissed her husband. "I gotta go."

Sam put his hand under Camille's chin and looked her directly in the eye. "You're going to fly up to the Island now? Tonight?"

"It's really important to me."

"You don't fly with anyone but Tony. And you never fly at night. Are you sure you want to do this?"

"I don't have any choice." Camille didn't even try to blink back the tears. Twenty years earlier, she had crashed while piloting an unfamiliar floatplane. Ever since, she'd been terrified to fly in the bouncy little planes and generally only flew when her friend Tony was at the controls.

Sam kissed her hard on the lips as a shower of purple, red, and blue fireworks burst overhead and the symphony belted out the *William Tell Overture*. "How do you plan to get to Kenmore? The traffic's impossible."

"We're taking the Whaler. It'll only take about an hour."

"Are you sure?"

"Yep. I have to go. And Tony found a pilot who can fly us up tonight."

"Okay, then call me when you get there." He kissed her again.

Camille ran down to her bedroom, frantically packed a duffel, and grabbed her laptop, then hurried out to where Robin waited on the deck next to the sixteen-foot Boston Whaler. "Hop aboard." Camille untied the mooring lines.

Camille's heart pounded in her ears as she navigated the boat through the narrow channel behind the row of houseboats. Robin's thick, curly ponytail was sticking out of the back of Libby's autographed Mariners spring training baseball cap. It was the thirteen-year-old's prized possession, and Camille knew what an act of generosity it had been to give it to Robin for good luck. She smiled through her tears.

Out on the lake, Camille slowly threaded the skiff between giant sailboats and huge cabin cruisers as wildly colorful fireworks exploded in the night sky. Trails of smoke and sparkling embers spiraled down around them while symphony music floated across the water. Camille pushed gently on the throttle and headed past the rowing club and under the drawbridge. The lights of UW Medical Center, Camille's alma mater, loomed on her left, and the waterfront community on Portage Bay, where Camille had lived years ago with Robin and Dallas, twinkled off to her right. Fireworks boomed behind her in the distance as she guided the boat into the Montlake Cut, its steep sides funneling her under another drawbridge. The slimy cement walls served as a canvas for all kinds of athletic-inspired artwork. "Holy Name class of 2017 rules!" shouted the north side in maroon and gray. The south side was purple and gold. "UW crew slew!" Camille thought of the many happier days she had spent cruising through the cut as part of the festive parade of yachts on the opening day of boating season, which took place on the first Saturday of May. Now, it wasn't until they had passed Husky Stadium and moved out into the stillness of Lake Washington that Camille realized what a dark, moonless night it was. It would be the worst possible situation for landing a floatplane.

CHAPTER THREE

Camille looked nervously out the tiny window into the inky nothingness as the floatplane taxied noisily out onto the lake. Steve, the young pilot, turned to Camille and gave her a thumbs-up. She forced her cottony, dry lips into a weak half smile in reply and gripped the arms of her seat with clammy hands as the plane bounced down the lake, gaining speed for takeoff. Camille sat up tall to see over Steve's shoulder and stared at the red gauges and dials glowing across the compact dashboard. She peered suspiciously at the fuel gauge. If only she had taken the time to check the fuel visually rather than trust the instruments, she would never have ended up in the icy Strait of Juan de Fuca that September afternoon many years earlier.

Camille took the bottle of Talking Rain seltzer from Robin's outstretched hand and tried, unsuccessfully, to moisten her mouth. Surely she could make it through the forty-five minute flight without passing out, she told herself as she noticed the familiar lightheadedness coming on. She closed her eyes and counted backward from a hundred.

When she came to, Robin was patting her face. "Camille, are you okay?" Robin shouted to be heard over the noisy engine.

Unable to muster the energy to respond, Camille simply nodded and tried to focus on something outside the plane. But the empty blackness forced a chill to settle over her torso. She knew the pilot needed some kind of reflection on the water to guide them down. Tonight there would be nothing.

It had been nearly twenty years since Camille's accident, but all the pilots in Tony's small fleet understood her terror. Steve raised his eyebrows and pointed down apologetically. She held her breath and nodded.

The tiny plane pitched slightly as it lost altitude. Camille searched in vain for a stretch of light reflecting on the water. She swallowed hard. The plane slowed suddenly as it skimmed across the silky smooth water. Without waiting for the plane to stop, Camille jerked open the door and drank in the dark salty air of Friday Harbor.

—

Camille felt like she was escorting Robin into an execution chamber as they walked up the steps into the square limestone hospital and past the red, white, and blue streamers hanging limply from the empty information desk. It seemed impossible that just hours ago Camille had been anxiously awaiting the fireworks. Now all she cared about was finding the intensive care unit in the dimly lit hospital.

The familiar smell reminded her of the chaos of Boston General. She vaguely remembered the "hit" of a really juicy trauma case. But now, here she was, just another terrified family member wandering down the vacant institutional corridors, hoping against hope.

Camille pushed through the doors to the intensive care unit and squinted at the bright-white hospital walls. Two men dressed in surgical scrubs huddled outside a patient room across from the nurses' station. The tall redhead had the familiar earpiece used by anesthesiologists to listen to a patient's heartbeat, and the doctor with the dark hair wore the blood-stained clogs of a surgeon.

The surgeon slammed the patient's chart into a rack mounted on the wall. "Where the hell did Willcox go? It's too dark for him to be golfing."

Who's Willcox? Camille wondered.

"What difference does it make?" the anesthesiologist answered. "He'd just get in the way if he were here."

Whoever he is, he's not going to win any popularity contests around this place.

"Okay, then . . . you wanna tell the family what happened?" the surgeon asked.

Oh God . . .

The anesthesiologist looked with disgust at his colleague and picked up the phone. "I'll page him."

A serious young nurse poked her head out of the room and shouted, "He's bottoming out again. We need you two in here! Now!"

The surgeon rushed into the room. "I'm right behind you, Meg."

The anesthesiologist followed but stopped short of crashing into a petite woman with short silver hair. He gently grabbed her by the shoulders and moved her aside. Dallas's wife, Gloria, leaned against the wall and covered her mouth as she sobbed.

Robin ran over. "Gloria! How is he?"

Camille had always considered Gloria to be one of the most outrageously brazen women she had ever met, but tonight, whatever it was that comprised Gloria's soul was nowhere to be found. She looked like she might at any moment turn into a pile of gray dust and blow down the hall. She folded herself into Robin's embrace.

Another nurse flew by, pushing a red crash cart. "I'm coming!" she yelled. "Excuse me. Please stay in the waiting room."

Camille recognized the tight voice of anxiety. It wasn't a good sign.

She and Robin took Gloria by the hand and guided her to the cramped waiting room, where they sat on one of the two matching yellow vinyl couches with curved metal arms. Camille's head was swimming. She clicked off the rerun of *Friends* blaring from the wall-mounted TV.

"He's all hooked up to tubes and wires. And he's so bruised and bloated," Gloria said.

"ICU patients always look like that. But it doesn't mean he's not going to make it," Camille tried to reassure her.

"Why is he all black and blue, then?" Gloria cried quietly. "He looks like he was in a street fight."

"That's from the DIC. It happens when the blood doesn't clot properly."

"What did the doctor say?" Robin asked.

"I haven't talked with the surgeon. I'm hoping he'll be available soon."

"What do you mean you haven't spoken with the doctor?" Camille got up and looked down the hall. "Which one did the surgery?"

"I haven't seen him in a while."

"He's not one of those docs working on him now?" Camille asked. "No."

"Well, where the hell is he?" Robin yelled. "I wanna know what happened. No one nearly dies from gallbladder surgery. Do they?"

Camille noted the commotion going on around Dallas's room. "Not usually, but I'm not that familiar with laparoscopic procedures. I'll call Sam and see what he knows." She dug in her purse for her cell phone.

Sam's voice sounded alert, not at all groggy from sleep. "I've been worried about you. You said you'd call when you landed."

"We just got here a few minutes ago."

"How's Dallas?"

"They're working on him."

"How's he look?"

"I haven't seen him yet." She changed the subject. "You know, when I was a nurse, I never worked on a post-op ward, so I know nothing about laparoscopic surgery. Do you know anything about it?"

"Are you kidding? I haven't seen any real blood since you taught me to suture twenty years ago."

"I figured as much. Do you think you could pop on your fancy doctor's UpToDate site and send me a few articles about laparoscopic cholecystectomies?"

"Will do. How's Gloria?"

"About as you'd expect."

"Jesus. Well, give her my love."

"I will."

Gloria looked up through puffy red eyes. "I remember the first time we met. Dallas was walking up the beach where I taught yoga at the spa in La Paz." She pulled her legs up onto the couch and wrapped her arms around them. "I was just getting ready to teach my morning class, and there he was, all scruffy from having just sailed down the coast." She smiled wistfully. "He was stopping off to provision for his trip to the South Pacific, looking for a laundromat." She wiped her tears with the back of her shaking hand. "Well, I told him there hadn't been a laundromat there for at least two years. He looked so disappointed. And he was so big and handsome, all tan with that thick silver hair."

"So, did you direct him to the closest laundromat?" Camille swallowed her own tears, grateful that Gloria was able to remember happier times.

"Are you kidding? I asked him to join my yoga class."

"And?" Camille had heard the story a thousand times.

"And he and I left together six months later to sail back up here."

The dark-haired doctor stuck his head into the waiting room. "Mrs. Jackson?"

Gloria jumped to her feet. "Yes?"

"You ladies can go in and see him for a few minutes. He's barely stable now, and we aren't very optimistic. We still haven't gotten his blood to clot."

Dallas lay on a bed in the middle of the well-lit room. A multitude of wires and tubes connected him to equipment that displayed all his bodily functions. A huge tube coming out of his mouth was taped to his cheek, causing his lips to contort to one side. His chest rose up and down in time with the mechanical respirator.

Robin burst into tears.

"It's okay. You can touch him." Camille wiped the tears from Robin's cheeks. "And talk to him. He can probably hear you." She put her arm around Gloria's shoulders and watched as the two women gingerly stroked Dallas's thick forearm.

Camille turned to the nurse. "I understand he had an aneurysm," she said quietly.

"He did, and unfortunately it got in the way of one of the instruments during surgery." The post-op floor nurse stooped down to measure the bloody urine in the bag at the end of a clear tube. "Mr. Jackson here is lucky that Dr. Willcox was on call last night. He's the best in town. We go to church together." She smiled. "The man's a saint."

Camille stood silently, rubbing Dallas's feet while Gloria softly sang the Penguins' "Earth Angel" into his ear.

Robin sank into the plastic chair at the bedside and rested her head next to Dallas's hip while the nurse took blood samples from the catheter in his neck.

"I'm going to go check my email and see if Sam's sent anything helpful," Camille whispered. "You two okay?"

Gloria smoothed Dallas's hair. "Go ahead, dear."

Camille looked at Robin, who bit her lip and nodded.

As soon as Camille was alone in the waiting room, she buried her face in her hands and tried frantically to remember anything Dallas had taught her about how to deal with a crisis of this magnitude. She knew he'd tell her to focus on the universal life force known to some as God and Allah or Mother Earth to others. And he'd apply the Buddhist concept of the dharma or Rumi's teachings on the universality of God to the situation. Camille breathed deeply and tried to pray.

The familiar pinging of an email notification on her phone broke the silence. She took out her laptop and began to read.

Outside, the purple haze of dawn crept over the woods near the hospital. She'd been so absorbed in the medical literature that she hadn't noticed the time passing. She rubbed her eyes, then got up stiffly from the hard little couch and splashed her face with water from the drinking fountain.

Unwilling to face the distinct possibility of Dallas's mortality, Camille reached her hands to the sky in sun salutation as part of the morning yoga routine he'd taught her so many years before. The second time through, she was interrupted by a loud, guttural scream emanating from Dallas's room. She turned and ran.

CHAPTER FOUR

It was a little more than an hour since Dallas had died. Camille walked up to the nurses' station. A bouquet-like arrangement of small American flags, put on the counter in anticipation of the Fourth, had somehow completely lost its oomph overnight.

"I'm Camille Delaney, here with Gloria and Robin Jackson." She blinked hard in an effort to shake the feeling of cotton candy trapped inside her head. "We're here to see Dr. Willcox."

"Is he expecting you?" the nurse said without looking up. The nurse's name tag was decorated in the familiar red, white, and blue theme.

"He should be. The ICU nurse called him early this morning and told him we'd be here at seven." Camille clutched the shoulder strap of her computer case, thankful she'd had a chance to review the latest research on laparoscopic cholecystectomies.

Nurse Nancy Jo Williams pointed to another vinyl couch. This one was burgundy and reminded Camille of dried blood. "Have a seat, then," she said officiously. The nurse turned back to her telephone conversation and snapped her gum as she sorted through the doctor's orders covering her desk. "He should be out in a little while."

As she turned away, Camille noticed a stack of medical records on the counter. Stamped on the top sheet was a big red "Expired" stamp. Dallas's name was clearly visible on the lower right-hand corner of the front page. Camille caught her breath and motioned for Robin and

Gloria to sit down. In a split second, she hoisted her computer case up, sending Dallas's chart flying from the countertop. "Oh my gosh. I'm so sorry! I'll get those."

The nurse didn't flinch. Camille flashed her an empty smile and held up her hand. She ran her hands through her hair, causing her gray tortoiseshell glasses to fly off the top of her head. She stooped down, grabbed her glasses, and began to comb through the mess of papers strewn across the sticky gray carpet that smelled strongly of disinfectant. From her vantage point, Camille noticed Nurse Williams's stocking feet and doubted that she'd feel compelled to jump up and help her out. Nevertheless, Camille wasted no time as she methodically skimmed through the records while pretending to straighten the pile.

Camille felt the tingly sensation of adrenaline dancing just below the surface of her skin. Because the surgery had taken place just the night before, the transcription department wouldn't have typed the operative report yet. She gathered up lab sheets with shaking hands, noting that Dallas had received eight units of blood and a bunch of plasma expanders and platelets.

After each procedure, surgeons always write a quick note from which they would later dictate. She tried to slow her shallow breathing as she looked for a handwritten doctor's note.

Nurse Williams glanced over her shoulder as Camille theatrically reorganized the chart. She signaled an okay sign with her fingers and listened as the nurse went back to an intense conversation with someone about upcoming nursing staffing issues at the hospital.

Ah-ha. There it was. Camille felt the tension begin to drain from her shoulders. This shit wasn't so hard after all. She closed her eyes briefly to calm herself, then opened them and tried to decipher the flamboyant purple handwriting. Willcox had scrawled that there was a great deal of bleeding and "extensive exploration was undertaken to determine its source." He had ultimately discovered an injury to the aorta and called in a Dr. Gonzalez to perform the repair.

Camille scanned the note, looking for a description of the aneurysm that had drained the life from her mentor. Why the hell didn't Willcox describe it in his note? She went back to the beginning and re-read it slowly, just to make sure. *What in the world?*

Anger replaced Camille's nervousness as she slowly stood up. Her lawyer instincts took over.

"Thanks," Nurse Williams said insincerely as she relieved Camille of the unwieldy stack of papers.

Camille approached Robin and Gloria. "Listen, you guys. I think it may be better if we don't let Willcox know that I used to be a nurse. Okay? And for sure don't mention that I'm a lawyer."

"We were hoping you could translate the jargon for us and see what the hell happened." Robin's voice had regained a bit of its edge.

"I will, but let's see how he explains this thing to us first. I think we may find out more if we play dumb."

Gloria cocked her head almost imperceptibly to the side and looked quizzically at Camille. "What do you mean that we may find out more? More what?"

There was no point in worrying Gloria and Robin. "Uh—well, sometimes doctors get defensive if they think they're being second-guessed."

"Whatever you think is best." Gloria was stately even in her grief.

Just as the trio got settled in the tiny waiting room, a handsome, late-middle-aged doctor strode confidently out of the door behind Nurse Williams. He had a perfect tan and sun-streaked, graying brown hair.

The doctor gave the nurse a boyish smile. "Attagirl, Nancy Jo. I knew you'd get those orders straightened out."

Camille could hardly believe her eyes as the doctor patted Nancy Jo Williams on the head and tousled her hair, then smoothed his crisp white lab coat. Camille watched with curiosity as the nurse rolled her eyes and clenched her teeth. Nurse Williams kept her head down and continued her paperwork.

"You must be the Jackson family. I'm Dr. Willcox."

Camille froze. The last thing she'd expected was a doctor who looked like he'd just stepped out of a *GQ* layout.

"You are the Jackson family, are you not?" He flashed a set of unbelievably perfect white teeth.

Camille gathered her wits. "Can we go somewhere private to talk?"

"Of course." Willcox's deep-blue eyes crinkled at the edges when he smiled. "Let me be the first to offer my condolences for your loss. Please come this way." Willcox graciously guided them down the hall to an opulently furnished sitting room. Camille looked around in disbelief. She had trained and worked in some of the most prestigious hospitals in the country, yet she had never seen a room that could compare to this.

The thick Persian rugs echoed the deep mahogany of the walls, which contrasted nicely with the tan leather couch and matching chairs. Bookshelves containing leather-bound editions lined the room. Camille recognized *Gray's Anatomy* and *Schwartz's Principles of Surgery*. Two walls held spectacular pieces of modern art lit by well-concealed ceiling lights. The paintings glowed with a depth of color she had only seen in original pieces in museums. *What the hell was going on here?*

Willcox sank into one of the overstuffed chairs and shifted to face the couch where Camille sat between Gloria and Robin. "Can I offer any of you a coffee?"

The couch was so soft, Camille felt as if her knees were going to bump into her chin. "No, thanks."

Willcox discreetly pushed up his sleeve and glanced at the Rolex watch nestled in the thick blond hair of his wrist. Over the Rolex was draped a heavy gold bracelet that matched the chain around his neck. He leaned forward with a look of utter sympathy and launched into a monologue about the unfortunate death of Mr. Jackson.

"As you know, Mr. Jackson has suffered for several years from severe dyspepsia," he said authoritatively. "His condition culminated yesterday after he ingested a large amount of saturated fat. This exacerbated his preexisting condition to the point that he sought emergency medical care here at Friday Harbor General." Willcox ignored the confused looks on Robin's and Gloria's faces. "After performing and interpreting many tests, including electrocardiography, gastric endoscopy, ultrasonography, magnetic resonance imaging, as well as computerized axial tomography, I determined that Mr. Jackson was undergoing an acute cholelithiasis attack, and I immediately took him to surgery."

Camille squinted and nodded somewhat skeptically.

Willcox continued, "As you probably know, I am a national expert in laparoscopic cholecystectomies, having performed thousands of them, both here and in California."

Thousands? In Friday Harbor? On San Juan Island?

"After I advanced the trocar, I noted the presence of bright-red bleeding, which is indicative of a hemorrhage." Willcox looked with consternation at Gloria. "I immediately opened the patient to determine the source of the bleeding and discovered the trocar had punctured an aneurysm on his aorta the size of a softball. I quickly called in a trusted vascular surgeon to repair the severed aneurysm." He lowered his voice. "Unfortunately, despite our best efforts, we were unable to save your husband."

"Aneurysm?" Gloria asked quietly.

Willcox cleared his throat and explained almost condescendingly, "The aorta is the very large high-pressure artery that circulates blood to the entire body from the heart."

Camille squeezed Gloria's hand as she slipped it into Camille's.

"Sometimes, the wall of the aorta is weakened, and the aorta expands like a weak spot in an inner tube," Willcox continued. "This is called an aneurysm."

Camille struggled to ignore the lump in her throat.

"To put it simply, your husband had an undiagnosed abnormality in the wall of his aorta that got in the way of the surgical instrument utilized in this very routine procedure," Willcox said hurriedly, without taking a breath. "There was no way to know it would be there so it could not have been avoided. I assure you we did everything humanly possible. Can I answer any questions for you?"

Willcox's pager went off, and he read the digital display.

"I'm very sorry. It seems I'm needed in the operating room. Please, make yourselves at home. If you need anything at all, just dial 4-4 on this phone." Willcox got up and took the time to hold each of their hands between his own as he gazed into their eyes. "Please don't hesitate to call." He pulled out a thin business card case and offered them each a card with the name *Andrew Willcox III* in gold foil lettering. There was no address, just a telephone number. Willcox closed the door quietly behind himself.

Gloria looked at Camille blankly. "I'm afraid I didn't follow much of that. Camille, do you have any idea of what the doctor just said?"

Camille nodded. "I'll translate for you when we get home. Let's get out of here." Camille stood up shakily and walked out into the hall, where she noted with curiosity that Willcox was heading in the opposite direction from the operating room.

Just as Camille was closing the car door behind Gloria and Robin in the parking lot behind the small hospital, she felt the full-body vibration of a noisy helicopter swooping over as it landed at the hospital heliport. Having spent years in the San Juan Islands, Camille knew the significance of a helicopter coming to the Island hospital. She bowed her head and said a little prayer for whoever was about to be medevaced off the Island for care, most likely at the trauma center at Harborview Medical Center in Seattle. But when she looked up, she was surprised to see that the helicopter didn't have the familiar Air Life Northwest logo; rather, it appeared to be a private aircraft. As she watched the flight crew open the door, she stopped in her tracks when Willcox and one of the docs she'd seen in the hospital loaded a couple of large picnic coolers into the helicopter and signaled to the pilot to take off. *He's not in the OR doing another case. He's heading out for a family picnic—probably out on one of the outer islands, where they have no stores so everyone has to bring their groceries and supplies in bins and coolers.* She instinctively grabbed her phone and took a picture of the call numbers on the helicopter.

CHAPTER FIVE

Camille stood in the cockpit of Dallas's sailboat enjoying the peacefulness of the early morning in the marina. The smell of bacon wafted from the thirty-foot Tollycraft powerboat moored directly across the dock. She could see a woman in the galley watching her two little boys prone on the dock, their fishing net poised to grab an unsuspecting school of minnows.

The scene seemed a million miles away to Camille as she climbed down the companionway into the cabin. The well-loved boat was the embodiment of Dallas. She remembered the countless hours she'd spent sitting in the cockpit, drinking ice-cold beer and handing Dallas tools as he worked on the boat's beechwood cabinetry. She struggled now to remember anything Dallas had taught her about death and dying.

Gloria wandered out of the aft stateroom, lit the propane stove, and put water on to boil. The sound of the coffee grinder cut through the silence like a jackhammer. "So, tell me what on earth that doctor said." She took out three pottery mugs.

"He basically gave us a very terse and extremely technical explanation of how he went to great lengths to act swiftly in Dallas's emergency gallbladder attack. He said he was able to make the diagnosis quite quickly, once he had run around ten thousand bucks worth of unnecessary tests." Camille shook her head. "Luckily, according to him, he was able to get Dallas into the operating room just in the nick of time.

But, unfortunately, Dallas had an aneurysm that got in the way of one of the instruments. It was a tragic, but unavoidable, complication of the procedure, at which, by the way, he is a self-proclaimed expert."

"Sounds like you don't believe him," Gloria mused.

Camille looked at her hands folded on the table in front of her. "I don't know what to believe."

"What exactly is an aneurysm?" asked Robin, who sat at the table across from Camille.

"An abnormal ballooning of the wall of a blood vessel. In this case, it was supposedly in the aorta, which is the large artery that takes the blood from the heart to the lower organs."

Gloria poured three cups of thick black coffee and handed one to Camille. "So, Dallas had one of these aneurysms?"

"Not necessarily." Camille gently fingered her favorite cup; the black one with the white lily on it. Dallas had bought it when he'd taken her on a sailing trip in the Canadian Gulf Islands several years earlier.

"What do you mean, not necessarily?" Robin demanded.

"Remember when I knocked Dallas's medical records onto the floor?"

Robin's face was soaking up the steam from her coffee. "Like a complete klutz?"

Camille smiled at the first bit of levity in an otherwise somber moment.

Robin filled her coffee with half-and-half until it was a light-tan color, then dumped in several teaspoons of sugar.

"The note Willcox wrote after the surgery didn't exactly mesh with what he told us this morning," Camille said quietly.

"How so, Camille?" Gloria asked.

Robin scooted over to make room for Gloria.

Camille blew on her coffee and took a sip. "First of all, the record showed that Dallas got eight units of blood and a bunch of IVs to increase his ability to clot. That seems like a lot to me. Unless Willcox didn't get in to repair the injury immediately, which would be hard to imagine, since the bleeding would be pretty overwhelming. And the fact that Dallas had DIC, the clotting disorder that made him look all bruised, makes me think that he bled a lot before the injury was detected."

"What's DIC?" Gloria asked.

"It's a clotting disorder that happens commonly when a patient gets blood transfusions. They have to give anticoagulants when they do several transfusions and then the blood loses its ability to clot. That's why Dallas was so bruised up."

"When did you become such an expert on diagnosing and treating surgical trauma? You sound like a goddamned surgeon," Robin said.

"I was a trauma nurse," Camille reminded her friend as she pointed to the computer on the floor at her feet. "And I had Sam email me those articles, remember?"

"Vaguely."

"And more importantly, I got a chance to skim Willcox's handwritten op note when I was picking up the records off the floor."

Robin cocked her head. "And?"

"And there was no mention of an aneurysm."

Gloria gently put her cup down on the well-worn table. "What are you saying, Camille?"

"She's saying that the asshole lied to us and said Dallas had an aneurysm when there wasn't one! Right, Camille?"

"I don't know," Camille said.

"But why would he lie to us like that?" Gloria asked.

"I'm not sure if he did."

Robin slammed her cup down, sending coffee flying across the table. "He's trying to cover something up. That's why!"

"He certainly could be," Camille agreed.

"Camille." Gloria's voice was shaking. "I need to know what happened to my husband. If there's been any impropriety, I want to know."

"We all do." Camille nodded.

"Will you please look into it for me? As an attorney?" Gloria's voice was clear, now, and determined.

"Jeez, Gloria. I'm way too close to Dallas. I couldn't be objective."

"Well, someone has to do it," Robin interjected.

"Maybe so, but not me."

"Who else, then?" Robin snapped.

"I know a bunch of plaintiff's lawyers who do this kind of thing all the time. I could act as a consultant, but I really can't get involved."

"I'd rather you did it yourself, dear," Gloria said.

"I can't . . . really. It'd be like a doctor treating her own family. And you know my firm wouldn't let a malpractice case through the front door."

There was silence for a moment, then Gloria got up and kissed the two women. Her eyes were sunken, ghostlike. "I need to get some rest. We'll discuss this later." She turned and disappeared into her stateroom.

Camille yawned. "I can never sleep in the daytime. I think I'll take a walk. Want to come?" she asked Robin.

"No. I kinda wanna be alone. I'll just stick around here."

"Okay." Camille kissed her friend. "Will you be okay if I take off for a bit?"

"Sure, go ahead. I'll be fine."

——

Camille wandered down the festive main street of Friday Harbor. She needed time to think. She passed a clean-up crew sweeping up Fourth of July firecracker remnants and headed up the stairway of an old wooden building, stopping in front of a narrow door covered with red rhinestones. The name *Ruby's* was spelled out in similar gems in old-fashioned script on a sign hanging from the eaves.

The rotund store owner had always struck Camille as someone she'd expect to see in a country western video rather than an aromatherapy store in Friday Harbor. Ruby's blondish-gray bouffant framed her cherublike face. And she wore a french-vanilla-colored loose fitting dress with metallic rivets that created a pleasant monochromatic look over a pair of creamy soft leather cowboy boots.

"Camille! Oh my God, darlin', I just heard about Dallas! What in heaven's name happened?" The New Age country western grandma rushed out from behind the counter.

Camille burst into tears. "I can't believe this, Ruby. I feel like I'm in a bad dream."

Ruby held Camille while she sobbed. "There, there, sugar pie."

The familiar Southern twang comforted Camille.

Ruby handed Camille a wadded-up Kleenex. "I just got off the phone with Gloria. She told me what y'all said about things just not addin' up."

"What do you mean?"

"To my way of understandin', y'all think maybe Dallas didn't even have an aneurysm. Camille, honey, you really must check into what happened. For Gloria."

"I can't, Ruby. Dallas was like a father to me. There's no way I could be objective, even if my firm would let me take a malpractice case." Camille collapsed into a chair in the back of the little store and sat looking out over the yacht harbor. "Besides, one of the reasons I got out of plaintiff's lawyering in the first place was because I got to the point where I couldn't deal with explaining to my clients that elderly people and women have no value in our so-called justice system."

"What on earth are you talking about, punkin?" Ruby sat down facing Camille.

"Listen, Ruby. The legal system has a bizarre way of deciding the value of a human life. I just can't fathom having to apply that kind of formula to Dallas."

Ruby rearranged the doilies on the arm of the chair once. Then again. She looked up. "Whatever do you mean?"

Camille pulled herself together, then slowly began to speak. "When someone dies, there's always the question of how much the survivors are to be paid."

Ruby nodded. "Of course."

"The problem is with the way the justice system makes that determination."

Ruby leaned forward and cradled her chin in her hand. "Go ahead, dear. Explain this to me."

"First, they determine how much the decedent earned. On a yearly basis."

Ruby gently chewed the nail on her pinky. "Okay." She nodded. "Then what?"

"Then they add a little something for what they call pain and suffering. Which is really just another way to see to it that the lawyers are paid."

"Are you telling me that the jury just awards the family the victim's lost wages? That's it?"

"Pretty much."

"So, in our legal system, we're each worth what we make? In a monetary sense?"

"Yep. I'm afraid so."

"This is appalling, Camille."

"I agree."

"You're saying that a housewife and mother is worth less than, say, a bank president?"

Camille nodded.

"That's ridiculous!"

"And an elderly person is worth even less because they earn basically nothing and have a shorter life expectancy," Camille added.

"It seems to me that because an elderly person has less time left, those years are worth all the more."

"I agree, but in our justice system, the golden years just aren't worth much."

"But can't a jury give the family as much as they want?"

"Yeah, but you wouldn't believe how they eat up the insurance lawyers' arguments about how much less the value of an elderly person or a housewife is. And it applies to working women, too. Since they typically earn less than a man—especially a white man—their cases have a lower value in the system."

"Lordy! I had no idea." Ruby shook her head.

"And the amount a jury awards is related to the skill of the lawyer trying the case. And since the elderly and women bring lower verdicts, the best lawyers won't take their cases. It's a vicious circle."

Ruby absentmindedly opened a cobalt-blue jar and inhaled deeply. A tart fragrance filled the air. "Well, surely something can be done."

"I kept hoping the public would get with the program, but it never seemed to happen. So, I quit. I just got sick and tired of explaining the inequities to my clients."

Ruby screwed the lid back on the jar. "And that's why you went into the divorce business?" She put the jar next to a green bottle perched on the windowsill.

"I wanted a change. I thought it'd be different with a real person on the other side. Not just an insurance company."

"What do you mean, insurance companies? I thought you used to sue doctors."

"I did, but I dealt directly with their insurance companies. They just like to parade the doctors in front of the jury for sympathy."

The bells on the door jingled, and Ruby headed to the front of the store to greet a young couple. "How do those people live with themselves, trying to convince juries that one life is worth more than another?" she clucked as she straightened the shelves on her way.

Camille followed close behind her. "Those lawyers are a different breed. In law school, we called them 'the generic boys.' They always sat in the front row, biggest suck-ups in the class." Camille narrowed her eyes in disgust. "Grew up to worship at the feet of the almighty billable hour."

Ruby took her position behind the ornate antique counter. "Well, Camille, honey, I can certainly understand your frustration with all this, but if y'all don't look into what happened to Dallas, who will?"

"Listen, even if I wanted to, I couldn't. My firm represents people in business matters and divorces. And lots of our divorce clients are doctors or doctors' wives. I can't take a medical malpractice case. My partners would never agree to it."

"You know something has to be done about this," Ruby said sternly. "And who says your partners get to make decisions about what cases you take?"

Camille sat on the stool in front of the counter where Ruby mixed her secret aromatherapy concoctions. "I agree that I should be able to take any case I want, but I can't. The senior partners have the last word." This wasn't the first time Camille had had to turn down a case because the partners said no. "To tell you the truth, I just can't think about it now."

"Of course, darlin'." Ruby turned to the rows of bottles behind her. "Let's see . . . I do believe a bit of lavender is in order. I'll mix you up a little potion."

Camille picked up a pamphlet on aromatherapy and wandered to the back of the store to test the various potions lining the narrow shelves. The exotic fragrances overcame her, and before she knew it, she had forgotten the familiar frustrations of the so-called justice system. She was lost in essential oils with names like *eucalyptus, bergamot,* and *ylang-ylang.* Maybe if she got just the right dose of one of them, she'd know what to do about Dr. Willcox. It was tempting to try to figure out what had really happened in that operating room. Maybe if she weren't so close to Dallas, she could investigate this whole thing objectively. Maybe her brain fog would soon lift, and things would start making sense. She popped the top off a small brown bottle and breathed in the pungent aroma. Or maybe this was just a bad dream.

CHAPTER SIX

Camille hurried past the icy-gray Chihuly glass sculpture standing alone in the white lobby of the prestigious law firm of Whitfield, Bahr, and Moses. Her high heels clicked across the marble floor, sending an echo throughout the cavernous waiting room.

The anorexic woman sitting behind the metal reception desk put two slender fingers over the microphone on her headset. "Sorry to hear about your friend."

Camille tried to smile and wondered how she would get through her first day back at the office. It had been gut-wrenching to say good-bye to Robin when she sent her on her way back to Sequim, on the Olympic Peninsula where she taught high school. "Thanks, Becky."

It seemed as if time had stood still over the past few days. She poured herself a cup of coffee from the service next to the lobby's lone purple orchid. She caught the faint fragrance of the flower as she turned to head for her office.

Camille's paralegal, Amy, sat in her cubicle, balancing a latte precariously in one hand while she searched for something on her desk. She cradled her phone against her ear with her shoulder.

"Laurel Nelson," she mouthed to Camille while making a motion like a quacking duck with her right hand. Amy rolled her eyes and shrugged. "Uh-huh . . . I see . . . Well, I'm not sure Camille can get to court that soon."

Without smudging her wet nail polish, Amy adeptly picked up a thick file from the midst of the piles of paper on her desk. "Laurel, I gotta go. Camille just came in, and she's late for a meeting . . . Sure. I'll tell her. Talk to you soon." She swiveled her chair to face Camille. "Laurel's soon-to-be ex wants to take the nanny with him and the kids to France next week."

"So?"

"So Laurel wants the nanny to go with her to Palm Beach and babysit the dogs so she can go out and party."

Dallas is dead, and all these people can think about is whether the nanny should go with the children or the dogs. "And what would she like us to do about this little crisis?"

"She wants you to go to court to get an emergency restraining order so her husband can't take the nanny to France."

"No, no, no." Camille backed up and waved her hands in front of her.

"Cha-ching. Cha-ching." Amy smirked.

"Get an associate to do it. Let one of them make an ass of themselves on the motions calendar."

"You got it." Amy handed Camille a file. "It was a really beautiful memorial service. Dallas would have loved it."

"Thanks. I think so, too." Camille flipped through the file.

"You know, I told you I could cancel your meetings this afternoon."

"No, I'd rather keep busy."

Amy followed Camille into her office, where stacks of documents were thrown about as if a hurricane had swept through. Amy inadvertently kicked over a pile of papers and stooped to reorganize the mess. "I loved the part where you and Gloria and Robin threw the lilies from the boat as it sailed out of the harbor. I cry every time I think about it. How many flowers were there?"

Camille lifted a pile of documents off her chair so she could sit. "Three hundred." She dropped the pile on the floor and sat down behind her long, custom-made Italian glass desk. She turned her white leather chair and looked at the gallery of family pictures on her credenza. Sam's handsomely chiseled features hovered over Libby's and Angela's most recent school pictures, and their Asian African American foster daughter's wide smile stood front and center. Grace's two front teeth had come out the day before the class picture, leaving her with a nearly toothless grin.

"How'd you guys get the service pulled together so fast? I thought it was only a Jewish tradition to have the service within forty-eight hours."

"It is, but Dallas was a student of world religions, and his will actually mandated that he be laid to rest no later than forty-eight hours after he made his transition. Makes sense to me." She twirled back around and shuffled through the papers haphazardly strewn across her desk. "Have you seen any of my glasses?"

Amy opened the second drawer of Camille's white lacquer credenza and surveyed Camille's outfit. "Black? Or gray?"

"Black."

Amy bit the drugstore price tag off the black glasses and handed them to her boss.

"Thanks." Camille didn't look up from skimming through the stack of legal papers on her desk as she reached for her phone on the second ring. "Ruby Rae is here?" Camille looked quizzically at Amy. "Um . . . Okay . . . Bring her up." Camille glanced at her watch.

"You have a packed calendar today. This had better be quick," Amy admonished her boss.

"Promise." Camille shrugged. "What on earth is Ruby doing here?" she asked to no one in particular as she turned to see her Island friend Ruby standing in her doorway. She was dressed in peach suede with fringe from head to toe. Camille and Ruby touched cheeks and kissed. Camille threw a stack of papers off the white leather loveseat and motioned for Ruby to sit. "Can I get you a cup of tea?"

"Hot water would be fine. I always bring my own." Ruby smiled as she pulled a tea bag from her purse and dangled it in front of her. "Look at this view." She gestured at Puget Sound sparkling forty-one stories below.

Camille turned to the coffee service on her credenza and poured Ruby a cup of hot water in a hexagonal white cup. "I'm so happy to see you."

"This is quite a place," Ruby commented as she stared behind Camille's desk at the black-and-white abstract paintings with streaks of red and yellow smeared unevenly across them.

Camille sat on her white Eames chair opposite Ruby. *I bet this place has never seen peach suede fringe.*

"My lord, darlin', how on earth do you get anything done in this mess?"

"It's more organized than it looks," Camille lied. "So, what brings you down to the big city?"

Ruby rummaged around in her oversized peach patchwork leather hobo bag. "I told Gloria I'd bring you these so y'all could take a look and see what happened." She pulled out a thick manila envelope. "It's Dallas's medical records," she whispered conspiratorially. "I just know something went horribly wrong here. You need to check into it."

"Where'd you get the records?" Camille asked quietly.

"I volunteer in the hospital, so I took Gloria down to the medical records department and had her fill out a records request," Ruby announced proudly.

"You know I can't sue a hospital or a doctor. I represent doctors. We've already had this conversation. The law business doesn't work that way."

"Well, there's something fishy about this doctor, Camille. I've done a li'l investigating myself."

Camille looked over her glasses at Ruby. "What investigating did you do?"

"Well, you can imagine that as the head volunteer at the hospital for the past several years, I can get access to most anything. Sometimes the administrator's secretary asks me to do her filing for her. So, I managed to find the files where they keep the doctors' credentials." Ruby grinned. "I figured we'd need more information on this doctor."

Camille leaned forward. "And . . ."

"And I found this letter from Harvard where he trained." Ruby held up an envelope. "Signed by a Dr. Irving. Any chance y'all know him?"

Camille raised her eyebrows. "I don't know a Dr. Irving, but I can ask Sam. He trained there too. What's fishy about a letter of recommendation?"

"Well, you know that you and I originally bonded years ago when we discovered that we both lived in Boston in the early two thousands. But you know I couldn't stand the weather, so I only lasted a couple of years." Ruby shivered. "I hate snow."

"Of course. How can I forget meeting you on the ferry back . . . when . . . like, ten years ago?" Camille refocused Ruby: "Are you sure no one knows you have this letter?"

"Exactly ten years ago. Good memory. And no. I made a copy and put back the original." Ruby's eyes narrowed. "There have been lots of complaints about this guy—I just don't think he's Harvard material." Ruby leaned back and crossed her arms. "So, over the past week, whenever I see Dr. Willcox around the hospital, I've been casually making comments about Boston and some of the restaurants and landmarks there. His wife, BJ, is an architect working on a big project on one of the outer islands, so you'd think if they lived in Boston, he'd be familiar with Faneuil Hall or the Custom House Tower or at least the JFK library." She shook her head. "But he's clueless."

"That's quite an accusation. Are you saying he falsified his credentials?"

Ruby shrugged. "Something about this guy doesn't add up. Of course, I haven't told Gloria. You're the only one who knows."

"Well, that's some good investigating, but I'm not sure what we can do about this theory of yours." Camille hadn't pegged Ruby for a crack investigator, but she was impressed.

"Camille, you need to take this case." Ruby was firm.

Camille cradled her head in her hands.

"Dallas was like a father to you," Ruby snapped. "And Gloria needs you. Someone has to hold this doctor accountable."

Camille had never seen this side of Ruby. "I can't, Ruby."

"Camille, you are a nurse and a lawyer. And you used to help victims of malpractice." It wasn't that Ruby was shouting or raising her voice, but her anger was welling up. "And you loved Dallas. If you won't at least investigate this, who will?"

"Look, Ruby. If my partners even knew these records were in my office, I'd have a lot of explaining to do."

"Dallas taught you the power of standing up for what's right and holding people accountable. And now you're trying to tell me that you will bow to a bunch of law partners and let them tell you what you can and can't do? Really, Camille?" Ruby's voice was tight.

Amy popped her head in the door. "Judge Rogers is on line three for the Johnson pretrial conference."

"Thanks, Amy. I'll take it at your desk." Camille looked at Ruby. "Wait here. I'll be right back. This should only take ten minutes or so." Camille felt like someone had just knocked the wind out of her. *What if Willcox lied about his credentials?* She almost bumped into Amy as she hurried out her door toward Amy's cubicle and picked up the phone receiver. "Camille Delaney for the petitioner, Ms. Johnson," she announced as Amy handed her the Johnson file. "Good morning, Your Honor."

When Camille returned to her office after the short conference with the judge, Ruby was nowhere to be found. But the distinctive soft peach leather hobo bag sat hauntingly on top of the piles of legal files haphazardly strewn across her desk. And the letter on Harvard letterhead was propped up on her chair.

Amy poked her head into the office. "I finished the Everett interrogatories. You want to see them?"

Camille didn't move. "In a minute."

"What's that?" Amy pointed at the peach bag.

"Dallas's medical records."

Amy came into the office. "No shit? Where'd ya get them?"

"My friend Ruby left them." Camille stared blankly at the bag on her desk.

"Listen, Camille, you are not getting involved in this thing." Amy crossed her arms. "Your partners would shit a brick if they even suspected that a malpractice case had crossed the hallowed threshold of this place."

Camille's eyes darted toward the door. "Of course I'm not."

She strode affirmatively across the room toward her desk, pulled out the manila envelope, and tore it open with an angry flourish.

"It's your ass if your partners find out. No self-respecting doc will hire you guys to hammer their ex if they find out you're screening malpractice cases against one of the brethren."

Camille looked Amy directly in the eye. "Well, then, lock the door." She expertly began scanning the records.

Amy complied.

Camille's heart jumped into her throat. "Oh God."

"What?"

Camille shook her head in disbelief. "He altered his record. I saw the handwritten note Willcox wrote the night of the surgery. It said he perforated the aorta and called in the vascular guy to fix it. There was nothing about a punctured aneurysm in his note."

"And?"

"And this dictated note says there *was* an aneurysm."

Amy looked over Camille's shoulder. "You're kidding."

"The vascular guy who came in to do the repair must have written a note . . . let me see if I can find it." Camille narrowed her gaze and began to methodically sort through the pages and pages of notes. "Okay, doctor's orders . . . nursing notes . . . progress notes . . . lab flow sheets . . ."

Amy neatly stacked the papers as Camille jumbled them on the floor in front of her. "Just a sec, Camille. Don't get them out of order."

Camille threw the last little pile of records on the floor. "I can't find a note from the vascular surgeon anywhere!" She slumped down, head back, arms flailed out to either side. "Shit. I can't believe this." She popped back up. "See if you can find an op report from a surgeon other than Willcox."

"Well, I can't find much of anything. Someone threw the records on the floor and made a big mess," Amy admonished.

Camille gathered the mess of upside down and sideways records off the floor and handed them to Amy, who patiently thumbed through the stack. Camille felt a twinge of the old familiar rush she used to get when analyzing an interesting malpractice puzzle. How many years had it been since she'd been this excited about a case?

She paced back and forth across the office. "Just see if there's a dictated op note or a handwritten narrative of the repair."

Amy plopped down on the floor and slowly sorted through the records while Camille hovered over her. "Is it possible that there's not a report by this guy in here?" Amy asked.

"Highly unlikely."

"That the report isn't here or that he didn't write a report?"

Camille sank down on the floor next to Amy, twisting to get comfortable in her tight skirt. "Well, I can't imagine a surgeon not documenting a procedure as important as an aortic repair. In fact, it would never happen. The note must be missing from the records they gave Ruby."

"What's the vascular guy's name anyway?"

Camille flipped to Willcox's op report. "Looks like it was the good Dr. Gonzalez. I'm gonna call him, see if he'll talk with me."

"You know he's not going to rat out one of his colleagues, Camille."

"He might. I'm calling him."

"Oh no, you're not," Amy said firmly.

CHAPTER SEVEN

Camille whisked through the cardio room of the gym, climbed on the StairMaster, and punched in the digital program. Before she started, she scanned the room, looking for her friend and investigator, Trish Seaholm. Camille couldn't wait to pick her brain about ways to check out Willcox and the other Friday Harbor doctors involved in Dallas's care, especially the consulting surgeon, Dr. Gonzalez.

Camille took a deep breath and looked out across the ship canal, where green treetops floated over the lavender mist of dawn. As she climbed the stairs to nowhere, her mind drifted back to a morning very similar to this one in a harbor where Dallas had first taught her to meditate. They sat together that morning in his dinghy and watched as the thick fog gradually transformed into a gauzy haze. Gulls cawed and sea otters sang for their breakfast as the sun broke through.

Camille was hooked. Since that day, few mornings went by that she did not meditate, often on the StairMaster, in the early morning.

As she exercised, Camille contemplated the contrast between the peacefulness of the sunrise on the water and the overwhelming sadness she felt at Dallas's passing. It was as though he were there, telling her to hold the grief as just another expression of the universe's great energy. But this morning she was completely unable to focus, so she directed her attention to the situation at hand.

In her mind, she reviewed the discrepancies between Willcox's handwritten note and the neatly transcribed operative dictation she'd read the day before. *Why wasn't there a note from the vascular surgeon who tried to save Dallas after Willcox punctured his aorta or aneurysm, if there was one? What if there was no aneurysm after all? Why would Willcox make up something like that? And what about his credentials? Or was Ruby grasping at straws?*

Camille felt a hand on her shoulder.

"Biceps, triceps, and shoulders today, my dear!" Trish had worked her way through the police academy as a personal trainer and worked out with Camille in exchange for Camille paying for her gym membership.

"Hey! You better be nice to me, or I won't tell you about the new investigation I have for you."

"Okay, grab the dumbbells. I'm all ears." Trish perched on a bench and leaned forward. "You gonna pay me?"

Camille paused. "Maybe." She mentally calculated the amount of her upcoming year-end bonus. It would be substantial—probably almost twice what Sam made as a university doc. "Yeah . . . Actually, yes. I will."

Camille went over the details of the case as she worked her way through her routine. As usual, Trish was ruthless, urging Camille to do "just one more."

Trish put the weights back on the rack. "Are you really going back into the malpractice biz?"

"No, but if it looks like there's something to follow up on, I'll refer it to one of my old trial lawyer buddies. Then I can just act as a consultant."

"Sure you will. I can just see you turning a big juicy malpractice case over to someone else to be lead counsel," Trish teased.

"I have to. My firm has rules prohibiting lawyers from taking any kind of case against a doctor. Period."

"We'll see." Trish handed Camille another set of weights. "So, have you run it by an expert yet?"

Camille closed her eyes and tried to shake off the picture of Dallas bleeding to death on the operating room table. "Three . . . two . . . one." She had to do something. "The girls have a swim meet today, and there's a university surgeon whose son just joined the team. I'm gonna try and see if I can talk him into looking at the records for me."

"I thought university docs weren't allowed to review medical records for plaintiffs."

"Well, that's the official position, but I've had occasional luck getting them to look at stuff. Off the record." Camille put the free weights on the rack and squirted a stream of water into her mouth from the plastic container with her daughters' school logo on it.

"How 'bout I go ahead and do a background check on the docs," Trish suggested.

"Start with Andrew Willcox the third. Says he's most recently from California. And Ruby got ahold of his credentials file, where there's a letter of recommendation from some guy by the name of Irving at Harvard. I checked it out, and there's a doc there by that name, but Ruby is convinced that Willcox never lived in Boston." Camille did a set of overhead presses.

"Ruby? Your friend who has that aromatherapy shop up in Friday Harbor? What does she have to do with this?"

"Small-town hospital—everyone knows everyone else's business. She's been surreptitiously quizzing Willcox on Boston trivia, and he's not doing all that well."

Trish laughed. "So, I have some serious competition in the PI biz?"

"Well, can you check all this out?"

Trish clicked on the Notes app on her phone and typed. "You got it. I can do that quickly. It shouldn't cost you too much."

"And while you're at it, can you find out who this helicopter is registered to?" She texted Trish a picture.

"Helicopter?"

"Yeah. It may be nothing, but someone whisked Willcox off in a helicopter the morning Dallas died."

"Why is that weird? Maybe he was going back to the mainland. Rich guys use the local helicopter service all the time."

"Well, it just seemed strange to me because he left the meeting I had with Gloria and Robin very abruptly, saying he had another case in the OR. Then, five minutes later, he's heading off for a picnic in a private helicopter."

"Picnic?"

"Yeah, he loaded a couple of coolers into the helicopter," Camille explained.

"So, he was probably going off to one of the outer islands where they have no stores . . . Could be Decatur, or Blakely, or Center," Trish mused.

"Exactly. Let's find out."

"Okay. I'm on it. I know that Tony moonlights doing helicopter charters. I'll start with him."

Camille finished her workout in record time. She was on a mission. If the university surgeon said nothing looked out of sorts, she'd let it rest. She showered quickly and headed for her car.

It was a fifteen-minute drive across the U District to the community swim club in the upscale neighborhood of Laurelhurst. Traffic in Seattle was a nightmare, even on a Saturday morning. Camille cursed herself for agreeing, for the third year in a row, to cochair the concession stand. How could she conduct an investigation if she had to spend the day making hot dogs? She gripped the steering wheel and darted in and out of traffic, determined to get her questions answered.

Running through the swim club parking lot, she threw on a bright-red apron and tied it crookedly behind her back. She hurried through the crowd of anxious parents and assumed her position behind the smoky BBQ, where oversized hot dogs popped their juices onto the sizzling briquettes. A half hour passed while Camille collected cash for junk food and sodas.

"I'll take one of those big dogs, hon."

Camille looked quizzically in the direction of the deep, somewhat familiar voice. *Hon?*

To her horror, she found herself eye to eye with Lorrey Lincoln, the slimiest of all the insurance defense lawyers in Seattle. Camille hadn't seen Lincoln since she last had a malpractice case five years earlier. He obviously didn't recognize her in her backward Mariners cap and apron stained with yellow mustard.

Lincoln smiled at her condescendingly. "Are they done? Or shall I come back later?" He winked at her.

She was speechless. "Oh sure. They're all ready." Camille grinned over her clenched teeth. "Here, let me get you one. Ketchup?"

"You bet! Lots of it!" His laughter stopped abruptly as ketchup squirted across the counter and all over his snappy white polo shirt.

"Oh my gosh! I'm so sorry!" Camille lied as she grabbed a dirty towel. "Here, let me get that for you." She wiped the greasy red mess all over his clean shirt. "Oh my! Look what I've done."

"Don't worry about it. I think I'll just go wash it off in the locker room."

"I'm really sorry, sir." She giggled at Lincoln's back as he hustled off.

A quiet crowd of people stood in line, staring at the scene that had just transpired. She shrugged and turned to her next customer. "And how can I help you?" Camille smiled at the tall Black woman with braided hair adorned with silver filigree beads.

"Hi, I'm Gigi, Kaitlin Richardson's mom." The woman had a knockout smile. "I signed up to help out at the concession stand. Is it safe to come in there?" Gigi pointed at the ketchup strewn across the countertop.

"It is now." Camille smiled. "Welcome."

"We just moved up from California. I understand Kaitlin's on the relay team with your daughter Angela."

"Hey, lady!" A little blond head poked through the crowd below Gigi's elbow, and glared up at Camille through thick glasses. "I gave you a ten-dollar bill for two candy bars, a hot dog, a Coke, and two licorice ropes, and you only gave me eighty-five cents back."

Camille winced. She was happy to cook the hot dogs and manage the stand, but having never worked retail a day in her life, she was dismal at making change. "Okay. How much do I owe you?" From the look of things, this kid probably had a much better grip than she did on the complexities of subtraction.

"Three dollars and fifty cents." The little girl glared up at Camille.

"Here you go. Don't spend it all in one place."

The little girl turned and disappeared as quickly as she had come.

"It looks like I'm not a minute too late." Gigi laughed as Camille held up the counter so Gigi could come behind. "I can even add and make change," Gigi added proudly.

"You're hired." Camille smiled. "In fact, I was hoping to get a minute to go and visit with . . . a friend. Any chance you could cover for me?"

"Sure, no problem."

"Great. Thanks a million." Camille ceremoniously handed Gigi the long, pointed hot dog fork, then removed her apron and placed it over Gigi's head. "I'll be back in a bit."

Camille scanned the crowd, looking for the young university surgeon. He was nowhere to be seen. She dejectedly climbed the bleachers, pulled a smashed turkey sub out of her canvas tote, and tried to get comfortable.

The crowd cheered for a little boy thrashing his way to the end of the pool. He was a good fifteen seconds behind his peers, but that didn't stop the team from chanting his name as he climbed out of the pool and into the arms of his waiting father. Camille smiled as the surgeon she'd Googled that afternoon wrapped his towheaded son in a Spider-Man beach towel. She gathered her belongings and began mingling her way down to the pool deck.

Dr. Richard Rosenberg sat down in a plastic lawn chair and was immediately surrounded by a cadre of overly suntanned single mothers.

"He's such a doll!" Lacie Dewitt gushed over little Christopher Rosenberg, her gold necklace glimmering against her leathery skin. She turned her head away from Richard and reapplied a thick coat of hot-pink lipstick.

Camille sat on the bleachers behind the doctor and watched as he politely listened to the single tennis ladies driveling on about the next club tournament. He clearly looked relieved when his son grabbed his dad's arm and pleaded for a hot dog. As the doctor excused himself and headed for the concession stand, Camille hopped up and followed him, taking her place behind them at the end of the line.

"So, how are you two enjoying your first swim team season?" she asked, trying to sound casual.

Richard smiled and responded, "It's our first step toward Olympic gold."

Camille held out her hand. "I'm Camille Delaney." She watched Richard shrink away ever so slightly and surmised that Dr. Rosenberg was worn out from being the most eligible bachelor at the swim club. "You work with my husband, Sam, at the U. He's in the department of epidemiology."

"Sam? You're Sam Taylor's wife?" Richard looked visibly relieved. "You have kids on the team here too?"

"Three college scholarships in the making."

Richard laughed. "What do they swim?"

"Oh, a little of everything. I can never quite keep track." She grinned and showed him the palm of her hand, which was smudged with ink from having written her daughters' swim events on it.

"Now, that's clever. I'll have to remember to use my hand for a pad next time." He smiled. "This is our first season."

"Well, I hope you like bleachers and hot dogs."

"Are you trying to tell me they don't have cushioned seats here like they do at the fancy country clubs?"

"I hate to be the one to break the bad news."

Camille waited while Richard ordered lunch, then ordered a bottle of lemon-lime Talking Rain for herself. Richard waited for her at the condiment table.

"Would you care to join us?" he asked.

"Sure, I'd love to." There was nothing like a married woman to provide cover for a reluctant bachelor. This could prove to be a mutually beneficial relationship after all.

Camille led Richard to a spot on the bleachers as far as possible from the singles zone.

Christopher wolfed down his hot dog and took off before his dad had finished meticulously spreading his pickle relish.

Yep, he's a surgeon. Camille smiled.

"See ya, Dad!"

"I was wondering . . . Do you know anything about laparoscopic cholecystectomies?" Camille asked hopefully.

Richard looked at Camille quizzically. "I did six of 'em yesterday—we do them robotically these days. Why do you ask?"

"That sounds like a lot."

"It may be for some. But I have several aspiring surgeons to teach. We really pack the patients in. What did you want to know about lap choles?" Like most doctors, Richard Rosenberg was much more comfortable discussing the finer points of surgery than listening to a play-by-play of some tennis match.

"For starters, I was wondering how often gallbladder surgery is done on an emergent basis."

"What's the matter? Do you get heartburn from the wonderful hot dogs they serve here?"

Camille laughed. "Hey, I'm the head chef of the swim-n-grill."

Richard winced, jokingly. "Then let me be the first to extend my compliments." He held up his half-eaten hot dog and wiped a drip of mustard from the corner of his mouth.

The PA system blared, "Girls fourteen and under fifty-yard fly. Swimmers on the blocks!"

"Just a sec. My middle daughter's in lane three." Camille stood and cupped her hands around her mouth. "Go, Libby!"

When the race was over, she sat back down. "As you know, Sam's a research doc, so he's no help when it comes to 'real medicine.' And I used to be a nurse, so I have just enough knowledge to be dangerous. We have a friend who had a complication during a so-called emergency lap chole."

"Hmm, I can't think of a reason in the world to do a gallbladder as an emergency, unless it ruptured or something, which is very unusual."

"Let me ask you this: How easy would it be to puncture the aorta of a two-hundred-fifty-pound man with a trocar?"

Richard leaned forward. "You're kidding. You'd have to be really whaling on that trocar to get it through the aorta of a guy that size. Who the hell was the surgeon?"

"His name's Willcox. He practices up in the San Juan Islands, in Friday Harbor."

"Let me get this straight. This guy's doing a supposed emergency lap chole in a two-hundred-fifty-pound guy, and he hits the aorta with a trocar?"

"And kills him."

Richard let out a low whistle. "A friend of yours?"

Camille nodded solemnly. "Very close friend."

"I'm really sorry. Ya know, it sounds kinda fishy. Maybe you should get the medical records. You might have misunderstood what happened."

Camille sized up Dr. Richard Rosenberg. He looked like a nice enough guy. *Might as well ask, the worst that could happen is that he'd say no. On second thought, the worst that could happen might be that he'd say yes.* She took a breath. "So, is there any chance you could look at the records for us?" Camille hollered over the din of the crowd.

"I'd be happy to."

Camille grabbed at her water to keep from spilling it all over herself as the whole bleacher section stood up to cheer. Camille jumped up to see her youngest, six-year-old Grace, on the block, ready for her breaststroke. Next to the block, her two older daughters looked almost identical in their matching team swimsuits and colorfully decorated caps. Sam came up behind them and put one arm around each girl. The threesome cheered so wildly as Grace dove in that Camille thought for a moment that her entire family would dive in and swim the race together. She held up her phone and snapped a picture just as Grace dove in.

"As long as there are no lawyers involved in the case," Richard added.

"That could be a bit of a problem."

"You've already talked to a lawyer?"

She was in it this far; might as well dive in all the way. "No. I am a lawyer. And I'm familiar with the university prohibition about its docs having contact with local attorneys," she added quickly.

Richard raised an eyebrow. "A nurse and a lawyer? Very impressive."

"I was just hoping you'd do it on the sly. No testifying or anything." She paused. "I'm really just trying to find out what happened. As the parent of one future Olympic swimmer to another?"

"You know, we aren't supposed to get involved with the 'dark side.' That would mean you or any of your buddies with cases against doctors who could possibly generate bucks for the U. On the other hand, they encourage us to help defend local guys who screw up. It's good for business, you know." Richard shook his head.

Camille held her breath.

"The whole thing's bullshit, if you ask me. It'd be my pleasure to take a look at your case. You have the chart?"

"Actually, it's in my car."

"I can't think of a better way to pass the time between events, if you want to go grab it."

———

Richard looked up from the records with a scholarly expression, his gold wire-rimmed glasses down on the tip of his nose. He poured himself a cup of coffee from a bright-orange Dora the Explorer thermos. "Coffee?" he asked.

"No, thanks."

Richard focused on the records for what seemed to Camille like forever. He flipped back and forth between pages a couple of times, then let out a low whistle. "Holy shit!"

Camille looked at him anxiously.

"Look at this blood pressure graph." He pointed. "See how it starts dropping about three minutes into the surgery? And the pulse goes up?"

"Yeah. Looks like he went into shock about five minutes into the case." Camille tried to forget she was discussing her friend.

"He sure did. Now what do you think a surgeon ought to do if the blood pressure drops and the pulse goes up like that?" Richard's voice had taken on the authority of a university professor as he lapsed easily into his teaching mode.

"Find the source of bleeding?"

"Bingo. And he better not waste any time. With pressures like this, the patient's obviously trying to bleed to death."

"So, what did Willcox do?"

"Not a whole hell of a lot. Look here! The patient's bleeding out, and this guy decides to make another incision to stick another trocar in through a different opening. We call 'em ports. Then he looks around for, let's see . . . He opens him at three twenty-five . . . That's what? Thirty-two minutes after he started! Jesus Christ!"

"When should he have opened?"

Richard looked over his glasses at Camille. "Half an hour sooner. Let's see if there's any blood loss recorded on the anesthesia record." Richard squinted and scanned down the page with his index finger. "Hah! Look at this, he lost fifteen hundred cc's, about a quart and a half, of blood before the guy opened him up! That's outrageous! This guy should be tried for murder."

It was Camille's turn to fall into the parlance of her profession. She was numb, on autopilot. "I take it that it's a violation of the standard of care for a reasonably prudent surgeon not to promptly open a patient who, during a laparoscopic procedure, demonstrates a significant drop in blood pressure and has a blood loss of fifteen hundred cc's?"

"If the question is whether this guy fucked up, the answer is yes."

CHAPTER EIGHT

Jonathan Bahr, the managing partner at Whitfield, Bahr, and Moses, ushered Camille into his large, walnut-paneled corner office. He strode across the handwoven rug, a thick manila envelope in his hand.

"Peg brought me this." He threw the envelope onto the highly polished table in the middle of the room.

Camille's stomach did a somersault as she tore open the envelope. "What the hell has Peg been doing in my office?" She clutched Dallas's records against her chest. "She's Francis's secretary, for God's sake. She has no business in my office."

"Well, be that as it may," Jonathan said in an even voice, "Peg's not going anywhere. She's been with him for almost thirty years. She runs this place, and she thinks you've gotten involved in a malpractice case." He folded his arms across his chest. "Now, I have some explaining to do to the senior partners. Please don't put me in an awkward situation, Camille. You've got to drop this. Now."

"These are my friend's records." Camille looked at Jonathan defiantly. "The one who died last month. I told his wife I'd look into what happened."

Jonathan winced.

"But I was very clear that if there was a basis for a suit, I'd refer the case out," Camille added quickly. "I told her we don't get involved in medical malpractice." She stepped back from Jonathan.

"Well, I think you'd better get these records out of the office." He moved toward the door. "And the sooner the better. If the rest of the firm gets wind of this, there'll be hell to pay. I don't have to tell you that we can't tolerate any damage to our reputation. Our business depends on our relationship with high-end professionals."

"I hear you." Camille's face flushed.

"I don't want to lose you. But I can only do so much."

"I appreciate that, Jothy, but keep that bitch out of my business. She's had it in for me since the day I walked through that door."

He dropped his voice. "Everyone knows Peg hates working for female attorneys. Like I told you when you started here, just give her a wide berth."

"Fine." She tucked the records under her arm and slammed the door behind her.

Camille found Amy sitting at her computer, eating a late-afternoon ham sandwich and playing Words with Friends.

Camille's voice was tight. "We have to talk."

Amy grabbed a light-blue legal pad and followed Camille into her office. "What's going on?"

"Look what Jothy just handed me." Camille dropped the stack of records on her desk.

"Oh shit. Where'd he get those?" Amy paused. "I told you this would get you in trouble."

Camille paced back and forth.

"Look, Camille, maybe this is a blessing in disguise. Why don't you refer the case out? You've gotten a review from an expert who says there was malpractice, so let it go."

"I can't." Camille swallowed to quell the rising tears. "I've got to find out who this Willcox guy is. I'd be surprised if he trained at Harvard, but I want to make some calls just to be sure. I'm going to call one of our old Harvard surgeon friends to see if he knows anything about Willcox."

"You really don't want to jeopardize your practice. You're making a shit ton of money here. You sure you want to risk that?"

"Just humor me. There aren't any plaintiff's lawyers in town who've got connections inside Harvard Medical School. I'm going to call an old doctor buddy and see what he knows about Willcox. Then I'll refer the case. I promise." Camille stuffed the records into her oversized black purse and hoisted it onto her shoulder. "I gotta go. Gracie has a cello concert in forty-five minutes."

As soon as Camille got off the elevator in the parking garage, she fished out her cell phone. "Hi, Gage. It's Camille Delaney. It's been forever! How are Barbi and the twins?"

"Hey, stranger! You're right—it's been forever for sure. We're all great. You guys?"

"We're good. Hey, I see you're in Detroit these days. How'd you end up there?"

"Well, where else would you expect to find a trauma junkie like me? Motown's happenin', babe, once you get used to it. Actually, it's not so bad. There's a golf course on every corner out in the burbs where we live."

"Golf? You?"

"Yeah, I'm getting old. The doc told me to lighten up on hang gliding. Old-guy knees, you know."

"Do you have a minute? Or are you on your way out the door? I just realized it's almost dinnertime back there." Camille wandered around the garage, looking for her car.

"Are you kidding? You should see the OR schedule in this place. I'm just getting my second wind. What's up?"

"I promise I won't keep you, but I'm working on this case, and I need some information. I think you can help."

"As long as you're on the side of truth and justice."

Whatever that means, Camille thought. "Of course."

"So, why do you need my help? Don't they have any surgeons out there on the West Coast, or does everyone just meditate away their ailments?"

"I need you for your brilliant mind. Why else? Here's the deal: there's this guy out here who calls himself a surgeon. Says he trained under a Dr. Irving." Camille got into her car. "Sam says he remembers him. I assume you knew him too?"

"Of course I know Irving. What's your doc's name? The one you're asking about? I probably knew him."

"Willcox, Andrew Willcox the third."

"Never heard of him. You sure he's not a soap opera character? The name's a bit much, don't you think?"

Camille smiled. "I'm not kidding; that's his name."

"And? You're defending him, I assume."

"Not exactly . . ."

"Hold on . . . you want me to help you sue the guy? I thought you said you were on our side."

"No, I said I was on the side of truth and justice."

"Same difference."

"Hang on; hear me out."

"Shit, Camille! I can't believe it. What does Sam think about this? Is it the money?"

"Not exactly. Believe it or not, it's an integrity thing."

"Whatchu smokin' out there, girl?"

Camille grinned as Gage lapsed easily into the street parlance of his native Harlem. "You really want a lecture on the civil justice system? How much time do you have?" Camille deftly navigated her car through the busy downtown traffic.

"How 'bout the abbreviated version of how a nice girl like you ended up on the dark side."

"You wouldn't believe some of the stuff I see. It's hard for mainstream medical folks to imagine how bad it can be out there." Camille sped up to make it through a yellow light. "Okay, tell me what you think of this: this Willcox guy perfed an aorta with a trocar while he was trying to do a lap chole on a two-hundred-fifty-pound guy."

"Hold on. He what?"

"You heard me, he perfed the aorta with a trocar."

"Do you know how hard he'd have to have been pushing on the thing to get it through the aorta, especially on a guy that big?"

"I have a pretty good idea, but that's not all. It took him thirty-two minutes to figure out what he'd done before he opened the guy up." A car honked at her as she waited for a herd of conventioneers with name tags hanging around their necks jaywalking in front of her, heading for the Sheraton.

"Thirty-two minutes! While the guy's bleeding to death? You gotta be shittin' me. What happened to the patient?"

"He died."

"I'm really sorry, but what do you want from me?"

"First of all, do you still know Irving?" She headed through South Lake Union and got stuck behind the streetcar that had been given the moniker "the SLUT" for South Lake Union Transit. Try as they might, the city council had been unsuccessful in redirecting the local tech workers to another nickname.

"Of course. He ruined the four best years of my life. I love the guy."

"Any chance you could call him and ask if he's ever heard of Willcox?"

"No problem. Tell me his full name again."

"Willcox. W-I-L-L-C-O-X. Andrew Willcox the third."

"When did you say he graduated?"

"I didn't, but he looks like he's around fifty."

"So, he would have been doing a residency at Harvard in the midnineties?"

"Yeah, I guess so."

"I doubt he was in Boston. I was there from ninety-six to two thousand, around the same time Sam was there, and I'd definitely remember him if he was in my program."

"Actually, it may be more useful to me if it turns out he never trained there at all. It'd mean he's lied about his qualifications."

"You're talking like a lawyer now, babe."

"Occupational hazard, I guess. Hey, give my love to Barbi and the boys."

"I'm being paged to the OR . . . I have your number. I'll call you back after I talk to Irving."

"Thanks, Gage."

Camille hung up the phone and turned down the narrow road where all the houseboat dwellers parked. *One step at a time,* she told herself. *If Willcox wasn't from Harvard, why had he lied about his training? And where the hell was this guy really from?*

CHAPTER NINE

It was a beautiful September day in the Pacific Northwest. The sky was a brilliant blue, and the water sparkled in return. The mountains proudly displayed their spectacular snowy peaks to the green forests below. And the clarity of the air was indescribable to anyone who had never experienced a sunny fall day in the San Juan Islands.

Ruby had left Camille completely unsettled for the past two months. And the opinion of Dr. Rosenberg hadn't helped. It had become hard to concentrate on her caseload—she would find herself in court, arguing about how her client couldn't possibly get along on only $20,000 per month, and her mind would suddenly wander to how she could figure out if the credentials letter in Willcox's file was real. Or who she could hire as an expert witness. But she couldn't leave her practice. It wasn't just the money. Or was it?

As often happened when Camille was facing one of those life-changing decisions, her mother abruptly reemerged. This time, she had announced that she was flying in from her family home on the Greek island of Lesvos, where she'd been living the past few years while she set up and ran an asylum project for Syrian refugees. She was heading to an urgent meeting in Friday Harbor with a group of her high-tech millionaire donors at one of their Island homes. They wanted an update on the progress of her rapidly growing project and to strategize the next steps in light of the changing political climate. Camille's mom popped back and forth between the Greek Islands and the San

Juans—or pretty much any place in the world—like New Yorkers shuttled back and forth to DC.

It hadn't taken much arm-twisting for Camille to convince Sam to join her for an unexpected weekend on their sailboat on San Juan Island. Their boat was moored next to Dallas and Gloria's boat in Friday Harbor—some people in the Northwest have vacation cabins, and others have boats moored in marinas in picturesque little harbors around the Islands. Camille loved their marine version of the RV life. Camille was looking forward to meeting her mom for dinner in Friday Harbor. She needed to think through her next career steps, and her mom was always her sounding board. And it didn't seem to be a coincidence that her mom had showed up at this exact time.

After their day-long sail in the cold, blustery winds, Sam gathered his papers and settled in to work on the speech he was giving at an upcoming symposium in London while Camille hurriedly layered on her fleece. She didn't want to be late for her mom's ferry. The plan was for them to meet and then walk together to the cabin that one of her mom's donors had offered her for her brief Island stay. Then they could go grab dinner in town. Camille kissed Sam goodbye, stopping to appreciate the scene she was regretfully departing—Sam and the dog alone with a thick, steamy pizza.

Pella Rallis never missed an opportunity to make an entrance, even if it was just disembarking from a crowded Friday evening ferry. Camille stood on her tiptoes and waved as her mom hugged a woman and her little girl, both of whom had likely been perfect strangers to her up until they had met by chance, probably in line for coffee or hot chocolate, on the giant ferry. That pretty much defined Pella—give her an hour on a ferry with a crowd of perfect strangers and, before they made landfall, she'd have made another friend for life. She had that way about her. Pella adjusted her world-worn backpack and broke into a slow jog toward her daughter, enveloping her in her arms. Camille didn't want to let go.

"I'm so glad you're here, Mama." Camille pronounced the word in Greek, with the accent on the second syllable.

Pella stepped back from her daughter's grasp, as mothers do. "Let me look at you." She put both hands over her mouth and blew a kiss at her daughter. "Beautiful—you are absolutely beautiful. I've missed you so much."

Camille felt the familiar empty ache, knowing her time with her mother would be short and intense. Then she'd jet off to care for others across the world. Camille couldn't remember the last time her mother made it to one of her own granddaughters' birthday parties or sporting activities. Sometimes it felt like everyone else mattered more to her than her own family. Maybe that was what made time with her mom so extra special. Camille vowed to savor every moment.

Mother and daughter walked in lockstep across the street and along the waterfront road toward the cabin. Pella was a natural beauty in the vein of Helen Mirren, and her Greek accent made her all the more stunning.

"Tell me, how's Gloria?" Pella asked as she held tightly to Camille's hand.

"Devastated." Camille felt the tears welling up. "She's trying to keep busy teaching her yoga classes, but Robin and I are trying to convince her to head down to her friend's place in Todos Santos for the winter. I'm hoping she'll leave after the Baja hurricane season, so probably early November."

"That's a great idea." Pella nodded.

It was a ten-minute walk, and by the time they reached the cabin, Camille had caught her mother up on the status of her investigation and what she was planning to do next.

It didn't take long for Pella to locate the hidden key in the garden shed, and they were inside the knotty pine living room within minutes of their arrival. Pella picked up a large white envelope and opened it.

"Well, how sweet is this? The Hellers had a platter of fresh oysters on the half shell delivered this afternoon along with some soup and a fresh baguette."

Camille marveled at how her mother's network took care of her—who just showed up to a cabin fully stocked with everything needed for an elegant fireside dinner? Sometimes it seemed like her own mother belonged more to her huge circle of admirers than to her own family.

"No need to go to town for dinner!" Pella announced happily.

"What's the latest on Lesvos?" Camille shifted the conversation to her mother's work as she took two plates off the open shelves while her mother leaned over to light the carefully placed logs in the stone fireplace.

"Over twenty thousand refugees and migrants on the Aegean Islands." Pella's long wavy gray hair was pulled into a bun that showcased her multiple ear piercings. She shook her head. "Twenty percent of the migrants are women, and thirty-five percent are children. Lots to do." Pella pulled the oysters and soup and a bottle of sauvignon blanc out of the fridge.

Camille poured them each a glass of wine while her mother turned the stove on under the pot of soup. "How many of those kids are unaccompanied?"

"Current estimate is seventeen percent." Pella knew her statistics backward and forward.

"How many lawyers are you managing over there now?"

"About a hundred and twenty-five at any given time. God, I love my volunteers—they work not only on Lesvos but also remotely from all over the world to represent these families who are just looking for a place to call home." Pella smiled as she put the baguette into the oven.

Despite her longing for more of her mother's attention, Camille was captivated by her mother's visionary leadership. She understood on some level that she was sharing this remarkable woman with the world for a reason. "How do you do it, Mom?"

"Do what?"

"How do you know what to do and when to do it?" Camille squeezed a wedge of lemon over the oysters and wiped a stinging twinge from her eye.

"Honestly, once you have a clear vision, it's just a matter of figuring out what needs to be done, and then everything just seems to drop into place." Pella cradled her chin in her hands. "How about you, darling? You must be completely unsettled. We talked about Gloria and your lawyering on the Dallas mess, but how are you actually holding up?" Pella rubbed Camille's back. "I miss him so much. It must be awful for you—you got to see him all the time. I only got my Dallas fixes when I came to town a few times a year."

"I miss him constantly. I can't stop thinking about him on the operating table. If he were here, he'd know what to tell me that would make the world make some kind of sense. I'm so glad you're here."

Camille smiled at her mother as she noticed some of the tension leaving her upper back for the first time in a while. She clearly felt safe in her mother's presence. "I don't know what to do, Mom. I have this fancy-ass office in a hoity-toity law firm. And I'm making a fortune. But I don't think it's enough." The fireplace crackled. "I think I want to do something more like what you do, really helping people, but I'm not you. I'm not a brainiac international lawyer. I'm not adventurous. I want to help Gloria with Dallas's case, but I can't do it without losing my job."

"You went to law school to be a plaintiff's lawyer and represent people who've been wronged. To be honest, I never fully understood why you did a one-eighty and switched gears after doing it for just a few years. And how on earth you ended up in such a corporate place, I'll never know."

It wasn't often that her mom offered such a bold assessment of Camille's life choices—it made her listen even more carefully.

"I'm tired of working with a bunch of middle-aged white men." Camille stopped to gather her thoughts. "Don't get me wrong. I like them—they've become friends—but I just don't want to spend my professional life being dictated to by this male-dominated hierarchy. I'm sick of being told what cases I can and can't take and having my cases valued only by how much money they bring into the firm. We never discuss the idea of using the law for good, like what you do."

"Tell me why you left plaintiff's litigation and joined the hierarchy in the first place."

"I was scared to work in a system where my livelihood would be dictated by a bunch of political hacks. You know better than anyone how politicians can change the laws that impact the kinds of cases we can take. They can pass a law, and poof, legal fees or damages are limited or a cause of action is gone. And to be honest, sometimes I don't trust my judgment about which cases to take and which ones to turn away." Camille opened a bottle of San Pellegrino. "Meanwhile, there you are, over there on your Greek island, fighting in court for asylum for hundreds of people. And their lives are at the mercy of immigration laws and courts around the world. I'm not sure I have the stomach for that. It's so sad."

"Well, me being a crazy asylum lawyer on the other side of the world is a far cry from your corporate loft. Don't you think there might be something in between that would be more satisfying?" Pella's smile was genuine. "And you have excellent legal judgment, so let's not even go there."

"To tell you the truth, I'm not sure I even want to be a lawyer anymore. The whole system sucks."

"Have a better idea? A better system?"

"And I can't just quit. We need reliable income, and plaintiff's lawyers go for months without being paid when they're working on a case. I'd be terrified. I'm afraid I couldn't focus on the work." Camille stabbed an oyster and devoured it in one bite. "In my line of work, we get paid by the clients, win or lose. I've become a master of the billable hour, and I'm pretty much the chief rainmaker at the firm. How do I give that up?"

Pella cocked her head. "I get that, but remember, to everything there is a season and a time for every purpose under heaven."

Leave it to my mother to quote some sixties song.

"So . . . what season are you in?"

"I think this is the season where you say, 'I told you so.'" Camille looked forlornly at her mother. The silence was notable and comfortable at the same time. "I'm just sick of my work being judged by a bunch of guys who only focus on the ever-present billable hour."

Pella was silent.

"I like most of my clients. And I know that they need help making it through really ugly situations as they disentangle in their divorces. But I also want to use the law for justice with a capital *J*. And my partners couldn't care less about that."

Pella dipped her oyster in the cocktail sauce and held it, dripping, in midair. "Do you want to change fields?" She was clearly hopeful.

"I don't know . . . I just want to feel like I'm making a difference. Like you." Camille paused. "And it's not just that I want to change my practice area. I just want to be able to take whatever cases I want, whenever I want to."

Pella gathered all her dormant trial lawyer skills, looking like she was preparing to cross-examine her witness. She leaned forward gently. "What did you like about being a plaintiff's lawyer the last time you did it?"

Camille topped off each of their glasses of wine. "Well, actually, I was working for some bigger concept of justice. And I used my nursing skills. I remember feeling like I was helping people in major life crises. They were scared and trying to navigate their way through an unbelievably confusing system."

Pella pulled the baguette out of the oven and tore off a chunk, dipping it into a shallow bowl of olive oil. "Tell me about some of those clients."

Camille smiled. Her mother had taught her that the best way to persuade is to let your witness do it themselves. "I know what you're doing." She laughed. "Let's see . . . I represented the family of a man who died after a doctor misdiagnosed a cancer. He left behind a wife with very little education and three kids. Their mortgage was foreclosed during litigation, and they had to move into a nasty little one-bedroom apartment because the mother didn't have the skills to support her family. When we finally settled the case, the mother was able to return to school and to afford a small house in the suburbs."

Pella tore another piece of bread and handed Camille half. "So, the system worked?"

"After a fashion. But not until after the mother was completely humiliated in her deposition. I honestly don't know what's worse, the original incident that brings someone to a lawyer or the indignities that are inflicted on them by the so-called justice system."

"Seems like you feel that you could make a difference if you had the freedom to take any case you want—even if you're suing a doctor."

"I think I'm just scared. I'm in a safe place. Money isn't a problem for once in my life. And, honestly, I'm not sure I have what it takes to be an entrepreneur. You're amazing, Mom. I'm not as good a lawyer as you. And I'm for sure not as brave."

Pella reached across the table and put her hand over Camille's.

Camille squeezed her mom's hand and continued. "You fight to get people freedom. All I can do is get people money. And money won't bring Dallas back."

"Of course not, but is there a better solution? Isn't that what the system's all about?" Pella queried her daughter.

"Yeah. Money. Period. Those responsible should pay."

"You know, the Bible discusses the principle of personal responsibility for wrongdoing. It's exactly what you've just explained to me."

"The Bible?" *Oh dear, Mother. Here we go . . .*

"Yeah. Just a sec, I'll bet there's one around here somewhere." Pella got up from the table, perusing the overloaded bookshelves surrounding the tiny living room.

While Pella searched the bookshelves, Camille scooped up two steaming bowls of crab bisque.

"All righty." Pella returned to the table with her head buried in the leather-bound volume. "Wouldn't Dallas be proud of us, talking world religion to solve your career challenges? Now, let me see . . . Where's that passage?" Pella rummaged in her backpack for her thick black reading glasses.

Camille waited as her mother flipped through the pages of the big old book.

"Here we go: Exodus, chapter twenty-one, verse eighteen." Pella smiled proudly. "Ya ready for this?"

"Go ahead." Camille took a slow drink of wine and closed her eyes, acutely feeling the loss of her friend and mentor.

"And if men strive together, and one smite another with a stone, or with his fist, and he die not, but keepeth his bed: If he rise again, and walk abroad upon his staff, then shall he that smote him be quit: only he shall pay for the loss of his time, and shall cause him to be thoroughly healed."

"Huh. The one who struck him shall pay his expenses and his medical bills. Sounds like our legal system . . . That's actually pretty amazing."

"It's not exactly a new concept, dear. If Dallas were here, he'd be explaining to us that we're each responsible for the effects of our actions on others." Pella closed the book. "I think justice is a calling."

"So, how did it turn into such a twisted and self-perpetuating system?" Camille asked thoughtfully.

"It's self-preservation. Once people create a system, it takes on a life of its own. And the principles upon which it was founded get lost in the egos of those who are dependent on the system they've created—kinda like your partners."

"Well, you're right about the justice system. Way too many people have a personal investment. It has nothing to do with justice. Only who can prove what."

"That's why we lawyers have to walk the walk, not just talk the talk." Pella looked at Camille, lawyer to lawyer.

"Sounds good but not so easy to remember on a day-to-day basis. Especially when you're trying to make a living."

"Camille, honey, you're having a crisis of conscience."

"I know that intellectually, but I have trouble remembering it when I'm in the middle of it."

"We all do. Remember when Dallas told us the story of the Ramayana? You were in nursing school, and we were having a picnic at the arboretum, in the Japanese Garden. I have such a vivid recollection of him telling us the story of how Krishna is driving Arjuna into battle on his chariot, and Arjuna is scared to death. He asks Krishna why the battle is taking place at all."

Camille nodded. "I love that you remember that afternoon." She held back the tears. "In the first few chapters, it becomes obvious that Arjuna's questions are really about life and death."

"That's right. The battle that Arjuna is headed into is not one of the outer world but in his own mind." Pella stopped and took a deep breath. "I still remember Dallas expounding on the fact that the battle in the story is a metaphor for the dichotomy between the material, outer, and inner worlds. It really made an impact on me. There really was no one like Dallas." She smiled tearfully at her daughter. "And here we are, all these years later, still learning this same lesson." Pella looked around the room. "It's almost like he's here with us now."

"So, I'm supposed to battle my fear of failure and my struggle about what it means to me to be a good lawyer." This time, Camille didn't even try to stop the tears.

"You're doing the right thing, asking yourself the hard questions. See if you can define the term 'good lawyer' in a way that's consistent with your own value system."

"I have a feeling I've been avoiding asking myself those same questions."

"Because?"

"Because I'm afraid of the answers."

—

Camille tried to be quiet as she tripped over Sam's foul-weather gear lying on the floor and made her way to the V-berth in the bow of the boat, where Sam and Jake snored in harmony. The boat smelled faintly of wet dog. She shook Sam. Jake looked at her disdainfully for disturbing a perfectly good guys' night. Then he yawned and nuzzled back into his position under the double sleeping bag.

"Wake up," she whispered loudly.

Sam turned over and groaned. "What time is it?"

"I don't know. Are you awake?"

"I am now. Are you coming to bed or what?" he asked sleepily.

"In a minute. We need to talk first."

"Can this wait till morning?"

"No." She shook him again. "This is important."

"Okay." He rubbed his eyes and squinted at her. "What's up?"

"I've decided to quit my job."

Sam's eyes suddenly focused. "How much did you and your mom have to drink tonight?"

"Apparently just the right amount. We were talking about values and doing the right thing." The words tumbled from Camille's mouth. "And I just noticed that there's nothing inherently worthwhile about me letting a bunch of middle-aged white guys tell me how I need to practice law."

Sam sat up in bed, his hair pointing every which way. "You're serious, aren't you?"

"Yup. When we get back on Monday, I'm giving my notice. I want my own office again."

"Camille, do you remember what it was like not to get a paycheck for months on end? How do you suggest we pay the girls' tuition?"

"I broke my previous billable hours record this year, so I'll be getting a huge partner distribution, and if I need extra money, I can use the girls' college funds until I settle Dallas's case."

Sam sighed. "Seriously? We're not using the girls' college funds to subsidize a new office for you. We can discuss this in the morning—after we've had a cup of coffee."

"We can discuss it anytime you want, but I'm not changing my mind. I'm going to get myself an office and take Dallas's case."

Sam flopped back on the pillows. "Jesus, Camille."

"I thought you loved me for my spontaneity."

Sam smiled sleepily at his wife. He pulled Jake up to his chest. "Fasten your seat belt, boy. We're about to get spontaneous."

—

First thing Monday morning, even the emaciated receptionist at Whitfield, Bahr, and Moses looked up as Camille charged through the austere lobby. She wound her way down the maze of hallways to where Amy sat, opening mail. Camille handed her a tall double mocha and wiggled her finger in the direction of her office.

Amy followed. "Yes?"

Camille perched on the arm of her white loveseat. "Just how happy are you working here at the fine firm of Whitfield, Bahr, and Moses?"

Amy raised her eyebrows. "Am I being fired?"

"No . . . more like promoted."

"To?"

"Well, how about office manager, paralegal extraordinaire." Camille swept her arm in an arc. "And anything else necessary for a small but extremely successful one-lawyer office."

She held her breath. She'd be sunk without Amy.

Amy laughed. "Camille, have you lost your mind?"

"Nope." Camille hoped Amy wouldn't detect the slight nervousness in her voice. "Congratulations are in order. I'm quitting. And you are cordially invited to join me."

"Join you where?"

"I dunno. Any ideas?"

Amy put her hands on her hips. "Did you go on another one of your yoga retreats this weekend?"

Camille walked behind her mammoth glass desk. "Nope, we went sailing. And I might have had dinner with my mom, who always has something to say." She smiled mischievously as she turned to look out over the Sound sparkling in the afternoon sun. *Please, please, say yes.*

"Well, I'm not a bit surprised that your mom is on board with this plan, but have you mentioned this to Sam?"

"Of course."

"And?"

"And he thinks we're going to go broke."

"Are we?"

"Of course not. We have our first case, and it's a winner. Jackson versus Willcox. How soon can we get it filed?"

"Well, I hate to be a stickler for detail, but we need some pleading paper first."

"See? I need you. Will you come with me?" Camille feigned a prayerful stance. "Please?"

"Can you afford me?"

Camille went over and stood directly in front of her friend and paralegal. "I can't afford not to have you. C'mon. It'll be fun."

"Have you told your partners yet?"

"No, I thought I'd wait till we find a place. By the way, can you find me a place while I go to the Island and start our first investigation?"

"Look, Camille, I'd love to go with you, but I'm not married to a rich doctor. I need a paycheck."

"Well, I'm not married to a rich doctor either. Sam works for the university, remember? And of course you'll get a paycheck. So, are you in?"

"Where do you want me to look for an office?"

"How about somewhere on the lake? So I can kayak to work. Let's make this a major lifestyle change."

"Do I get my own kayak?"

"You drive a hard bargain." *She's gonna come.* "What color do you want?"

"Green."

"It's as good as done."

"Okay. Count me in."

"Fantastic! Now would you please draft me a resignation letter and, while you're at it, draft a lawsuit against Willcox and Friday Harbor General. We'll file it as soon as we get ourselves set up. I'm going to go call Trish and see if she was serious when she offered to go undercover in Friday Harbor."

CHAPTER TEN

Camille awoke abruptly to the familiar symphony of raindrops harmonizing with the creaking houseboat as it swayed slowly back and forth on its moorings. She'd been in the new office in Fremont for a few weeks and still had dreams about family law motions court. How long would it take for her to realize that those days were behind her? And so were the billable hours—at least for now, until she could wrangle some clients. And the certainty of a paycheck was fast becoming a distant memory.

She knew from the damp chill that a marine front had blown in overnight. It was dark. Very dark. She could barely make out the shadow of the Boston Whaler dancing hauntingly in the mist outside their bedroom window. Fall. Fog. Football season. Time to trade tank tops for turtlenecks. Camille pulled the thick down comforter around her chin and snuggled up next to Sam. She had a few more minutes to relax until she had to get up and head out to catch the ferry for a noon meeting with Dallas's family doctor.

Because Dr. Hennesey had been on vacation for the entire summer, Camille had anxiously waited for September to roll around. And since Willcox's explanation for doing a so-called emergency gallbladder surgery was that Dallas had long suffered from gastric pain, Camille was especially curious to hear what Hennesey had to say about Dallas's health history.

She got up and quickly made a smoothie. Then she took off down the dock.

Camille's phone rang just when she was getting on the Anacortes ferry. "Your new office couch is being delivered today," Amy announced. "You want me to use your credit card for the delivery charge?"

"Sure." Camille did a mental calculation of the amount she'd spent to get the office up and running. Thankfully, Amy knew how to find furniture on clearance. So far, they were pretty much staying on budget. "That'd be great." She turned off her engine as directed by the deckhand on the ferry. "I'm not sure what time I'll be back today. Can you call Trish and see if she has any background info on any of the docs in the OR with Dallas: the assistant surgeon, the vascular guy, and the anesthesiologist?"

"On it." Amy hung up.

—

Dr. Henry Hennesey's clinic was located in a converted farmhouse that smelled of mildew and Betadine. Camille shuddered at the dust-covered baseboards and directed her attention to the man who looked vaguely like the Pillsbury Doughboy. She tried to sit still so the spindly chair wouldn't squeak beneath her.

Hennesey chewed his fingernails as he bounced in his scuffed-up leather chair. "Let's see . . . Dallas's last physical exam was . . . uh . . . about two months before he died." He flipped to the lab slips at the back of the chart. "Uh . . . cholesterol was somewhat high, which indicates moderate to severe hardening of the arteries, normal for a man of sixty-five." He turned another page thoughtfully. "He was slightly overweight but not enough to worry about, and . . . let's see . . . his prostate blood test was normal."

Hennesey closed the chart. "Look, Ms. Delaney, Dallas was a faithful patient of mine for many years . . . A great man. It's such a pity. Unfortunately, I was away all summer. I . . . I'm sure Dr. Willcox did everything he could," he stammered. "Did you know he trained at Harvard under Dr. James Irving, a world-famous surgeon?"

"Well, that's impressive." Camille wondered if anyone at Friday Harbor General had actually checked with the state licensing board to see if he'd *really* trained at Harvard. "Dr. Hennesey, I'm curious," Camille said innocently. "It's my understanding that Dallas had to have surgery to treat an inflamed gallbladder, and I guess I thought that you'd have expected him to have complained of some kind of ongoing symptoms. You haven't mentioned a history of any stomach pain. I'm a bit confused."

A faint pinkish glow crept up Hennesey's milky-white face. "Excellent question, Ms. Delaney." He got up abruptly and opened the window. "Are you warm?" He removed his white coat with his name embroidered on the pocket and loosened his tie.

"I'm fine," she said without taking her eyes off him. He wasn't going to avoid her questions that easily.

Hennesey settled uneasily back into his chair. "Stomach pain is such a common complaint for men of Dallas's age, I imagine I probably just hadn't bothered to record it in his chart. But just because I didn't write it down doesn't mean Dallas didn't suffer from right upper outer quadrant pain. In fact, now that you mention it"—he nodded and held up his index finger—"I think I recall Dallas mentioning abdominal pain over the years." Hennesey avoided eye contact with Camille as he opened the chart.

A medical assistant stuck her head into the office. "Doctor, your next patient is waiting."

Hennesey quickly stood and tightened his tie. "Well, I guess duty calls."

"But, Doctor, surely if Dallas had a problem with gastric pain, you'd at least have made a few notes about it, wouldn't you?"

"I'd love to discuss this further, but I really must be getting back to my patients."

Camille got up and took a few steps, placing herself between the doctor and the door. "Mrs. Jackson is wondering if Dallas really needed the surgery in the first place. She doesn't remember him having any trouble with stomach pain."

"I'll take a closer look at my records and give you a call." He tried to step around Camille.

She grabbed Dallas's chart. "I'd like a copy of the records." She handed the doctor a release.

Hennesey glanced at the paper. "It . . . it would be easier if we just emailed them to you."

"I'll wait."

———

Andrew Willcox stood in his huge kitchen overlooking the San Juan Channel. The sun peeked out from behind a cloud, reflecting for a moment on the deep-blue water before disappearing behind a bank of gray clouds. Willcox finished off his PowerBar, then picked a perfect pear out of the sterling silver fruit basket in the middle of the cooking island. As if anyone in the house actually knew how to cook. He methodically peeled the pear over the vegetable sink, careful not to leave anything out of place. As a surgeon, he valued meticulousness in every aspect of his life. He pushed the peel down the disposal and wiped off the granite countertop as his phone lit up. He always answered it on the third ring.

Hennesey skipped the pleasantries. "This is Hank. I just got out of a meeting with a lady lawyer about the Jackson case. Andy, you know as well as I do that Jackson didn't have cholecystitis. And so does the lawyer. She asked a bunch of questions. Like his pre-op symptoms. And his history. And—"

"Shut up, Hank! What do you mean you had a meeting with a lawyer? What was her name?"

"Delaney, Camille Delaney. The medical release she left me says she's from Seattle. I have her office address."

Willcox grabbed a pad and scrawled *Camille Delaney* on it. "What the hell do you think you're doing discussing one of my patients with a lawyer!"

"I have nothing to hide. I was at a rodeo in Ellensburg when the guy died."

"Look, I can prove he had a hot gallbladder. I performed a multifactorial battery of diagnostic tests on him. And you've seen the pathology report. Don't you *ever* discuss one of my patients with a lawyer. Ever. Do you understand me?"

Willcox hung up and dialed his assistant, Vic Jones. "We need to set up a surveillance on a lady lawyer in Seattle. My old Chris-Craft cabin cruiser is just coming out of the yard. Pick it up today and get down to Seattle stat. You can moor it in some marina down there and stay on it while you figure out what the hell is going on with the lawyer."

"Okay, and who am I setting up surveillance on?"

Willcox looked at the pad. "Camille Delaney."

"Got any more info on her?"

"Nope. Just that she's a lawyer. You can Google her address. Hennesey says her office is in Seattle."

Willcox looked up to see Dr. Carl Burton banging on his front door. Burton was the local pathologist who served as Willcox's surgical assistant after training as a surgeon in his first career. Willcox hung up on Vic and waved Burton in.

Burton pushed past Willcox and slung his briefcase onto the kitchen island. "BJ got an email from the real estate agent in Arizona." He took out his laptop. "The property next to our retirement community is going up for sale for eight million. We—"

Willcox interrupted. "That'll have to wait. There's some lady lawyer asking questions about the Jackson case."

"So what?" Burton didn't look up from logging on to his laptop. "We checked him out. He was unemployed. Old. And no dependent kids. No lawyer is gonna take a case like that—there's no money in it. And besides, there's no case to pursue. The op report says there was an aneurysm that you had no way of knowing was there, and that kind of complication is"—Burton made air quotes—"a known risk of the procedure. Calm down."

Willcox paced across the kitchen. "I hate lawyers. I don't want to have to deal with this!"

"You won't. My path report describes an aneurysm, and I deleted Gonzalez's op report from the hospital computer." Burton rolled his eyes. "So, what's the problem?"

"The problem is that we need inventory, and I don't want to draw unwanted attention to our operation right now."

"Vic has another trauma case lined up for Friday night."

"Yeah? Who?"

"There's a guy named Westchester who lives out on Wellesley Road. Been on disability for a broken hip," Burton said.

"Kids?" Willcox asked.

"Nope, just him and his old lady. Living off the system. And they're not married. She couldn't bring suit if she wanted to."

"Car accident?"

"I think so."

"Sounds good to me. Keep 'em rolling." Willcox chuckled. "Might raise some questions with the lawyer nosing around in our business."

"Are you kidding? People get in car accidents all the time. Especially guys who drink too much. I can put a toxicology screen in his chart with an elevated blood alcohol—that'll stop people from asking questions."

"Car accident." Willcox nodded approvingly. "Okay, I need to call Vic and tell him to put off his trip down to Seattle for a few days."

"Seattle trip?"

"Sending him down to keep an eye on the lady lawyer."

"Well, tell him we need a one-car spin out. And let's do it tonight. We can't wait until Friday. Time is of the essence."

Willcox changed the subject. "How much more do we need to get that property in Arizona?"

"BJ thinks we can get it for seven point five, so we need another two in addition to the money we're getting from the refi. At that point, we'll be totally liquid."

Willcox nodded.

"By the way, your wife's a fucking genius." Burton referred to BJ Willcox with notable admiration. "She's got us a ton of negotiating room by keeping all that cash in the bank just ready for us to make a move."

Willcox dialed Vic. "Slight change in plans. We need that accident tonight for the inventory, then you can head to Seattle the day after tomorrow."

"Got it," Vic answered. "That guy out on Wellesley Road? I thought we were doing him on Friday."

"Tonight." Willcox was firm.

"Okay. If he's in town, I should be able to make it happen. It'll probably be late. He tends to stay out drinking until midnight or so."

"Okay, so we have a busy night. There's a little girl who's going to be pretty happy tomorrow."

Burton shook his head. "And we've got actual paying patients waiting on a liver, a heart, a pancreas, and another kidney." He pulled his cell phone out and dialed Net Copters. "We need a helicopter in Friday Harbor tomorrow. Seven a.m. pickup, with drop-off over on Brigantine Island by Decatur." He paused. "Yeah, I know there's a last-minute charge. Put it on our account—Andrew Willcox." He slammed the door behind him.

Willcox looked at his watch. It was just after lunchtime in Arizona. He took a breath and dialed, hoping he could catch her before she left for her art class. He took a dog-eared picture out of his wallet and gazed into the clear blue eyes. It had been too long.

———

Camille sat in her car on the bow of the ferry and watched it cut through churning black water as it headed out into the San Juan Channel. She cracked her window just a bit to let in the smell of cold sea air and pulled out a purple legal pad so she could organize the evidence she'd discovered so far. Before she knew it, the ferry attendant was knocking on her window, telling her to start her car. Time to disembark in Anacortes. She headed out of town in the increasing drizzle. Just as she passed Snow Goose, her favorite vegetable stand that was closed for the season in the wintry gray farmland of the Skagit Valley, Ruby called to report that Willcox and the hospital administrator were livestreaming on a local community Facebook page. Ruby put her phone near the computer so Camille could hear it.

"And the doctor is going to be telling us about a revolutionary new surgical procedure that he says is *guaranteed* to get rid of that nasty heartburn we all experience at two o'clock in the morning," the hospital administrator said proudly. "Right, Doc?"

"Hey, Ruby, can you write down the time and name of the Facebook page so I can find this later?" Camille asked. "I'm driving."

"Sure, honey," Ruby responded.

"You bet," Willcox said. "I guarantee if *I* do this procedure at Friday Harbor General, you *will* get rid of your heartburn."

"Gee, Doc, with a *guarantee* like that, we can hardly wait to find out all about this cutting-edge procedure, if you don't mind my pun." The administrator was obviously pleased with his play on words.

"Well, Tom, as we all know, heartburn is something everyone suffers from at one time or another. And more so as we age."

"Tell us what causes heartburn, Dr. Willcox."

"Sure, Tom. The medical term for heartburn is *reflux esophagitis.*"

Another chuckle. "No wonder they call it heartburn."

Camille rolled her eyes. *Everyone thinks they're Anderson Cooper.*

"Reflux is just what it sounds like: the contents of the stomach swish up into the tube that our food travels down, which is the esophagus."

"I failed science; now I know why I ended up on the administrative side of medicine."

Willcox laughed gratuitously.

The drizzle turned into a driving rain as Camille merged onto I-5 South. She turned the windshield wipers to high and cranked up the defroster.

"And now what does medical science have to offer us in the way of treatment?" Tom asked.

"There's a great surgical procedure that can be done quite simply, with minimal recovery time. It's called a laparoscopic Nissen fundoplication."

"Whoa, Doc. Come again?"

"In the business, we just call it a lap Nissen, Tom."

"So, what all's involved?"

It began to hail, and traffic slowed to a crawl. Camille strained to hear as staccato beats rang on the roof of her car.

"Basically, we just thread a tiny fiber-optic camera through a hole in the skin into the area at the top of the stomach and locate the valve that's become weakened. Then we use tiny instruments to tighten the opening between the stomach and the esophagus."

"And presto chango, no more heartburn?"

"That's pretty much it."

"We have lots of questions in the chat, Doctor. Let's scroll through and get some answers."

So that's where he gets all his patients. Cutting-edge procedure? Shit, they've been doing lap Nissens for decades. And how come no one in the medical business knows it's a potential violation of the Consumer Protection Act to guarantee a surgical result? It seems like maybe some continuing education would be in order for these two yahoos.

"Thanks, Ruby," Camille said. "That little discussion just might come in handy at some point."

CHAPTER ELEVEN

To say Camille was shocked when the assistant surgeon, Max Gonzalez, had agreed to meet with her would be an understatement. In all her years as a plaintiff's medical malpractice lawyer, no treating doctor had ever even answered her call, let alone come to a meeting. Not surprisingly, the anesthesiologist had flatly refused Amy's request to schedule even a brief call with Camille, because doctors who are colleagues never criticize each other, ever, or hardly ever. So, the fact that Dr. Gonzalez had not only agreed to meet but had arranged to do so at his brother-in-law's B and B on a totally different island in the San Juans was beyond intriguing.

When the day of the meeting finally arrived, Sam convinced Camille to let him come so they could make a romantic weekend of it.

Angela stopped brushing her black hair long enough to help Camille pile the duffel bags and backpacks from the front porch of the houseboat onto the dock cart. "Where'd you get that ugly purple leather jacket?" she asked her mother.

"I got it at the Nordstrom sale. And it's aubergine, not purple." Camille turned away from Angela and pulled a prescription bottle out of the front pocket of her jeans. She popped a low-dose Valium in preparation for the flight to the Island.

"Well, if you got it at that sale, you can be sure you'll see it on every street corner in Seattle this winter. You should take it back."

"I like it. I'm keeping it."

"You'll be sorry." Angela flung her hair over her shoulder and pushed the cart up the dock. Camille grabbed the door to close it and shouted up the stairs to Robin, who had come to town from her place in Sequim. It was always a win-win when she came to town for the weekend. The girls loved hanging out with her, and Camille and Sam usually got some time alone. "Thanks for watching the girls! Call us if you need anything!"

"It's going to be a blast!" Robin responded. "I got us tickets to the WNBA championship game tomorrow night. Can't wait!"

"I'll let you know what I find out from the mysterious Dr. G.!"

"It had better be good," Robin shouted.

Camille shut the door and hurried to catch up with Angela, stopping to admire the vintage Chris-Craft cabin cruiser that had arrived a couple of weeks ago and was moored in a slip fifty feet from her bedroom window, across the narrow canal from her houseboat. It seemed strange that she still hadn't met the owner—most people on the lake went out of their way to be friendly. But the guy on the cabin cruiser almost seemed like he was avoiding the neighbors. Still, Camille waved at the silhouette of the stocky man standing on the stern who grabbed the dock line and quickly jumped off the boat without taking his eyes off her. She turned to see if he was looking at something behind her. But no, he was staring right at her. She picked up her pace and broke into a run up the dock, with Jake nipping at her heels.

It was less than a five-minute drive to the small cement block building that stood under the weathered "Island Air" sign where Tony stood waiting.

"Where's Sam?"

Camille let Jake out of the car and looked around. "What? Sam, late?" She and Tony shared a knowing laugh. "While we're waiting, I have a question."

"Shoot." Tony smiled.

Camille took out her phone and showed Tony the picture she had taken of the helicopter the morning that Dallas died. "You know who this belongs to?"

Tony took the phone. "Yeah, it's part of the Net Copters fleet. I moonlight for them and sometimes take folks up to islands where they don't have room for a landing strip."

"Like . . ."

"Well, lately I've done a few charters to Brigantine Island over by Decatur. There's a big new compound over there. And sometimes the folks I take over seem pretty sick. That's why they charter a copter. They can't handle the water taxi." He paused. "Turns out they're part of one of those Make-A-Wish things, where dying people get to go on some kind of luxury vacation. Seems super sweet, and so sad."

"Any idea who owns the place?"

"I don't know for sure, but I do know that the architect is BJ Willcox, who's married to one of the doctors over in Friday Harbor. I shuttle her back and forth every once in a while. I'm pretty sure she managed the entire building project, which was finished last spring. Her doctor husband goes over every once in a while. I think he helps with the medical care."

Camille raised an eyebrow in curiosity.

"And those outer islands have no stores or services," Tony explained, "so they always end up schlepping all kinds of coolers and bins of groceries, which increases the charter fee, so it's a win-win for me. A Friday Harbor church has fundraisers to pay for the food and extras. BJ and her husband are big in the church, so they're pretty involved with the charity that runs the place."

"Any idea who funds it?" Camille asked as she walked Jake over to the bushes for one last potty break.

"Not sure exactly, but you know as well as I do that these islands are packed with all kinds of Seattle tech millionaires with mad getaways. They keep me busy flying them all over the Islands. I know lots of them have been pretty involved in nonprofits."

"You got that right. My mom was up here a few weeks ago for some kind of summit called by a bunch of her funders."

"Must be nice," Tony mused.

The conversation was interrupted by Sam squealing into the parking lot.

Tony opened Camille's trunk and threw a backpack over each shoulder. "How long are you two planning to be gone, anyway?" He grabbed a case of wine out of the trunk as a burly guy with a thick silver earring jumped out of his car. He put on a pair of aviator sunglasses and pulled his hood up over his head and a gaiter up over his mouth and nose as he walked toward the dock where the floatplanes took off.

"Here, let me help," the guy offered as he took the case of wine from Tony. "It's freezing down here on the water." He pulled on his gloves.

Sam nodded and looked up. "Feels like a marine front is blowing in." He grabbed the two duffel bags.

"Where y'all headed?" the guy asked.

"Friday Harbor, on San Juan Island," Tony responded.

Tony grabbed the case of wine from the guy and hoisted it into the cabin. He stopped and looked up. "Gonna be a nice sunset. Thanks for your help." He flipped down the step so Camille could board.

Camille stood frozen in front of the plane, her eyes unfocused.

The familiar smell of Tony's clove cigarette brought Camille slowly back to reality.

Camille put her foot on the step and stopped to check the weather. Then she climbed in.

"Shall we?" Tony reached in and tightened Camille's seat belt. "You okay?" He gave her a knowing look. "This should be an easy trip. The water was pretty smooth up there this morning."

"I'm fine," she lied and grabbed Sam's hand with one hand and patted the muscular greyhound with the other.

"Full tank!" Tony announced.

Camille smiled. She appreciated the extra care Tony took to reassure her about the fuel level. If only she'd known to switch tanks that afternoon twenty years earlier.

"Ah, an Island weekend sans children. Not bad for a couple of old married farts." Tony closed the door and pulled twice on the handle to show Camille that it was safely locked.

The plane shuddered as Tony fired up the engine.

Camille paused for a second, unsettled, as she watched the guy on the dock holding up his phone as though he was taking a picture of them. He faded from view as the plane taxied out onto the lake.

"Did Amy tell you what this trip was about when she made the reservations?" Camille asked.

Tony took his parka off as he waited for a floatplane to land in front of them on the lake. "Just that you want me to drop you off at the marina tonight, and then tomorrow I take you guys over to the new bed and breakfast on the other side of Shaw Island. Sounds romantic."

"Not 'us guys.' Just me."

"What about Sam?"

"I have a meeting at The Islander," Camille responded.

Tony grabbed the radio and announced his intention to take off. "November nine-two-seven Whiskey Juliet preparing to take off to the north from Lake Union." He turned to Camille. "It's going to be a few minutes. There's a line out here today." He popped his headset off. "So, what's the meeting about?"

"I'll tell you if you promise to keep it quiet. Besides, you need to know what's going on, just in case."

"Sounds intriguing."

"One of Dallas's doctors has agreed to meet with me to talk about Willcox, your Brigantine Island pal. He's the one who messed up Dallas's surgery. But he wants it to be a secret. So, he suggested we meet at The Islander. Apparently his brother-in-law owns the place."

Tony looked at Sam and changed the subject. "Are you sure this is safe? Why does this guy need to meet in some remote B and B?"

"Ask the boss." Sam pointed at Camille.

Tony's radio crackled, and he put on his headset, listened for a few seconds, and tossed Camille and Tony each a pair of disposable earplugs to drown out the noise. He pushed his headset off one of his ears so he could listen for when they were clear for takeoff. "Well?"

"Well nothing. I'll be fine," Camille insisted.

"Are you just going to let her go meet with this guy by herself? How do we know he's on the up-and-up?"

Camille tore open the plastic wrapper of the bright-orange earplugs with her teeth. "He's a doctor, for God's sake."

"So was Jack Kevorkian, but I wouldn't want my wife at some isolated B and B alone with the guy."

"See, dear? I'm not the only one who questions your sanity. Tony's got a point, you know. I still think we should stick around."

"I told you the guy's never gonna talk if I show up with an entourage! Why do you think he went to the trouble of setting up this meeting so no one would see us together?" She theatrically stuck the earplugs in her ears to end the conversation once and for all.

The plane floated effortlessly up off the lake and banked over the 180-foot-high Aurora Bridge, heading west before banking north to the Islands. Camille breathed a sigh of relief. She almost allowed herself to enjoy the trip until she noticed that the sun had disappeared behind a layer of misty clouds. She knew how easy it was for a pilot to get disoriented in the fog. *Stop it,* she admonished herself, *Tony's got instrument ratings up the kazoo.*

—

The Colonel looked out over the expansive Friday Harbor Marina. He had been the harbormaster there ever since he retired as an army helicopter pilot. The shelves in his drab office were lined with military precision. He grabbed the Taster's Choice that he had positioned between the nondairy creamer and the neatly closed box of sugar, took the jar off the shelf, and mixed a heaping tablespoon into a Styrofoam cup along with boiling water from his electric teakettle. He washed and dried the spoon and put it away before replacing the coffee jar exactly where it had been. Then he repeated the procedure with the creamer, then the sugar.

The Colonel assiduously avoided all unnecessary contact with marina tenants. People were basically untrustworthy. His life centered around his old airplane radio, and he spent most of every day listening to the local air traffic.

The static almost drowned out the abrasive ring of his landline. "Harbormaster," he said gruffly.

"Well, hello, Colonel!"

The Colonel had learned to tolerate Andrew Willcox the third.

Willcox continued, "The Chris-Craft looks great! Your man Mike really outdid himself on the teak this time. Tell him he can take her out cruising anytime he likes, after Vic brings it back up from Seattle. Mrs. Willcox and I have no plans for any winter cruising. I'm afraid she's still a California gal at heart."

And why would I care about his old lady?

"Thanks for the offer, Dr. Willcox. I'll let Mike know." The Colonel felt he owed Willcox ever since he had performed emergency surgery on the Colonel's sister shortly after the doc arrived in Friday Harbor a few years back. And the Colonel always repaid his debts. He wondered what the doc wanted from him this time.

"There's a woman coming in by floatplane today, with her husband and a greyhound dog." Willcox's voice sounded typically hollow. "I need to know where she goes when she gets off the plane. I want to keep an eye on her while she's on the Island."

The Colonel paused. The debt he felt he owed Willcox had been paid several times over. Now it was only about money.

"There's a hundred bucks in it for you, my man."

"One fifty."

"Keep me posted."

The Colonel hung up the phone and turned up the volume on his air traffic radio.

—

The flight to the Islands was as smooth as Tony had predicted it would be. And thanks to the miracle of modern medicine, Camille was even able to glance out the window from time to time to see the Islands spreading out below her like blotches of green across an abstract painting. A ferry glided past the narrow Mosquito Pass as a pod of whales crossed its bow, creating streaks of white in the sapphire water. Camille always considered an orca sighting to be a sign of good luck.

As they approached Friday Harbor, Tony turned to Camille and held up his index finger, making a circling motion. He raised his eyebrows inquisitively toward the flamboyantly sun-streaked sky framing the Olympic Mountains. She nodded. Anything to put off the inevitable landing. Tony headed out over Haro Strait, flying in smooth, loopy circles so they could savor every last drop of the spectacular sunset. Sam kissed Camille on the cheek as they gazed over at the snowy purple mountains awash in the pink glow of dusk.

Much to Camille's relief, Tony was right about the landing. As soon as they glided to a halt at the dock, he gave Camille a big smile as he opened his door and pulled on his fleece ski cap. "Man, it's cold when the sun goes down!" He threw the line to the dock attendant.

Camille smiled. "Do you have time for a drink with us?" The dog jumped agilely off the float.

"You bet." Tony hoisted Camille's case of wine onto his shoulder and headed up the dock. "This should get you through the weekend," he joked.

Camille elbowed him playfully. "We're replenishing for winter."

Tony smiled. "I'll be over soon. I gotta go sign out first."

Camille had always figured the Colonel's demeanor was due to some type of posttraumatic stress disorder from unimaginable atrocities during his tours as a pilot and POW in Vietnam, so she always tried to greet him with a warm smile, even though he typically ignored her. But today he responded with an icy stare that caused Camille to shiver as if she'd been hit by a cold wind. She watched through the dirty, fogged-up window as the Colonel picked up his phone without taking his eyes off her.

—

"Willcox here." The voice sounded arrogant, as always.

"This is the Colonel. That lady you were wondering about? She landed six minutes ago."

"Excellent."

The Colonel grabbed his logbook. "Island Air flight five zero two landed in the harbor at seventeen ten. Same plane as your guy sent me a picture of forty-three minutes ago. Passengers were a man, a lady, and a gangly looking dog."

"Where'd they go?"

"Took up residence on a sailboat in the Harbor, slip number C one-oh-four. Vessel name, *Sofia*. Forty-two-foot sloop-rigged." He didn't bother giving Willcox the boat model; he wouldn't know the difference.

"Who owns the boat?"

"Taylor. It's been moored here since 2010. Owners live in Seattle."

"Address?"

The Colonel didn't respond.

"Another hundred?" Willcox was impatient.

The Colonel put his feet up on the desk. "Two."

"Fine."

"It's 17657 Fairview Avenue East, number twelve. Pay their Friday Harbor Marina fees in full once a year. Six thousand dollars."

"That's her. Thanks, Colonel. Keep an eye on the broad for me, would you?"

"Affirmative."

CHAPTER TWELVE

The next morning, Jake gently nuzzled Camille awake from the first really deep sleep she'd had since Dallas's death. The gentle rocking of the sailboat was the absolute best prescription for insomnia. She rolled over and stared for a few minutes at her peacefully sleeping husband, then grudgingly got bundled up and grabbed Jake's leash. "Shh!" she quietly admonished the whimpering greyhound. "Hurry up, boy. Let's go." A cold blast of crisp fall air greeted them as they climbed up the companionway.

Camille and Jake jogged up to the parking lot just in time to see Gloria warming up her vintage Dodge Rambler. Camille grabbed the mug of steaming hot tea off the top of the car. "Don't be driving off with this on your roof!"

"It's a chilly one, isn't it?"

Camille cradled the mug in her hands for warmth. "It sure is. Where are you off to at this hour anyway?"

"I'm teaching an early-bird yoga class. Gives me a reason to get up and get going."

"Good for you." Camille gave her friend a peck on the cheek. "You'd better get in the car and drink your tea before it gets cold."

The Colonel pulled into the parking lot just as Gloria turned the corner. He stopped and peered intently at Camille and Jake before marching erectly toward his office on the service dock.

Camille realized how ridiculous she must look standing alone in the parking lot wearing the flamboyant hand-painted paisley silk pajamas she'd bought in Friday Harbor as a birthday joke for Sam. Over the pj's she wore a hot-pink fleece jacket. Her hair stood on end, bordered by Angela's multicolored ski band. A shivering greyhound pulled against the leash in her right hand, and she held a plastic bag of dog poop in her left as her cell phone vibrated from deep within her pocket. She pulled off her right glove and tapped to answer. It was Amy.

"You know that nurse consultant you asked me to call? She did a search on aortic aneurysms and found out that the national expert just happens to be guess where?"

"It's a little early for guessing games," Camille joked.

"University of Washington!" Amy announced proudly. "Some guy by the name of Dr. Roberts. Google him; you'll find a huge, long list of research papers. The nurse is sending us a bunch for you to review."

"Perfect! See what else you can find out about him."

"On it."

"And is everything okay at the office?"

"Yep! All good. You ready for your big meeting with Gonzalez? Need anything from me?"

"Yeah, did we get the new credit card yet? I'm running a little low on cash."

"Haven't seen it yet. Are we okay, money-wise?"

"Yep." *Kind of.* Camille did some mental math. "My bonus should be coming in anytime, and our new credit card has a pretty high limit."

"Well, thank God for that." Camille could hear the relief in Amy's voice.

She changed the subject, not wanting Amy to worry about finances. "I can't wait to hear what Gonzalez has to say."

"Me either. Call me when you're done. I'll be here, drafting the interrogatories you wanted."

"Thanks! Will do. Talk to you later today." She hung up and turned to Jake. "You and I are a sight to behold, pal." She crunched across the gravel parking lot in her yellow rubber sailing boots. She turned to wave at the Colonel and was taken aback to see him focusing on her with a huge pair of binoculars.

—

Willcox fumbled for his phone. He swore as he knocked a half-full snifter of last night's brandy onto the thick mauve carpet.

"What?" he snapped.

"Colonel here. I have an update on the broad."

Willcox grunted and muted *The Today Show*. His stomach churned and his head throbbed. He belched loudly.

"Subject and husband left their boat last night at twenty forty-five."

Willcox hit the remote, and thick velvet curtains opened to display a spectacular scene of white caps chasing each other across the swirling gray water of the San Juan Channel.

"They went for dinner on another boat moored in the marina."

Willcox mustered a weak smile. "Who owns the boat she had dinner on?"

"For another hundred."

"Jesus! Okay. Another hundred." Willcox clenched his jaw.

"Hold the line . . . Jackson. Dallas Jackson. I knew the guy. Died last summer. Wife still lives on the boat. She and the subject were having a conversation in the parking lot at oh-six fifty-two this morning."

Willcox's hangover faded momentarily. "The lawyer had dinner with Jackson's widow?" Shit. Willcox abruptly hung up the phone and bolted out of his leather recliner. This was about to get a lot more complicated.

—

Camille was met with the aroma of Sam's special super-strong coffee when she climbed down the companionway.

"Hey, Amy found me an expert at the U. Do you know a Dr. Roberts? He's some kind of superstar research jock. I can hardly count the number of journal articles he's published."

Sam handed Camille a cup of coffee. "It's a big medical center, Camille. Pretty sure a lowly epidemiologist like me wouldn't have much opportunity to cross paths with a famous research star."

"I'm going to download some of his articles and read up before my meeting with the vascular surgeon today."

Sam lathered a piece of toast with peanut butter. "Are you sure you really want to have this meeting? There's something creepy about you having to meet on another island. Doesn't that seem a little weird to you?"

"You and Tony know where I'll be, and I'll text you if I have any trouble. I'll be fine." Camille settled in with her laptop to skim a few of the articles authored by Dr. G. A. Roberts. Amy was right, he was double-boarded in pathology and cardiology and wrote articles about aortic aneurysms. He was exactly who Camille needed to talk to about the case.

A few hours later, Camille and Sam were once again boarding Tony's floatplane for a short hop over to the neighboring island.

Tony turned to give Camille the familiar thumbs-up as he announced his flight plan.

"November nine-two-seven Whiskey Juliet announcing takeoff from Friday Harbor to the east for a hop, skip, and a jump over to Shaw, just south of Neck Point."

Before they gained much altitude at all, Camille squeezed Sam's hand as he pointed down at a pristine white beach house surrounded by long covered verandas. The laughing green-and-white striped awnings that shielded tourists from the intense western heat of late summer afternoons had been silenced for the season. The plane landed in the midst of a monochromatic watercolor in various shades of gray.

"Are you sure you want to go through with this?" Tony asked as soon as he turned off the noisy engine.

Camille's eyes focused intently. "Open the door. I'll be fine."

Sam stroked her cheek. "Be careful. What'll you do if anything happens?"

"We've been over this a hundred times, Sam. I'll be in a public place. I'll text you if I have even the slightest concern, and if anything happens, I'll start screaming. Just like we taught the girls when they were little. Remember Officer Nick, the guy who came to school and gave the safety lecture every year? If someone grabs you, start yelling to attract attention."

"Silly me. I thought those lectures were intended to protect our kids from being kidnapped. It didn't occur to me that I'd be having this discussion with you."

"Sam, I have to go now." She stepped carefully off the plane float onto the dock. "I promise you nothing's going to happen." She shut the door a little more forcefully than she anticipated. *Adrenaline,* she told herself as she waved apologetically to Sam, whose forehead was pressed up against the fogged-up window.

Camille wondered if this was how her mom felt as she walked into a refugee camp to interview witnesses for an asylum trial. Well, not exactly like this. She scanned the perfectly manicured flagstone path to the wide porch of The Islander Bed and Breakfast. She stuck her hands deep into her pockets as she passed the large rhododendron skeletons that framed the walkway and hesitated. Suddenly, she felt terribly alone. Maybe this was a bad idea after all. She looked around for an easy exit just as a handsome man in his midthirties solicitously opened the door.

"Thanks." She forced a smile and nervously scanned the sunroom behind him, where a line of tables with checkered tablecloths were lined up in front of a river rock fireplace that opened into a parlor. The fire crackled wildly, drawing Camille in from the cold. She glanced back to see the beginning of a squall building out on the bay, then marched into the hauntingly cozy scene.

Her host looked disarmingly like a young Brad Pitt. "You must be Ms. Delaney. Dr. Gonzalez is right around the corner."

Camille fought to open her clenched jaw. "Thank you."

The man smiled. "Follow me. By the way, I'm Fredrick, Dr. Gonzalez's brother-in-law."

"Nice to meet you."

Fredrick led Camille through the sunporch and around the fireplace to where a Latino man with thick curly black hair stood in a small alcove surrounded on three sides by windows framed in white woodwork.

"You must be Ms. Delaney." He held out his hand. "Max Gonzalez."

He certainly looked harmless "It's Camille, and it's a pleasure to meet you." *I hope.*

"Please. Sit." Dr. Gonzalez pointed to a white wicker chair covered in vintage sage-and-blue floral fabric.

There didn't appear to be anyone else in the place. "Thanks so much for agreeing to meet with me. What a lovely setting." When she noticed that Fredrick had silently disappeared, she felt another surge of adrenaline dancing right beneath her skin.

"Can I get you anything? Coffee? Tea?" Dr. Gonzalez turned to a silver coffee service on the sideboard. "It's fresh. I promise."

Camille relaxed ever so slightly in response to the doctor's broad smile.

"Coffee would be great, thanks." *Max Gonzalez is kind of cute. Then again, so was Ted Bundy.*

"Cream or sugar?"

"No, no thanks."

The queasy feeling in Camille's stomach reappeared as Max Gonzalez sat down in the matching chair across from hers.

"So . . . your secretary tells me you and your family have a sailboat you keep up in the Islands?" Dr. Gonzalez tried to make small talk.

"We do. It's moored over in Friday Harbor. It's the best weekend getaway place ever, and we love it. How 'bout you? Do you have a boat?" Camille tried to look nonchalant.

"I'd love to, but I'm still paying off school loans. And we have three kids under five. We'll definitely have to wait a few years before we even think about a boat."

Camille was beginning to like the young doctor. He was more than cute. He was really cute. Especially when he laughed. Just as Camille scolded herself for getting a bit too comfortable, the doctor's cell phone rang. Camille reevaluated her reaction to Gonzalez as he turned away and grabbed a pad from his pocket to scribble notes about one of his patients. Just then, the sound of door chimes filled the cozy B and B.

"Coming!" Fredrick hollered as he hurried toward the door. "Who on earth?" He looked through the peephole and opened the door for a muscular man with a hood pulled up, framing his face. He shoved back his hood and pushed his aviator sunglasses up on his head as he stomped his feet to kick the dirt off his dark-green rain boots in the entryway. A thick silver earring caught Camille's attention. The boots were a giveaway; the guy was probably a local fisherman. He did look vaguely familiar, but she couldn't place him. Maybe he was one of the locals who sold fresh salmon at the Sunday market in Friday Harbor. As the fisherman followed Fredrick out to the sunporch, she began to relax. It felt safer with another customer around. Camille watched over Dr. Gonzalez's shoulder with relief as the man ordered lunch.

Camille and the doctor chatted for a while about nothing more important than the weather, obviously sizing each other up when the doorbell rang again. She watched with amazement as her husband pushed past Fredrick into the parlor.

"Any chance we could get a cup of coffee and an early lunch?"

What on earth is he doing here?

Fredrick tossed his thick wavy brown hair, which was cut bluntly just above his ears. "You bet! We aim to please."

Sam plastered on a phony smile as he scanned the room.

"Come with me. We have a killer sunporch, and Neil has just started the fire. It's fabulous!" Fredrick pointed down the hallway.

"Come on, hon," Tony fussed at Sam. "He just loves these old houses. We just bought a great old place on Queen Anne Hill in Seattle. So, of course, now Sam's always looking for decorating ideas." Tony rolled his eyes and crossed his arms. It was all Camille could do to keep from bursting out laughing. Sam and Tony had apparently decided to protect her by masquerading as a gay couple looking for someplace to have a romantic early-afternoon repast.

"So, how far along are you in your investigation of the Jackson case?" Dr. Gonzalez asked Camille quietly.

"Well," she answered cautiously, "I've spoken to a surgeon at the University of Washington who wonders how it could have taken so long for Dr. Willcox to discover that the aorta was perforated." Camille cringed inside as she waited for a response.

"Because he's an idiot. That's why."

Camille was stunned. Granted, it'd been a few years since she'd handled a med mal case, but in all her years of practice, she'd never heard such a stinging criticism from a doctor about a colleague. And the energy behind the statement was close to pure hatred. If this guy was for real, she was sitting on a gold mine. *Take it slow.*

Camille noticed a giant black yacht cutting across the bay, leaving a stream of bubbling, cauldron-like water in its wake. "Tell me, how long have you known Dr. Willcox?" she asked.

"Too long. Actually, I came to town three years ago. From New Mexico. I grew up in Las Cruces and trained at U Arizona Medical Center. Willcox had just arrived when I came to town."

Camille watched as two men in yellow slickers moored the big yacht, dwarfing the small dock.

Gonzalez went on to explain how he and his wife had looked forward to living in the Islands near her family, including her brother and his partner, who owned the B and B. But he had never been able to establish a busy practice, since Willcox had a lock on most of the referral sources throughout the local medical community. Gonzalez lamented the fact that Willcox was doing more surgery up on this sleepy island than some doctors down in Seattle.

"Where does he get all his patients?" Camille asked.

"Anyone who comes to the hospital with heartburn or an upset stomach gets operated on. Whether they need it or not. As you may guess, guys on vacation tend to eat and drink too much and get epigastric pain, uh, heartburn. Then their wives get nervous, thinking it's a heart attack, and off they go to the emergency room, where Willcox charges in to save the day. Just in the nick of time, one hour later, and the guy's gallbladder would have burst, he tells the wife—after he's ordered every conceivable test known to medical science."

Camille grimaced. "That's awful."

"And he's the world's worst surgeon to boot."

"What's the hospital doing about it?"

"They love the guy. He's their cash cow. And the Island population has exploded, especially after some developer sued the county to change some zoning laws so they could build a densely populated retirement community out on Lime Kiln Point. Rumor has it that they're planning to build another place close by. Everyone in town is up in arms. But at the same time, more older people moving up here means more medical care is needed. I hear the hospital was silently lobbying to change the zoning laws with the Lime Kiln Point developer. It was quite the local political drama. So, anyway, the hospital was about to start recruiting surgeons when Willcox magically appeared on the scene. His timing was perfect. Then when the administrator saw Willcox's surgical numbers after he'd been here for a few months, he about wet his pants."

"But you'd think they'd do something about his complication rate."

"You'd think so, but the hospital rakes in the bucks every time he orders diagnostic tests or does procedures or surgery."

Camille focused on the doctor with narrowed eyes. "But they must know what's going on."

"Hey, times are tough in the medical biz these days. As you probably know, most health care facilities are hurting for patients. Jobs are at stake. Everyone from administrators on down is sitting on pins and needles. The only way they can justify their existence is by increasing revenue for the hospital. His complication rate is high but not so bad that anyone can convince the hospital administrator to do anything."

"Well, surely the docs have raised some concerns."

"Yeah, but the administrator attributes the increasing complication rate to the increase in the aging population that's moving up here into the retirement place. And it's kind of true—there's just more care needed."

"Hasn't anyone run some statistics to prove that his complication rate is unacceptable?"

"Remember, Willcox is the answer to the administrator's prayers. His job is safe as long as the hospital's in the black, which it is for the first time in almost—"

The veranda door slammed shut, interrupting Gonzalez midsentence. At first Camille couldn't place the deep-blue eyes peering right through her. But when the man shoved back his rain-soaked hood, her heart jumped up into her throat. The overly sincere grin Willcox had schmoozed her with last summer had been replaced by a menacing sneer. She looked searchingly at Gonzalez and gauged the distance to the door.

"And just what do you two think you're doing?" Willcox's voice cut through the toasty scene like an icicle.

Gonzalez shot out of his chair and back into the corner, like a caged animal, the bravado draining from his face as Willcox's arrogant presence filled the room.

Camille gathered her wits and stood up on very shaky legs.

Willcox ignored Gonzalez and turned to Camille. "Ms. Delaney. How nice to see you again." He smiled gratuitously. "I'm happy to announce that your little investigation is over as of now."

Camille looked to Gonzalez, who stood frozen by the bank of windows. She held her breath.

Willcox stepped so close to Camille that she could feel his warm breath on her face.

"And how is little Gracie doing in cello this year? Mrs. Hizar is known to be one of the best teachers." He winked. "That Gracie is a lucky little girl."

Camille tried to keep her knees from buckling as she took a step backward. *How the hell does he know who Grace's cello teacher is?*

"What's going on here?" Sam's sudden presence in the midst of the nightmarish situation made it all the more surreal.

Willcox turned to him. "Hello, Dr. Taylor. I'd suggest you take the little woman and go home now. This case is officially closed."

Gonzalez looked at Sam quizzically.

"Ah, I take it you two haven't met." Willcox pointed at Sam. "Dr. Gonzalez, meet Dr. Taylor, famous research epidemiologist from the University of Washington."

Camille caught and held Sam's worried gaze, then looked out the window to see the guy with the aviator sunglasses who had just been having lunch at the next table untying the giant black yacht. She looked back at Willcox.

"This meeting is over. You two can hop, skip, and jump your way back over to Friday Harbor." Willcox stood threateningly in the middle of the room. "Now."

Sam spoke up. "C'mon, Camille. Let's go." He placed a hand gently on her lower back.

Camille pulled away. "No. Dr. Gonzalez and I haven't finished our coffee yet." She glared up at Willcox, who looked down at her as if she were a pesky rodent.

Sam grabbed Camille's arm. "I really think we'd better be going."

Tony wandered in from the hallway and stopped. "Uh, the weather's starting to kick up out there. We best be off." He paused, looking expectantly from Sam to Camille, then tossed the keys up and caught them with one hand.

Camille was jolted back to reality. For the first time, she recognized the significance of the brewing storm. Her fear of flying mingled with her rising sense of panic over Willcox's familiarity with her family.

Willcox walked over and opened the door for Camille. "After you." Willcox feigned a bow.

Camille glanced over at Gonzalez, who was glaring at Willcox.

Willcox leaned over and whispered in Camille's ear loud enough for Sam to hear. "It would be so sad for little Grace if I were to see you and Dr. Gonzalez together again." He walked away.

Sam's grip on Camille's arm tightened. "That's it. We're outta here." He dragged her out the door toward the red-and-white plane rocking on its floats in the shadow of the giant black yacht.

CHAPTER THIRTEEN

"Get in. Let's go." Sam grabbed Camille by the arm.

She held the plane strut to keep from falling into the frigid water as Sam pushed her aboard the plane.

Camille felt a wave of nausea as the plane lurched forward over a rolling carpet of whitecaps and lifted off before she could locate both ends of her seat belt. The noisy engine made it impossible to carry on a conversation, so Camille and Sam sat still, holding hands. Tightly. The five-minute ride back to Friday Harbor seemed like forever as Camille continuously swallowed the bile that crept up into her throat with each inadvertent altitude drop. She pressed her face into Sam's shoulder as they rocked down to a bouncy landing in front of the marina.

Camille opened her eyes and tried, unsuccessfully, to focus on something outside the rain-blurred window as the plane taxied quietly to a stop.

"So . . . what the hell happened back there?" Sam blurted out as soon as the engines quieted down.

Camille felt clammy all over. "Apparently Willcox doesn't want Gonzalez talking to a lawyer."

"Okay, enough private investigating. Do you think you can get your old job back?"

Camille drew back from her husband's steady gaze. "Are you crazy?"

"Look, Camille. I don't know exactly what's going on up here, but I do know that whatever it is, it's not worth it. And I'm sure your mother didn't intend for you to put her granddaughters directly in Willcox's crosshairs when she talked you into walking out on your cushy practice."

"Leave my mom out of this. This is about holding the guy who killed Dallas accountable. It's about justice."

"Okay, well, let someone else be the justice warrior here." Sam opened the door and hopped off the plane. Grabbing the line Tony threw to him, he jerked the plane violently toward the dock.

Camille stood next to her husband in the rain. "Remember when we were in Atlanta for your fellowship at the CDC? And I decided to go to law school so I could make a difference in the world?"

Sam cleated the line to the dock. "Shit, Camille, this is no time for you to get on a soapbox."

"It's exactly the time for me to get on a soapbox. Gonzalez clearly inferred that Dallas wasn't the first one Willcox had killed. And I have a strong suspicion he won't be the last."

"So, you've done a great preliminary investigation. Give the case to Midvale and Covington. They love big, messy cases like this, and they have the resources to process them. We don't need this shit."

"I'm not giving this case to anyone! Trish and I can handle it just fine on our own!" She stormed off, leaving Sam standing on the dock. He swore as a wave crashed over his feet.

———

Camille stepped up the companionway ladder to open the hatch for Trish as she entered Gloria's sailboat. Camille had camped there after Sam had abruptly decided to go for a solo stormy afternoon sail.

"I came as soon as I got your text. What's up?" Trish asked as she threw her backpack onto the quarter berth in the aft stateroom of Gloria's boat, where she had offered to stay while Camille and Sam were in town. "Three's a crowd." She winked. "Where's Gloria?"

"She has a yoga class, and Sam and I had a fight, so I thought we should debrief here." Camille pulled a shot of espresso from Dallas's pride and joy, his La Marzocco Italian espresso machine. She began to foam the milk for a latte.

Camille recounted her afternoon at the bed and breakfast up to the altercation with Sam on the dock. "How the hell did he know about Grace's cello?" Camille asked. "He wouldn't dare drag my kids into this thing. Would he?"

"He's either been following you or had someone doing a background check. Or probably both."

Camille handed Trish the latte and grabbed her own. "Maybe Sam's right. Maybe we are in over our heads. I'm not sure it makes sense for me to continue financing this investigation. What if the system is right, and they won't pay Gloria much for the loss of a sixty-five-year-old guy?"

"We're doing fine. And this is about justice, not only money."

"That's easy for you to say. I'm the one about to use up all my bonus money paying for this operation. And now I'm apparently risking my kids' lives in the process."

"This guy is a big fish in a little pond. Control freaks like him don't like to venture far from their home turf." Trish sat on the banquette at the handcrafted built-in table in the cozy galley. "I can't imagine someone like that coming after you or your family in Seattle," she said as she put her feet up on the opposite banquette. "But I'll call my buddy at Seattle PD and give him a heads-up. And you make sure you use that fancy alarm system I helped you pick out last year, okay? In fact, I'm gonna upgrade it for you. I can save you a bunch of money if I do it myself."

Camille sighed. "Okay."

Trish blew on her latte to cool it down.

"Enough about my day. Tell me what you've found out up here." Camille got up and found a bag of Gloria's homemade chocolate chip cookies and put it on the table.

"Thanks." Trish popped half a cookie in her mouth. "Let's see. I reconnected with your friend, Ruby. Like you said, she has a pretty good overview of the community. And she introduced me to the woman who owns the shop where you bought Sam those ugly paisley silk pajamas for his birthday last summer. Name's Lydia. Soloist in the church choir, past president of the PTA, yadda yadda yadda. Your basic all-around busybody." Trish licked the foam dripping down the side of her cup. "And I joined the local choir, at Lydia's suggestion. Good way to get to know folks in a small town."

Camille nodded.

"And by the way, I had no idea how international this sleepy community is. So many people from South Asia—mostly Microsoft and Amazon peeps. Then there's a contingent from Jamaica, I think. They show up intermittently at the local tavern to watch cricket."

"So, what do they have to do with the Willcox situation?" Camille asked.

"Nothing. That's why I haven't really gotten to know them, but I was just noticing how this place is growing. And the new retirement communities are really starting to pop up. Before long, we're not going to recognize this place."

"So, what about Willcox?" Camille coaxed.

"I'm in the choir with his wife, BJ. She mostly keeps to herself. But I'm hoping to dig up some dirt on her husband from their fellow parishioners."

"What about other cases he screwed up? Gonzalez told me about his complication rate. Bad, but not bad enough to raise too many eyebrows."

Trish scrolled through the notes on her iPhone. "Let's see . . . There was a woman who died during a hysterectomy . . . a guy who died unexpectedly during surgery a month before Dallas . . . and a man who was killed in a suspicious car accident. The thing that strikes me from a legal perspective is that all the patients were either old, so the case would have no significant value, or if they were young, there were no dependents or spouses to bring suit."

Camille nodded.

"Then there's this woman in my aerobics class," Trish went on. "Rumor has it that her husband had a lung removed, and he's being treated in Everett now. I heard there's a question of whether he really needed the surgery in the first place. She's considering a lawsuit."

"What?"

"Yep. Turns out he was on chemo and went down to Everett for a second opinion. They looked at the slides, and no cancer. I'll check that one out further."

"That'd be great."

Trish looked at her notes. "Also, I'm not sure if it's related to anything, but I think Willcox may have been building some kind of family compound out on Brigantine Island over between Decatur and Lopez Islands. Remember that place that burned down a few years ago? I think they're rebuilding it. His wife, the architect, is back and forth all the time, working on the place."

"Yeah, Tony told me he drops folks off over there every once in a while. He thinks it's run by a nonprofit organization where dying people go for a luxury vacation in the Islands. Pretty sure BJ Willcox designed it, and Willcox must volunteer over there, but that seems a bit out of character for this guy," Camille noted.

"So, the whole project is some kind of nonprofit? Something doesn't ring true with those two. He's not the charity type."

Camille nodded. "Can you check it out?"

"Will do, and get this!" Trish changed the subject. "Do you remember last summer the girls met those twins and they were hanging out together when you all were up here on vacation in August? You're never gonna believe who they are!"

"Those two guys they went kayaking with? I think they still play online games with them. They seem sweet."

"Yep! They're Willcox's kids. They go to boarding school back east somewhere and just come to the Island for vacations."

Camille cradled her head in her hands. "Oh my God. You're kidding." She looked up. "I want this guy outta my family's life."

Camille reached down to pet Jake, who was leaning up against her, almost knocking her over. "Shoot. He needs to go out." She threw Trish the leash. "And I need some exercise."

Trish looked at her phone. "Okay. I'm going to grab a veggie burger. Don't want to be late for choir practice. I'll walk you up the dock."

—

Every Thursday at five o'clock sharp, the Colonel stopped at Derby's, the tavern located just at the top of the dock in the marina. He preferred to go by himself, but today the kid had invited himself along. He sat on his stool at the end of the bar and waited for the bartender to bring him his usual. Mike ordered a Redhook.

The Colonel hunched over his drink as he watched the lawyer and a blonde walk up the dock together with that big dog in a stupid-looking jacket. The lawyer stopped while the dog relieved itself on the tire of a car that looked to have been abandoned for the season. The blonde continued across the street and pushed through the heavy oak door.

Mike nudged the Colonel. "See that blonde who just walked in?"

"Yeah. You know her?"

They watched as the blonde took a seat by the window over by the pool table, where a group who appeared to be from somewhere in the Caribbean were racking up pool balls as they watched a cricket game on the big screen.

"New girl in the choir, Patsy Swanson. Up here from Walla Walla on sabbatical. She's a teacher."

"How much do you know about her?"

"Jeez, cool it. I'm not gonna marry her or anything. But don't you think she's hot?"

The blonde gave her order to the server and turned to watch the game.

"How long have you known her?" The Colonel's tone was harsh.

"She's been here a few weeks, I think. She's got a great voice, and her body won't quit."

"Keep your pants on."

"Give me a break," Mike snapped.

Just then, BJ Willcox showed up and air-kissed a couple of the pool players. She laughed as she took a beer from a tall man with dread-locks, who winked at her in return. BJ grabbed a pool cue and broke the rack straight on. The group clapped as two balls rolled into pockets in either corner. BJ pumped her fist and surveyed the table. "Five ball in the corner pocket." She pointed with her cue.

The Colonel turned back to Mike. "Where does she live?"

"Who?"

"The blonde!" The Colonel was impatient.

"In the marina on a boat. I can almost see into the portholes with the binoculars from the shop." Mike leered.

The Colonel watched as BJ Willcox turned to the blonde and asked her if she wanted to play. The blonde declined, reminding the doctor's wife that choir practice was starting in half an hour, and they had to hurry. Clearly these two knew each other.

The Colonel turned to Mike. "What dock's she on?"

"The blonde? C Dock. What the hell difference does it make to you where she lives?"

Holy shit. "Slip?"

"One-oh-four. Is this some kind of test?"

Bingo! "Just haven't seen her around. That's all." The Colonel knew he could get a few Benjamins from Willcox for this little twist of fate.

"Well, it's my business who I date. And I think I may be in love." Mike slammed down his beer mug and nodded at the bartender.

The bartender stopped in front of the two men. "How 'bout you, Colonel?"

"I'll have another shot of Wild Turkey—no, make it a double."

"What's got into you?" Mike asked.

"Nothing. Listen, I gotta make a call." The Colonel got up stiffly from the barstool and headed to the back of the bar so he could talk in private, stopping to borrow a smoke from the bartender as he headed to the drafty back door, searching in his phone for Willcox's number. He grimaced at Willcox's familiar condescending tone.

"I'm calling this report in from Derby's joint down at the marina." The Colonel's military precision never failed. "The subject just walked up the dock at seventeen twenty-two." He lit the cigarette. "She was with a member of the choir."

Willcox was groggy. "Hang on—you woke me up. I was in the OR all night last night." He cleared his throat. "What member of the choir?"

The Colonel paused. *Wonder if he knows his old lady is hanging out with the lawyer's blond friend.* "Some girl named Patsy. Says she's here on sabbatical from Walla Walla."

"Isn't that the killer blonde Mike's been dating?"

"Yup. Apparently he's been tryin' to get in her pants for some time now."

The line was silent.

"Doc? You there?"

"Yes, yes, Colonel. I'm here. Thanks for the report. Anything else?"

"Maybe."

"Two hundred?"

"Three." The Colonel exhaled a plume of smoke out the back door.

"Okay. Three it is," Willcox said impatiently.

"The blonde lives on a sailboat in the harbor."

"Can you find out her slip number?"

"C one-oh-four. It's the lawyer's boat." The Colonel smiled. He knew Willcox would eat this shit up.

"Thanks for the report. I assume you'll continue to watch those two. Closely."

The Colonel considered adding the additional tidbit about the blonde and the doctor's wife hanging out at Derby's and decided against it. He'd hold that back for later. "Over and out." The Colonel clicked off his phone and ground out his cigarette on the floor.

—

Willcox got out of bed and threw a navy-blue smoking jacket over the expensive hand-painted paisley silk pajamas his wife had bought him for his birthday. He hit the autodial.

"Get up!" he shouted at Burton who had assisted him in the late-night surgical case.

"I'm trying to sleep here." Burton was clearly frustrated.

"Not anymore you aren't."

"What the hell's going on?"

"You know that new chick in the choir, the blonde?" Willcox asked.

"Are you calling me in the middle of my nap to tell me about your latest wet dream?"

"She's been living on the lawyer's boat at the marina. Who the hell is she?"

"Whose boat?" Burton yawned loudly into the phone. "Who lives on what boat, and why do I care?"

"The blonde from the choir. She lives on the lady lawyer's boat down in the harbor!" Willcox nearly shouted.

"And why can't this wait till tomorrow?"

"Don't you think it's a bit suspicious? This chick shows up outta nowhere and gives us some line about being a teacher from Walla Walla. Then she turns up on the lawyer's boat? We gotta check her out."

"Well, let's have Vic get busy in the morning. He can make some calls. I think you're overreacting cuz she likes Mike better than you."

"I got a bad feeling about this chick."

"Look Vic's got surveillance going down in Seattle to watch the lawyer," Burton said flatly.

"Actually, he's back up here for an assignment tonight. Gonna scare that prick Gonzalez into shutting up."

Burton interjected, "Then have him do the same for the lawyer. If anyone needs to be scared off, it's her. We're not going to let some broad and her sidekick cut into our operation. There's too much money to be made. Vic'll get her to back off."

"Okay. I'll see you in the morning. We have a couple of simple kidneys. The team flew up yesterday. They're ready to go."

The line went dead.

Willcox heard the ping of a new email announcing itself from his laptop. He opened it to see an email from his local real estate agent.

> Dear Dr. Willcox,
>
> Your wife had requested that I keep an eye on the market in hopes of procuring the lot next to your parcel out on West Side Road. It has come to my attention that the couple who owns the twenty-acre piece at Lime Kiln Point just bought a huge property over on Decatur Island, so it's my guess that they'll be selling their San Juan piece sometime this spring. It's a one-of-a-kind piece, so I expect the asking price will be around ten million.
>
> As we discussed earlier this year, the seller doesn't know that you, as the owner of the adjacent parcel, are interested in the piece. If he learns this, he'll clearly raise the price of the land because he would understand the value to you of owning adjacent pieces. I suggest you consider forming another corporation in Mrs.

Willcox's maiden name again through which you can make an offer. It is my understanding that you will be able to offer cash, with no contingencies. I recommend you take steps to effectuate this immediately, so that I can make an offer on your behalf when the owners get serious about the sale, probably in the spring.

Very truly yours,

Walter French

Willcox called Burton back. "We got another problem."

"Now what?" Burton was irked.

"That piece out by Lime Kiln Point is going to hit the market in a few months. We need it. After we got the hospital to pressure the zoning board to allow us to develop the retirement place, I'm pretty sure we can get them to help us extend it to the adjacent piece. We can get another forty half-acre lots on that parcel."

"How much?"

"Ten," Willcox snapped.

"Shit. Talk about bad timing."

"We don't have the dough for this one right now. We need three million more to snap that one up." Willcox paused.

"Okay." Burton was clearly awake now. "We need that piece if we want to increase the hospital census up here." He paused. "Good thing we have a few months to pull a deal together."

"Thanks to BJ's strategy, we just did the refi on the Arizona property, but we need that to import more folks to increase our census out in Tarrington. BJ has been negotiating with the owners of that piece. We have money in the bank, but BJ doesn't want to use it just yet." Willcox paused, then added, "She's right. We need liquidity now for sure."

"How about the choir girl? She's single. And young and healthy. Perfect protoplasm," Burton mused.

"Car accident?" Willcox suggested.

"No. We just had a guy in a car accident," Burton said decisively. "And we don't need the money quite yet. Not until spring. I have an idea, but I need a little time." The phone went dead.

CHAPTER FOURTEEN

A chilly mist hung over the marina as Camille climbed aboard the creaking sailboat. She groped to open the companionway door. Time to kiss and make up. She stepped into the warm, cozy cabin.

Sam and Tony sat on opposite sides of the table, an empty Häagen-Dazs container between them. Camille's shoulder muscles tightened as Sam looked up at her. It had been a long time since they'd had a fight. She stood in the middle of the salon, staring at her husband.

Remarkably, Tony took the hint and excused himself. "I think I'll head over to my brother's place. I'm going to crash there tonight."

No words were exchanged between Sam and Camille as they waited for Tony to close the hatch.

Sam raised his eyebrows. "So?"

Camille sat on the counter in the galley. "Look, I have to finish what I've started. Just bear with me."

"Camille, this has gotten completely out of hand."

"He's not gonna hurt anyone. He's a big blowhard."

"I can't believe you're saying this!"

"Let's make a deal. I'll promise to get out of this if anything at all suspicious happens. Just give me a little more time."

Sam shook his head. "I don't know. Our kids are being threatened, and you're going to run out of money to pay Amy and now Trish. And we have tuition due."

Camille walked over and kissed her husband. "I'm sorry I stormed off this afternoon."

Sam took his wife in his arms. "Do you have any idea how worried I was?"

"Can we finish this discussion tomorrow?"

It was a night of candlelight, wine, and music. And no interruptions . . .

———

"Jesus Christ!" Willcox yelled to no one in particular as he picked up his phone on the third ring. He needed at least some sleep in order to be on his game in the morning for surgery. He looked at his clock. *One a.m.*

"Willcox here," he snapped.

Vic Jones didn't identify himself, he just offered his report. "Just got back from Gonzalez's clinic. I've got the chart note you wanted from the Jackson case."

BJ rolled over and put the pillow over her head as Willcox turned on the bedside light. "How can we be sure he won't notice the chart note is missing?"

BJ pushed the pillow off her head and opened one eye. "Put him on speaker," she instructed.

"I pretty much tore up the place. It looks more like a junkie broke in looking for drugs than a well-oiled break-in," Vic responded.

"Good man." Willcox nodded at BJ. "Get rid of that note."

"Ten four," Vic answered, and the phone went dead.

Willcox switched off the light and pulled the covers over his shoulder, trying to screen out the glow emanating from BJ's phone. "Can you turn that damn thing off? Who the hell texts in the middle of the night?" Willcox turned away as BJ shoved her phone under her pillow.

"G'night," she said.

———

Camille awoke to the familiar aroma of Sam's famous coffee. She smiled sleepily as he handed her two steaming hot mugs, then ran back to the galley and arrived with her favorite: bagels, lox, cream cheese, capers, and onions. Sam climbed back into the double-zipped sleeping bag in the cozy V-berth. Camille was in heaven.

Sometime in midafternoon, Camille's cell phone rang. She jumped out of bed, slipped on a pair of sweatpants, and wrestled her T-shirt from her husband's playful grasp. The empty plastic plate clattered to the ground.

It was Amy calling to let Camille know that they'd just received a copy of Willcox's licensing packet, and she was emailing it over now.

Time to get back to work. Camille dialed her friend Gage in Detroit.

"Do you have a minute?" Camille asked when Gage came on the line.

"I've got a few. I'm between cases. Just finished digging a bullet out of some woman's belly."

"I can't believe you're still such a big jock. Most guys outgrow the excitement, you know."

"I guess I'm still strung out on the hit you can only get from a good trauma case in the OR, which is just as well since all of the old recreational drugs seem to be off-limits for us old farts. Hey, I talked to Irving last week. He's never heard of your guy."

Camille smiled. "So, he didn't train at Harvard?"

"Not in the department of surgery."

Camille looked at the document Amy had just sent. "Shit. That letter we got from Willcox's file at the hospital—the one from Harvard—he used that same letter in his state licensing application."

"That's bold. How'd you figure that out?"

"I just got a copy of his application from the state licensing board."

"Guy must have some kind of cojones to forge a letter from the godfather of laparoscopy. And submit it to the state."

"No kidding. I gotta tell you, Gage, there's something very strange going on here. I just can't put my finger on it."

"Well, let me know if I can be of any more assistance. My next case is ready. It's a lap chole. How's that for ironic . . . and b-o-o-o-ring?"

"Thanks for your help. I'll be in touch." Camille clicked off the phone.

Sam hollered from the V-berth. "Who was that?"

"Gage Bryant. He's helping me figure out where Willcox really trained. I just got his application for licensing from the state, and he lied about his training. To the state."

"Isn't that some kind of fraud?" Sam sat up in bed.

Camille climbed into bed and handed him her laptop, opened to the Harvard letter. *Maybe he'll get interested in the case if he's part of the team.* It was worth a try.

Sam grabbed his glasses and read the letter. "He trained under Irving at Harvard? What year? Maybe we were there at the same time."

Camille snatched the laptop back. "Gage checked with Irving, and he's never heard of Willcox."

"So, how'd he come up with this letter?" Sam asked.

"It's obviously a forgery."

Sam looked at Camille quizzically. "You'd think the hospital would've checked his references before granting him privileges."

"Not necessarily." Camille paused. "You know, Gonzalez said yesterday that the hospital was pretty desperate for a surgeon when Willcox came on the scene. I'll bet they were so happy to have him show up, they never bothered to check him out."

"But the bylaws of most hospitals require the credentialing committee to check out the new docs before granting them privileges."

"Yeah, but remember that case I had with that ER doc who lied and said he'd done a residency, and we found out he'd barely graduated from med school?"

"Yeah."

"And that was in a small-town hospital in eastern Washington. Just like Friday Harbor General. Actually, it was a similar situation; they were short on docs over there too. I have a hunch some hospitals are so excited to have a warm body, they're a little lax on the old bylaws."

Sam took a deep breath. "God, I'm glad I work in a medical center. These little community hospitals give me the creeps."

Camille noted with encouragement how Sam had suddenly taken an interest in the case. "Aren't you just a little bit curious to find out where Willcox is really from?"

"Actually, I am. I can't believe someone would be so bold to forge a letter of recommendation from James Irving, of all people. He'd shit a brick if he found out."

CHAPTER FIFTEEN

"I'll get it!" Angela yelled as she ran downstairs to answer the doorbell. "Mom! I can't get this stupid alarm off!" Angela banged on the hallway wall next to the pad for the alarm that Trish had helped Sam upgrade to a high-tech system with motion sensors after the aborted meeting with Dr. Gonzalez resulted in Willcox issuing thinly veiled threats to their kids.

"You need to reboot it," Libby yelled at her sister.

"Ugh! I *hate* this thing." Angela plopped down on the stairs as Libby commandeered the alarm system.

"There. You just have to wait for the green light and the beep." Libby turned to go back to her bedroom as Angela opened the door.

"I can't believe you came!" Angela exclaimed.

Camille spread the last piece of french bread with garlic butter and looked up, almost slicing through her finger as the Willcox twins and a younger boy entered her living room.

"Mom? Are you okay?" Angela asked worriedly.

"I . . . I'm just fine." Camille held her finger under cold water.

"You remember the twins from last summer, on the Island? They taught us to kayak. And this is their friend Carlos."

"Yes, of course. Nice to see you, boys. Angela, can I talk to you for a minute? Out on the deck, please." Camille turned to Robin, who had come to town for the annual Christmas celebration, and handed her the garlic bread. "Can you put this in the oven?" she asked as she ushered her eldest daughter outside.

"What's the matter?" Angela asked.

"You didn't ask me if those boys could come to the party."

"You told me I could invite a few friends over for the Christmas carolers." Angela's tone was defensive.

"Okay, but next time let me know who you're inviting." There wasn't much she could do at this point.

Robin and the taller of the twins were deep in conversation when Camille and Angela reentered the kitchen. "So, your families have always lived in the same towns all of your lives?"

Camille paused. *This might be my big break.* She listened intently.

"Yep, our dads work together. They're doctors. Before we moved here, we lived in two different states, and we were born in another country," the shorter twin bragged.

"Okay, let me guess where you've lived. Give me a hint." Robin loved a good parlor game.

"I'm gonna change. I'll be right back," Angela assured her guests apologetically. "You can talk to my mom and Robin," she shouted over her shoulder as she ran downstairs.

Great idea. Camille smiled to herself.

"No problem." The boy turned his attention back to Robin and looked up and smiled ever so slightly. "Let's see . . . Here's your clue: home of the Bryant-Denny Stadium."

"Oh my God!" Libby yelled and came running in from the study. "I love the Crimson Tide!"

Camille laughed at her middle daughter. It was typical of Libby to burst into a room without bothering to say hello or welcome her friends.

Robin looked at Libby blankly.

"Um . . . they won something like seventeen national championships," Libby stated authoritatively.

The twins' friend, Carlos, nodded proudly and lifted up his sweater to show off his bright-red Alabama football jersey.

"You guys lived in Alabama?" Robin continued the game intently. "I don't think I've ever known anyone who actually lived in Alabama."

Camille looked at the boys in disbelief. *Alabama? Willcox was from Alabama?* "So . . . when did you live there?" She tried to act smooth.

"When we were little. Before we moved to—"

"Hey, wait. I'm gonna guess!" Robin interrupted and hit Carlos on the arm playfully. "Libby got the first clue. Give me another."

"I have one!" the short twin offered. "But you can't answer." He wagged his finger flirtatiously at Libby.

"Okay." She giggled.

Robin and Camille looked at each other, raised their eyebrows in unison, and smiled knowingly. It was extremely out of character for thirteen-year-old Libby to give a boy the time of day, never mind actually flirt with one. Maybe those hormones were finally kicking in after all.

"Home of Peoria," the boy announced proudly.

"Illinois!" Robin shouted.

"Nope!"

"I know!" Libby squealed in delight. "Arizona! You lived in Arizona!"

"I said you weren't eligible. You cheated."

"I did not! Anyone knows that Peoria is in Arizona. It's where the Seattle Mariners' spring training camp is. We go there every year. Did you live close to the stadium?" Libby asked excitedly.

"Not too far. We got to see a lot of games there. That's when I became a Mariners fan. But I've never really lived in Arizona. My parents make me go to this stupid boarding school in Connecticut."

Camille looked at Robin, who smirked in return. She couldn't wait to tell Trish that they could check off the first two items on their to-do list. She had determined two of the recent states where the Willcoxes had lived—and neither was California, which is where Willcox told everyone he was from. And it had just taken about three minutes.

"What are your names again?" Camille asked casually.

"I'm Al, and this is my twin brother, Bert," said the tallest twin. "We all go to boarding school together cuz our parents think the schools in the little towns where they live are lousy."

"What kind of doctors are your dads?" Camille knew about Willcox but was genuinely curious about Carlos's dad.

"Our dad's a surgeon, and Carlos's dad is a pathologist. He used to be a surgeon too, but now he mostly just looks at specimens in the lab."

"And does autopsies of dead people," Carlos proclaimed proudly.

"Hey!" Robin interrupted. "You guys never gave me a clue so I could guess the other country where you lived."

"Oh, right. Let's see . . . ," Al responded. "That's a hard one. The dish they have there is called *oil down*, and the country is called the Spice Isle."

Robin chewed her nails, thoughtfully. "We're gonna need another clue."

"They play lots of cricket—and they speak creole."

"It must be in the Caribbean."

"You're warm, but you need to be more specific."

Camille flushed with excitement. "Grenada!" *The home of the off-shore medical school attended by students who couldn't get into programs back in the States,* she thought. "You must be from Grenada."

"How'd you guess?" Carlos looked dumbfounded. "No one I know has ever even heard of Grenada."

"I guess I just read your mind." It all fit together. Willcox must have trained in Grenada and forged a letter of recommendation from Harvard to cover up for his lack of meaningful credentials.

Camille looked at Robin, who stared at her in disbelief. "I can't believe you guessed Grenada. How'd you figure that out?"

"Just a lucky guess."

"No, really. You must have had a reason to guess Grenada," Robin persisted.

"I said it was a lucky guess." Camille quickly changed the subject. "The carolers are going to be at the end of the dock at seven o'clock sharp. We have to get this bread in the oven."

"I can't believe you got Grenada, of all places. How'd you figure that out?"

"Let's drop it, Robin . . . Sam! Have you walked the dog? We have to leave in ten minutes!" Camille hollered downstairs to her husband. "And tell Grace to wear her warm parka. It's in the dryer! On second thought, I'll find it for her." Camille wanted to get out of the kitchen in order to avoid Robin's probing inquisition.

The sound of the Christmas carols began faintly, from afar. Then, one by one, a parade of narrow vessels appeared. First, a bright-pink boat, then a yellow one, followed by a turquoise one, and a varnished wooden boat. "God rest ye merry, gentlemen . . ." echoed across the lagoon, and the Christmas lights all around the lake twinkled in response. "Let nothing you dismay . . ." Camille found it enthralling. "Remember Christ our sa-a-vior was born on Christmas Day." Well, not so enthralling once the level of inebriation of the kayakers became evident. But still, very festive.

Every year, a gang of brightly attired kayakers paddled around Lake Union, stopping at every houseboat community to sing Christmas carols, where they enjoyed treats prepared by the dock's residents before moving on to their next appearance.

The head kayaker handed a stack of laminated sheets of Christmas carols up to Sam, who was standing closest to the edge of the dock. He passed the sheets around to his neighbors and belted out in harmony with the kayakers. "Hark the herald angels sing, glory to the newborn king!"

Some of the kayakers had battery-powered Christmas lights adorning their stocking caps. Others had plastic wreaths attached to the decks of their boats. And one fellow had a tropical Hawaiian palm tree complete with a wind-up hula dancer grinding away on his aft deck. *How very kitschy,* thought Camille as she looked out over the sea of happy carolers.

"Hey, counselor!" yelled one of the kayakers in the back.

Camille squinted across the water and recognized her swim team pal, Richard Rosenberg. "Hey, Richard! Merry Christmas!" She elbowed Robin. "See that guy back there? He's the surgeon who helped me at the swim meet."

"The goofy-looking one with the reindeer antlers on his head?"

Camille yelled to Richard, "Tell Christopher Merry Christmas for me!"

"Or Happy Hanukkah, as the case may be." Richard laughed over his shoulder as he paddled off to the neighboring community dock for the next performance.

CHAPTER SIXTEEN

Camille stood in front of the mirror, surveying herself in the tight vintage black sequined dress that she had spent way too much money on. Caroling kayakers in polar fleece one night, the Children's Hospital Christmas Gala in a little black dress the next.

Sam grabbed Camille from behind. "Very sexy shoes!"

"Enjoy it while you can. I only wear 'em till midnight, then they turn into bunny slippers, and the prince and princess climb into their warm and cozy bed and snuggle together happily ever after."

Sam pretended to remove his colorful silk bow tie. "So, you want to skip the party and go right to the happily-ever-after part?"

"Hey, it's your party. You call the shots."

"I suppose the Sittas might get their noses out of joint if we didn't show up to sit at their table." Sam sighed wistfully.

Camille extricated herself from her husband's arms and threw her faux fur jacket over her shoulders. "Okay. Then quit teasing me, and let's go."

"I'm right behind you." He gave his wife a big, puppy dog grin. "But let's come home early, all right?"

"Whatever you say. These are your people, not mine." Camille giggled as she followed him to the front door.

"We're leaving!" Sam hollered up the stairs. "I'm turning on the alarm. Do *not* open this door for anyone."

"We won't!" Libby yelled.

"I have the Ring app on my phone, so we'll know if you open this door or disable the alarm."

"Jeez, Dad." Angela looked over the stairwell. "What do you think's gonna happen? You're going to scare Gracie."

Sam blew Angela a kiss. "Just humor me and watch out for your sisters. Okay?" He punched the code into the panel and opened the door for Camille.

"Good ni-ight!" The red light beeped as the door closed behind them.

—

Camille and Sam walked slowly up the spiral staircase into the ballroom of the exclusive Columbia Tower Club, on the seventy-fifth floor of the tallest building in Seattle. The city lights blanketed the ground below. Camille was a pro at networking these events. This evening she had given herself a single goal. To meet, or at least find out as much as possible about, the mysterious Dr. Roberts, the university hotshot who had authored several articles about aortic aneurysms. She made a visual sweep of the elegantly decorated dining room.

"I'm going to schmooze around and look for that guy from cardiology who wrote those articles I told you about." Camille was all business.

"Can't you relax, just for one night?" Sam suggested.

"I'll find you at the end of the cocktail hour, dah-ling. Ciao!" Camille plucked a fluted glass of champagne from the silver tray that floated on the fingertips of a white-gloved young man and headed into the noisy sea of cocktailers. She was on a mission.

"Merry Christmas, Camille!"

"Merry Christmas, Jim." Camille shook hands and offered her cheek to the rotund chief of orthopedics at Children's Hospital. Dr. Jim Voss's face glowed with the ruddy complexion of one who appreciates a good glass of wine. And tonight there were many glasses of good wine to be appreciated.

"We really enjoyed the cabernet tasting at your house last month. Can't wait for the zin next month." Camille smiled and turned to keep from being derailed.

Another tuxedoed gentleman caught Camille's eye. "Happy Holidays, Heber. And give my best to Dawley." She offered her cheek to the world-renowned toxicologist.

"Bob, how are you?" Another social kiss. Bob Halladay's wife, Midge, had a patent pending for a new drug rumored to revolutionize the treatment of arthritis.

He squeezed Camille a bit too tight. "You look ravishing tonight."

Camille pulled away. "Where's Midge?"

"She's around here somewhere!"

Camille kept moving gracefully through the crowd. "Give her my regards."

She passed her friend Kip Davenport, a prominent local gynecologist who was deep in discussion with Cathy Swain, her neighbor and the chief of gynecology at the university. "Hey, watch it. Here comes the token lawyer!" Davenport laughed.

Camille smiled and waved; she didn't have time to joke around.

Ah-ha, cardiology, straight ahead. Doctors were notorious for hanging together in little pods with other specialists. You find one cardiologist, you find them all. "Molly! How nice to see you." Camille touched cheeks and kissed the air next to the ear of Molly Duncan, the grande dame of the heart transplant anesthesia team.

"Merry Christmas, Camille." Molly turned from her conversation with Martin Zhao, who had recently left academic medicine to open a chain of pharmacies. Camille looked at Dr. Zhao curiously. Rumor had it that his wife had gotten into some kind of legal trouble and may have even ended up in prison. Tonight he had a young sequined blonde on his arm.

Dr. Duncan appeared to be relieved when Camille broke into her conversation. She'd greeted Camille warmly. "How nice to see you," she said loudly while rolling her eyes toward the mismatched couple. "And how are the girls?" Dr. Duncan's voice got more gravelly as the years progressed.

"Very teenage."

"Thank you," the doctor mouthed expressively.

Camille always thought the tall, pencil-thin woman with the concave cheeks of a high-fashion model looked more like a retired ballerina than a high-powered anesthesiologist.

"Ah, I remember well the day that our youngest left for college. Take heart. You only have . . . let's see . . . Grace must be about seven?"

"Six."

"Well, that's only, what? Twelve more years. On second thought, you better have another drink." Molly removed the empty glass from Camille's hand and replaced it with a fresh drink. "Here you go, my dear."

Camille diplomatically changed the subject. "Hey, do you know a guy named Dr. Roberts? He wrote a couple of terrific articles about aortic aneurysms that I've been reading for one of my cases. I'd love to meet him."

"Of course. I do . . . and *she's* brilliant. We're very lucky to have gotten her. She's bringing in a ton of research money: worth her weight in gold. And she's single—barely survived a brutal divorce down in California. Do let me know if you know anyone." Molly scrunched up her shoulders and giggled like a schoolgirl.

"Is she here? I'd love to meet her."

"I don't think so. I think she's in New York, lecturing at Columbia— or is it Cornell?"

"Oh shoot. I was really hoping to meet her tonight. I couldn't get an appointment to see her until March!"

"I think her big grant proposal is due at the end of February. I wouldn't bother her until then, dear."

"Here's to women who get fully funded grants!" Camille raised her glass in another toast. "I'd better go find Sam. I have no idea where we're sitting. Merry Christmas!" Camille turned to make her way through the crowded room full of stiff men in black and white punctuated by women in glitzy gowns. Every few feet, she kissed another drunken man and complimented his wife on her gown. Her feet were already killing her.

Camille was limping ever so slightly by the time she spotted Sam across the room. She took a breath and headed through one last group that, thankfully, she didn't recognize. No one to feign interest in for a minute. She wandered slowly toward her husband, who she noticed looked particularly splendid this evening in his tux. She hoped they'd be able to get home at a decent hour to spend some time together, just the two of them.

"Hey, Camille! Merry Christmas."

Camille turned toward the vaguely familiar voice. Richard Rosenberg broke away from the posse of doctors mingling around the grand piano.

"Happy Hanukkah!" Camille laughed. "I can't believe it. I haven't seen you since the regional swim meet, then I see you two nights in a row!"

"Small world, isn't it?" Richard looked at Camille's high heels. "I'll bet your feet are killing you. You want to go over and sit at one of those tables by the window and catch me up on your investigation of that San Juan doc?"

"How'd you know?"

"My wife used to hate wearing those things. Every time we went out, she'd stand around for about a half hour, then drag me over to sit on the outskirts of the party so she could kick them off under the table."

"I knew I would have liked that woman."

"You two would have been great friends. I miss her so much." Richard looked out the window and watched the ferry gliding gracefully into port, thousands of feet below. "So . . . tell me, how's our case going?"

"Our case." That's a good sign. "Actually, it gets more interesting all the time."

"How so?"

"We've moved from plain old medical malpractice to fraud since I first told you about the case. And I have an appointment with a doc at the U who's an expert in aneurysms. You know a Dr. Roberts? Not sure of her first name. She goes by G. A. Roberts in her journal articles."

"I don't know her personally, but she's a gold mine for the U. It was huge when they announced her move up here from Stanford."

"Wow. Good to know. So bummed she's not here tonight." Camille smiled as she glanced over at the registration table. "Oh my God, see that guy over there? With the dark curly hair?"

"Yeah, standing with the woman with the half grown-out perm?"

"Yeah." Camille smiled. No man she'd ever known could properly identify a grown-out perm. "He's the vascular surgeon from Friday

Harbor who tried to repair Dallas's aorta after Willcox impaled him with the trocar."

"Dr. Gonzalez?"

"How'd you remember his name?"

"His name was in the chart I reviewed last summer. I remember all kinds of irrelevant stuff. I'm a great partner for Trivial Pursuit."

Camille reluctantly slipped her shoes back on. "C'mon. I'll introduce you."

Richard grabbed Camille's empty glass and signaled a waitress for another. "Hey, wait up!" He hurried to keep up without spilling the two glasses of champagne.

"Dr. Gonzalez?" Camille smiled broadly. "Camille Delaney. We met at your brother-in-law's place on Shaw Island last month . . . to discuss . . ."

Gonzalez's eyes darted from Camille to Richard. He stepped back. "The Jackson case. How could I forget? How nice to see you." Gonzalez shook Camille's hand a bit too hard. "And what brings you to a Children's Hospital event?"

"My husband's chair of infectious diseases at the U."

Gonzalez turned to the woman standing next to him. "My wife, Chrissy. This is Camille Delaney, the lawyer I told you about."

"I've heard all about you." The doctor's wife smiled sincerely. "I really respect what you're doing. It won't be easy, you know."

"It never is." Camille paused. "I'd like to introduce you to Dr. Richard Rosenberg. He's a surgeon at the U."

Richard handed Camille her glass of champagne and reached out and shook Gonzalez's hand warmly. "A pleasure."

"Actually, we've met," Gonzalez said. "I've taken quite a few of your continuing ed classes. I especially enjoyed the laparoscopy meeting I attended last summer."

"Thanks."

"Richard has been helping me with the Jackson case."

"Is that so?" Gonzalez fixed his gaze over Richard's shoulder, as if he were looking for someone.

"What a mess." Richard shook his head knowingly.

Gonzalez turned to Camille and told her about how his office had recently been broken into. Camille grimaced. If Gonzalez thought the break-in was related in any way to her case, she'd be dead in the water.

"You know I'd really like to help you, but I'm just not willing to get any more sideways with Willcox than I already am. I have enough trouble with my practice as it is."

"What do you mean?" *Please, please don't let Willcox scare you off,* Camille pleaded internally.

"I'm having a hell of a time getting referrals from the local docs ever since you and I met."

Camille noticed that Gonzalez had completely shredded his cocktail napkin.

"And like I told you, I have kids and a mortgage."

"I understand." This might be the last chance she had to talk to this guy. "But let me ask you just one thing. Did Dallas have an aneurysm?"

"I think I see our hosts coming in." Gonzalez began to walk away.

Camille followed. "Willcox told us the morning after the surgery that Dallas had an undiagnosed aortic aneurysm that he hit with the trocar."

Gonzalez stopped and turned to Camille. "I really don't want to get involved in this."

Camille rushed ahead, spilling a bit of her champagne. She planted herself in front of Gonzalez. "I saw Willcox's handwritten note the morning of the surgery, and it said that the aorta was perforated by the trocar. Nothing at all about an aneurysm. And you're the only one besides Willcox who knows what really happened in there."

"Look, I already told you I don't remember the case that well. I just remember your friend bled a lot."

"There wasn't a note from you in the chart. Do you keep separate records on your cases?"

"You do, don't you, honey?" Chrissy asked.

Gonzalez shot his wife a nasty glance and looked across the room. "Our hosts just arrived. We should go tell them we're here." He stuck out his hand to Camille. "I wish you the best of luck. Really."

"Thanks." Camille tried frantically to think of another angle.

Gonzalez held out his hand to Richard. "Nice to meet you. I meant it about your lectures. And I'm relieved to see that Camille has the big guns behind her on this case. She really has her hands full with this one."

Richard smiled. "I have a feeling that Willcox may have met his match."

Gonzalez took a couple of steps toward his friends, then paused. Camille held her breath.

Gonzalez turned to her. "You know, if your friend had just had a simple aneurysm, I'd have been able to save him." He walked away into the sea of Christmas cheer.

CHAPTER SEVENTEEN

Camille glided up the escalator at the hospital at UW Medical Center and into the bustling lobby, where a mélange of men and women in long white residency coats mingled with those in the shorter coats of medical students. Staff in blue scrubs hurried by officiously, and orderlies rushed around, carrying stacks of patient charts or pushing wheelchairs. Camille glanced at her watch, thankful that she had just enough time to grab a latte before her meeting with Dr. Roberts. This wasn't the first time she'd tried to get a university doc to help her in a case, but it was the most important. Hopefully, Doc Roberts wouldn't be a stickler for policy. Camille crossed her fingers.

"Camille?"

Camille turned to locate the friendly voice. She never knew who she'd run into at the lobby of the medical center. At the end of the latte line stood Gigi, wearing a stylish orange anorak.

"What brings you to the hospital at this hour? You must be looking for Sam."

"No, I know exactly where he is. He's driving the girls' carpool this morning." She laughed.

"Lucky you to have someone to coparent with. I don't think my ex even knew where Kaitlin's school was."

"Hey, I didn't know you worked down here." Camille changed the subject. She didn't have time to hear about another failed marriage. "Last month when we were at a swim meet, I thought you said you had to leave early for some kind of biochem lecture, so I assumed you worked over in the biochemistry department."

"I do lecture up there sometimes, but my office is here, in the research wing."

Camille looked at her watch. "Oh damn! I gotta go." She grabbed her latte. "I'm late for my meeting. You still want me to drive Kaitlin to the meet tomorrow?"

"That'd be great."

"We should be home by seven."

"I'll pick her up at your houseboat, then!" Gigi shouted as Camille took off jogging toward the research wing.

"See ya!"

Camille hurried down the long, institutional green hallway, balancing her latte carefully to prevent it from spilling as she squeezed into the packed elevator.

Camille passed the faded posters representing grants procured by many of the brain trusts behind the green doors, as the research geeks were affectionately dubbed. The Department of Pathology looked like all the other offices in the worn-out research wing. Directly outside the chairman's corner office was the standard lineup of pictures of middle-aged white guys, who, at one time or other, had held the title of department chair. The similarity between these guys and the executive team at her former firm was not lost on Camille.

Dr. Roberts's office was next to a line of tables overflowing with books and research projects that had obviously outgrown the facility. She rapped her knuckles gently on the open door. A serious young man sat behind a desk, speaking on the phone. He pulled a pencil from behind his ear and pointed it at the chair next to the door in the cramped office, then cupped his hand over the phone and told her that the doctor was running late.

Stacks of medical journals surrounded the assistant's desk. Camille noticed journals of both cardiology and pathology. There was no question about it: this was the doctor she wanted, or needed, to have on her team. The meeting had to go well.

"Dr. Roberts must keep busy reading all those journals," Camille said.

The secretary shook his head in what appeared to be genuine admiration. "Yeah, she's pretty amazing. She's board certified in both cardiology and pathology."

"Jeez!" There weren't many doctors who had that type of double board certification. Camille couldn't believe her luck. This woman was practically in her own backyard. *She's going to look at the slides,* Camille told herself confidently.

The secretary picked up the phone as it buzzed. "Yes, she's right here. I told her you were running late. Okay. Okay. I'll send her in." He looked up. "She's here. Right through that door." Another pencil point.

Camille's heart pounded. *So much for supreme confidence. Maybe I could just grovel.* She opened the door and stopped cold.

"Camille? What are you doing here?" Gigi sat behind a cluttered desk, and her eyes opened wide in a look of utter surprise.

"Gigi?" Camille looked at the ID badge hanging from Gigi's white lab coat. It read *Georgia Ann Roberts M.D.* "You're Dr. Roberts?" She stood perfectly still. "You never said you were a doctor. I've been trying to meet you for the past three months!"

"I thought you knew I was working on a big research grant for the department of cardiology. And by the way, I had no idea you were involved in medical lawsuits."

"Shit, Gigi. You're famous! Why didn't you tell me? And I thought your name was Richardson."

"Kaitlin's last name is Richardson, not mine. What about you? I thought you were Taylor."

"Sam and the girls are. I'm Delaney."

"Well, now that we finally know each other's names after all these months, sit down and tell me what on earth you want to talk with me about. I understand you've been very persistent. I've been trying to dodge you for months."

Camille sat on the straight chair next to the door without looking behind her. "I still can't believe you're *the* Dr. Roberts. What a trip. I can't wait to tell Sam."

"Sam knows who I am. I see him in the cafeteria all the time."

"You're kidding! He's such a guy. He'd never stop to wonder why you were hanging around the medical center cafeteria." Camille gathered her wits. "Well, you're probably busy. Let me tell you why I'm here."

"Please do, and by the way, I've got some time to chat. My grant's on its way to Washington as we speak. I was going to take the day off, but I decided to come in and get caught up on my mail and my reading. And I have a meeting with some lawyer who won't seem to take no for an answer." Gigi grinned. "So, shoot."

"Okay, here goes. I'll try to be brief. I represent the wife of a man who died during what should have been a routine lap chole." Camille stopped and reconsidered her approach. There was no point beating around the bush with Gigi. "Actually, the guy who died was a very, very dear friend of mine."

"I'm really sorry, but I hope you're not here to talk to me about cholecystectomies. I haven't even thought about them since med school."

"You sound like Sam. The chole is only the beginning; it gets more complicated." Camille decided to cut to the chase. "The surgeon said he hit an aortic aneurysm with the trocar, but there's evidence that my friend may not have had an aneurysm after all. And if he did, I thought that as an expert on aneurysms, you could figure out whether it would have been big enough to get in the way of a trocar during a laparoscopy."

"So, you want me to look at the slides?"

"If you would." Camille said a silent prayer.

"I'm sure with Sam being on the faculty here, you're familiar with the university's policy about not allowing its docs to have any interactions with plaintiff's lawyers."

Camille swallowed. "Of course . . . I . . . I was just hoping you could take a quick look at the slides. Off the record."

Gigi shook her head. "I really can't."

Camille ignored the comment. "The pathology report says there was a big ol' aneurysm. But I'm not so sure whether Dallas had an aneurysm at all. That's why I called you. I don't know who else could evaluate an aneurysm case like this."

"Are you saying that you think the pathologist lied?" Gigi cocked her head and frowned.

"It's possible."

Gigi was silent.

"And I have a feeling that Dallas didn't need gallbladder surgery in the first place, so I was hoping that you'd take a look at those slides too."

"Why on earth do you think that?"

"Well, this doc's a real piece of work. My investigator has uncovered a bunch of other cases he may have screwed up, and I have a feeling those may just be the tip of the iceberg."

"I can't imagine a hospital would put up with someone who's had that much trouble. He couldn't possibly be that bad."

"And it turns out that he forged his licensing application."

Gigi sat back abruptly. "This sounds like a movie script. How'd you find out he forged his application?"

"He listed that he went to Harvard, but the chief of surgery at Harvard—"

"Irving?" Gigi interrupted.

Camille looked at Gigi with surprise. "You know Irving?"

"Godfather of laparoscopy? You bet. I lectured with him at a multi-specialty conference in Denver last year. And he's coming to town this spring to speak at the annual surgical society meeting."

"Small world."

"So, did Irving know your surgeon?" Gigi got back on track.

She looks interested. Camille allowed herself to be hopeful for the first time during their conversation. "Said he'd never heard of him."

"How can a surgeon lie about his credentials and then perform negligent surgery without getting his butt kicked off the hospital staff?"

"You wouldn't believe what goes on in small-town hospitals. And this is definitely not your run-of-the-mill malpractice case."

Gigi shuffled through some papers on her desk and looked at her calendar. "Look, Camille, I'm fairly new around here. It's really too early for me to be bucking the tide. I'd be in deep shit if my chairman found out. And to be perfectly honest, I have to tell you I'm no real fan of the legal system. No offense."

"I don't blame you." Camille tried to cajole her. "I'd be lying if I didn't say I share your disgust with the system in general. But once in a while, a doc really does screw up, and the family deserves to be compensated."

"Yeah, but how do you balance that with the effect that lawsuits are having on the health care system?" Gigi stood up. "Everyone knows that costs have gone up because of the number of medical malpractice suits being filed."

Camille reluctantly got up. "Or so they think."

"C'mon, Camille. It's a known fact that there's a litigation explosion in this country." Gigi walked toward the door. "We're suit happy. Everyone wants to be compensated for the least little inconvenience."

"You believe all that insurance company propaganda?" Camille got ready to spout statistics about the failures of so-called tort reform.

Gigi opened the door. "Listen, I have to admit I don't exactly like being told what to do by the powers that be, but I'm afraid my hands are tied."

"Gigi, I really need your help on this thing."

"Please don't put me in this position, Camille. I have my career to consider." Gigi shrugged awkwardly. "I am not going to get involved in a lawsuit," she said definitively. "No offense, but I'm still recovering from my last scrape with the legal profession—I'm still paying off my divorce lawyer down in Cali."

"Ouch. Sorry to hear that," Camille said.

"It was definitely not something I want to go through again." Gigi changed the subject. "I'm glad to be here, minding my own business and doing my research."

Camille thought for a moment about the portraits of the department chairmen out by the elevators. "Don't you find yourself exhausted by the middle-aged white guys whose pictures fill these hallways telling you what you can and can't do?"

Gigi looked at her friend. "You have no idea."

"Actually, I do. I just left my high-end law practice to get out from under this exact same kind of smothering."

"Well, keep in mind that you don't have the added burden of being a Black woman in medical academia."

Camille winced inside. She hadn't meant to compare her white privileged self to this kick-ass Black scientific rock star. "You're exactly right. I don't have your experience in that regard, and I'm sorry if it sounded like I thought I did."

Gigi shook her head. "I hear you, though. It's cool what you did. Maybe someday I can do the same, but I do kinda need a medical center to support my work, so lighting off on my own really isn't an option."

"I get it. And I'm sorry you have to deal with these assholes."

"Thanks. Me too. And I'm sorry that I can't get involved in a lawsuit."

"They're not going to know. They can't track your every move."

"I can't take the risk. I've worked too hard to get where I am, and there's no way I'm going to throw it away." Gigi went over to the door and held it open for Camille. "I need to get back to work. I'm really sorry, but you need to find someone else to help you." The two women shared a knowing look. "Maybe some old white guy who can buck the system. But not me."

The mug shots of the former department chairmen seemed to be laughing at Camille as she walked past them. "I'll be back, assholes," she said aloud and slammed her open hand against the elevator button so hard that it hurt.

CHAPTER EIGHTEEN

It was always chaos after a swim meet. Camille directed Libby to stuff the dirty, wet towels into the dryer and turn it up to high. Meanwhile, little Grace proudly danced around the living room, displaying her two blue ribbons while Angela checked voice mail.

"I invited that surgeon from the swim team and his son over for dinner tonight." Camille tried to get Libby's attention as she and Trish pored over Libby's computer at the island in the open kitchen.

Trish turned away from the screen. "How come?"

"I've been getting to know him better, and I'm hoping to talk him into actually testifying against Willcox."

"Fat chance. He's from the U."

"Never say never." Camille squinted to see the computer screen without her glasses. "What are you guys up to anyway?"

"Playing a game and talking to Carlos. Wanna say hi?" Libby asked.

"Of course. Hi, Carlos! How's the fancy Connecticut boarding school?" Camille spoke loudly at the computer as her daughter's fingers flew across the keys. Camille remembered how she'd learned to type fast—back in the early days of AOL when there was a per-minute charge for online time. That was some expensive flirting. A split second later, Carlos responded in the chat, *Hi, Mrs. Taylor. How's it going out there in Seattle?*

"Great, just great." She pulled Trish from her stool.

Trish followed curiously. "What's up?"

"That's the pathologist's kid!" Camille whispered excitedly.

"Burton?" Trish mouthed.

Camille nodded.

"Watch this," Trish whispered and perched on the bar stool next to Libby, who Camille figured was typing at least a million words a minute. *So, who do you think will be the starting pitchers for the Mariners at spring training?*

Carlos's response appeared instantly on the screen. *They have a couple of new guys that are supposed to be hot, but I've never heard of the old guy they just drafted. I can't believe he's worth all that money. Can you?*

"I gotta start dinner," Camille said.

Trish turned to Libby. "Ask him what it was like living in Arizona. I've always wanted to live someplace that's nice in the winter."

Libby typed *Here's my friend Trish*, and passed the keyboard to Trish and said, "Here. Ask him yourself."

Age? Sex? the universal teen internet greeting glowed at her from the chat on the screen as a car crashed on the racecourse in the background.

None of your business! Trish typed. *So, tell us about Arizona.*

The weather was good, but the town where my parents lived was really, really boring.

What town was that? Trish asked.

Tarrington.

What was so boring?

Bunch of old farts in trailers.

What about Alabama? Trish turned back to Camille and shrugged. *I heard you used to live there too. Does everyone down there have those thick Southern accents?*

Sure do, y'all. It was nicer than Arizona in a way, except no baseball.

What was the name of the town where your parents lived in AL?

Norton. It's the Schitt's Creek of Alabama. But with mostly old people and tourists. No idea why anyone would want to go there.

"Hey, it's my turn!" Libby grabbed the keyboard from Trish.

"Okay, okay. Sorry for monopolizing your boyfriend." Trish slid the keyboard back to Libby and patted her on the head as she got up to carry the platter of chicken out to the deck, where Camille was firing up the grill.

—

"Pay dirt." Trish put the chicken down next to the grill on the covered deck and held up her hand for Camille to high five. "It's Tarrington, Arizona, and Norton, Alabama." Trish grabbed the wine opener and the bottle of chardonnay Camille had taken out to the deck. She poured herself a glass and pulled out her phone to take notes on her recent find.

The doorbell rang. "That must be Richard. Come in!" Camille ran back inside and looked over the balcony to the foyer below and was surprised to see Gigi peeking her head in.

"I'm here to pick up Kaitlin. Is she ready?" Gigi closed the door to keep out the pounding rain.

Camille felt like an animal with her prey cornered at the bottom of the stairs. "She's in Angela's room." Camille bolted downstairs to the bedroom area. "I'll get her." She paused. "Do you have time for a glass of wine?"

Gigi refused to look Camille in the eye. "No, thanks. We've gotta get home."

"I have white or red." *That was a stupid thing to say.*

"Thanks anyway." Gigi shifted from one foot to the other. "Kaitlin!" she yelled over Camille's shoulder. "Let's go!"

Kaitlin appeared, swimming gear tumbling from her sports bag.

"Thanks for the ride, Camille," Kaitlin said politely.

"Any time." Camille smiled and put her hand on the doorknob. "Are you sure you don't want to stay for dinner? I'm making my world-famous spicy BBQ chicken."

"Can we, Mom? Please?"

"Not tonight, honey." Gigi moved past Camille and out the door. "Thanks for taking Kaitlin to the meet. I'll be happy to drive next time."

"That'd be great."

"Good night." Gigi pulled up her hood and headed out into the downpour.

"Night." Camille closed the door gently and trudged back up into the lively kitchen scene. She opened the deck door and was greeted by the hickory smoke of the BBQ mingled with the rain. Her breath evaporated in a cloud of fog. She wasn't going to give up on Gigi this easily.

As Camille diligently tended the BBQ, the doorbell rang again. That had to be Richard. He'd probably bomb out on her next, she thought dejectedly.

Camille covered the fiery grill and went in to greet Richard and his son. She stopped abruptly when she saw Angela introducing Gigi to Trish, who had stopped chopping onions long enough to shake Gigi's hand.

Camille came back inside, tentatively.

Gigi pushed back her rain-soaked hood. "My battery died," she offered sheepishly.

Angela ignored her mother's entrance. "Trish's a private investigator," she announced proudly to Kaitlin and Gigi.

"Nice to meet you." Gigi gave Trish the most beautiful smile.

Trish stood perfectly still.

Uh-oh. Trish's in love. "Will you change your mind about that glass of wine?" Camille asked hopefully.

"White, I guess." Gigi stood in the middle of the room, dripping wet. "How embarrassing. I just got that thing tuned up."

"It's no problem. Sam can go out and jump your battery. But please reconsider and stay for dinner. We have a ton of food." Camille handed Gigi a glass of chardonnay.

Trish came up behind Camille and hugged her. "And believe it or not, this woman is a hell of a cook." She kissed Camille on the cheek.

Gigi paused.

"Come on." Trish went over and gently removed Gigi's jacket, then led her by the hand to a stool at the counter in front of the heavy-duty Viking range. "Sit."

Gigi complied.

Trish went back to cutting onions. "You don't want Sam having to go out and get his great wavy hair all wet. Let's wait for the rain to stop." She wiped her eyes with a kitchen towel.

"You're grilling in a rainstorm?" Gigi questioned no one in particular. "In March?"

Trish pointed at Camille. "She's Northwest born and raised, and no PNW native lets a little rain squall deter them from a good BBQ dinner."

Camille dumped a bag of mixed greens into a giant salad bowl. "Gigi's a pathologist at the U, and I'm trying to convince her to look at Dallas's slides." She tried to sound nonchalant as wayward pieces of greens floated to the floor.

Trish looked firmly at Camille, then turned to Gigi. "Don't mind her." She cocked her head in Camille's direction. "She's got a one-track mind."

Gigi relaxed, just a bit.

"Trish, can you help me with the chicken?" Camille asked.

"Sure." Trish followed Camille out into the stormy night.

Camille closed the door behind them and leaned on it. "You gotta help me."

"What?" Trish asked.

"I think she likes you, and we need for her to review the slides. Remember what I told you about how my meeting with her went sideways."

"Please tell me she's single." Trish put her palms together in a prayerful stance.

"Actually, she's recently divorced—I heard it was ugly."

"I promise I'll be nice. But do I get combat pay for having to flirt with the most gorgeous woman I've ever laid eyes on?"

"Go!" Camille pushed Trish back into the kitchen ahead of her. "And don't you dare break her heart."

"Here," Trish teased Gigi, "you might as well make yourself useful." She put a box of Triscuits, a plate, and a wedge of Gorgonzola in front of Gigi. "You are officially in charge of appetizers."

"This is definitely within my cooking repertoire." Gigi laughed. "But don't push your luck. This is as far as I go."

Trish glared playfully at her new pal. "Boiled any good water lately?"

"Hey!" Gigi laughed. "I'll have you know I can make scrambled eggs and toast. And I do several versions of mac and cheese."

"I see, and what versions would those be?" Trish raised an eyebrow, feigning skepticism.

Gigi rolled her eyes. "Let's see . . . There's the blue box and the red box . . . And Pasta and Company down at U Village has a new frozen mac and cheese in a tin pan. That's for special occasions."

Camille looked at Sam, who stood in the doorway smiling and shaking his head incredulously. She shrugged.

"So . . . is being a private investigator as cool as it sounds?" Gigi asked as she finished lining up the crackers crookedly on the plate.

"It's pretty groovy," Trish answered, raising her glass in a toast as the doorbell rang.

"Come on in. It's open!" Sam yelled over the balcony.

Richard Rosenberg and his son, Christopher, tromped in—the little boy's iPad hidden under his jacket to keep it dry. "We brought our own entertainment. I hope you don't mind."

Camille got Christopher a pop, took him into the TV room, and plugged his iPad into the TV. "Gracie! Christopher's here! He brought games!"

Gracie scrambled onto the couch next to her friend. "What'd ya bring?" she asked as Camille closed the door gently.

"And this case is one of the most interesting cases I've ever worked on, because there are so many interwoven facts." Camille heard Trish lecturing Richard and Gigi as she came back into the room.

Camille slid into the kitchen, trying not to interrupt the conversation flow, and haphazardly threw mushrooms, onions, and pesto into the risotto.

The two university doctors' mouths were hanging open. Camille knew that talking to a private investigator was about as far outside their reality as having a conversation with a professional wrestler. They were leaning forward on the counter, and Trish was on a roll.

"So, now what are you going to do?" Gigi asked Trish.

"Well, I want to see what I can find out about the towns where Willcox and Burton lived before they came to Friday Harbor. Any common threads or similarities between the towns. Stuff like that."

Gigi looked like she was getting into it. Camille bit her lip hopefully, trying not to look too enthusiastic. *Keep it up, Trish.*

"Well, Carlos mentioned that both of the other places they lived were full of geezers. Kind of like you, Sam." Trish punched Sam in the arm playfully.

Sam shot Trish a fake grin. "Very funny."

Trish turned to Camille. "Where's your laptop?"

"Downstairs in our bedroom, in my briefcase in the armoire."

Trish grabbed Gigi by the elbow. "C'mon. I'll give you a houseboat tour."

Gigi didn't object as Trish guided her down the curved staircase, turning to shoot Camille a wide-open smile and giving her a thumbs-up. "Got her!" she mouthed and took off.

—

Trish theatrically opened the antique armoire in Camille and Sam's cozy espresso-brown bedroom.

Gigi looked around. "Well, this is certainly romantic."

Trish smiled as she plopped on the bed and flipped open Camille's laptop.

Gigi put her hand on Trish's shoulder and leaned up against her. "You know her password?"

"I'm pretty much Camille's tech expert. She's helpless without me." Trish rolled her eyes and logged on while Gigi waited.

"Let's see, how do you spell Tarrington?" Trish typed in the name of the town and waited.

A few clicks later and they stared, transfixed, as artwork downloaded and a photograph of a desert mountain scene slowly appeared.

"It's beautiful," Gigi said.

Trish slowly scrolled down and read: "Tarrington, Arizona, is fifty-five miles northwest of Phoenix, halfway between Carefree and Interstate 17 on the way out to Black Canyon City; nicknamed Shangri-la by its residents; home to Desert Cactus Estates; one of the preeminent retirement communities in the state. For additional information, click on the icons below."

"Click on Health Care," Gigi prompted.

They waited as a picture of a white, Southern antebellum-type building came into focus.

"That's got to be the ugliest medical center I've ever seen," Gigi said.

Trish smiled to herself. Gigi was hooked. Trish read aloud: "Wellington Hall, fifty-five private rooms, a surgical suite second to none, and a world-class diagnostic center and laboratory."

"Go back and click on Demographics."

A nicely formatted page appeared next. "The average age of the Desert Cactus Estates resident is sixty-five years young! Each winter, the foothills come alive with the familiar sound of rumbling RVs returning to Shangri-la."

"Let's print this and check out Norton, Alabama." Trish hit Print.

Another web page came up. "Norton, Alabama: the fastest-growing retirement community in the southeast," Trish read. "Well-kept secret jewel, blah, blah, blah; home of world-class Sparkling Gulf Medical Center focusing entirely on the care of seniors."

"What about demographics?"

"More geezers," said Trish as she read the paragraph directly under a picture of a gray-haired couple riding bikes along a picturesque boardwalk.

"We'd better get back upstairs, or I'm afraid we might find ourselves staying down here all night."

Trish put her hand on Gigi's back and guided her to the kitchen, where Camille was setting out a tray of marinated artichoke hearts, roasted red peppers, and pickled asparagus surrounded by various types of olives.

"What'd you find out?" Camille asked as she refilled her guests' wineglasses.

Gigi and Trish looked at each other as Gigi munched on a pickled asparagus. Trish smiled flirtatiously. "Well, it's interesting how similar the places Willcox used to live are."

"In what way?"

"They're both basically tourist towns, mostly for seniors," Trish answered.

"Hmm . . . I guess Friday Harbor could be characterized as a tourist town too. But I don't know about the geezer factor," Camille said.

"Hey, Camille, I don't want to burst your bubble, but your friend Dallas may just fit the definition of geezer to some," Richard said.

Libby barged into the kitchen. "Hey, Mom, did you order our tickets for spring training? It's an early game on Tuesday."

"I did. Aren't you proud of me?"

"Spring training? I'm jealous," Richard remarked enviously.

"Are you guys Mariners fans?" Libby asked.

"Are you kidding? We're total converts."

Ah, the way to a man's heart is through his favorite sport. "Ever been to spring training?" Camille asked.

"I wish."

"Why don't you guys come with us? We're heading down on Monday," Camille suggested, hoping she could get close enough to Richard to convince him to testify against Willcox.

"Hey, yeah. That'd be cool!" Libby shouted.

Richard nodded thoughtfully. "Well, it's an idea. It's my week off call—I was just going to work on polishing an article I'm writing that's due by the end of the month. I can do it from anywhere."

Camille held her breath.

"And Camille and I can check out Desert Cactus Estates." Trish nodded eagerly. "And you too, Gigi. It'll be fun."

"I don't know if I could get away with this little notice." Gigi looked wistfully at Trish. "But thanks anyway."

"C'mon, you won't have to get involved in the Willcox thing if you don't want to," Trish whined jokingly.

"Just make it part of your research project," Richard suggested. "Then you can write it off."

"Maybe the players on the senior golf tour could offer their unnecessary parts for my aortic aneurysm study." Gigi laughed.

"Exactly what are you researching, anyway?" Trish asked innocently.

"Well, I take samples from aortic aneurysms and do a bunch of tests on them to see what causes some people to survive and what causes others to die from a rupture."

"Where do you get body parts for your studies?" Trish asked.

Gigi perked up. "I have different hospitals around the country send me samples."

"I guess you're always on the prowl for new hospitals to give you tissue," Trish offered.

"Sure," Gigi answered coquettishly. "I'm always looking for new specimens." She opened her eyes wide at Trish.

Camille wasn't sure whether Gigi was more interested in Trish or the specimens. She guessed that they might be one and the same.

"I have an idea." Trish pulled up her stool and leaned her elbows on the counter. "I happen to know of a hospital down in a picturesque little retirement community in Arizona. They have a nice, modern medical center that caters to its residents, all of whom are over fifty-five. What do you want to bet they'd love to participate in your little old research project?"

"Not a bad idea. But I'd need a research assistant to accompany me." Gigi smiled at Trish.

"No problem. I'll starch my lab jacket, and I'm all yours," Trish said as she grabbed Sam's glasses off his face and pulled her hair back in a clip. "How's this?" She looked at them, ever so slightly cross-eyed. Like a chameleon, right before their eyes, Trish had transformed herself into a somewhat nerdy research assistant.

"Very cute." Gigi pushed a wayward lock of hair from Trish's face. "So, if I were to say yes, when would we be leaving?"

"Monday morning," Libby piped up quickly.

Gigi raised an eyebrow. "Hmm."

"C'mon," Trish urged.

"I can take Kaitlin out of school for a few days." Gigi smiled mischievously. "I may just be able to pull it off."

Camille spoke up. "You don't have to—it's teachers' conferences this week. That's why we scheduled the trip now."

Gigi nodded. "Good to know. I can never keep track of the school schedule up here. Seems like every time I turn around, it's another day off for something."

Trish turned to her newfound friend. "So, is it really true that you can't look at Dallas's slides?"

"I really shouldn't. The U has an ironclad policy against its docs getting involved in lawsuits."

"They'll never know. Just do it after hours." Richard shrugged.

"Why can't you look at slides from here?" Trish turned to Sam. "You must have an old microscope around here somewhere."

Gigi laughed and cocked her head at Sam. "Yeah, Sam. I'm sure you have an old Leica around here someplace?"

Sam shrugged. "Um . . . nope, but if I had an extra ten grand, I could put one in the armoire for home use."

"Ten grand for a microscope?" Trish raised her eyebrows.

Camille interjected, "Looks like it's going to have to be an after-hours trip to the medical center."

Trish turned to Gigi. "We could really use your help," she pleaded.

"How'd you get dragged into this?" Gigi asked Richard.

"Camille is hard to say no to." Richard held up his hands as though he were giving up. "And I'm just not all that into caving to department chairs whose ivory tower lives are so detached from reality. This guy is a danger to the community, and I have no problem helping to stop him."

"Well, that's easy for you to say as a male doc. You don't have to deal with the backlash I would. I'm a Black woman scientist working in a world of old white men. I'm so sick of all of it. I just want to do my science."

"As much as I hate to say this, Gigi is probably right. She has lots to lose if she helps out in a lawsuit against another doc," Trish interjected. "I ended up leaving the SPD after being taunted over and over for being gay."

"SPD?" Gigi asked.

"Seattle Police Department. It was my dream job," Trish said wistfully. "But I just got sick of the politics and struck out on my own."

"And not that it's the same, but I haven't looked back after leaving the bad boys I used to work with," Camille offered. "But I get it. You don't have the option of opening up your own university lab."

Richard looked at Gigi thoughtfully. "You do know what a coup it was for the U to convince you to move your research up here, don't you?"

The group turned to Gigi.

Richard continued, "She was on the landing page for the med center website. I'm here to tell you that most of the docs in the research wing are in awe of you, Dr. Roberts." Richard held up his wine in a toast.

The group lifted their glasses in admiration as Gigi looked pensively out the window, lost in thought.

"You brought the U a ton of research money," Richard stated authoritatively. "I bet your grant is bigger than most of the dinosaurs up there in pathology have ever dreamed of getting. Do you really want to let them dictate what you do?"

"Well, I do have to admit that I'm curious about the slides." Gigi refocused on the task at hand.

"As any good doctor would be," Richard offered. "Let's look at this like scientists. We have a puzzle to solve. Can't we put the whole lawsuit thing aside for a minute? I, for one, am actually curious about what the slides might show."

"How about this?" Trish said conspiratorially. "Gigi, you can look at the slides, with no commitment to do anything more. If it looks like there's something to pursue, you can help Camille find an expert who can actually testify." She cocked her head at Richard. "Some white guy like Richard."

Richard feigned indignation. "She has a point." He smiled.

Gigi nodded. "I could do that. Just a quick slide review. That's it."

Trish turned on the charm full bore. "And remember, Camille can sue the U if they give you any shit. And I'll act as your own personal bodyguard. I'm very, very protective."

"Okay, okay," Gigi whispered.

Camille smiled. "Thanks, Gigi."

"But you have to come up to the medical center at night, when there's no one around."

"No time like the present," Camille said eagerly. "How about tonight?"

"Tonight?" Gigi stammered.

"Sure. We're only ten minutes away." She turned to Sam and Trish. "You guys can do the dishes," she teased.

Trish nodded. "Totally. We got you covered."

"My car broke down, remember?" Gigi reminded them.

Trish looked at Sam and Richard. "Looks like you two are on KP tonight. I'll take Gigi to the hospital and wait."

"Well, if I'm going to Arizona early Monday morning, I have some lab work to finish up before I go." Gigi smiled. "If you drop me off now, Camille can meet me at my lab around ten, and then I'll stick around for a bit to get caught up. I can take an Uber home."

Trish grabbed her coat and Gigi's jacket.

Gigi turned to Camille. "Okay if Kaitlin spends the night tonight?"

Sam smiled. "As long as she's willing to be on KP with us." He looked around the messy kitchen. "We have our work cut out for us."

Trish grabbed a baggie and put a few pieces of BBQ chicken in it. "Dinner to go!" she announced as she formally presented it to Gigi with a flourish.

Gigi reached around Trish and swept a handful of crackers and cheese into the bag. "I'm starving."

"Okay. We're outta here." Trish looked at Camille. "You meet Gigi in her lab at ten."

"Perfect." Camille smiled. *One step at a time.*

CHAPTER NINETEEN

Camille pushed through the thick green doors and into the darkened research wing of UW Medical Center. She walked past the mug shots of the former department chairmen. "I'm ba-ack," she snarked at them. Warm light emanated from under Gigi's door. She knocked.

"C'mon in." Gigi ushered Camille into her small private lab. For the first time since Camille had known her, Gigi actually looked like a doctor, in her surgical scrubs, her braids twisted in a tight bun on top of her head.

"I can't believe you talked me into this." Gigi locked the door behind her.

Camille scanned Gigi's lab, taking note of the plaques perched precariously between overflowing stacks of journals and scientific paraphernalia tumbling from the shelves. "Hey! Nice digs. Richard was right. You must be bringing in some serious grant money to get a lab like this!"

Gigi was all business as she held out her hand nervously. "Slides?"

Camille handed Gigi a small wooden box, which Gigi immediately placed on the lab bench. She opened it and placed a slide on the microscope stage.

"Huh. How old did you say Dallas was?" Gigi asked as she flipped the lens to a higher power.

"Sixty-five."

"Let me see another one." Gigi put on her glasses, tilted her head back, and looked at the label affixed to the slide.

Camille leaned over Gigi's shoulder.

Gigi perched her glasses on her head and returned her attention to the microscope. She held out her hand without looking up. "Give me another," she said curtly.

Camille felt like a nurse again. She placed a slide firmly in Gigi's outstretched hand, as if they were in surgery.

Gigi slowly went through the procedure to sharpen the focus. "Huh."

Camille couldn't contain herself. "What?"

Gigi was all doctor. "This is weird." She slipped the slide out and put the other one back. More focusing.

"Well?" Camille asked urgently.

Gigi slowly turned away from the microscope, and put her hands on her knees. She leaned forward. "If this specimen is from a sixty-five-year-old man, I'm Beyoncé."

"What do you mean?"

Gigi looked back into the microscope. "The vessels on this slide are too smooth," she said without looking up. "The internal lamellae is too elastic to have come from someone in their sixties. These slides came from someone way younger than your friend."

Camille's heart began to race. "Are you sure?"

"Look." Gigi swiveled the teaching eyepiece toward Camille. "You took histology in nursing school. See the nice, even wavy line just below the surface? If this were from an older person, you'd see more atrophied, calcified tissue." She looked up. "There's no way this is Dallas's gallbladder."

Camille gazed into the microscope. "Oh my God."

"I can hardly wait to see the aneurysm." Gigi flipped open the box.

Camille held her breath as Gigi played around with the microscope.

"This is more like it. Lots of evidence of atherosclerosis. Now, this specimen definitely came from an older person."

"But how do we know if the aneurysm is really from Dallas?" Camille wondered aloud.

Gigi knitted her brow. "Why wouldn't it be?"

"If you're telling me that the gallbladder slides aren't Dallas's, why should we believe that the aneurysm slides are his?" Camille stumbled over her words. "Remember, there was no mention of an aneurysm in Willcox's handwritten note, and Max Gonzalez inferred that there was no aneurysm when I spoke with him at the Christmas fundraiser."

Gigi looked at Camille expectantly.

"There's gotta be a way to tell if these are his slides," Camille urged.

Gigi sighed. "Let me take a look at the medical records." She flipped to the back where the lab results were filed. "He was an organ donor, wasn't he?"

"Yeah, why?"

"Well, you're in luck." Gigi turned to her computer. "I can't believe I'm doing this." She shook her head.

"Doing what?" Camille asked curiously.

"This computer's hooked up to the National Organ Donor Bank. I did my first fellowship on transplant tissue typing. Everything is cataloged by number in order to protect confidentiality. Hang on. Dallas's tissue typing data should come up in a sec."

Camille shifted from one foot to the other as numbers and scientific data filled the screen.

Gigi turned to Camille. "Did Dallas ever have any problems with his kidneys?"

"Not that I'm aware of. Why?"

"How about his eyes?"

Camille shrugged. "He just wore reading glasses."

"Huh." Gigi stared at the screen.

"What's wrong?" Camille leaned over, frantically trying to decipher the data for herself.

"Well, it's unusual for a donor to only donate skin. It's usually all or nothing, unless they've had kidney disease or something that would make them unable to donate."

Every fiber in Camille's body was on alert. "That computer says Dallas just donated skin?"

"Uh-huh."

"That's impossible!" Camille gripped the counter and sat down. "Robin and I went over the list of organs that would be donated. They said that since Dallas was basically healthy, they could use his kidneys, his liver, his corneas . . . Let's see. Not his heart." Tears welled up in her eyes. "I . . . I don't remember what else, but I know it wasn't only skin."

Gigi went from doctor to friend in a heartbeat. Her voice was soft. "Well, it says here that the only tissue harvested was skin."

Anger replaced sorrow as Camille leapt back to her feet. "That's bullshit! If his organs weren't sent to the organ donor bank, where the hell did they go? And why did they have Gloria sign all that paperwork if they weren't going to donate his organs?"

Gigi got up and put her hand on Camille's shoulder.

"I have to know if this slide came from Dallas. You've got to help me!"

Gigi plopped back down onto her stool. "I can't." She crossed her arms emphatically.

"C'mon. Please help me." Camille choked back the tears.

"Look, the only way to tell is to go down to the main lab, and the security down there's too tight." Gigi looked up at Camille. "Camille, I agreed to do a quick review of the slides. Not do a full-blown tissue analysis."

Gigi walked over to the window and looked out at the houseboat lights reflecting on Portage Bay. The big old houses lining the parallel streets on the north side of Capitol Hill glowed warmly over the still water. "I always dreamed of an office with a view like this."

"Please help me," Camille pleaded. "Those department assholes can't touch you. They wouldn't dare."

"My dad died of an aneurysm." Still facing the window, Gigi hugged herself and rubbed her upper arms as if she were trying to keep warm.

It was Camille's turn to comfort her friend. "I'm so sorry."

"He never got to see me graduate from med school."

Camille took a step closer. "That must have been hard."

Gigi's shoulders slumped. "He could have survived if he'd been in a medical center," she said angrily.

"Where was he?"

"In a small town up near Mount Shasta in California. He was a minister."

"What was he like?"

"He taught me everything meaningful that I know."

Camille handed Gigi a tissue from the desk. "I know what you mean. Dallas was my life teacher. Kind of like the father I never had."

"My dad was one of those guys who always stood up for the most marginalized," Gigi went on. "Whatever you do to the least of my brothers and sisters, you do to me," she said in a booming voice. "That was his favorite Bible verse."

The two women stood shoulder-to-shoulder for a moment, watching a big sailboat cut across the smooth, dark water and go under the open drawbridge.

"I'll understand if you don't want to get involved any further in this thing. You've worked hard to get where you are. I know it would take attention away from your science if you had to deal with cranky department chairs—even if you'd come out victorious."

"But then again, I have to live with myself. And a big, fancy education doesn't mean much if you can't use it to help someone. There are other Dallases out there—the least among us. And people like him and my dad deserve excellent medicine. Maybe we can prevent this from happening to anyone else." Gigi blew her nose as the drawbridge closed behind the boat. She turned back to her lab bench and picked up the slides. "Let's see if the aorta sample they sent you really came from Dallas." Gigi walked over to the door. "We don't have enough on this slide to do a straight tissue type." She sounded like a doctor again. "I'll have to do a blood type match. It's spooky down in the main lab at night. I'll do it if you'll come down there with me."

"What about the security?"

Gigi looked at Camille nervously. "We'll fake it."

"You're sure you want to do this?"

"I can hear my dad preaching. You do what's right, then put up a fight." Gigi drew a shaky breath. "Here, put these on." She threw Camille a pair of scrubs as Camille threw her purple leather jacket on the chair.

Camille almost had to run to keep up as Gigi pulled her key card out and buzzed them through locked doors with signs warning "Authorized Personnel Only." As they wound their way through the Department of Pathology maze, Camille poked her head into labs with vials of various colored chemicals surrounding rows of microscopes. The scientists' screen savers danced eerily in the darkened rooms.

"In here." Gigi veered into a short hallway and hit the automatic door opener mounted on a wall beside a set of surgical doors. She unclipped her ID badge and slid it through a box that looked like a credit card machine, then turned and unclipped the badge hanging from Camille's lab coat and ran it through.

"Whose ID is this?" Camille asked as she replaced the badge.

"My chief resident. He's on vacation."

Gigi ushered Camille into a long lab with rows of microscopes standing on black-topped lab benches under huge ventilation hoods. *It smells like my college chemistry class.* Camille watched Gigi pull out the slides and grab a couple of vials off the shelf, busily initiating what appeared to be a rather detailed science experiment. Camille nervously wandered around the lab, stopping to look at family pictures pinned on personal bulletin boards. Jokes clipped from newspapers and scientific journals were taped to the wall.

Camille took a breath and tried to imagine herself as a famous scientist working late into the night trying to discover the cure for SARS. Just then, a couple of men in full surgical attire pushed open the heavy swinging doors and loudly interrupted her fantasy.

The taller of the two men sized up Camille, then turned to Gigi. "What're you doing down here this late?"

Camille detected a note of hostility in his voice.

"Oh . . . just finishing up the tissue typing for that paper I'm trying to get to the *Journal of Pathology* by next Friday." Gigi seemed to glare back at him.

Camille turned away and unclipped Gigi's chief resident's name tag and stuck it into her pocket.

One of the doctors turned to Camille.

"Oh jeez. Forgive me," Gigi stammered. "Lester Noonan and James Wandel, meet Deb Henry. Deb's up from California."

The two men looked at each other. "What a fabulous hostess you are," Wandel said sarcastically. "Bringing your houseguest to the lab on a Friday night."

"She's a doctor," Gigi said hurriedly.

Camille bit her lip, recognizing for the first time what Gigi was up against at the U. These two were dripping with something close to contempt.

"Huh. Where do you practice, Dr. Henry?"

"California." Camille grabbed a book sitting on the bench in front of her and flipped it open, trying to look like she was searching for some rare histological phenomena.

"Where in California?"

"Where?" Camille thought back to Gigi's wall of plaques. "Stanford . . . I'm at Stanford."

He took a step closer to her. "In pathology?"

He's not buying this. "Yup. Hey, Gigi, can I take another look at one of those slides?" Camille looked over Gigi's shoulder to avoid confronting the inquisitive man.

Gigi turned off the microscope. "Sure. You can see it when we get back upstairs."

"I can't wait to see more of those calcifications."

The doctors looked suspiciously at the two women.

Camille grabbed Gigi's arm and gave her a gentle pull. Gigi stood and quickly pocketed the loose slides scattered across the black lab bench. "Yes, it's unusual to see that amount of calcification on tissue from such a young patient. I wonder if he had premature atherosclerosis," Gigi commented in a scholarly tone.

The tall doctor took a step closer to the two women.

"Gigi, it's almost ten thirty. I have an early meeting tomorrow," Camille said.

"Oh my gosh! Let's get out of here."

Camille could hear the slides tinkling against each other in Gigi's pocket as she pushed Gigi gently toward the door. "Nice to meet you both!"

It was all Camille could do not to break into a full run as they turned the corner.

"Who were those guys?"

"A couple of big-gun pathologists."

"Well, I see what you mean about being up against the hierarchy. Wow. Those guys were real assholes."

"Yeah, and at the same time, their science is amazing. They're working to create systems to prolong blood storage."

"Sounds fascinating," Camille said sarcastically.

"It's actually important for small community hospitals that don't have access to blood banks. That way they can store O negative blood on premises for emergency surgery."

"Does the tall guy have some particular reason not to like you?"

"James Wandel is hardly my biggest fan. I got the research position that he thought he had in the bag. He's never gotten over it. Why do you ask?"

"He was looking at you weird. That's all. So, what about Dallas's tissue?"

"Don't know. I didn't get to finish the test."

Camille's heart sank. She followed Gigi through the interconnecting hallways back to her office, where they closed the door and exhaled loudly together.

"Listen, Camille, I have a ton to do if I'm going to get out of town by Monday. I need to finish up here. I'd offer to go back down there and recheck the slides, but I just can't."

Camille was silent.

"We can check them when we get back, okay?"

"You sure you don't want me to give you a ride home?"

Gigi held the door open for Camille. "No. Thanks anyway. I'll grab an Uber."

Camille turned to Gigi as they walked together to the elevator. "I really can't thank you enough for helping me like this."

"Let's just pray that those two jerks don't figure out who you are," Gigi said as the elevator doors glided closed.

Camille got out of the elevator and hurried down the long tunnel connecting the medical center to the underground parking lot. She was relieved that they were leaving town soon. The stress of the past few months was finally getting to her. She was exhausted.

Maybe I can finally quit worrying about the girls, she thought. Just for a week. They'll be a thousand miles away from Willcox and his goons. *Maybe Sam and I can even steal some time alone.* Lately they'd been too distracted for any kind of romantic interlude, with Sam jumping out of bed to check on the girls every time the houseboat creaked.

Camille walked out of the tunnel and across the dark, empty parking lot to the stairway leading to the lower floor. She'd been in this lot a thousand times when she was at UW nursing school. But back then, the nurses always left the hospital together in a big group, after their shift. Tonight she felt very alone. Camille looked cautiously behind the door before entering the cold cement stairwell. She bounded down two steps at a time, her nerves on edge.

A colorful display of red and blue flashing lights greeted her as she exited the stairwell underground. Camille drew in a quick breath, hoping the cops were just responding to a car break-in and not something worse. As she gingerly walked past the police car, she noticed a woman with short dark hair in the back seat holding an ice pack to her face, while a female officer tried to comfort her. Camille could see that the woman's clothes were torn. She said a quick prayer for her and picked up her pace as she neared her familiar dark-green Explorer.

"Excuse me, miss."

Camille jumped and turned to face a very young police officer. "Yes?"

"I'm sorry. I didn't mean to scare you. Can I have a minute of your time?"

"Sure, how can I help?"

"There was an incident just now, and we're wondering if you noticed anything unusual on your way down here."

An incident? How subtle. "What happened?"

"I'm not at liberty to release that information, ma'am." The young officer stood by awkwardly as Camille stared at the woman in the police car.

"Ma'am?"

Camille was in a fog. "Uh, I'm sorry. I . . . uh . . . I just came down through the tunnel. I didn't see anything." She stood silently as an aid car, its siren blaring, pulled up next to her Explorer.

The officer took out a clipboard and clipped a long yellow form to it. "Can I have your name and address please?"

"Is she a nurse?"

He nodded. "She got off shift early. Should have called for a security escort." He shook his head as he handed Camille the clipboard. "If you wouldn't mind, it'll just take a minute."

"Sure." Camille took the clipboard in her shaky hands and sat sideways in the back seat of the police car as the medics gently helped the woman onto the gurney.

She reached in her purse and pulled out a business card to attach to the form, straining to hear what the woman was telling the police officer as they wheeled her to the ambulance.

"He kept calling me a whore lawyer," she sobbed.

Camille froze.

"And he told me that if I spoke to the police, my children would pay." She buried her head in her hands as the officers furiously scribbled notes.

The female officer held the woman's hand. "Nothing's gonna happen to your children. I promise."

"I don't have any children." The woman's sobs were gut-wrenching. "Oh, God help me!" the woman screamed as they shut the ambulance doors behind her.

An uncontrollable shiver shot through Camille's body. *Lawyer? If she spoke with the police, her children would pay? It had to be a coincidence.* But just in case, she shoved her business card back into her purse and hurriedly filled out the form by hand. "Here you go." She held out the completed form. She had to get home. Now.

The officer took the clipboard and handed her one of his cards. "Thanks. If you think of anything later that might help us out, please give me a call."

"Certainly, Officer."

"Someone from the department will most likely be calling you within the next few days."

Before the officer climbed into his car, he stopped and shouted over the roof of his car to Camille. "Ma'am, did you happen to see a bald man, about five seven, stocky build, around here tonight?"

"No."

"Okay, thanks—just checking." The officer waved at her and started his car. "Keep an eye out, and be careful, ma'am. Lock your doors." The officer slammed his door and drove away.

In that moment, Camille's headlights caught and illuminated a torn and bloody purple leather jacket exactly like hers that had been hidden under the police car. She swallowed hard to keep the nausea at bay. Her heart raced as she considered for a moment the advisability of retrieving the jacket to give to the police. Then she revved her engine and squealed out of the parking lot, her eyes glued to the rearview mirror. *If she talked with the police, her children would pay?* She sped through two red lights, leaving the rumpled-up jacket on the cement floor of the garage.

When she reached home, Camille searched the shadows by running her headlights past the shrubbery surrounding the parking lot. She quickly took off her jacket, turned it inside out, and hopped out of the car and into the rain. The dumpster was at the top of the dock in a darkened wooden enclosure. She held the creaking door open with her foot as she stretched to throw the wadded-up jacket into the trash The heavy lid slammed loudly as she ran full speed down the dock to her houseboat, where she closed the front door quietly, hoping Sam wouldn't notice her dripping wet and without a jacket. There was no point in telling him anything before she had all the facts. He'd just freak out.

"That you, hon?" Sam's voice came from the upstairs living room.

Camille squeezed back tears as her fingers danced across the alarm pad. She looked out the front window and double-checked the dead bolt on the front door. Twice.

"Just a sec. I'll be right up. Are the girls home?"

"Grace and Libby are in bed, and Angela and Kaitlin are online with some boys playing a game."

"I'll just go check on them."

"Is something wrong? You seem upset. Did everything go okay with Gigi?"

"It was fine. I'll explain it in the morning. I think I'm just a little stressed about not being ready to leave on Monday."

Sam came to the top of the stairs as Camille was checking on Angela and Kaitlin. "Have you seen my keys?" he asked. "I can't find them anywhere. I had to walk home and climb in through the window. I almost fell in the lake."

Camille dropped the carry-on suitcase she was struggling to get out of the storage closet. "Your keys are missing?"

"Yeah, and my master key to the department was on that ring."

"What about your house key?" Camille yelled.

"Everything was on that ring. And if someone loses a master key, they have to rekey the entire department. Last time that happened, it cost almost ten thousand dollars. And the person who lost the key had to pay half."

She crumpled to the floor. "Your house key is missing?"

CHAPTER TWENTY

Andrew Willcox took off his linen sport coat, turned it inside out and placed it over his arm, and waited as the limo driver put his luggage into the trunk. He breathed in the warm desert air.

The driver held the back door open. "Sir?"

Willcox slid into the deep, tufted gray leather seat and turned on the TV to catch the local Phoenix weather report. He had a tee time early the next morning.

"Where to, sir?"

"Tarrington, out past Carefree." Willcox sat back to enjoy the forty-five-minute ride to the rural community north of Phoenix. He'd actually be seeing her in less than an hour. He could hardly wait. It had been so long. He fingered the long jewelry box in his breast pocket.

The ring of his cell phone interrupted his reverie. "What?" he snapped.

"I took care of the broad last night," Vic Jones announced flatly.

Willcox sat up. "Huh?"

"Had a little meeting with her in a dark parking lot."

"And?"

"And I don't think we should expect any more trouble from her or the blonde."

Willcox hung up and exhaled slowly. *Thank God.* His stomach did a flip-flop as he looked up and saw the sign welcoming him to Carefree slide past outside the tinted window. Just fifteen minutes more.

—

Willcox strode toward the lavish luxury VIP suite of Rebekkah's Manor. A hush fell over the nurses' station as he walked by. The ward was decorated in a Caribbean theme, with bright splashes of hot pink and turquoise and a number of seascapes.

"Hello, Doctor." The nurse's accent matched the Caribbean décor. "You're here early."

"Good morning." Willcox tried to be civil, but he was too excited for small talk. It had been so long.

"Rebekkah is going to be so excited to see you. And what beautiful orchids! I'll go get a vase."

Willcox whisked down the hall and into the entryway of the huge suite. The walls were hand-painted with a trompe l'oeil scene of a tropical garden, and the carpet was a rich green. The effect was stunning. Willcox felt as if he were entering his own secret garden. He paused and stared at the tiny woman curled up in the pink satin sheets he'd given her for her birthday.

"Mother?" he whispered.

A pair of blue eyes fluttered open and closed from deep within the woman's chalky gray face.

He gently took her hand and ran his forefinger up and down the lacy purple veins. "I'm here, Mother." He knelt at her side.

She smiled and squeezed his hand weakly.

It gave him butterflies.

"It shouldn't be long, Mother."

The woman looked up and motioned her son to help her sit.

He lurched for the intercom. "Get someone in here now! We need some pillows. Feather pillows. Hurry up!"

Once she was situated, he removed the thin strand of diamonds from the box and hooked them at the back of her neck. He handed her a mirror.

She placed her open palm over the necklace and smiled. "It's lovely."

He kissed her cheek, remembering her thick, flowing blond hair. She had been spectacular in her younger days.

She took a few shallow breaths. "I took my name off the transplant list, Allie."

"No. No." He panicked. "No! I'm sure we'll get a suitable match soon."

"No, honey. I'm tired. I don't want to fight anymore."

Willcox sat softly on the bed. He wasn't about to let her go. He couldn't. "You're tired. It's to be expected. You'll feel better after the transplant. You always do." He held his mother's hand to his lips and kissed it.

His mother looked out the window. "Isn't the desert beautiful in the spring? I've always loved the flowers." She smiled. "And this spring is especially lovely." She closed her eyes. "My last spring."

"Stop saying that, Mother." Willcox choked back his tears. "Let's talk about your garden."

"Ah, yes."

"You were quite a gardener in your time." His voice cracked.

"That I was." The woman closed her eyes briefly, while her son caressed her face. "I remember the orchids they had in Grenada. You gave me the biggest bouquet I'd ever seen when I came down for my first transplant. Do you remember that, Albert?"

Willcox smiled. "Only the best for my queen."

"When I woke up from surgery, I thought I'd died and gone to heaven. I never saw so many rare orchids in one place."

Willcox tried to burn the image of his mother into his memory. She was so beautiful. "We'll find a match, and you'll wake up in a room just like that one in Grenada. I promise."

"No, honey. I'm all through."

"No, Mother. You're just not feeling well. Things will be better soon."

She held her hand over his. "Really, darling. There are lots of young people with beautiful lives ahead of them. That little boy in your charity ward here, he needs a kidney more than I do." Willcox's mother looked adoringly at her son. "You're so incredibly generous to help so many children. I've lived long enough to see what you've made of yourself. I'm tired now."

It wouldn't be so hard to find two kidneys, one for the kid and one for her. "Mother." A tear escaped and wound its way down his cheek. "You know I can't go on without you." She'd change her mind—he was sure of it.

The tiny woman looked at her son with eyes like lasers. "You have to, Allie. I've expected a lot from you, and you've always delivered. We've lived a life we never dreamed possible. That son of a bitch in Alabama deserved everything he got."

Willcox nodded silently. Memories of his mother working double shifts every day in the rancid so-called nursing home raced through his mind. It wasn't until he was an adult that he had found out about the circumstances of his conception at the hands of the fat old slug who owned the place. The Emerald Palace was Willcox's first purchase. The creep's family had sold out cheap after the guy died during surgery. Willcox had explained that he'd done everything humanly possible to save him.

And Mother had the second in a long line of kidney transplants. It had been a perfect match: poetic justice at its best. All those doctors' kids in the fancy suburbs who'd teased him relentlessly throughout elementary school back in Alabama had been at his mercy when he returned as the town's only surgeon. The hospital had been trying to recruit a surgeon for a year before he showed up.

"You've come a very long way from the hills of Alabama. Don't stop now. You've almost made it."

"I'll try, Mother."

"No, Allie. You will not try. You will succeed. You and BJ will own the largest empire of retirement communities and boutique surgical transplant centers in the world. You two can help so many people."

"But it won't be worth a thing without you." She had no idea how many people had been helped by the unsuspecting surgical patients at the local hospitals.

She dozed off.

Willcox watched her chest delicately rising and falling as she slept. His mind drifted back to Grenada, where he and his high school sweetheart, Billie Jo, had first met Bertolini. He had to give BJ credit for coming up with the plan. He had been desperate to get his mother out of the public hospital, where she lay dying of kidney failure. And it was Billie Jo's idea for him to do a fellowship in transplant surgery. That way he'd have an "in" with the transplant list for his mother. When that didn't work, he and BJ concocted a plan to get her a kidney themselves. BJ suggested he approach Bertolini and suggest that Bertolini could provide the necessary pathology reports to support the diagnoses to justify the removal of a kidney. It was brilliant. And as BJ pointed out, there was no reason for the plan to be limited just to his mother. No one really needed two kidneys, and the bureaucrats at the organ bank didn't seem to give a shit about all the wonderful people who were too far down on the list.

His mother awoke. "Allie." She smiled sleepily.

"Shh." He stroked her hair and watched her look out over the colorful garden.

"All of your homes are so beautiful." She sighed.

He had to hand it to BJ. Her plan to set up retirement communities for active seniors and use the patients for donors was certainly brilliant, but her designing and building the surgicenters out in the middle of nowhere was the coup de grâce. As long as they imported the construction crews, and then the surgical teams, no licensing officials would even know they existed. The San Juan Islands and Tarrington were definitely way off the beaten path. No one would ever find them there. And besides, BJ had convinced him to do a few charity cases each year, so they were actually helping the poor.

His mother interrupted his self-congratulatory reverie. "Can you cover my shoulders?"

"Look, Mother." He pulled the soft white blanket up. "I have a plan. I'll see to it that the little boy gets the next match. And then we'll get one for you." He had never told her exactly how she had been so lucky to get her transplants whenever she needed one.

"Ah, my darling." She held his face in her hands. "You know it takes too long on the waiting list. My luck has finally run out." She closed her eyes.

No, Mother. Your luck never runs out, Willcox thought as he watched his mother drift off again. He put his head on her shoulder and wept. He would not let her go.

———

Camille headed toward the breakfast buffet set up next to the bubbling fountain in the hotel lobby. They'd gotten in late the night before, and she still felt a bit bleary. She refilled her coffee cup for the third time and wished for a real Seattle latte as she returned to the table.

Gigi certainly didn't look like she'd just gotten five hours of sleep. In fact, she looked distinctly like the famous research doctor that she was. She wore a conservative khaki pantsuit with a stiffly starched white blouse open at the collar. Her glasses hung on the ever-present chain around her neck, and her braided hair was pulled back into a ponytail at the nape of her neck. There was no way that the chief of surgery would refuse Gigi's request to add Wellington Hall as her next study participant.

"Well, that's a far cry from the red palazzo outfit you wore on the plane!" Camille stopped braiding Gracie's hair for a moment and was taken aback at a flashing similarity between Gracie and Gigi.

Gigi moved toward Grace. "Here, let me do that."

Camille stepped aside, grateful for the friendship that had developed between Gigi and Gracie—the more Black women role models she could surround Gracie with, the better. She marveled at the motherly way Gigi tied off Grace's braids and kissed her on the cheek.

"Hey, Trish!" Libby shouted. "When did you get glasses?"

Camille barely recognized Trish as she wound her way over to their table, her stick-straight bangs pulled haphazardly up in a plastic clip.

"Trish!" Angela screamed in horror. "You look like such a nerd! What are you doing with lipstick on? And those glasses! They're vintage!" She made a face as Trish pushed a pair of oversized tinted purple glasses back up onto the bridge of her nose.

"I'm going to work as a lab assistant." Trish tugged at her too-short gray pants and tried to straighten the bow on her pink flowered blouse.

Camille gave Trish a thumbs-up signal as she rolled her eyes. "Where did you find that shirt?"

"Château Value Vill-ahj." Trish turned to Gigi. "So, how do I look?"

"Like a lab assistant," Gigi replied with unabashed admiration.

Camille smiled at how hard and fast Trish and Gigi had fallen for each other.

Richard ran into the dining room, dragging his son by the hand. He crammed a doughnut into his mouth and handed one to Christopher.

"Mom! Dad's eating bacon! And doughnuts," Libby announced loudly.

Sam sheepishly covered his plate that he'd stacked high with all the things he never got to eat at home.

"We gotta go. Now!" Libby was adamant. "The Mariners start signing autographs at eight thirty, before they start their morning stretches. Hurry up!"

Camille kissed her family as they filed past her. She patted her husband on the butt and playfully plucked the handful of bacon from his to-go plate. "Love you."

He took back the bacon. "Me too." He gave her a sappy smile and kissed her.

Richard stuck a couple more doughnuts into his pocket and turned to Christopher. "We get to eat in the car on the way to the game." He looked at Camille. "Hey! Later today we can look at some medical records on my laptop."

"Whose medical records?"

He took a few steps back toward her as Christopher pulled him toward the door. "I did a computer search, and it turns out that a handful of Willcox's patients ended up at the U."

"He referred patients to the U?"

Richard shoved half a doughnut into his mouth and shook his head. "It looks more like they either self-referred or were referred by other docs," he said with his mouth full. "But they'd all been treated by Willcox at one time or another."

"Interesting."

Richard took off after Sam and the girls. "Let's go, Chris." He waved to Camille. "See you after the game!"

———

Camille headed back to her room. It had been a shitty week. Thank God she could finally let her guard down. She passed the hotel gym and decided to do a quick round on the StairMaster before checking in with Amy.

Camille glanced up at the big-screen TV. *Just forty-five minutes, then it's back to work.* She began to pump away.

On the TV, a perky young woman chatted with an older man with hair plastered back from his face. They sat a bit too close to each other on a lime-green couch set in front of a fake window looking out over the chemical-green Tarrington golf course surrounded by a cactus-studded desert landscape. Something about the kitsch of a homey local TV show made her smile.

Camille took a deep breath and got ready to meditate as the closed-captioning appeared below the TV duo. Out of the corner of her eye, she noticed the white letters of the words "laparoscopic surgery" in the black band of type sliding silently along the bottom of the screen.

Camille automatically slowed her pace. She craned her neck as if she could actually hear the interview.

"This will be our last call this morning." The woman's fake smile stretched her lips across her teeth. "Hello? You're on the air with the doctor."

An all-too-familiar face framed by graying blond hair filled the TV screen.

Willcox!

Camille gazed intently at the affable-looking doctor leaning back in his chair, fingers laced casually around his knee as he responded to the caller.

Camille read the closed-captioning as Willcox flirted with the female cohost, and the male cohost squared his shoulders in a not-so-subtle attempt to put himself physically between his colleague and the charming doctor by blocking their view of each other. "I'd like to thank our guest, Dr. Ashley Wellington of Wellington Hall. For an appointment with Dr. Wellington, please call 1-800-A-W-S-C-O-P-E."

Dr. Wellington? Un-fucking-believable.

The stair climber had stopped, but Camille didn't even notice. The woman stared at her guest. "Wellington Hall is located out past Carefree on the way to Black Canyon. And just as soon as we get off the air, I'm going to call and get my mother an appointment with Dr. Wellington. Do you think you could pull any strings to get her in soon, Doctor?" The woman leaned forward to see around her male cohost and smiled coquettishly at Willcox.

"I'll certainly see what I can do, Delia." Willcox pointed his index finger at her and winked. "Now I'm off to Wellington Hall. I have surgery this afternoon."

Holy shit! Willcox? Surgery? At Wellington Hall? Today? Camille flew off the StairMaster and raced down the hall to her room, where she quickly grabbed her phone and dialed Trish. Her face fell as she heard the muffled ring of Trish's cell phone in the next room.

CHAPTER TWENTY-ONE

Gigi had never seen such an outlandishly decorated hospital: red velvet to the max. The hallway leading to the doctors' dining room, where she and her "assistant" were to meet with the chief of staff, was lined with Victorian tables and sideboards. Each piece held an antique lamp, many of which involved some sort of elaborate shade, mostly pink, with fringe—it was vaguely reminiscent of an Airbnb she'd stayed in in New Orleans when she'd given a presentation at a conference a few years back.

Dr. Reginald Radnor greeted Gigi and Trish and guided them through the stares of the middle-aged white guys in the ostentatious doctors' dining room. She'd have this guy eating out of her hand by the end of lunch.

"I was just reading your paper on dissecting aortic aneurysms in patients receiving immunotherapy. Fascinating piece of work," Radnor said as he held out Gigi's chair.

"Thank you, Dr. Radnor. I've been looking forward to seeing your facility." Gigi squinted at a heavy gold-framed portrait of what appeared to be some kind of Confederate general. "It's . . . really something," she said as a chill went up her spine.

"I know, the décor's a bit much, but beggars can't be choosers. We have a very generous benefactor whose wife is an architect. She designed the new wing and then insisted on updating the décor."

Radnor ordered their lunch, then opened the folder he'd been carrying with him. "Here we go. I have a printout of the statistics, just as you requested, Dr. Roberts."

"Please, call me Gigi." She smiled. *This should be a piece of cake.*

"Okay, Gigi." Dr. Radnor smiled sincerely. "Let's see, where was I? Ah, yes . . ."

The overhead page boomed: "Dr. Avon. Dr. Lynn Avon. Dial 4-7-8. Dr. Avon, dial 4-7-8."

Gigi perked up. "Is that Lynn Avon, the pathologist?"

"Uh, yeah. Do you know her?"

"If it's the same Lynn Avon I'm thinking of, she was one of my star residents at Stanford." Gigi smiled confidently at Trish and nodded very subtly.

"I'll bet it's her. I'm pretty sure Lynn's from California." Radnor seemed pleased about the connection. "Small world, isn't it?"

"It sure is." Gigi nodded. "How long has Lynn been on staff here?"

"Oh, she's with Phoenix General. She just rotates up here to cover for our pathology department. One of our guys spends his summers in Wisconsin. So, Lynn is with us in the summer and whenever else we need help. She's been trying to get on here full time, but the budget won't allow it at the moment."

The waiter brought the threesome each a perfectly plated salade Niçoise.

Gigi couldn't get over how often she found herself running into former students during her travels.

"Dr. Radnor, Dr. Radnor, please call 3-7-9. Dr. Radnor, call 3-7-9." The overhead boomed.

"Excuse me just a minute." He picked up an imitation old-fashioned telephone on the credenza. "Dr. Radnor here. Yes . . . I'm doing her at one this afternoon . . . I see . . . Well, it'll have to wait . . . Four o'clock would be fine." Radnor hung up and turned to Gigi. "We're in luck. I thought I'd have to cut our meeting short for my one o'clock bowel resection, but I got bumped by a nephrectomy. If you don't mind, I need to call my wife and let her know I'll be late for dinner." Radnor used the phone again. "By the way, would you like to join us for dinner, Gigi?"

"I'd love to. Thank you."

Trish leaned over and quietly asked, "What's a nephrectomy?"

"Kidney removal," Gigi whispered.

Trish made a face.

"Where are you staying?" Radnor asked.

"Out at Squaw Peak."

"Ah, there's a lovely restaurant in the hotel. We can meet you there. Say, at eight?"

"That'd be great."

"Oh, here's our benefactor now." Radnor pointed to the tall man with graying blond-streaked hair. He was wearing a crisply starched lab coat and had just entered the dining room, filling it with his presence. The man walked over and stood directly behind Trish.

"I've scheduled an emergency nephrectomy that has priority over your one o'clock case," he announced loudly.

"So I hear."

Gigi looked at the pompous surgeon and then at Trish, who had bolted toward the restroom without turning back.

"Dr. Roberts, meet Dr. Ashley Wellington. Dr. Roberts is the lead researcher on a multicenter study involving the pathophysiology of aortic aneurysms."

"It's a pleasure to meet you, Dr. Roberts," Wellington said stiffly. "I've heard some of your podcasts. What brings you to the Valley of the Sun? Spring training or just a little well deserved R&R?"

"Dr. Roberts contacted us to see if we can participate as a tissue harvesting site for her study."

Wellington's smile was replaced by an icy glare. "Tissue study? Here at Wellington Hall?"

"It's quite an honor to be asked." Radnor beamed.

Wellington boldly pulled up a chair. "So, Doc, where are you practicing now? Rumor has it you left Stanford rather abruptly."

Gigi couldn't remember the last time she had felt such overt hostility. "I'm at the University of Washington. They offered me a full floor for my lab, and you should see the view!" She tried in vain to elicit a smile from the ice king.

"Huh. You left Stanford for the view in Seattle?" Wellington sneered. "That's a new one."

Gigi leaned forward, placed her elbows on the table, and cradled her chin in her hands. "The full professorship didn't hurt either."

Radnor interrupted. "Uh, Dr. Roberts was just telling me about the study methodology."

"Oh, she was?" Wellington sat back, folded his arms, and looked at Gigi. "Let me guess. You want us to do all your grunt work. We screen the patients. We do the surgery. We prepare the specimens. And then you get all the credit. And we don't get a red cent. Sounds fair to me."

Before Gigi could prepare a retort to this asshole, the overhead paging system blared: "Dr. Wellington, Dr. Wellington, please report to surgery. Dr. Wellington, please report to surgery."

"I guess someone's got to go practice real medicine." Wellington pushed away from the table, almost knocking his chair to the floor. He didn't say a word as he walked out the door, his white coat flying behind him.

Gigi got up from the table. "If you'll excuse me, I think I'll go powder my nose."

"Of course. I . . . I don't know what to say about Dr. Wellington. I'm sure he must have had a hard night."

"Don't worry about it. I'll be right back." *Who the hell was that guy?*

Gigi bent down to look under the stalls in the women's restroom. "Trish? Are you in here?"

"Shh!" came the disembodied voice. "Is the coast clear?"

"What the hell are you doing?" Gigi whispered loudly.

"Is he gone?"

"Is who gone?"

"Willcox!" Trish whispered.

"Willcox?" Gigi almost shouted. "What are you talking about?"

"Shh! Get in here!" Trish opened the door of the stall where she was sitting on the toilet, her legs curled up under her. "Turn around, so your feet point the right way."

The door to the restroom swooshed open and closed. Trish put her finger to her lips while a woman locked herself in the adjacent stall. When the woman washed her hands, Gigi twisted her head to see Trish, who was perched behind her on the back of the toilet.

As soon as the woman left, Gigi hissed, "What the hell's going on?"

"Willcox is here. He was right behind me. The guy Radnor wanted to introduce to you."

"You're shitting me. Wellington is Willcox?"

"It looks that way. And he knows me, so I need to get out of here before he sees me."

"Well, that shouldn't be too much of a problem since he just got called to the OR."

Trish climbed down off the back of the toilet seat. "I'm not taking any chances. Give my apologies to the good Dr. Radnor. I'll meet you in the car."

—

Camille jumped out of the terra-cotta tile shower and wrapped herself in a fluffy hotel towel. The humidity in Arizona was so low, she was almost dry by the time she reached the ringing phone.

"The insurance adjuster for the Jackson case is on the line. Shall I put her through?" Amy asked.

"Yeah, sure." Camille slipped into a white terry-cloth bathrobe.

"Winnie Douglas here," the woman at the other end of the line barked.

Camille leaned up against the hard bathroom vanity. "Hi, Winnie. This is Camille Delaney."

Winnie skipped the pleasantries. "I'd like to discuss the possibility of putting the Jackson case into mediation in the next couple of weeks."

"I'll talk to my client about it." Camille was noncommittal.

"Listen, Camille, we've both been around the block a few times. You know as well as I do that you're not going to hit a home run on this one. What've you got? A sixty-something-year-old guy with no income. There's no way a jury's going to deliver a significant verdict, even if you do win on liability, which is far from a sure thing."

Camille paced back and forth in the spacious bathroom. "Obviously we have differing opinions, once again."

"Willcox hit an aneurysm. Shit happens. It's a known complication of the procedure. Period."

Camille shook her head.

"And you're not going to be able to admit any evidence of Willcox's prior difficulties. It's not relevant. No judge is ever going to allow it. Your negligence is thin, and damages are limited at best. This is not a big case, Camille."

"I'll get back to you."

"Tell you what. I'll go ahead and get a mediation scheduled. The committee wants the case settled soon. Otherwise, we're looking at a full-blown defense and the offer to settle is off the table for good. Let me know if your client says no; otherwise, I'll assume the mediation's a go."

The line went dead. Camille hung up the phone, went out onto the deck, and leaned over the railing, looking down at the desert landscape. She didn't even have a pathology expert to testify against Willcox. Yet. And going to mediation without an expert wasn't exactly a great way to get the insurance company to come up with the big bucks. Something had to give. And soon.

CHAPTER TWENTY-TWO

Willcox drained his martini and fidgeted impatiently as he waited for Burton to show up with the details of their upcoming real estate deal. The cocktail crowd was just beginning to filter into the Palo Verde Room at the exclusive Boulders Resort. He watched with envy as a helicopter landed on the helipad just next to the first tee. Three young people jumped out, and one young man turned to hold his hand out to help a fit, older, gray-haired man climb out of the aircraft. Willcox chuckled as the old guy slapped the hand away, hopped out, and ducked as he hurried across the tarmac and into the lounge of the restaurant, where he was solicitously greeted by the maître d'. Willcox sat back. Someday, he'd have peons like that falling all over themselves, waiting on him.

Burton hustled across the round dining room and took a thin file folder out of his black leather portfolio as he sat down. "I just got off the phone with BJ. It seems the owners of the property next to ours down here in Arizona have an opportunity to purchase a piece immediately adjacent to a strip mall they developed out in Mesa. All of a sudden, they want to sell. We need to move quickly."

"So, when do we make the offer?" Willcox asked impatiently.

"The price has gone up a million. So, we need more cash. And if we use it all on the Arizona project, we won't be able to get the piece on the Island."

"Shit. We need to develop the San Juan project in order to keep our census up," Willcox said. "I was thinking. We gotta have another 'complication' before we head back up north." All his mother needed was a kidney. The rest could be used to raise money for the Arizona property. And thankfully, BJ had made them promise that they'd keep all their cash in the bank so they would have the flexibility to close on either piece at a moment's notice. A few million more in cash wouldn't hurt.

Willcox watched as the maître d' circled Mr. Big and his team, elaborately showing them the label of an obviously expensive bottle of champagne. Mr. Big nodded approvingly as the maître d' officiously and gently opened the bottle and began to pour. Then Willcox returned his attention to Burton, who was explaining that they would be well advised to cool it up north for a while since there was already a disciplinary proceeding brewing up there. Maybe they should just focus on Arizona for the time being, he suggested.

Willcox couldn't shake the image of himself garnering the same kind of attention as Mr. Big. At the rate they were going, he could have his own damn helicopter in just a few more years. No more charters with cheap, fake leather seats. He looked back to Burton. "What do you suggest we do about the practice up north?"

"I just told you. We take it easy for a while. As it stands, we've actually done quite nicely with our choles and Nissens, but obviously the real money's in harvesting. And the turnover at the marinas and little resorts ain't gonna supply us with enough protoplasm." As always, Burton knew the statistics backward and forward. "If we really want to kick ass up there in the summertime, we gotta import more donors."

"How do we do that?"

Burton pulled a letter out of another file folder and handed it to Willcox. "As you can see, BJ just got word that we have the zoning to build a resort—which we'll market as a fifty-five and over destination but not a retirement community. And that zoning only applies to that exact piece out on Lime Kiln Point. So, BJ and I were talking—even though we started our operation up there intending to develop another retirement community, which typically keeps us in supply, it'd actually be better to do some type of resort." He stroked his chin. "The zoning up there is never going to allow us to build the kind of project we can get away with around here."

"But we just refinanced the San Juan piece to finish the surgicenter over on Brigantine Island."

"It'll wait. We still have cash from that refi so we can use it to get the build-out done for the resort. BJ has the plans ready for the zoning board, but she hasn't submitted them yet. Not sure what the holdup is."

"Who's gonna tell BJ we need to pull back a bit up north?" Willcox grabbed a breadstick and broke it in half.

"She knows the numbers better than either of us. She'll understand. She's the one who makes us keep liquidity so we can afford to build up north and move quickly when a property comes on the market."

Willcox nodded.

"You're wife's a genius on the financials." Burton's admiration was genuine.

"So, we back off while we're building the resort up there and get going again once it's built."

"Yep. And besides we need to keep a bunch of dough ready for when BJ gets all the permitting done in Friday Harbor. I figure it'll take about a year or so to complete."

"You're saying we stay in Arizona for a full year?" Willcox was clearly on board with this plan. "Way better golf courses here."

"Yeah, but we do one more round up there. We have patients waiting over on Brigantine Island."

"Agreed, but we've got one on the list down here tomorrow, right?"

"Yep. Vic's got my nemesis under surveillance. I think we can get her done in the next forty-eight hours. Then we head back up north." Burton was pleased with the plan.

"Okay," Willcox responded. "Then let's focus on increasing our census down here by putting in more of those little trailer stalls. The place can keep expanding to stretch as far as the eye can see. We'll never run out of inventory. And as long as we keep putting everything in BJ's maiden name, no one will ever figure out who's behind the purchases."

—

Gigi sized up Dr. Radnor. *I'll bet the guy likes his cocktails. A few stiff drinks, and he'll tell me anything I want to know. Patience.*

"I invited your friend Lynn Avon to join us. I hope you don't mind." Radnor smiled.

"Of course not, that'd be great." Gigi nodded.

Radnor's cell phone rang just as the waiter came over to take their drink order. "We'll just see you when you get here, then." He put the phone back in his pocket. "Lynn's running a bit late," he explained. "Listen, Gigi, before we go any further, I want to apologize again for Wellington's behavior today." Radnor placed his hand on his chest as if to say, "Mea culpa."

"Don't worry about it." She shrugged. "Really. I'm sure he's under a tremendous amount of stress, as we all are in these days of managed care."

"You're very understanding. Wellington has a great deal of clout around here since he donated such a large chunk of money to remodel the hospital. So, we all tolerate him to the best of our ability."

The waiter came to the table and theatrically snapped each of their napkins onto their laps.

"I understand."

"Well, I'm happy that he didn't succeed in scaring you off. I was afraid you'd turn around and walk out after he gave you such a hard time." Radnor chuckled with relief.

"I'm not one to be put off by someone like Wellington." Gigi changed the subject. "Did you happen to bring the numbers we were discussing today?" *Let's get through with the aneurysm charade and on to what the hell Willcox is doing down here.*

"Right here." Radnor nodded to the waiter to bring him another Manhattan.

For the next twenty minutes, Gigi and Radnor huddled together, going over details of the aortic aneurysm study, with Jody Radnor trying to look interested in the minutiae of the extensive research requirements.

When Radnor was on his fourth Manhattan, Gigi decided to broach the subject of Willcox's competence. "So . . . I see from these statistics that Dr. Wellington has had his share of unfortunate outcomes this year. I guess it could be a statistical anomaly." *Follow me, baby.* She crossed her fingers.

Radnor sat back in his chair and stared intently at Gigi for about fifteen seconds, then polished off his Manhattan in one gulp and put his glass down hard. "Ashley Wellington the third has always had more than his share of complications."

Jody Radnor glanced nervously at her husband, whose facial spider veins had turned a deep shade of reddish purple. Jody appeared to be wincing as she looked at Gigi.

Gigi ignored Radnor's wife. "What do you mean?"

Radnor flagged down the waiter and ordered a bottle of wine.

Gigi leaned forward ever so slightly, trying not to look too anxious. "You know, it's no problem from my vantage point."

"No, I'm sure it isn't. In fact, our golden boy doesn't even do vascular surgery, so you won't have much to do with him anyway. But, to tell you the truth, I'd like the opportunity to discuss our situation with someone who's more objective than I am."

Jody Radnor put her hand on her husband's arm, obviously trying to get his attention.

Gigi smiled gratefully as he shook his wife off. "I'd be happy to offer any help I could," she said.

"Thanks, but I don't honestly know what you could do."

Jody leaned forward and faced her husband, her back to Gigi. "She can't do anything at all, Reg. Let's let it rest."

Gigi craned her neck to see around Jody Radnor. "Well, like you said, sometimes it helps just to have a different perspective."

Jody sat back. "It's too complicated." She glared openly at her husband, who held his glass up for the waiter to pour him the cabernet.

Jody turned to Gigi. "You really don't want to get involved in this, Dr. Roberts." Her voice was crisp and cool.

Radnor spoke up. "Dr. Roberts is from Seattle. She doesn't know anyone around here. We can talk to her about Wellington."

Jody ignored Gigi's presence. "You've had enough trouble with Wellington. Let it go."

"I want another perspective on the situation."

"For what?" Jody threw down her napkin. "What possible difference could it make to discuss that man with anyone? It won't make any difference, and you know it."

After a brief pause, Radnor looked at Gigi. "Ashley Wellington appeared on the scene here not too long after Desert Cactus Estates was completed. Before he showed up, we were just another small-town hospital, doing a bit of this and a bit of that. I had a typical general surgery practice. Nothing fancy. Beautiful home in the desert, nice friends. Golf every Wednesday."

Gigi nodded, trying to look concerned.

"Then one day a cadre of developers showed up. Before we knew it, we were smack in the middle of a huge retirement community. Trailers stretched as far as the eye could see. Then came the strip malls and fast-food restaurants." He swirled his wine forlornly.

Jody interjected. "Look, Dr. Roberts, I don't know why you're so interested in Dr. Wellington. But my husband is almost ready to retire, and we don't want to cause any disruption here. Please, please don't ask him to go up against Wellington. He's a very powerful man around here."

Gigi was speechless.

Radnor continued as if his wife had never spoken. "Business at the hospital began to pick up to the point that we needed another surgeon to help keep up with the population explosion. Like magic, Wellington shows up.

"And before you know it, he donates a ton of dough to remodel the hospital and get all kinds of pricey high-tech equipment, and we're off and running. Mind you, no one but Wellington knows how to use most of the newfangled equipment, and there's a big brouhaha when the other local surgeon and I go and get trained to use it. By that time, Wellington's been doing a bunch of laparoscopic surgery, and we're up to our ears in surgical complications." Radnor waited while the waiter brought the salads.

"At first, I figured the procedure was so new that anyone doing it would run into unexpected complications. But after we all learned to do them, no one was having as many complications as Wellington. He even started having intraoperative deaths. I'm telling you, we had no idea what to do; here was our benefactor playing slice and dice with our newfound snowbirds."

"Enough, Reginald," Jody snapped. "He's had a few too many. Forgive him. I'm sure he doesn't mean to infer that Dr. Wellington has had anything to do with the deaths at the hospital."

Gigi looked at Jody. "Of course not." She could almost hear the theme song to *The Twilight Zone*. Same story, different town. "Why didn't the credentialing committee step in?" she asked.

"This is where it gets almost hard to believe." Radnor poured himself another glass of wine. "The hospital had been recruiting a new surgeon for over a year when Wellington showed up. Before long, he and his wife were in the church choir and pillars of the local community. He quickly built up a strong referral network."

Gigi tried to appear nonplussed, but she could feel her pulse pounding in her ears.

"And unfortunately, the credentials committee is heavily weighted with his new friends who certainly don't seem very enthusiastic about taking on their buddy, who'd recently become the hospital's namesake."

"What was the administrator doing about his complication rate?" Gigi asked.

"Well, as the population of the community increases, so do the hospital admissions, so the administrator chalks up the complication rate to the fact that there are so many more surgeries being done."

"My word, he has the entire community locked up." Gigi was breathless over the eerie resemblance between the two scenarios. "What'd you know about him before he came here?"

Jody sat back in her chair, closed her eyes, and shook her head.

"He came very highly credentialed. Harvard, no less. The committee was tripping all over themselves to grant him privileges."

"Interesting."

"Ah, there's Lynn." Radnor stood up and pulled out the chair opposite from Gigi.

The plain-looking, slightly overweight pathologist hurried over to the table and hugged Gigi. "It's so good to see you! Sorry I'm late. And, yes, I'd love a glass of wine. Thank you, Reggie." Lynn's eyes crinkled up at the corners when she laughed.

"Hang on, I'm getting to it." Radnor poured Dr. Avon a generous glass of wine. "I was just singing the praises of our fine benefactor." He passed the last of the grilled scallop appetizer to Lynn, who soaked up the remaining sauce with a piece of bread.

"I hope you guys were done with this." Her voice was husky and her laugh soulful.

"You bet." Gigi directed the conversation back to the subject at hand. "The story of your benefactor is really something." She rolled her eyes, feigning exasperation.

Lynn tore herself another hunk of french bread and slathered it with butter. Without waiting to finish chewing, she said, "So, what d'ya think?"

"Well, it sure looks like you have your hands full."

"Not me. I'm just part time up here." Lynn stuck her tongue out at Radnor playfully. "For the time being anyway. Now, tell me, Reg, what on earth does Wellington have to do with the good Doc Roberts's research project?"

"Not a damn thing." Radnor was obviously beginning to feel the effects of his rising blood alcohol level. "I jus' started in on him," he slurred.

"Well, you're probably boring the shit outta my pal here." Lynn dismissed Radnor with a wave of her hand.

"No, really, I'm always fascinated by community hospitals' quality assurance problems. I spend a ton of time traveling to hospitals just like Wellington Hall." Gigi paused. "Well not exactly like Wellington Hall." She smiled. "I have to say, the physical layout is one of a kind."

Lynn let out a huge guffaw. "That's putting it mildly. We work in a goddamn Twelve Oaks mansion from *Gone with the Wind* out here in the middle of the Painted Desert. It's the ugliest fucking building in the valley."

Gigi laughed. "You said it, not me. But, honestly, architecture aside, your situation with Wellington isn't all that unusual," she lied.

"Well, you haven't heard the rest of the story."

"Do tell . . ." Gigi focused on her former student.

"Well, Wellington is only half the problem. We have this goofball pathologist who's become Wellington's right-hand guy. Ever heard of a pathologist scrubbing in the OR?"

"I'd have to say no to that one." Gigi wondered if her nose would start to grow.

"Dr. Bertowski used to be a surgeon," Radnor explained, "but he had some kind of car accident and got nerve damage in his hand. Had to quit surgery. But he still likes to scrub, so Wellington kind of adopted him as his own personal assistant."

"I can't personally imagine scrubbing in on a case," Lynn said. "Shit, I wouldn't know a Richardson retractor from a Simpson forceps."

"Jesus Christ, forceps are for delivering babies." Radnor rolled his eyes.

"See? What'd I tell you?"

"So, what's the problem with this pathologist? What's his name again?"

"Bertowski," Lynn said quickly. "The guy's a maniac, that's what. Insists on having his very own lab. Keeps it all locked up, even when he's in there. Won't let anyone, even the regular cleaning people, in. I tried to borrow a few supplies from him once, and he almost bit my head off."

"And lemme tell you, that's a missake. No one takes on Lynn Avon and lives to tell about it." Radnor was noticeably sloshed.

"And that's not all!" Lynn was hot. "That shithead Bertowski keeps trying to cut me out of my work. Wellington won't let anyone read his slides but Bertowski. The two of 'em are inseparable. Fuckin' Frick and Frack."

As dinner wound to a close, Gigi asked Lynn if she'd like to have a cappuccino with her in the bar. They had to talk. Alone. Gigi felt certain that Lynn would help get them into the hospital computer so they could see what Willcox had been up to in Arizona.

Thankfully, Radnor indicated that he had an early case the next day, so they were home free. After saying goodbye, Gigi stopped and called Trish and Camille to come meet them in the piano lounge. A strategy session was definitely in order.

———

Gigi hastily made introductions all around and launched into a lengthy explanation, telling Lynn their real reason for coming down to Wellington Hall.

"So, which of you fine women is going to meet me at the hospital and check out the computer?" Lynn asked without missing a beat. "I can't tell you how much easier my life would be without that little slimeball Bertowski. I could finally get on here full time."

Trish spoke up. "Gigi's not going in there. She's got too much to lose."

Gigi breathed a sigh of relief. She'd had her fill of undercover work.

"And Camille doesn't have the investigative skills," Trish continued. "I'll do it."

"No, I think I should go." Camille's voice was uncharacteristically soft.

"Camille, you don't know the first thing about self-defense. You can't go in there," Trish admonished her.

Camille sat up straight, trying not to think about the scene with the nurse in the purple leather jacket in the university parking lot. "Nothing's going to happen to me in a busy public hospital. And besides, Trish, you don't know what to look for. I'm the one with the medical and legal knowledge." Camille set her jaw. "I have to go. It's gotta be me."

———

Willcox waited until the third ring to pick up his phone. "Willcox here."

"It's me," Vic Jones reported curtly. "The lady doc just left Squaw Peak. You guys ready?"

"Yep. Carl is particularly looking forward to this one," Willcox responded.

"Got it. Shouldn't be too difficult. She lives way out in the desert. Another drunk driver single-car accident on a long lonely road."

"Good man. Over and out."

She could easily bring in a few million.

Willcox called Burton. "Get some rest. We're going to the OR first thing in the morning—it's gonna be a long day. I'm calling in the surgical crew over at the Manor—they gotta prep my mom and that little boy—and we have one waiting on a heart and another needs a liver. I need to call BJ and let her know we'll have a few million more in the bank by nightfall."

CHAPTER TWENTY-THREE

Willcox held the hands of the inconsolable woman and gazed into her eyes. "There's really nothing we can do, Miss Avon. Your sister hit a tree head-on and sustained a major head injury." He looked over the woman's shoulder at the pathologist lying among the equipment in intensive care. She had the familiar gaze of death. Her chest rose and fell in time with the noisy respirator. Not long now.

The round-faced woman slumped back onto the bench outside her sister's room.

Willcox sat down next to her. "I can't tell you how sorry I am for your loss."

"I just talked to her a few hours ago. She was on her way home from dinner with an old friend."

That was her first mistake. He patted the woman's hand.

She covered her face with her hands. "I don't know what to do."

"Your sister was a fine doctor. I'm sure she'd want others to be able to benefit through her untimely death. She appears to have been a very healthy specimen."

The woman was clearly horrified. "Specimen?"

Willcox continued quickly. "She was a . . . a very special woman to all of us here at Wellington Hall."

And as luck would have it, a single, childless one at that. No one with standing to bring suit. This one is almost too easy.

Willcox amped up the charm. "I'm sure you're aware that there are many, many wonderful people on organ donor lists."

The woman sobbed. "But how can you be sure? How do you know for sure she won't come out of it?"

"We can tell by the electroencephalogram. She has no brain waves." Willcox glanced at the clock behind the nurse's desk. He had a kidney to do in five minutes. "Time is of the essence, you know." He handed the woman a clipboard with the forms on it. "I had the honor to know your sister. I know she'd want you to sign."

The woman blew her nose and scribbled her name at the bottom of the page.

—

Vic checked the door to Burton's office to make sure it was locked, then crawled under the lab bench and dialed the combination to the safe. He carefully withdrew several slides and handed them to Burton, who labeled the slides "Rosa Antonio."

"Here. Stamp the requisition with a delivery time of eight thirty-two." Burton directed Vic as he picked up the hospital dictation phone and began to speak as he glanced at his watch: seven fifteen; he had to be in the OR in fifteen minutes. "Patient: Rosa Antonio. Hospital number"—he looked at the requisition slip—"98-7321. Gross appearance: large, irregularly shaped kidney weighing three hundred and forty grams and measuring eighteen by twelve by nine centimeters. The kidney is enlarged, and its surface is oscillated with cysts throughout. Some of the cysts are soft and contain fluid."

"When do we do the doctor?" Vic asked as he rinsed out the familiar Styrofoam cooler.

Burton clicked off his Dictaphone. "Shh." He clicked it back on. "The renal capsule is removed, and the cystic appearance is accentuated. On bisection, the specimen has normal parenchyma replaced with cysts throughout. These have thin walls and contain a yellowish, clear fluid. There are no tumors present. Representative routine sections taken. Gross impression: severe polycystic kidney disease. Microscopic exam reveals thin-walled cysts and remnants of renal medulla and scattered glomeruli with minimal inflammation and no evidence of malignancy. Diagnosis: polycystic kidney."

He tossed the Dictaphone onto the bench and looked at his watch. "Let's go. Mrs. Antonio awaits." He looked at Vic. "The doc will be turned off and sent to my lab in a couple of hours. The Manor team will be ready by noon." He grabbed his monogrammed lab coat and jogged off.

———

Camille hopped out of the car and crossed the opulently landscaped parking lot toward the imposing building and her early morning meeting with Dr. Lynn Avon. Willcox would never recognize her in Trish's long blond wig with thick bangs hanging down over her forehead. The fashionable tortoiseshell glasses were making her dizzy, even though Trish had sworn the lenses were clear. She shifted in an effort to get comfortable in the lab coat that was just a tich too tight under the arms. *I can't believe I'm doing this,* she thought as she crossed through the hospital lobby and down the wide, antique-lined hallway.

Ah-ha! Path lab dead ahead. Camille picked up her pace and quickly located Dr. Avon's office. Since she was a few minutes early, she wandered over to the window and looked out at the green lawn bordered by an English country garden and two thinly foliaged willow trees. The landscape was oddly out of place in the austere desert.

Lynn's screen saver flickered and startled Camille. It was a picture of Lynn and a shorter version of her, probably a sister, in mountain climbing gear, their arms around each other. They sat, laughing, on top of a huge rock wall. Lynn was supposed to be here to meet her at seven thirty. Camille looked at her watch. It was seven forty-five.

A clipboard holding a month's worth of OR schedules hung on a bulletin board by the door. The first thing that came to Camille's attention was the word "vacation" written in bold red ink across Willcox's column. Apparently he was going to take off the following week. *He's in the choir with Trish, so he probably needs to be back for the big St. Patrick's Day service on Sunday.* She flipped to the current OR schedule and ran her finger down the list, looking to see if Willcox and Burton were in the OR today as expected. If they were, she could relax. They wouldn't be around to identify her.

Yep. Seven thirty. Nephrectomy. *Oh God. Another kidney on the auction block.*

Lynn must be running late. Camille decided to take herself on a department tour. But first she wanted to be sure Willcox was actually in the OR. She picked up the phone.

"Hi. I'm calling from the floor. We're just wondering when to expect Antonio back up here. Do you think she'll be here before noon?" Universal nursing language for "we're busy and hoping the patient isn't coming back to the floor before everyone goes out on their staggered lunch breaks."

"Hang on." The OR receptionist's voice echoed over the intercom. She came back on the line. "They're doing her now. Sorry. She'll be up right around eleven."

"Thanks anyway." Camille felt a distinct chill shoot up her spine.

Might as well check out the place. She tried to look casual as she walked lightly down the hall. The next door down had a bronze plaque that read "Dr. Bertowski, Chief of Pathology."

Why not? she thought boldly. She slowly turned the doorknob to Burton's lab. To her surprise, it swung open. She looked in. "Dr. Bertowski?" she said softly. Then a bit louder, "Anybody here?"

She turned and closed the door behind her. Her chest tightened.

Like everything else in Wellington Hall, Burton's lab smacked of *Antiques Roadshow.* Camille ran her hand over the impressive microscope standing on the highly polished mahogany lab bench. A brand-new Leitz. She wondered how much that'd set them back.

Camille surveyed the lab, not looking for anything in particular, when she noticed a set of slides on the counter by the door. She read the label. *Rosa Antonio . . .* Jesus Christ, Antonio was still in the OR. Camille caught her breath and picked up the stamped requisition form. She glanced at the gold inlaid clock sitting on Burton's desk. It was five after eight. The requisition indicated that the specimen had arrived in the lab at eight thirty-two.

Camille picked up the hospital dictation phone and hit Rewind. Burton's deep voice pierced the silent lab: "Patient Rosa Antonio. Hospital number 98-7321. Gross appearance: large irregularly shaped kidney weighing three hundred and forty grams and measuring eighteen by twelve by nine centimeters. The kidney is enlarged, and its surface is oscillated with cysts throughout. Some of the cysts are soft and contain fluid . . ."

While she was listening to the supposed polycystic kidney diagnosis, she noted a Styrofoam ice chest lined with plastic sitting open on the floor next to the refrigerator. She felt the color drain from her face.

Camille looked down, trying to decide what to do next, when a safe hidden in the wall under the lab bench caught her eye. She stooped down to check it out.

Her stomach did a flip-flop as a man in full surgical garb came in and closed the door behind him. Camille's mouth went dry as she heard the loud click of a key slipping into the lock and the sound of a dead bolt echoing throughout the lab. The man kicked the cooler out from under the lab bench a bit and dropped something into it. Camille squeezed her knees up to her chest and held her breath. From her vantage point on the floor, she was at eye level with a plastic bag that held a smooth hunk of tissue about the size of a grapefruit. It was surrounded by ice.

The man was humming a country western tune to himself, his bloody surgical shoes facing away from her. She heard the shovel in the ice maker: one scoop. She closed her eyes tightly: two scoops. She exhaled while the man noisily dumped the ice into the Styrofoam ice chest. The plastic bag presumably containing Rosa Antonio's kidney crinkled as two more scoops of ice were added. The hum turned into a song as the man taped the container closed and left the lab, locking the door behind him.

Camille sat silently for a few seconds, shaking uncontrollably, her back against the wall. She held her breath and waited long enough to convince herself that he wasn't coming back, then crawled out from under the table and ran to the door. She jiggled it.

It was secured with one of those double-keyed locks that require a key to open even from the inside.

Her heart began to race.

—

Trish rolled down the window of the white Taurus, her eyes glued to the emergency room door, where she and Camille had agreed to meet. She perked up as a stocky bald-headed man hurried out carrying a Styrofoam cooler. He hopped into a silver BMW two-seater with personalized license plates: *AW.* It had to be Willcox's car.

Thankful that she and Camille had decided to drive separate cars, Trish pulled out, hanging back in traffic so he wouldn't realize she was following him. She had a feeling this guy might lead her to wherever it was Willcox was selling organs. Then she could call one of her old friends at the FBI so they could shut this operation down. But being unnoticed became more difficult as the BMW headed up through the dry brown foothills as they neared the Black Canyon turnoff to Interstate 17. She passed a gun range on the left and almost rear-ended the BMW as it abruptly turned down a driveway that led behind a red rock outcropping. Trish slowed to see the driver waved through a security gate surrounded on both sides by thick stone walls topped with tightly wound razor wire more commonly found in Fallujah than in the desert hills of the Southwest. Trish continued down the road, wondering what on earth was behind the rocky terrain. She did a U-turn back to the driveway, where she noticed a small marble sign carved in flowery cursive that read "Rebekkah's Manor." Shit. It looked more like a prison than a manor. Whatever the hell it was.

Just as she opened her phone to take notes, her cell phone rang.

"I have a little problem here," Camille whispered.

"What do you mean 'little problem'?"

"I kinda got locked into Burton's lab."

"What! Where's Lynn?"

"She must've gotten hung up. She didn't show, so I took myself on a tour of the department. And you're not gonna believe this. While I was in here, a guy came in with a kidney, packed it in a cooler, and took off."

"Was it Styrofoam?"

"Yeah, why?"

"I'll tell you later." Trish directed her attention to the situation at hand. "What the hell were you thinking, going into Burton's lab?"

"It was open. You would have done the same thing."

"So, now what are you gonna do?"

"Wait for you to come rescue me."

"I'll be there in fifteen minutes."

"What do you mean, fifteen minutes? I need to get out of here. Preferably *now*."

"Sit tight." Trish was already speeding through the picturesque landscape.

"So, what do I do in the meantime?" Camille's whisper had taken on a frantic tone.

"Let me think . . . Is there a window?"

"Yeah, but I'm not exactly on the ground floor."

The desert sagebrush flew past in a blur. "What floor are you on?"

"It's the first floor, but it's up off the ground level. You know how the entire place sits up kind of high."

"Is it too high to jump?"

Camille leaned over to the window and peered out, trying not to be seen by the gardener mowing the lawn. "Yeah. Way too high."

"Hang on. You're obviously not going to get out of there by yourself. I'm almost there. Exactly where are you?"

"Beats me."

"Well, what's outside?" Trish asked impatiently.

"An English country garden . . . and . . . a couple of anorexic willow trees."

"Is there something you can put in the window where you are to let me know which one it is?"

Camille surveyed the lab and noticed a fake putting green. "I'll put a yellow golf hole flag in the window."

Trish roared down the driveway, past the outdoor patio, and across the chemically induced green lawn. She located the garden and the willow trees and, glancing up, spotted a yellow flag perched lopsidedly on a diagonal in the window. She pretended to look at the flowers on the bush outside the window.

Trish glanced up and smirked at Camille, whose panicked visage popped up from below the windowsill. She hastily directed Camille to climb down and stand on her shoulders. Trish admonished Camille to close the window before dropping down. But just as Camille tried to get her footing, the sprinkler system surged on at full force. Together, they fell back onto the lawn.

"Senoras!" hollered a maintenance worker. "Tha spreenklers!"

"Thank you!" Trish grabbed Camille's hand and raced across the lavish lawn, leaving the golf flag hanging haphazardly out the window.

When they reached the circular drive in front of the hospital, Trish whispered under her breath, "Meet me back at the hotel," and walked casually away.

———

On her way to the car, Camille had to walk past the outdoor smoker's section for hospital staff about thirty feet from the ER door. As she turned to avoid the heavy smoke, she heard one nurse talking to another.

"Did you hear what happened to Dr. Avon?"

Camille stopped abruptly, pretending to rummage in her purse for her car keys.

"They said her blood alcohol was under the legal limit. I don't know how she could hit a tree head-on."

Camille's knees went weak.

"Did she die?"

"Her sister just signed the authorization to turn off life support. They're doing her organs now."

Camille's peripheral vision went black and began closing in. She couldn't breathe. She had to get out of there. Mustering every ounce of her strength, she propped herself up against a light pole on the end of the row of cars where she had parked. Pushing off from the pole, she stumbled the twenty feet to what she thought was her rental car, but the key didn't fit in the door lock. Shit. For the first time, she noticed with dismay the number of white midsize rental cars that were parked in the hospital lot in this resort town. She frantically looked around as the heat shimmered off the pavement in the hot morning sun. Her heart pounded in her ears as she lurched down the row and hit the fob so the car alarm would hopefully let her know where the hell her car was. The car alarm noise sounded like it was at the end of a long tunnel. Camille turned toward it and ran.

———

There was no way Trish was going to return to the hotel without finding out what the hell was going on at that high-security desert compound. She almost ran a red light as she scrutinized her GPS in an effort to figure out the route she and the BMW had followed earlier that day. Racing across the desert, she texted Camille and told her she'd be late.

Stakeouts were all the same. Hours of sheer boredom punctuated by the thrill of a possibility—just to have your hopes dashed. Then, when least expected, something might happen to make it all worthwhile. *Thank God for audiobooks,* Trish mused as she tried to keep her focus on the gate into the compound with razor wire from her hiding place just off the road behind a stand of cacti.

Just as she was about to give up, a stream of cars exited the massive security gate and turned right in front of her. Instead of continuing with her stakeout, she decided to follow them.

Three of the cars ended up in front of a small tavern with a fake horse-hitching rail out front. Trish watched three men and two women get out of their cars and enter the bar. They looked somewhat out of place. All five were Black, and two of the men had long dreadlocks. She pulled into the parking lot in the back of the wood-frame building and glanced around to be sure no one was looking. Then she opened her backpack and pulled out the familiar long auburn wig. She took off her blue jean jacket, wadded it up, and stuffed it into her backpack, and slipped on the red Arizona Cardinals satin jacket she'd bought at the gift shop in the Phoenix airport. She perched a pair of Gargoyles sunglasses on her head and replaced her Reeboks with a pair of clunky red platform sandals. *Just a tich of makeup, and you're a regular Cardinals' fan,* she told herself as she hastily lathered on the hot-red lipstick, brushed on a little too much blush, and headed into the Western-style saloon.

When Trish's eyes finally adjusted to the dim light of the cramped little bar, she noticed the group gathered around the pool table, where a game of cricket was being broadcast on the big screen, a scene hauntingly similar to Derby's up in Friday Harbor. The taller of the three men immediately noticed Trish and winked. She smiled and took a seat at the bar and grabbed a menu, surprised to see a list of all kinds of unfamiliar Caribbean dishes.

The guy who'd just winked at her sauntered over to the bar where she was sitting.

If it isn't Bob Marley, all dressed up like a real cowboy. Is it my imagination, or is this the same group that watched cricket at Derby's up in Friday Harbor?

He put his arm on the back of her barstool. "Give the lady whatever she wants, Jose. It's on me." The guy's voice had the distinctive patois of someone from the Caribbean, which fit with his dreadlocks but not so much the cowboy getup. Trish shot the man a cool look and started to order a Chivas, then glanced at the menu and reconsidered. "Give me a premium rum, straight," she said, without taking her eyes off him.

Yep. These are the same cricket-watching pool players from Friday Harbor. And they're friends with BJ Willcox. Trish was on full alert, thankful for the wig as she self-consciously pulled the long red hair over her shoulders—not that this man would ever recognize her. She'd never actually spoken to any of them, but still . . . As any well-trained cop would do, she gauged the distance to the door and considered her getaway options.

The Jamaican cowboy nodded with approval as the bartender poured her a glass. Then he pulled up a stool next to her. "You new around here?"

He doesn't recognize me. "Maybe." She delicately took a sip. "Wow. This is amazing!" She nodded at the bartender and held up her glass to toast with the cowboy, noticing with curiosity that he and his pals were all drinking flavored seltzer water, seemingly out of place for the setting.

Trish reached down to grab her bag so she'd be prepared to run if necessary and caught her breath. The cowboy was wearing the familiar blood-splattered clogs commonly worn by operating room staff.

Trish self-consciously placed her cocktail glass on the bar as the Jamaican cowboy scooted closer. It wasn't often to see a bar like this filled with teetotalers.

"So, what brings someone from Jamrock out here to the desert?" Trish asked flirtatiously, her heart beginning to pound with curiosity and just a little fear.

"Nice try, but not Jamrock. We're from the Island of Spice." The guy tipped his seltzer toward his friends playing pool across the room.

Well, he's not from Jamaica. What's the Island of Spice? she wondered.

She lifted her glass. "To . . ." She cocked her head.

He clicked her glass. "To Grenada!" His smile was huge and friendly.

Trish almost choked on her rum. She coughed. "To Grenada."

The cowboy's pager interrupted his toast. He unclipped it from his belt and held it up sideways to read the digital display. "They're ready for us!" he shouted to his friends and turned to the bartender. "Can we get our order to go, please, Jose?"

"Really? We just finished our morning case," complained one of the men as he racked up the pool balls.

"They said we'd be busy today, but I didn't think they'd have everyone prepped so soon." One of the women shook her head.

Trish cocked her head toward the cowboy. "See ya round?"

The cowboy nodded. "Yup, gotta go back to work." He was all business as he walked back over to the pool table area and grabbed his sweatshirt. "C'mon, Doc. We have a long day ahead." He gave a sideways hug to one of the women who was putting away her pool cue.

Doc?

"I'm right behind you." Her broad smile displayed her brilliant white teeth.

The cowboy ushered his crew out and lagged behind to wait for the brown-bag lunches the bartender was gathering together hurriedly. "See you guys tonight?" he asked expectantly.

"I doubt it, Jose. Might be an all-nighter for us. Maybe we'll see you in the morning for breakfast." He laughed as he closed the door gently behind himself.

Trish turned to the bartender. "Where are they off to in such a hurry?"

Jose picked up the empty seltzer bottles the customers had lined up neatly on the bar. "Those guys are nurses, and the two women are doctors. Real nice folks. All from some island in the Caribbean."

"Any idea what brings them here?" Trish tried to determine the chances of some random group of Grenadian docs and nurses showing up in both towns where Willcox practiced. And she was sure that if they were practicing medicine in Friday Harbor, she'd know about them.

"Nope, but as soon as I got to know them and they became regular customers, I learned to cook island food so they'd feel at home." The bartender proudly held up his menu.

"Is there a hospital out here?"

"Not that I know of. They don't talk much about their work, so I don't ask. They're great customers, very polite and good tippers, even if they don't drink much. They're always standing by, ready for some kind of medical emergency." He smiled.

"How many nurses and doctors hang out here?"

"Quite a few. Why do you ask?"

Without skipping a beat Trish answered, "I'm thinking of moving out here with my mom, and it'd be great to know if there's a good medical facility around."

"Well, I'm no help in that arena, but I'd be happy to make you some lunch." He shoved the menu across the bar.

Trish looked at her watch. "I'll take whatever's quick and that I can get to go." She smiled.

CHAPTER TWENTY-FOUR

Camille, Gigi, and Trish sat on the balcony of Camille's hotel suite debriefing the events of the past twenty-four hours. They were clearly shaken by the loss of Gigi's friend Lynn.

"What the hell is that Caribbean medical crew—assuming that's what they really are—doing down here *and* in Friday Harbor?" Gigi asked angrily.

Camille shook her head. "Well, it's certainly not a coincidence."

"My hypothesis is that they're doing surgery out at that compound surrounded by razor wire. They say they're from Grenada, which is where Willcox trained." Trish's voice was clear and intense. "And I just followed a kidney out there this morning. It's got to be some kind of transplant center."

"They can't just plop a surgical center out in the middle of nowhere—they have to get accreditation and licenses." Gigi shook her head incredulously.

Trish interrupted. "Well, that probably explains the razor wire and why it's out in the middle of nowhere."

"Why do you think they're doing surgery there?" Gigi asked.

"First clue was the bloody clogs," Trish announced. "Then one of them called the other 'Doc.' And then I chatted up the bartender, which is how I learned that they're all doctors and nurses."

"Oh my God," Camille gasped, recognizing the potential significance of a Grenadian surgical team waiting to perform a kidney transplant in some kind of surgical fortress surrounded by razor wire.

"How do you know they're from Grenada?" Gigi was clearly impressed with Trish's investigative skills.

Camille held her breath as the terrifying story was coming together in her mind.

"Well, the first tip was their accents, which I originally thought were Jamaican, but then one of them actually told me they're from Grenada," Trish explained.

"We need to stop this monster!" Camille interjected. "I'm certain that someone is going to get a kidney that, until earlier this morning, belonged to a nice woman by the name of Rosa Antonio."

"Who's that?" Trish asked.

"The seven thirty nephrectomy," Camille said quietly. "I saw it on the surgery schedule right before the kidney ended up in the cooler in Burton's lab."

"That one's probably already safely ensconced in its new host." Trish looked at her friends. "Pretty sure they did that one before I met them—they said they had just come from the OR, and the timing would line up with the BMW carrying the Styrofoam cooler I followed this morning."

"Oh my God." Camille put her hand up in front of her mouth. "This thing has gotten entirely out of hand. This guy has to be stopped before he kills anyone else."

Gigi put her head down. "I can't believe Lynn's dead. Do you think he killed her?"

"Well, it sounds like it was an actual car accident, but it seems like there's a better than even chance that her organs didn't make it to the organ bank." Trish rubbed her girlfriend's back. "I'm so sorry."

Gigi grabbed a tissue and rubbed the tears from her eyes.

Camille looked at Trish. "If they're removing organs at Wellington Hall and transplanting them at that compound—what do they call it? Rebekkah's Manor—what are they doing up in the San Juans? And how does the team from Grenada fit into this picture?"

"Well, let's look for similarities. Both of the hospitals are in remote rural communities, and we know that they look for places where there are lots of older folks." Trish was all business.

"So, if they're taking organs to that desert compound to be transplanted, how long would organs last if they had to be flown down to Arizona from Friday Harbor in time to transplant them?" Camille asked Gigi.

Gigi jumped in. "If they have to helicopter them to Sea-Tac, or even Boeing Field, then get them to Arizona, and then try to get them from the Phoenix airport out to that compound, I don't see how it's possible."

Trish looked at the team. "So . . . what if they have a place near Friday Harbor?"

Camille stopped short as a chill went up her spine. She remembered seeing Willcox hopping into a helicopter immediately after Dallas's surgery. With a cooler.

Almost in unison they said, "Brigantine Island."

"That explains why Tony drops off so many sick folks there." Camille could hardly catch her breath.

"And why BJ Willcox has been working on a construction project over there," Trish added. "She's an architect, you know."

Camille was silent for a minute, then said slowly, "That medical crew is the transplant team. They must fly up for cases on Brigantine . . ."

"That would explain why they show up intermittently in Friday Harbor—and they always come in by boat in a fancy Grady-White. They're probably coming over for some R&R. There's nothing to do over on Brigantine Island," Trish said slowly. "The whole private island thing sounds interesting until you realize you're basically all alone out there. They probably get bored over there waiting."

Camille picked up her phone. "I need to call Gloria and tell her we may not be able to get her any money after all. We need to shut this down and, when we do, all hell's going to break loose, and Willcox's insurance company won't pay Dallas's claim after they find out Willcox essentially murdered him."

Gigi interrupted. "What do you mean they won't pay?"

It was Camille's turn to be the scholarly one. "Insurance policies cover people for negligent acts. But you've all heard of policy exclusions, right?"

The two women nodded.

"Well, one of the exclusions is that they don't cover for intentional acts or criminal acts."

"So, if Willcox's insurance company finds out that he's been killing patients, they won't pay the claim?" Gigi asked.

Camille looked at her friends. "Exactly. And now I'm going to have to call Gloria and tell her we can't take the chance of pursuing this thing any further. It's too risky."

Trish held her hand over Camille's phone. "But if we're going to report this to the authorities, we should at least try to wrap up our part of the investigation. I'm not sure they're going to believe this. We need to gather as much evidence as we can."

"You sound like a cop," Gigi said with a twinge of admiration.

Trish stayed focused. "Let's go ahead and check to see if there was a patient with an aneurysm at Friday Harbor around the time that Dallas died. That might explain where the hospital got the tissue samples they sent us."

"Patient diagnoses are usually tracked by the hospital computer," Gigi explained. "If we could get into the computer up there, we might be able to find a patient with an aneurysm."

Trish jumped up and abruptly grabbed her phone. "I'm gonna call Ruby."

"Why Ruby?"

"She can go over to the hospital and get into the computer."

"Brilliant." Camille nodded. "She knows the password since she enters lab results for the nurses as part of her volunteer job."

Trish dialed the phone. "Hi, Ruby? It's Trish . . . Arizona . . . It's hot. How 'bout up there?" Trish sat on the edge of her chair. "Listen, I have a huge favor to ask you." Trish gave Camille a thumbs-up. "Okay . . . ready? We need to get some information out of the computer over at the hospital. Do you have time to run over there? Great. I really appreciate it . . . Call me when you get there. And be careful. If anyone's around, don't do it. I can get the info another time . . . Bye now."

Suddenly Richard burst into the room without knocking. His eyes were wild with excitement. "You are *not* gonna believe this!"

"What?" Camille had never seen Richard so worked up.

He thrust his laptop in front of Camille. "Check this out. These are all of the cases where Willcox was the previous treating doc. And I reviewed several of the charts to see what was going on."

Camille tried to grab the laptop. "Let's see!"

He playfully slapped her hand away. "Slow down. It won't make any sense to you. Let me explain it."

"Bossy, bossy."

"This is really weird," he said breathlessly "It looks like a bunch of Willcox's patients have ended up at the U over the past few years. But none of them were actually referred by Willcox himself."

"So, how'd they get to the U?" Gigi asked.

"Referrals from other community docs mostly."

"For?" Camille raised her eyebrows.

"For back pain most often."

"Back pain?"

"Back pain."

"That's strange, don't you think?" Camille looked at Gigi, who nodded in agreement.

"It gets stranger," Richard said.

"Yes?"

The words tumbled from Richard's mouth. "Listen to this: There were six patients who all presented to the U with back pain over the past two years. All of them had seen Willcox for a workup before undergoing a laminectomy. Surgery on their spine," Richard explained to Trish.

"I know what a laminectomy is," Trish said impatiently.

"Sorry. Anyway, Willcox diagnosed all six of them with polycystic kidneys and recommended against the laminectomy."

"You got me there. What kind of kidneys?" Trish asked.

"Poly-cys-tic. It's a rare, inherited kidney condition where the kidneys lose their normal anatomy and become replaced by fluid-filled cysts," Richard explained. "Eventually they become completely non-functioning, and the person ends up on dialysis or hopefully receives a transplant." Richard barely stopped for breath. "But I haven't even gotten to the weirdest part. Each of them had had a kidney removed by Willcox, but none of them got any relief from their back pain, so they kept seeking medical help." He paused.

Camille's mind was racing. "Go on," she urged.

"All six of them eventually wound their way to the university and underwent diagnostic workups that showed some kind of disc problem. And all of them underwent laminectomies at the U, and they all basically got better."

"So, what'd the workup on their kidneys look like?" Gigi asked.

"You ready for this?" Richard locked eyes with Camille. "They all had absolutely identical lab findings."

"What do you mean?" Trish asked.

"I mean that the blood tests and CAT scans that Willcox relied on to make the diagnosis of polycystic kidneys were exactly the same in each patient."

"How exactly the same do you mean?" Gigi asked slowly.

"I mean the same hematocrit, the same hemoglobin, the same bands, the same eosinophils, the same neutrophils . . . And the path reports are identical too. Quite simply, they're duplicates of the same report."

Camille felt the air suck out of her lungs like she was in a depressurized airplane. Her friends didn't look much better.

"And I take it that the chances that six different guys would have exactly the same lab results and have a kidney removed, then end up with laminectomies is pretty remote?" Trish asked suspiciously.

"Pretty much statistically impossible." Gigi stared straight ahead.

The jangling of Trish's phone brought Camille up short. Trish grabbed it. "Hello? Hi, Ruby. Where are you? In the admitting office. Log on to the computer . . . Good. Now, can you do a search of the surgical census for aneurysms? Okay, I'll hold." Trish whispered to her friends, "She's looking."

"For what?" Richard asked curiously.

"Other patients who've been treated at Friday Harbor for aneurysms," Trish said softly.

"There is? When was it?" Trish turned to Camille and said, "Bingo! June tenth." She grabbed a piece of paper and scribbled the name August Gianelli.

"I have an idea," Gigi said as she held out her hand for the phone. "Let me talk to her a minute."

"Ruby? I'm going to give the phone to my friend Gigi. She's a doctor; she wants to talk to you."

"Hi, this is Gigi. Can you pull up the patient's chart?" She looked at Camille. "Great . . . now scroll back to the lab section and find the autopsy report . . . Who signed it? Burton." She looked knowingly at Camille and Trish. "Okay. Look under the organ donor section . . . Is there a long organ donor number? It probably starts with 20-51 . . . Just a sec." Gigi grabbed a pad and pen. "Let me read it back to you. It's 20-51-2975386. Thanks a million, Ruby. Bye now."

Gigi took over. "I need your laptop." She directed Trish in an unusually authoritative voice.

Trish complied and pushed her laptop across the table to Gigi, who quickly logged on. The others looked over her shoulder as she flew through the prompts by typing in one secret code after another. Finally, the screen lit up to welcome Dr. Roberts to the National Organ Donor Bank.

Camille grabbed the pad and slowly read off Gianelli's organ donor number. They held their breath as the screen flickered, the cursor indicating that the search was continuing. Finally the number appeared at the top of the screen in bold letters, under the word Profile. Gigi stopped halfway down the screen and read aloud, "Skin only . . . Oh my God."

Camille stood up. "We're done. Who do we call, Trish?"

"Just a minute. We have time to solve this ourselves." Trish had the look of a detective who didn't want to be taken off a case. "Didn't you say that you saw on the OR schedule that Willcox was scheduled to be on vacation next week?"

"Yeah," Camille said slowly.

"And he's not going to be back in Friday Harbor until St. Patrick's Day, right?"

"Uh-huh."

"Well, as long as he's not doing surgery, he can't really hurt anyone, can he?"

"No," Camille said thoughtfully.

"Then by my count, we have until the St. Patrick's Day service—that's ten days—to get the case settled. After that, he'll be back in action in Friday Harbor, and then I'll call one of my detective friends."

Camille stopped to think for a couple of minutes. "Okay, but no more surgery for this guy. If we even get an inkling that he's heading into an operating room anywhere, we call the authorities."

"Are we sure we have enough evidence to get the case settled in a week?" Gigi asked.

"We will if I subpoena Max Gonzalez for a deposition." Camille picked up her phone.

CHAPTER TWENTY-FIVE

It was 9:00 a.m. and Camille sat in a busy Starbucks kitty-corner from Seattle's elegant Fairmont Olympic Hotel, where the national surgical symposium was just getting started. It was hard to believe that Irving had been scheduled to speak at the symposium for over a year and that Richard was chairing the Sunday morning session. Maybe her luck was changing. Camille checked Outlook and noticed that her meeting with Richard and Irving was set for nine thirty, not nine o'clock.

Just enough time to have the much-dreaded conversation with Gloria about the value of Dallas's case and the urgency of settling it as soon as possible. She hated having to discuss the legal system's unconscionable way of valuing a human life, especially in relationship to Dallas. But time was of the essence. She pulled out her cell phone and dialed Gloria in Mexico.

"Hi, it's me, Camille," she said when Gloria came on the line.

"Good morning, dear. How's our investigation coming along? I've been praying for resolution every day."

"Well, your prayers may have been answered. The insurance adjuster wants to take the case to mediation, so that has been set for Friday. Can you be back up here by then?"

Camille could almost see Gloria's serene smile at the other end of the phone. She knew the upcoming conversation would shatter that serenity.

"Of course, dear. And I'm glad you called. As you can imagine," Gloria said quietly, "I've been meditating and praying about how to approach this entire situation." Camille could hear Gloria take a deep Kundalini breath. "I understand all that you've told me about how your system works."

Camille winced in response to Gloria's description of the system as "hers."

"And I can't say I completely disagree. For example, I agree that there's no amount of money that could begin to replace Dallas in my life."

"Of course not."

"But on the other hand, money's all we have to give to someone who's lost their life partner. I know you've explained that the system values a person's life by figuring out the amount of money they would have made and then they add some unknown amount for so-called pain and suffering . . . which I personally find repugnant."

Camille closed her eyes and saw Dallas sitting in the cockpit of his boat, waiting for her and Sam to come back from a sail on what had originally been a moderately windy day. But a gale had blown in, seemingly out of nowhere, and Dallas had obviously been worried. He jumped up as they fought the wind and current in the marina. Relief was written all over his face. A tear snaked its way down Camille's cheek as she remembered Dallas's smile, a smile that came right from his soul. How was she supposed to explain to Gloria that the life of this hugely loving presence was limited in the eyes of the justice system, simply because he wasn't a big wage earner? Maybe Sam was right. Maybe she couldn't be objective in this thing.

"You know, I keep wondering," Gloria continued. "If you can't put a value on someone's life, how on earth are you supposed to put a value on pain or suffering, for God's sake?" Thankfully, Gloria didn't wait for an answer. "Let's assume for a moment that I want Willcox's insurance company to pay me for what I lost. How would I go about determining what to ask for?"

Camille took a breath, ready to speak.

But Gloria continued, "I've finally figured out how the insurance company can make it right and how I could use this blood money to benefit some less fortunate than I. I'm going to purchase some acreage out on Lime Kiln Point. It's owned by a nice couple who sold a biotech company for millions, and they have agreed to sell me a small parcel before they donate the rest to the San Juan Land Conservancy. They'll give it to me at a huge discount so I can create a shelter for women reuniting with their children after prison. They said they'd help me set up a nonprofit so they can get a tax deduction."

Camille grinned. *Dallas would love this idea.*

"As it turns out, the owners are being aggressively pursued by some investors who are trying to build a fifty-five and over resort there. They say they're confident they won't have any trouble getting the necessary zoning permits and the approval of the city council. They're about to submit their plans soon.

"But the Bloomfields are very excited to donate most of the property to the San Juan Land Conservancy after they carve out the area where their living compound is and sell the small plot to me for only eight hundred thousand dollars. It's the perfect solution. We'll be surrounded by acreage that's a land conservancy, and there's a view of Haro Strait and—"

Camille gently cut her off. "So, Gloria—"

Gloria interrupted her right back. "So, I need to net eight hundred thousand dollars after I pay you whatever attorney fees and costs you've incurred," Gloria instructed Camille sternly.

Camille sat silently for a moment. "Dallas would be thrilled." Now, how was she going to explain that Dallas's case would likely settle between a hundred and fifty thousand and two hundred thousand, or maybe more now that there was so much evidence of malfeasance? "Um . . . If we weren't able to get the full eight hundred grand, do you think we could raise some money for the balance? We could have some fundraisers."

"Maybe I could convince them to wait, but the Bloomfields have already short platted the piece, and they want to move on. They're going to build over on Decatur Island. So pretty and remote over there," Gloria said calmly. "Look, I know you called to explain to me that we can't get anywhere near that amount of money for a case like this. And if we need to go to trial, so be it. I'm sure the jury will appreciate our plan."

"The jury will never hear about the shelter," Camille said quietly. "It won't be allowed into evidence."

"Why not?"

"It's not relevant to the value of Dallas's life. None of this is admissible into evidence. All the jury will hear about is how much money he would have made and how much you'll miss him."

"Why do they call this a 'justice' system anyway?" Gloria's voice was sharp.

"I'm not the right person to ask."

"So, what do you suggest?"

"Listen, Gloria, I'll email you some sample verdicts and settlements."

"What difference does it make what other cases have settled for?"

"Well, unfortunately, the way we value cases is by comparing them to what other juries have awarded other wives who have lost sixty-five-year-old retired husbands."

"Well, tell me what you think we can get, then."

"I don't honestly know. This has gone far beyond any malpractice case I've ever seen."

"How so?"

Camille gathered her thoughts. "Well, we have pretty strong evidence that Willcox and the pathologist, Carl Burton, have been operating a highly illegal operation out of Friday Harbor General Hospital. It involves the possible sale of human organs." She winced, waiting for Gloria's reaction.

"Go on," Gloria said firmly.

"I hate to even have to discuss this with you, Gloria."

"I've already lost my husband, Camille. How much worse can it get?"

"I think we can prove a cover-up."

"How so?"

Might as well get it over with. "While we were reviewing the information in the National Organ Donor Bank, we noticed that they had only received skin from Dallas."

"No, no, dear. We specifically discussed Dallas's wishes with the doctors. We asked that all possible organs be donated."

"I know you did. But what I'm saying is that all of his organs didn't make it to the organ donor bank."

Gloria paused. "Why not?"

"We've discovered that several of Willcox's other patients' organs haven't made it to the donor bank either. And we have reason to believe that Willcox has actually removed healthy kidneys from some of his patients."

"Why on earth would he do that?"

Camille took a deep breath. "We think he may be selling organs on the black market."

"Oh God."

Camille waited.

"Are you suggesting that Willcox let Dallas die so that he could sell his organs?" Gloria whispered.

"We think it's a distinct possibility."

"And he's done this to others?"

"We think so."

Another long pause. "How do we put a stop to this?"

"We're doing all that we can to gather enough information to take to the authorities. But we're walking a fine line. Our hope is to get the case settled on Friday, then contact the authorities immediately. We can't take any chances by letting Willcox continue to perform surgeries. We don't know when he may victimize another patient."

"Of course not. But do you think we can really get the case settled this week?"

"We can if we can prove that Willcox falsified the records. Then the insurance company will be concerned that we may inflame a jury, and the value of the case increases. They get scared shitless when their insureds face allegations of falsifying medical records. My guess is that they'll pay a lot to settle this case."

"Well, whatever you do, don't endanger anyone else. If we can't get this case settled in time, I'll just have to live with it, but we need to really try to get this done. So many women and their children would benefit."

"I hear you, and I know how much Dallas would love this idea. We'll do our best to get you as much money as we can for your shelter and then shut down Willcox before he hurts anyone else." Camille tried to convince herself that she could leverage her network to help fundraise for the balance needed to get the shelter built.

"Okay . . . I can't thank you enough. You know you're the only one who truly understands who and what Dallas was all about. I'm positive that if you're given the chance, you'll convince that insurance adjuster of his value as a person."

Camille hung up and noticed Richard standing in the latte line with a distinguished-looking gentleman wearing a red bow tie and a herringbone sport coat. *Right out of central casting,* thought Camille with a smile, her days in Boston fondly bubbling up in her memory.

After a few minutes, Richard came over and said, "Camille Delaney, it's my pleasure to introduce you to Dr. James Irving."

Camille stood to shake hands with the scholarly looking gentleman, who peered at her intently through thick glasses. "Thank you so much for meeting with us," she said. "Please sit down."

"No problem at all. It's almost time for lunch back in Boston. I've been up since three a.m. your time, you know. Never do seem to adjust to this time zone out here." He looked around absentmindedly, like he was in a foreign country. "Dr. Rosenberg has told me a bit about your dilemma with that fellow up in Friday Harbor on San Juan Island—beautiful place, the San Juans. We rented a cottage up there a few years back." He quickly turned back to the subject at hand. "Tell me how I can be of assistance in your case here."

Camille explained that Willcox claimed to be from Harvard, but their investigation had discovered that to be untrue.

"I certainly never had a resident by that name."

"Well, does the name Carl Burton ring any bells?" Camille asked. "Or Bertowski? Skinny fellow with a disarmingly deep voice. He's a pathologist—"

"Pathologist? Carl Burton you say? We had a guy named Bertolini. Carlos Bertolini. Left Boston in 2003. Thrown out on his ear, I should say."

Camille drew a breath. *Carlos? That had to be more than a coincidence.* Camille smirked at Richard and sat forward on her chair. "This guy is about five six and one twenty. And he sounds like James Earl Jones."

"Ah . . . the infamous Carlos Bertolini."

"What can you tell us about him?"

"Oh, my dear, where do I start? But first, do tell me what Bertolini has to do with this mess."

"He fraudulently read a path report as an aneurysm when there wasn't one."

"I see, and the pathologist is either Bertolini or his identical twin. What'd you say he goes by up here?"

"Carl Burton."

"It has to be the same guy. Of course he'd keep his initials so he wouldn't have to get rid of all his monogrammed shirts." Irving shot Camille a look of disgust.

"What was he like?" Camille asked.

James Irving clearly relished an audience. "Carlos Bertolini applied for a surgical fellowship in transplant surgery at Harvard in 1986. But he didn't make it past the first cut. What an attitude that young man had. I personally saw to it that he didn't even get invited back for the customary second interview." Irving sat back and crossed his arms. "He was so bright, but at the same time, he lacked even the most rudimentary of social skills. It was money, money, money. He even asked how much he could expect to make as a Harvard-trained transplant surgeon during his fellowship interview!

"To make a long story short, he abruptly switched his plans and decided to go into pathology—even though he'd recently completed a surgical residency somewhere down south. First, he was hell-bent on joining my team that was studying tissue rejection in transplant patients, and then he switched gears and applied to the Department of Pathology, which accepted him into their program. They told me they couldn't resist his 'stinging intellect.' Couldn't have cared less about his lack of conscience. They needed help on a huge, complicated research project on the treatment of drug-resistant tropical diseases." Irving stopped and laughed. "Bertolini was totally distraught when he found himself enlisted into the tropical disease research rather than the transplant team." He took a sip of his latte. "So, imagine our surprise when Bertolini actually discovered a drug that would treat Coral Fever, an extremely virulent tropical disease that's fatal if not treated within eight hours. He got an incredible grant offered to him by the pharmaceutical company that was sponsoring the research." Irving pulled out a pipe and chewed on the end. "So, he was a hero for a while." Irving pointed at his latte cup. "Can I have another one of these? This is very Seattle, isn't it? Sitting here, drinking lattes at Starbucks."

The guy isn't half as intimidating as he appears, Camille realized with a smile.

Irving thanked Richard, who shortly returned with another round of lattes.

"Let's see, where was I?" Irving seemed to enjoy the suspense. "I guess I was just about to get to the part where I had a grant to study the mechanism of tissue rejection in organ transplantation, which, as you can imagine, had Bertolini totally pissed off—here I was, doing the research he had intended to do. It was a terrific coup for the university. I was responsible for accumulating the data over a four-year time period. The research was funded by the same company that Bertolini had done the tropical disease research for, and much to my chagrin, they had insisted that Bertolini handle the pathology data. Well, in January 2002, I was presenting my paper at the international society meeting in Chicago. Very prestigious, you know." He smiled smugly at Camille and paused. "The air was thick with anticipation. I was at the podium, and suddenly out of nowhere, I get an email from an anonymous sender that stated our data had been falsified. The email contained a complicated code that if applied to the study results would demonstrate the data was entirely unreliable.

"Well, all hell broke loose. The code was deciphered, and lo and behold, it did unravel the entire study. The drug company immediately yanked the funding. As you can imagine, my name was mud. Not just at Harvard, but I'd been disgraced in front of an international symposium of my peers.

"Now, luckily, I had been quite well respected for many years, so most of my colleagues supported me when the investigation began to piece together what had actually happened. It was like a Rubik's Cube. The university finally discovered that Bertolini had been methodically falsifying the data by misreading the pathology slides from the study participants. And true to form, he had done a brilliant job of it. Rather than just willy-nilly mixing up the results, he had actually manipulated it to generate plausible conclusions that didn't raise any suspicions. Looking back, I can say that if Bertolini had used his mind for something other than revenge, he would have made a real name for himself in the world of pharmaceutical research. As it was, he ended up not just getting bounced out of Harvard but got his license yanked for good. Last I heard, he was teaching in some offshore medical school somewhere off the coast of South America, I think."

"Jeez, what a story. I take it you were obviously able to salvage your reputation?"

"The investigation took the wind out of my sails for a bit. At about that time, we were just beginning to get involved in some laparoscopic robotic surgery research. I was ready for a change, so I spent some time traveling overseas to Europe to hone my skills. And voilá! I found a new niche. I love it. And I still get to travel and lecture as much as I always did. That's not to say that if we had been having this conversation twenty years ago, I wouldn't have told you I was ruined. I was sure the world had ended. But time marches on." The doctor paused to reflect, then looked up. "So, how in the world do you think Bertolini ended up in this neck of the woods?"

"It seems that he's partnered up with Willcox in some scheme to falsify Willcox's path reports. Which is hauntingly consistent with what you've been explaining."

Camille put down her latte so Irving wouldn't notice that she was shaking. It was becoming abundantly clear that the scope of this investigation was exploding. Suddenly, she felt an acute awareness that it was up to her to stop these two before someone else got killed.

CHAPTER TWENTY-SIX

As soon as her meeting with Richard and Irving was over, Camille rushed to her car to drive Grace's Brownie troop over to the troop leader's for their meeting. As she was dropping off the girls, her phone rang. It was Gigi announcing that she'd gotten the big grant she'd been waiting to hear about.

"But there's a catch," Gigi added.

"What is it?" Camille hopped out of the car, picked a Brownie cap out of a puddle next to the car, and handed it to a little redhead.

"Remember those two guys we ran into in the lab that night we were looking at Dallas's slides?"

Camille waved to the troop leader standing in the doorway. "Yeah." How could she forget?

"Well, remember that one guy, James Wandel, whose job I supposedly stole?"

Camille kissed Grace goodbye and gave her a hug and automatically glanced up and down the street, looking for anything out of the ordinary as Grace skipped up the walkway. "The tall, creepy one?"

"You got it. It turns out the asshole wrote me up for allowing an outsider into the lab."

Camille caught her breath. "I thought we told them I was some kind of visiting doc."

"We did, but apparently we left one of Dallas's slides on the microscope stage in the lab, and they tracked it down to Friday Harbor

General and found out the patient was involved in a lawsuit, and the shit hit the fan."

"Jeez, Gigi. I'm really sorry." She'd promised not to get Gigi in trouble, and now she'd jeopardized her career.

"They issued a formal reprimand and decided that the grant I submitted has to be coinvestigated by another professor."

"That sucks," Camille said dejectedly as she pulled out of the driveway. "It's your grant. You're the one bringing in the big bucks."

"Yeah, well it sucks even worse that Wandel has been assigned to be my coinvestigator. They think of it as a slap on the wrist. But I'm not taking it that way. I'm sick of having to jump when they say jump. The deck is stacked against me. I doubt they'd even think twice if one of them took a colleague into the lab just to look at some slides, even if there was a lawsuit involved."

"What are you gonna do?"

"Beats me."

"I'm really sorry, Gigi. Maybe we can sue them or something."

"No offense, but I don't think I need any more help from you at this point."

The line went dead.

—

The music from *Saturday Night Live* jarred Camille out of her internal brainstorming session about what she could do to get Gigi out of the jam with the university. Camille felt completely responsible for the whole mess. She shifted under the covers of her big, comfy bed and hit Mute on the remote when she heard footsteps outside the front door. She jumped up and looked out the window before checking the alarm and grabbing her phone. Just in case.

Camille's heart pounded in her ears as someone jiggled the front doorknob. She began to dial 9-1-1.

"Camille?" Sam hollered from the front hall where Camille could hear him aggressively hitting the keys to the alarm.

"Sam?" Camille collapsed on the bed and exhaled. "I thought you were staying at the hospital. It's your on-call night."

Sam walked over, turned off the TV, and planted himself firmly in front of it.

"What are you doing?" She held her arm out and tried to aim the remote around Sam to get the TV back on in an effort to calm herself down.

Sam stood steadfast. "We have to talk." He held up a slashed purple leather jacket. "Recognize this?"

Camille's blood pressure began creeping up again. "It was hanging on the coat stand in my office when I came back from the lab tonight. And apparently whoever left it there wanted to make sure I saw it, so they put it in the middle of the office. Where's that purple jacket of yours?"

Camille swallowed hard and stared silently at her husband, trying to hold back tears.

"Someone broke into my office, Camille. There's top-secret classified infectious disease data in there. You know that." He sat on the end of the bed. "Do you know anything at all about this?"

Camille shook her head.

"I've gotta report my lost key to the department now. It's gonna cost us about five grand. And I don't have to tell you that with you not working, that's a huge problem."

"I've got a few new divorce cases."

"Let me guess. Domestic violence cases for people who can't afford to pay you. Right?"

Camille paused. "They can pay. Just not now."

"Look, I know how important it is to you to solve the Dallas mystery. But we can't afford not to have your income right now. We have tuition due in a couple of weeks, and we don't have any cash on hand. I'm a university doc, not some hotshot private practice guy."

"We can borrow from the retirement account." Camille cringed in anticipation of Sam's reaction.

He looked like he was going to explode. "We are *not* going to borrow from our retirement account to pay our living expenses."

"Give me just a little while longer. I can get this case settled. Max Gonzalez's deposition is Wednesday, and we go to mediation on Friday."

"Dr. Gonzalez made it perfectly clear to you that he isn't willing to take on Willcox. He's got enough troubles of his own without getting

Willcox any more pissed off at him than he already is. I suggest you make some calls and see who has time to take the case over from you. You gotta get out of this thing. Now."

———

Willcox leaned his new set of Ping clubs behind his reserved tee at the Boulders driving range. His mother was definitely on the mend, so he could finally take time off to play eighteen holes.

Burton arrived when Willcox was halfway through his first bucket of balls. "We got a call from the agent on the Island today," Burton announced.

"And?" Willcox asked without leaving his driving stance.

Burton polished his driver with a monogrammed towel. "And there may be another offer coming in on the Island property next week."

"So, what do we do now?"

"Well, we can't exactly finalize our offer since we're committed on the Arizona piece."

"Shit."

"It never occurred to me that there'd be any interest in that place up on the Island. It's clearly overpriced."

"Apparently not that overpriced." Willcox hit a ball straight to the two-hundred-yard flag. "What do we need to do to get this thing done?"

Burton looked at Willcox before turning to address the ball.

Willcox stepped back and took a sip of his Bloody Mary, moving the celery stalk to keep it from poking him in the eye. He chuckled as Burton struck the ball. "Nice . . . if you were playing a hole with a dogleg left."

Burton ignored Willcox's comment, stuck his butt out, and wiggled his shoulders before hitting the ball hard to the left again. He angrily teed up another ball.

Willcox interrupted Burton in mid swing. "So?"

"Jesus Christ! Give me a break, would you? I'm thinking." Burton practiced his swing.

"Okay, like this." Willcox strode confidently up to the tee and hit Burton's ball three hundred yards straight down the driving range. "You're not following through. Keep your head down."

Burton forcefully dumped the bucket of balls over and put another one on the tee, his brow knit in full concentration. He sliced it to the right this time, then turned to Willcox. "We should have the money no later than middle of next week. Assuming everything with the blonde goes according to plan."

"Good." Willcox's cell phone rang, and he answered it.

"Hello, Andrew? This is Lorrey Lincoln. Got a minute?"

"Sure. Hang on a sec." He muted his phone. "It's the lawyer who's representing me on the Jackson case." He unmuted and spoke into the phone. "What's up?"

"The plaintiff's lawyer has subpoenaed one of the witnesses in your case for a deposition this week, and I just realized that I hadn't talked to you about him yet. His name's Gonzalez, Max Gonzalez. He assisted you in the case. You have any reason to believe that he'll say anything unfavorable about the surgery?"

Willcox sat on the bench behind the tee. "Gonzalez is a prick."

"Got any dirt on him in case he turns on you?"

"He's not smart or brave enough to even dream of hurting me." Willcox tilted his head back and dumped a package of honeyed peanuts into his mouth. "If he gives you any shit, just ask him why he screwed up the Jackson case. If he hadn't barged into the OR and demanded to take over the case, the patient would probably still be alive. He's the one who killed the guy. Not me." Willcox laughed a throaty laugh. "Tell him we have an expert ready to testify against him. We have nothing to fear from that little weasel. If he takes me on, he'll be sorry."

"I like your style, Doc. I like your style." Lorrey chuckled. "Any reason to think he'll have anything out of the ordinary to say about the case itself?"

"Nah. He didn't even write a note."

"No note?"

"Nope. Check the record."

"Great. By the way, we're scheduled to go to mediation this Friday. It's simply a cost–benefit decision. But as you know, it's ultimately your call. The guy wasn't worth more than a hundred. No income, shortened life expectancy due to the aneurysm. It'd cost more to defend the thing than to settle it. But I wouldn't blame you if you don't approve of the settlement. I could kill 'em at trial."

He had to hand it to Lincoln. Making that pitch to take the case to trial. *Only way he made any dough was to work the hell out of the thing. The guy's probably billed the insurance company at least a couple hundred grand.*

"Settle it. My wife, BJ, will handle the details." Willcox hung up.

CHAPTER TWENTY-SEVEN

Camille turned her office upside down looking for her briefcase with the notes for Max Gonzalez's dep. It was scheduled to begin at Lorrey Lincoln's office in twenty minutes. She hit the intercom. "Have you seen my briefcase?"

"It's out here. I was just getting it packed for the dep," Amy responded.

"Great. I'll be right out." The phone on Camille's desk rang just as she slid on her trench coat. She looked at the caller ID. "It's Jothy," she hollered to Amy, who was standing in the doorway. "Can you tell him I'll call him back?" She took the briefcase. "I gotta run. I'm late."

Amy ran in and picked up Camille's phone, waving goodbye to her boss. "Amy Hutchins here."

Camille was just pulling out of the parking lot when Amy ran up and knocked on the window. "I have Jothy on my cell. You might want to take this call. He says it's important!" Amy was out of breath from running. "It's about Jackson."

"Jackson?"

Amy nodded and handed her phone to Camille.

Camille was curious for sure. "Jothy? What's up? This better be good. I'm late for a dep."

"I just got finished seeing a new divorce client by the name of BJ Willcox. Sound familiar?"

Camille put her car in park. "You're kidding me."

"Nope. And she gave me something to give to you. Says it'll help you on one of your cases."

"What is it?"

"First you gotta tell me how you're gonna thank me for this."

"A latte?"

"Bigger."

"Bottle of wine?"

"Bigger."

"Dinner at Canlis for the four of us," she suggested.

"With a bottle of Leonetti?"

"You got it."

"I'll call my wife."

"So?" Camille asked expectantly.

"So, I'm holding an operative note dictated by one Max Gonzalez for a surgical procedure on a Dallas Jackson."

Camille gasped for air. "Jesus Christ!"

"It's being emailed as we speak."

Camille turned to Amy. "Check my email. Quick!"

Amy ran inside and returned holding a newly printed page in one hand and a pair of glasses in the other. Camille snatched them both and skimmed the document.

"Make that a week in Hawaii . . . for your entire family."

"I think I'd prefer to go alone with Linda."

"Okay. I'll pay for the babysitter. Better yet, I'll babysit your kids myself. Listen, Jothy, I gotta split. I'm on my way to take Gonzalez's dep. You have no idea what this means to me."

———

"Hello, Dr. Gonzalez." Camille greeted the handsome doctor who was standing in the lobby of Lincoln and Associates, tightly clutching a subpoena.

"Hello." He held out a clammy hand.

"I'm sorry to have to resort to a subpoena, but . . ."

He looked away.

The receptionist, who Camille had known for years, pointed down the hall. "Camille, you're in conference room two."

"Thanks, Shirley."

"Follow me, please, Dr. Gonzalez." Camille opened the door to the conference room and greeted the smarmy insurance defense lawyer with the chipmunk-like cheeks. Camille couldn't remember ever having been so anxious to begin a deposition.

"Good morning, Camille. Welcome back to the world of medical malpractice. It's been a long time." As an afterthought, Lincoln looked at the young doctor. "And you must be Dr. Gonzalez. I'm Lorrey Lincoln." He blinked furiously behind a pair of bright-turquoise contact lenses.

"And this is Winnie Douglas, the claims adjuster on the file." Lorrey pulled out a chair for a hard-edged woman with an outdated asymmetric haircut.

Gonzalez shook hands hesitantly with each of them. "Nice to meet you."

"And this is Cleo Tracey. She represents the hospital," Camille introduced the woman at the far end of the table.

"I'm ready whenever you are," Camille told Diane, the court reporter.

"Okay. Raise your right hand. Do you swear or affirm that your testimony will be the truth and nothing but the truth."

"I do," Max answered solemnly.

Camille spoke while she opened her notebook and organized her papers. "State your name for the record, please."

"Max L. Gonzalez."

He was clearly nervous, so the first order of business was to get him calmed down.

She started with a few softball questions. "Dr. Gonzalez, can you please briefly outline your professional training, beginning with your undergraduate education?"

Max loosened his tie as he and Camille got into a kind of rhythm.

"As you sit here today, do you have an independent recollection of this particular case?"

He nodded. "I remember this case," he said softly.

The court reporter interrupted. "You need to speak up please," she said sharply.

Gonzalez cleared his throat. "I said I remember the case."

"Okay. Please tell me when you were first called in to consult on this case."

"I was at home, having a Fourth of July picnic with my family, when my phone rang. It was one of the nurses from the hospital."

Camille put down her pen and looked deeply into Gonzalez's eyes. "What did she tell you?"

"That Willcox had punctured some guy's aorta with a trocar."

"And what did you find when you got to the hospital?"

"I found a patient who was bleeding rather profusely after having his aorta perforated."

"Tell me, Doctor, what were your clinical findings when you finally scrubbed in?"

Gonzalez's eyes darted from Camille to Lincoln. "I discovered a perforated aorta."

"Was there an aneurysm?"

Gonzalez looked at his hands twisting together on the table in front of him. "I'm not sure . . . I don't remember."

Camille's pulse quickened. "Doctor, did you write a note after you finished the procedure?"

"Of course. I always dictate a note."

"Did you bring Mr. Jackson's chart in response to my subpoena?"

"Yes," he said slowly, "I did."

Gonzalez slid the chart across the table.

"I don't see an op note in here."

"My . . . my office was broken into last fall. Someone pulled most of my charts off the shelves and made a complete mess of the place."

"Was Mr. Jackson's chart one of those that was pulled off the shelf?"

"It was." He shrugged. "I think the op note may have gotten lost in the shuffle after the break-in."

Camille swiveled her chair around and bent over to open her briefcase. She turned back around and opened the file folder she held in her hand.

She handed a single piece of paper to the court reporter. "I'd like to mark this as exhibit one to the deposition." She handed Lorrey a copy, then handed the exhibit to Dr. Gonzalez. "Dr. Gonzalez, is this a true and correct copy of your operative dictation on the Jackson case?"

Gonzalez's cheeks flushed. "It appears to be."

"Doctor, can you decipher this note for us?"

"It basically says that I looked around and determined that the patient had a perforated aorta. I quickly clamped and tied off the ancillary bleeders, then I turned my attention to the aorta and began to repair the perforation."

Camille sat up as straight as she could and leaned forward across the table. "What significance does the fact that Mr. Jackson was suffering from DIC have to you as a surgeon?"

"You typically don't see disseminated intravascular coagulation immediately after a patient suffers a traumatic injury."

"How much blood had Mr. Jackson lost by the time you arrived?"

"Let's see . . . It looks like the blood loss was fifteen hundred cc's." He drew a shaky breath.

"So, would you agree with me that Mr. Jackson had been bleeding for quite a while before you were called in?"

"Yes, it looks like it."

"And what is the significance of an estimated blood loss of fifteen hundred cc's?"

"Well, it means that the patient is bleeding to death."

Camille held Dr. Gonzalez's note in front of her and pulled her glasses down off her head. She quickly skimmed the note, then opened her three-inch binder and located Willcox's operative report. The loud click of the binder echoed in the large conference room. She deliberately removed the note and handed it to Diane. "Could you please mark this as exhibit two?" She waited while Diane stamped the document. "Doctor, I'm handing you Dr. Willcox's op note. Do you see about halfway down the third paragraph, where Dr. Willcox discusses hitting an aneurysm with the trocar?"

Max looked Camille directly in the eye. "I do."

"I didn't see any mention of an aneurysm in your note. Did you diagnose Mr. Jackson with an aortic aneurysm?"

"No."

"And why is that?" Camille asked loudly.

"Because . . ." Gonzalez paused. "I guess it'd be because Mr. Jackson did not have an aortic aneurysm. He simply had a perforated aorta. I tried to repair it. I was unsuccessful."

Camille nodded. "And you know why your repair was unsuccessful, don't you?"

"Objection! Leading the witness!" Lorrey shouted proudly, knowing full well that in a deposition, where no judge is present, that his theatrics were woefully unnecessary. His objection would just be for the record in the event the deposition was later used in an actual trial.

"Go ahead, Doctor," Camille said in a level voice.

Gonzalez looked at the floor. "I have a pretty good idea."

"Why don't you tell us, then." Camille looked sharply at Lorrey.

"Because Willcox waited over a half hour to call me in."

"If Mr. Jackson had had an aneurysm, would you have charted it?"

"Of course."

Camille pushed her glasses up on her head. She looked at Max for a second while he took a long drink of Coke, as though he were dying of thirst.

"Now, Doctor, it's my understanding that Dr. Willcox has had more than his share of unfortunate outcomes at Friday Harbor General. Isn't that correct?"

"Objection! Vague and ambiguous." Lorrey's chipmunk jowls were flexing and releasing.

"I . . . I guess you'd have to define 'more than his share,'" Gonzalez said softly.

"Well, were you aware that Dr. Willcox removed a man's lung for cancer, and it was later discovered that he didn't have cancer?"

Gonzalez shot Camille a look of surprise. "Yes. I heard about that case."

"And how about the woman who died during a routine hysterectomy? Did you also hear about that case?"

He raised an eyebrow. "Yes."

"Okay. And how about the man who died mysteriously after a one-car accident?"

"Yes." He sighed. "I remember that one."

"And there are others, aren't there?"

"I guess so."

"Now, Dr. Gonzalez." Camille raised her voice indignantly. "Isn't it true that a hospital has an obligation to protect the public from harm at the hands of a doctor practicing at that hospital?"

Gonzalez waited a moment. "The hospital credentialing committee has an obligation to monitor the privileges of the doctors on its staff to assure that those doctors are practicing safe medicine."

"You've had occasion to come in and perform repair surgery on Willcox patients, haven't you?"

"Yes." He sighed.

"How many times?"

"I couldn't tell you."

"More than ten?"

"Yes."

"More than twenty?"

"Yes."

"More than fifty?"

"I really wouldn't know."

"Would it be fair to say that it's not unusual for you to get a call from the OR informing you that Willcox needs you to come in and bail him out?"

"Object to the form of the question. Argumentative!" Lorrey threw his hands in the air.

"You can answer the question, Doctor," Camille stated authoritatively.

"No, I guess I wouldn't consider that to be unusual."

Camille pressed on emphatically. "In fact, you'd consider Dr. Willcox's complication rate to be somewhat excessive, wouldn't you?"

Gonzalez fidgeted in his chair. "I think so. Yes."

"Thank you, Doctor," Camille snapped. "Now tell me, just what did you do to try and protect the public from Dr. Willcox?"

"I beg your pardon?" Gonzalez looked shocked.

Camille pushed her notes away and leaned forward and said slowly, "What did you do to fulfill your obligation to protect the community? Or do you not consider yourself liable for sitting by and knowingly allowing Willcox to continue to operate on innocent patients?"

Gonzalez lowered his gaze and took a slow breath. He looked up at Camille and stared at her for ten seconds. "I have had several discussions with the administration about Andrew Willcox," he said tersely.

"Why?"

The doctor paused for at least a minute while Camille stared at him intently.

"Because, in my opinion, Dr. Willcox is not a particularly safe surgeon."

"Dr. Gonzalez, are you familiar with the standard of care for a surgeon practicing surgery in the state of Washington in 2020?"

"Yes, I am."

Lorrey jumped to his feet. "Objection! Objection!"

Camille ignored the theatrics. "Go ahead, Doctor."

Max's eyes darted to the court reporter. "I forgot the question . . . Could you . . . Could I please have it read back?"

The court reporter complied. "Are you familiar with the standard of care for a surgeon practicing surgery in the state of Washington in 2020?"

"Yes, I am familiar with the standard of care."

"And, Doctor, do you have an opinion about the surgery performed by Dr. Willcox on Dallas Jackson?" Camille asked.

Gonzalez scratched the back of his neck. "Yes, I guess I do have an opinion."

"And what is that opinion?"

"Object to the form of the question!" Lorrey tried to stare down the doctor.

"My opinion is that Dr. Willcox was negligent in his treatment of this patient." Gonzalez shook his head dejectedly as he exhaled.

"Can you explain specifically how Dr. Willcox violated the standard of care?"

Winnie Douglas shifted in her seat and glanced angrily at Lorrey, then scribbled a note to him on her legal pad. He read it and shrugged in return.

Gonzalez looked out the window. "A trocar is a very sharp instrument, and it's of paramount importance that the surgeon be cognizant of the placement of the trocar when he's introducing it." He sounded as if he were reading from a textbook. "As you know, the aorta's located in the back of the patient, so in a patient such as Mr. Jackson, it'd be about six to eight inches down from the skin. There's no way you should ever push a trocar in so hard that you go through the patient all the way to his aorta."

Camille smiled gratefully. "Do you have an opinion as to whether Dr. Willcox should have recognized that he had perforated the aorta sooner?"

"Well, I guess I'd have to say that a surgeon should have known that a patient with the vital signs of Mr. Jackson was in shock."

"What did the standard of care require Dr. Willcox to do when he noticed that Mr. Jackson was in shock?"

"He should have opened the patient immediately."

"What specifically should have alerted him to open this patient?"

"His pressure was ninety over fifty-five, and his pulse was one fifty, and his blood loss was fifteen hundred cc's."

Lorrey and Winnie were scribbling notes back and forth furiously.

"What should a reasonably prudent doctor do in such a situation?"

"He should have performed a laparotomy immediately."

"And what is that, Doctor?"

"You make an incision up the middle of the patient so that you can explore to find the source of the blood loss."

"Doctor, in your opinion, if Dr. Willcox had immediately opened the patient, would it have been possible to save him?" Camille took a drink of water so that no one on the other side of the table would notice that she almost choked on her words.

"Yes. If Mr. Jackson had simply had a perforated aorta, and I was called in promptly, I could have saved this patient."

Touchdown. Camille took a deep breath and smiled. "Thank you, Doctor. I have nothing further at this time."

"Dr. Gonzalez, my name is Lorrey Lincoln, and as you know, I represent Dr. Willcox in this matter." Lorrey flipped to his neatly typed outline that had no doubt been prepared by one of his underlings. He shoved it aside.

"Dr. Gonzalez, take a look at this." Lorrey slid a copy of the autopsy across the table. He waited for Max to finish looking at the document.

"Turning your attention to page two, can you read the second paragraph and tell me what it says?"

"It says the patient had an aortic aneurysm."

"Uh-huh! Yes, it does, doesn't it?"

"Yes."

229

"How do you explain that the pathologist who did the autopsy diagnosed an aneurysm if in fact there was none?"

Gonzalez shrugged his shoulders. "I guess you'd have to ask a pathologist."

CHAPTER TWENTY-EIGHT

Camille bounded out of her car and raced down the alley and through the mysterious pink door that was the only identifying feature of the appropriately named Pink Door restaurant located on Post Alley in the Pike Place Market. She stood at the top of the long staircase, looking down over the kitschy décor, and waved to Trish and Gigi. There had to be some way to get Gigi to testify. It was her only chance.

"How'd Gonzalez's dep go this morning?" Trish asked as soon as Camille was within earshot.

"You're not gonna believe this." Camille shook her head. "He creamed Willcox. So, now I have the expert witness I needed—even if he's a reluctant expert."

"What do you mean?"

"He testified that Willcox violated the standard of care in his treatment of Dallas."

"Why do you think he changed his mind about testifying?"

"Maybe it had to do with my not-so-subtle threat to sue him for his part in Willcox's continuing to kill innocent patients."

Trish grinned. "So, what'd Lorrey do?"

"Almost popped his fluorescent contact lenses out onto the conference room table." Camille laughed. "Then he tried to make it look like the case will boil down to a swearing contest between Gonzalez and Willcox."

"What do you mean?" Gigi asked.

"Well, as far as they know, there's no evidence that corroborates Max's testimony that there was no aneurysm."

"That's bullshit," Gigi snapped. "And by the way, I had it out with my chairman this morning. There's no way he's gonna dictate to me who I have to work with on my grant! I'll take my marbles and go to another university if I have to. I'm not going to work with James Wandel on anything. Period. I'm pretty much done being pushed around by a bunch of old white guys."

Camille had never seen Gigi really mad before. "What made you change your mind?"

"I just kept thinking about what you guys keep telling me. I'm the one who did the science to justify the grants I bring in. I'm going to own it."

Camille was impressed. "You're sounding like my mom. She runs an international asylum project, and one thing I've learned from her is that once we've paid our dues and reached the pinnacle of our profession, we need to set an example for other women."

"And we need to do what our heart tells us," Gigi added. "Your mom and my dad would have made a good team."

"So . . . ," Camille said with anticipation, "what's next?"

"Well, no one is going to tell me who I can and can't testify for." Gigi raised her glass of wine. "Here's to the truth, the whole truth, and nothing but the truth, so help me God."

"You know you could be giving up something you've worked for your whole career," Camille reminded her friend.

"I hate to get all corny, but do either of you know how the Hippocratic oath begins?"

Trish and Camille looked at each other and smiled. The three women said in unison: "First do no harm . . ." They clinked their glasses.

Gigi said, "What kind of doctor sits by and lets Willcox continue to kill people? Not this one."

Trish put her arm around her girlfriend and kissed her on the cheek. "You're so cool. Isn't she great?" Trish beamed.

"You'll testify?" Camille asked.

"I have to. If anyone hated the system, it was my dad. He'd never let me rest another day if I didn't." Gigi looked up. "See, Daddy. I told you I'd do it."

"I can't tell you how grateful I am, Gigi. But as you know, the mediation is on Friday. Can you give a deposition tomorrow?"

"No problem. I can have my chief resident cover for me."

Camille pulled out her cell phone.

Trish turned to Gigi while Camille was on the phone setting up the dep. "I'm going back up to the Island this weekend to see if I can get any more information on Willcox's other victims."

"So, you're going up there for the whole weekend?" Gigi asked.

"Yeah, wanna come? Gloria is in Todos Santos for the winter. We can stay on her boat. It's really romantic."

"Sure, Kaitlin's going to her dad's for the weekend. I can fly up after my dep." Gigi turned to Camille. "What are you guys doing this weekend?"

"Sam's got to cover the infectious disease hotline this weekend for his fellow so he can go to a family wedding. And I'm gonna help with the St. Patrick's Day Dash over at Green Lake—the girls are running in it this year." Camille looked at her watch. "And speaking of St. Patrick's Day, I've got a shitload of cookies to bake this afternoon with Gracie's Brownie troop. I gotta go." She pecked her two friends on their cheeks and took off up the staircase leading out of the restaurant.

—

Camille stood in her kitchen and ran her sticky fingers through her hair. She cursed herself for forgetting to turn on the timer for the batch of cookies smoking in the oven while the cadre of little girls, covered with flour from head to toe, noisily decorated the well-intended but slightly misshapen shamrock cookies with green icing and sprinkles.

"Fire! Fire!" Grace ran around frantically. "Stop, drop, and roll, you guys!"

The house filled with the shrieking of six year olds as they gleefully practiced their fire drill. Jake came storming upstairs to check out the hysteria and quickly joined in by howling and frolicking on the floor with the girls.

Camille barely heard her phone ringing above the din. Scrambling to pop in her EarPods, she headed out onto the deck with the smoking sheet of cookies before the smoke alarm went off too. The cookies sizzled in a pouf of steam as they hit the ice-cold water, where grateful ducks rallied around for their afternoon snack.

"What on earth is going on?" Amy shouted. "It sounds like you have a thousand Brownies massacring a flock of wild mallards over there."

"Thank you very much for the editorial comment." Camille closed the sliding door to damper the noise. "I happen to be in complete control of the situation. Things are going quite smoothly, thank you."

"I have Winnie Douglas on the phone. She's anxious to speak with you. I can put her through, if you'd like."

"Just a sec." Camille poked her head in the door and shouted, "Hey, Angela! Can you please take over for a few minutes? I have an important call." She closed the door again, and said, "Go ahead." She wiped her hands on the towel she'd thrown over her shoulder.

The insurance adjuster's flat voice replaced Amy's friendly tone. "What's up?"

"I'd like to discuss the upcoming mediation."

Sure she would. "Okay."

A short girl with thick wire-rimmed glasses came out on the deck and held up a half-baked cookie. "Do you think these are done yet?"

"Hang on, Winnie." Camille put her hand over the phone. "Give them five more minutes. And don't forget to set the timer." She ushered the little girl back into the kitchen and closed the door behind her. "Sorry about that. Now you were saying?"

"We've finished our investigation, and although we feel that the case is defensible, we realize that there's always a risk in going to trial, so we'd like to see if we can't reach a reasonable compromise on Friday."

Camille was all ears. "Okay." *This ought to be interesting.*

"I'd like to tell you our analysis of the case, then you can give it some thought and respond if you'd like."

Camille slipped on the hooded sweatshirt she had tied around her waist and sat down on the Adirondack chair on the deck. "Okay, shoot."

"Well, first off, I don't have to tell you that the potential jury verdict range for a sixty-five-year-old man with no income is limited at best. Like seventy-five to a hundred thousand, max. And of course the jury's going to take into account what kind of person the decedent was, as well as his spouse."

Camille stood up and paced back and forth across the deck to keep warm.

"As you know, the likelihood of a jury giving money to any plaintiff is directly related to how much they feel about them as a person. We've done a rather thorough background search on both the decedent and his wife. And I think what we've discovered further limits the value of the case." The adjuster's voice was openly hostile.

What on earth could anyone find to criticize Dallas or Gloria about? "Why don't you tell me what you've got, and I'll discuss it with my client."

"Fine. Let's see . . . You may be unaware that Mr. Jackson had, shall we say, a rather colorful past."

"How so?" Every muscle in Camille's body was on alert.

"In 1978, Dallas Jackson was arrested in San Francisco for possession of LSD. He received probation. Then in '79, he was arrested twice for trespassing on the Presidio army base. He resisted arrest and was charged with assaulting a police officer. In 1980, he was investigated by the FBI for inciting disturbances of the peace. After that, he lived as a fugitive in Mexico on a sailboat."

Oh for Christ's sake. Camille shook her head in disbelief.

"Then he disappeared for several years. He finally ended up moving to Seattle in the late eighties. And did you know that his first wife was killed in some kind of freak accident? Very suspicious. Clearly, the man had a propensity toward antisocial behavior and violence."

Fugitive in Mexico? Camille almost broke out laughing. "You're kidding. You don't really think you can convince a jury that a peace activist in the seventies was some kind of sociopath." She decided to hold back on explaining how Dallas's first wife, Robin's mother, had died in a tragic diving accident in the Sea of Cortez. She didn't want the adjuster to somehow twist that against Gloria.

"I'd hardly call him a peace activist," the adjuster said coldly. "We believe we can make an argument that he actually killed his first wife."

"What?" Camille yelled; it was all she could do not to hang up.

"Four arrests and a wife who was killed in a suspicious accident? We can at least pique the jury's curiosity," she said with a hint of satisfaction.

Camille grabbed the deck railing. "No one is going to buy that, Winnie. Dallas Jackson did not kill anybody."

"Gloria Jackson was an abused child whose mother ended up serving a ten-year prison sentence, leaving Gloria with her elderly, neglectful grandparents."

Camille caught her breath. She had no idea if Winnie was making this up, but it did line up with Gloria's interest in helping mothers reunite with their children after the moms were released from prison.

"Now, Gloria herself was the victim of domestic violence at the hands of her first two husbands and was even hospitalized a number of times in the mideighties and early nineties for injuries incurred as a result of spousal abuse." She paused for effect. "I can send you the arrest records if you'd like."

Camille could hear Winnie flipping the pages of her notes. "Let's see, she's been in counseling a number of times over the years in an effort to break her pattern of choosing abusive men and was ultimately institutionalized at a sanitarium in Mexico, where she met Mr. Jackson. Since she's been in Friday Harbor, she's been regularly visiting a women's shelter, presumably for continued counseling."

"She volunteers there," Camille responded calmly, still wondering if there was even a kernel of truth in Winnie's recitation of Gloria's childhood and early marriages.

"That may be your explanation. But I promise you we'll be presenting evidence to the contrary. You know as well as I do, Camille, that there are just some women who keep going back to abusive relationships, and Ms. Jackson was one of them. He was an asshole, and she's lucky to be rid of him."

"Okay. Let's say, for the sake of argument, that she was a victim of domestic violence. It's not relevant in this case. No judge will allow prejudicial evidence like that."

"Of course it's relevant. She's going to be asking the jury to compensate her for losing her loving husband. And if the jury finds out what a jerk he was, they aren't going to give her a dime. She's clearly better off without him."

"What are you talking about?" Camille snapped.

"Look, the guy has a history of violence; he's been arrested a number of times. And she has a habit of getting involved with abusive men.

We have an expert who will testify that the decedent's wife is a typical battered woman, and that more likely than not, Mr. Jackson was just another in a long line of abusive relationships. Admit it, Camille. We'll get a defense verdict on this one. He didn't even have a job. Did you know that she supported the bum by teaching yoga? Give me a break."

The woman was a true bottom-feeder. Camille didn't trust herself to respond civilly to what she had just heard. She took a deep breath and counted to ten.

"Are you there?" Winnie asked flatly. "Give it up, Camille. Get this thing wrapped up and move on to a case where you're at least doing the right thing for someone."

Camille just about snapped, then caught herself. "I've scheduled the deposition of another expert for tomorrow."

"Well, I'm sure that will be fascinating . . . And by the way, I hope you're not relying too heavily on Dr. Gonzalez. I'll be bringing in testimony from other doctors in Friday Harbor who will say that he's not exactly a surgical genius. In fact, the hospital was getting ready to put him on probation when this case occurred."

"I'll tell you what, Winnie. Let's get Dr. Roberts's dep done, and then we'll talk. Okay?"

"See you tomorrow. One way or the other, we should know by Friday if your case is worth the pleading paper it's filed on."

CHAPTER TWENTY-NINE

Tony balanced on the float of his plane, untying the mooring line with one hand and holding a smoldering clove cigarette in the other.

"So, who's the new squeeze?" he yelled to Trish as she ran down the dock, her backpack thrown awkwardly over her shoulder.

"What new squeeze?"

"The chick in the flashy red Mercedes sports coupe." Tony pointed to the parking lot with a knowing smirk.

"Oh, just some *doctor* from the U." Trish kissed Tony on the cheek. "Let's go. We wouldn't want to make all these nice people late, Captain!" Trish jerked her head in the direction of the plane full of passengers all buckled in and waiting, not so patiently, for her to climb aboard.

Trish looked down over the Islands and watched the powerboats streaking past the sailboats, their wakes leaving an ever-expanding triangle on the glass-like water. As they approached the Island, Trish could see Willcox's ostentatious mansion standing just a bit north of the harbor.

As soon as the plane taxied up to the dock, Trish hopped out and breathed in the crisp salt air.

"C'mon over for a glass of wine tonight, if you have the time," she said to Tony as he tied the plane to the pier.

"Actually, I have a date with a nurse from the hospital at seven thirty."

"Why don't you bring her by with you? You can have a drink, then go out by yourselves."

"Okay. That'd be great."

"See ya!" Trish pranced down the dock and watched as the grumpy harbormaster picked up a landline phone.

———

Gigi sat directly across the table from Lorrey Lincoln. She wore a striking royal-blue suit, and her braids were threaded through hundreds of carved gold beads. She looked completely at ease.

Lorrey looked smugly at Camille, then turned to the court reporter. "Swear the witness."

"Could you please raise your right hand, Dr. Roberts?"

Gigi complied. "Do you swear or affirm that your testimony will be the truth, and nothing but the truth?"

Gigi locked her calm eyes onto Lorrey's turquoise contact lenses. "I do."

"State your name for the record." Lorrey's left eye began its familiar twitch.

"Georgia Roberts."

Camille let her attention wander as Lorrey flew through the preliminaries.

"Dr. Roberts, have you ever given sworn testimony before?"

"Yes."

Camille snapped to attention. Uh-oh.

Lorrey grinned. "Sure you have. Great way to supplement a university salary isn't it, Doc?" He looked at Winnie knowingly. "So, tell me. On how many occasions have you testified?"

"I'm not sure I can give you an exact number."

Camille cringed. She'd assumed from her conversations with Gigi that she hadn't been involved in the legal system. And she knew Lorrey would make mincemeat of Gigi if he could characterize her as a hired gun.

"Well, was it more than ten?"

"Oh yes."

"More than twenty?"

Camille tried to look nonchalant.

"Sure."

"Fifty? Have you testified more than fifty times?"

"I don't think it would be more than fifty."

"Now, Doctor, why don't you tell us a little bit about the times you've testified under oath." Lorrey grinned at Winnie. "And be sure to include how much you've been paid for that testimony."

"Okay." Gigi turned to Camille and shrugged. "I was the lead researcher in several organ transplant projects before I got the grant to study aortic aneurysms. And I was appointed by the president to serve on a number of committees involving the organ transplant funding. One of my responsibilities was to testify in front of congressional committees. So, I've testified in Washington frequently over the past ten years. I just can't remember how often. And I've never been paid. It's an honor to be appointed to such a prestigious position. I do it at my own expense."

Camille bit her tongue in an effort to keep from smiling. She focused her gaze out the window at the clouds on the lake. Cumulonimbus. Dallas had taught her that the tall, puffy clouds signaled serious weather ahead.

Lorrey tried, unsuccessfully, to hide his disappointment. "Now, Doctor, I understand Ms. Delaney has hired you to testify as an expert witness in this matter."

"I have *agreed* to testify as an expert witness, yes."

"Why don't you tell me what Ms. Delaney has asked you to testify about today."

"Ms. Delaney approached me to review the slides she received from Friday Harbor General Hospital in an effort to determine whether Mr. Jackson had an aneurysm."

"Where'd she get the idea that he might not have had an aneurysm?"

Camille opened her mouth to object, but Gigi answered before she had a chance. "I have no idea what Ms. Delaney was thinking. Presumably she wanted me to make that determination."

"What did she provide to you?"

"She brought the slides she had received from the hospital in response to her request."

"Mr. Jackson's slides?"

"The slides were labeled *Jackson*."

"Did you look at the slides?"

"Of course."

"And did you determine whether the slides were of an aneurysm?"

"Yes, the slides were of an aneurysm."

"Of course they were." Lorrey smiled at Winnie. "Now, did Ms. Delaney show you any other slides?"

"Yes. She had some slides, also labeled *Jackson*, that were of a gallbladder."

"Okay, and did those slides demonstrate an inflamed gallbladder?"

"Yes."

"Okay . . ." Lorrey looked puzzled. "So, Doctor, do you have any testimony that is in any way helpful to Ms. Delaney's case?"

"Yes, I think so."

"And what would that be?" Lorrey looked condescendingly at Gigi.

"Well, I believe it's helpful to Ms. Delaney's case that none of those slides came from Mr. Jackson," Gigi said casually.

Lorrey furrowed his brow.

"Objection. Lack of foundation," interjected Cleo.

"What do you mean, they didn't come from Mr. Jackson?"

Camille smiled slightly. Lorrey was blinking fast. The contact lenses must be acting up again.

"I mean that none of the tissue specimens came from Mr. Jackson."

Cleo didn't look up from her note-taking. "Same objection."

Lorrey blinked uncontrollably. "Dr. Roberts, on what evidence do you base your opinion that the slides allegedly did not come from Mr. Jackson?" His voice was shrill.

"The slides I reviewed could not have come from a sixty-five-year-old man."

"How on earth could you know the age of the patient a specimen came from?" Lorrey shouted indignantly.

"It's quite easy. The tissue in the gallbladder slides labeled *Jackson* showed no signs of the aging process. No atherosclerosis. No calcifications. In fact, the histological appearance of the slides I examined was clearly that of a young person. Smooth-walled vessels, elastic internal lamellae. It was clear that the gallbladder slides couldn't have come from Mr. Jackson, so last night I compared the blood type of the specimen to that of Mr. Jackson."

"And?"

"And I discovered that the specimen came from a person with B positive blood . . . and Mr. Jackson was A negative."

Gigi turned and stifled a smile at Camille, who swallowed and blinked hard to keep a tear from escaping. She reached down and pretended to look for something in her briefcase. Gigi had really come through.

Lorrey rifled through the papers he had stacked in front of him. He extracted a typewritten sheet. "Dr. Roberts, why don't you tell us why you left Stanford."

"I was offered a full professorship at the University of Washington, and I was ready to make a move, so I accepted the position."

"Isn't it true that you were involved in a rather nasty and expensive custody battle over your daughter?"

"Objection," Camille said sternly. "What possible relevance does Dr. Roberts's divorce have to these proceedings?"

"It goes to bias and motive."

"How could Dr. Roberts's personal life possibly have anything to do with her bias or motive to testify as an expert witness in this case?"

"Dr. Roberts, isn't it true that divorce became extremely long and dragged out since your husband accused you of being an unfit mother to your daughter due to your homosexuality?" Lorrey pounded the desk.

"That's enough, Lorrey! I'm instructing the witness not to answer the question. This is out-and-out harassment, and I will not allow her to be subjected to your innuendoes."

"I'm entitled to ask questions that go to bias or motive for testifying."

"And this has nothing to do with any potential bias of this witness."

"Well, you can take that up with the judge at a later date, but right now I am going to finish this deposition." Lorrey set his oversized jaw.

"Not if you're going to pursue this line of questioning, you're not."

"Tell it to the judge, Camille. Your objection is noted. Now, Dr. Roberts, were you or were you not asked to leave Stanford due to your emotional instability over your newfound homosexuality?"

"Don't answer that, Dr. Roberts!" Camille stood and grabbed the phone on the credenza. "Amy, get me Judge Cranbrook on the phone. Tell her we're in a dep, and we have a discovery problem. I'll hold." Camille turned her back on Lorrey and watched a fishing boat maneuver under the drawbridge. "Good afternoon, Judge Cranbrook. This is Camille Delaney. I'm calling on the case of Jackson versus Willcox. And I'm in a deposition here with Mr. Lincoln, who represents the defendant, Dr. Willcox, and Cleo Tracey, who represents Friday Harbor General Hospital. I'll put you on speakerphone, if you don't mind."

"Hello, everyone. This is Judge Cranbrook. Please be brief, counsel. I'm in the middle of a trial here."

"Hello, Your Honor, this is Lorrey Lincoln."

"And Cleo Tracey."

"Okay, what can I do for you, counsel?"

"Mr. Lincoln is taking the deposition of one of the plaintiff's experts, Dr. Georgia Roberts, who is a professor of cardiology and pathology at the University of Washington Medical Center."

"Good afternoon, Dr. Roberts."

"Hello, Your Honor."

"Go ahead, counsel."

"Mr. Lincoln has been unconscionably harassing this witness regarding her sexual orientation."

"I beg your pardon?" the judge responded sharply.

"He's making disparaging comments about the sexual orientation of the professor. And asking extremely personal questions about her divorce and child custody situation."

"Mr. Lincoln, is that correct?"

"It goes to the bias of the witness, Your Honor." Lorrey glared at Camille.

"This is an expert witness testifying on a scientific matter, I assume?"

"Yes, Your Honor," Camille answered.

"Mr. Lincoln I don't see how any part of this witness's personal life is relevant whatsoever to her opinion in this case. Please explain why you see it otherwise."

"Your Honor, this is a discovery deposition," Lorrey whined. "I have a right to pursue any line of questioning that would lead to the discovery of admissible evidence."

"And how could the witness's sexual orientation possibly lead to the discovery of admissible evidence?"

"I'm entitled to explore the witness's bias or motive."

"How on earth do you think this may relate to bias or motive?"

"I believe the witness lost a great deal of money in her divorce, and she's selling her testimony to pay her legal bills."

"I've heard enough. Mr. Lincoln, you will refrain from asking any personal questions of this witness. Ms. Delaney, please don't hesitate to call back if any of this continues. Good day, counsel."

Lorrey leaned forward on the table and raised his voice. "Dr. Roberts, are you being paid by Ms. Delaney here to provide testimony in this matter?"

"Ms. Delaney has offered to pay me for my time. But I have directed her to forward whatever money she feels would be appropriate for my services directly to the National Organ Donor Transplant Foundation."

Lorrey bounced back in his chair and glared at Gigi.

"Dr. Roberts, do you have any basis for your belief that someone at Friday Harbor sent the wrong slides?"

"Yes, I do."

"And what is that?"

"I had an opportunity to review data from another patient who actually had an aneurysm and was operated on at Friday Harbor General. And as it turns out, the slides that were labeled *Jackson* were really from the other patient."

"And do you know the name of that other patient?"

"It's August Gianelli."

"Where is Mr. Gianelli now?"

"He died."

The two defense lawyers continued to take notes without looking up.

"At Friday Harbor General Hospital." Gigi paused. "Under the care of Dr. Willcox."

CHAPTER THIRTY

Trish greeted Tony and the petite woman with the chin-length brown hair as they climbed down the narrow stairway into the boat.

"I'm Trish. Nice to meet you." Trish held out her hand.

"Hi. Sally Berwyn."

"Wine? Or beer?" Trish held a bottle in each hand.

"Wine'd be great, thanks."

Trish grabbed a corkscrew as Tony and Sally sat on the banquette. "So, I hear you're a nurse over at Friday Harbor General."

"Yeah. I just came up to work for the summer in the ER, since that's the busy season. But I kinda like it up here, so I decided to stay through the winter."

"And how do you find it?"

"Peaceful. I love the solitude here in the winter. But I'm afraid my tenure at Friday Harbor General's about up."

"How come?"

"Well . . . Let's just say I'm glad to be heading to grad school this fall."

"What do you mean?" Tony asked.

"I can't exactly work in a place that I don't feel is providing adequate care. There are a few docs up here that I wouldn't let touch me if I were gasping my last breath."

"Like who?" Trish asked.

"I shouldn't name names, but . . . there's this arrogant guy who treats everyone around him like they're his personal slaves."

"I think I know who you mean. I'm up here on sabbatical, and I joined the choir just for fun. I gotta agree with ya, the doctors I've met through the choir are really something." Trish paused, hoping Sally would feed her more information.

"Like?" Sally asked expectantly.

"Well, there's this guy named Willcox. What a piece of work . . . I can't imagine letting him anywhere near me."

"Me either," Sally agreed. "Something about him, I can't exactly put my finger on—"

"And there's something strange about his wife, BJ," Trish interrupted.

Sally looked at her watch. "When did you say our reservation was, Tony?"

"Seven thirty. Jeez, that's in ten minutes. We gotta split. Thanks for the wine, Trish." He stood and ushered his date up the companionway. While Sally was putting on her boots, he stuck his head down the hatch and whispered, "You shoulda told me you wanted to interrogate her. I'da brought one of those big, bright lights, and we coulda shined it in her face."

"Was I being too nosy?"

"Not any more than usual, I guess." A smile crept across Tony's face. "So? Do you like her?"

"Well, she's not my type."

"Shit, Trish. I'm not trying to fix you up with her!"

"I know! I was joking. She's very nice. And I think she likes you."

"You do?"

"We're gonna be late!" Sally laughed as she hollered from the dock.

"Gotta split. See ya tomorrow?"

"Sure. And I like that she's a little bossy. You two have fun." Trish slid the hatch closed and went below.

—

Camille hurried into the espresso shop across the street from the office building on the edge of the Pike Place Market where the mediation service was located. Late, as usual. Robin stood up and waved at Camille. "I have your latte!" She held up the steaming cup.

Camille hugged Robin and Gloria and sat down. She pulled a file out of her briefcase. "So, are we ready?"

As always, Gloria carried herself like royalty. "Do you really think we can get this done today?"

"They have no idea that we have to get it done now. As far as they're concerned, we'll take this thing all the way to trial. Be sure you don't let on to the mediator that we're out of time on this. Besides, I think the insurance company definitely wants to put this behind them. Remember, they're faced with the proposition of going to trial with a doctor who's lied in his medical record and a hospital that sent false slides in response to a subpoena. Not to mention that Gonzalez testified that Willcox let the patient bleed to death before calling him in. And the hospital has to deal with the fact they failed to take any measures to protect the community from the monster. And to top it off, Trish called me this morning and told me that one of the family docs in Friday Harbor reported Willcox to the disciplinary board, and they've been moving forward with charges against him and, quite possibly, the hospital. I'd say, on balance, they're very anxious to settle this mess."

"What do you mean the disciplinary board is going to file charges?" Robin asked.

"Trish spoke to a woman at the disciplinary board named Lois Birmingham, and she looked up Willcox in the computer and couldn't believe that no one has filed a statement of charges against him. Apparently, the guy who's in charge of the state disciplinary file on Willcox is about to retire, and he's too lazy to do any of the paperwork. Lois said she'd take over the file."

"Is that good for us?"

"Yeah, it puts more pressure on them. Apparently, Lois called Dahlquist, the hospital administrator, yesterday to find out what's up with Willcox's privileges. The timing's perfect. Willcox and the hospital both know that the disciplinary board is breathing down Willcox's neck and that it's just a matter of time before the hospital goes down in flames with him."

"Great!"

Gloria finished off her latte. "I called the people who own the property and told them that we may be in a position to put together a deal this weekend. They said they've been getting a lot of pressure from that developer to sell it to him."

"How nice of them to hold off till you can come up with some money."

"They can only wait a little bit longer, as they've got some rather pressing obligations. As much as they like the idea of helping me with my shelter, I think it's now or never."

The three women gathered their things and crossed the street to the mediation office. In the elevator, on the way up, they ran into their mediator, retired Superior Court Judge Frank Maunders.

"How's the sailboat? You guys gonna race the Vic-Maui this year?" Frank asked Camille, referring to the trans-Pacific race from Victoria, British Columbia, to Maui.

"We're planning on it. How about you?" She smiled.

"If my wife can get away. I think she may have a trial that week."

Camille turned to Gloria and Robin. "Frank, I'd like you to meet my clients, Gloria and Robin Jackson."

"My pleasure." Frank shook both of their hands warmly. "I was sorry to read about your loss. Mr. Jackson sounded like a special guy."

Gloria looked Frank straight in the eye. "He was."

Frank stepped back and held the elevator doors for the three women. "I'll see you in conference room three. I need to go get my materials."

Gloria looked at Camille. "Seems like a very nice man."

"He is, but remember, he does a large number of mediations for the Pacific Northwest Medical Insurance Company."

"Meaning he's in their hip pocket," Robin snipped.

"Not exactly, but close," Camille answered.

"Is there anything in this system that is what it seems on its face?" Gloria asked sincerely.

"That's a good question. I'd have to say no. Every little thing that goes on in this so-called justice system is replete with hidden agendas and competing interests both above and below the surface."

The receptionist led the three women down to a windowed conference room. "Judge Maunders will be right with you. There's coffee, tea, or pop right here." She pointed to a sideboard loaded with refreshments.

Judge Maunders strode confidently into the room and sat at the head of the long table. After briefly explaining the mediation process, he stood and told the women that he would go down the hall to get the defendant's first offer.

"So, we just sit?" Robin asked.

Camille got up and poured them each a tall glass of water from the crystal pitcher sitting on the ornate sideboard. "Pretty much."

Frank returned after fifteen minutes, sat down, and said, "The defendants feel that you've significantly overvalued your case." He rubbed his eyes. "They've offered twenty-five thousand dollars."

"What?" Robin shouted. "They kill my father and offer to buy us off for a measly twenty-five grand?"

Camille held up her hand at Robin. "It's part of the game."

"They're just responding to your substantial initial demand," Frank explained to Robin patiently before turning to Camille. "Camille, don't you think three and a half million was a bit high for this one? I'm sure the decedent was a helluva guy, but I don't have to tell you there's never been an Island County jury verdict anywhere near seven figures for an unemployed sixty-five-year-old retired guy, no matter how terrific you think he was." Frank leaned back in his chair.

"This isn't your average retired-guy death case, Frank." Camille folded her arms across her chest.

"Well, maybe you can tell me why."

"First of all, we have a colleague of the defendant who testified in his dep that the defendant's a walking time bomb. That's more than a bit unusual, don't you think?"

"Of course. But it doesn't mean they'll pay seven figures."

"Then, we have the hospital sending fraudulent slides in response to a subpoena. I don't think a jury'll like that. Do you?"

"Of course not, but your evidence is a bit complicated on that one. They may not believe your expert."

"A full professor at the university who's on the Presidential Commission on Organ Transplantation, and is testifying in return for me sending her fees to a charitable foundation?"

"You're kidding? Nice touch." Frank nodded in admiration. "How the hell did you get a university doc to testify for a plaintiff?"

"It seems I found one who got a little pissed off at the system."

"And she still has a job?"

"The U isn't likely to kiss off a twenty-five-million-dollar grant just because the recipient has a conscience."

"You've got some good points. I'll go share your position with the other side. Do you want to respond to the twenty-five?"

"Not really. I'll come down if they make a good faith offer."

"Don't do this to me, Camille." He shook his head. "It's Friday. I don't need Lincoln down my throat so early in the day."

"Okay." Camille looked at Gloria. "We'll come down by twenty-five thousand. But at this rate, we're going to miss the St. Patrick's Day Dash on Sunday."

"Fine. I'll be back." Frank grabbed his monogrammed coffee cup and his yellow legal pad and took off.

Robin got up and stretched. "Is this all we do all day?"

"It gets a bit more interesting as the day progresses, but this is basically it."

By midmorning, the defendants had offered $100,000, Camille had reduced her demand to three million, and Frank had started to look a bit pasty.

"What do you want me to tell them? It sounds to me like you guys are dealing with two entirely different cases."

"Is Willcox in there?"

"The defendant? No, but his wife is here. As far as I can tell, she's his business manager, and she has authority to respond to offers and to settle."

"His wife? Seriously?"

"I know. Strange, huh? But she seems entirely up to speed on the case. And she has ready access to the doctor on her phone."

"Well, ask Mrs. Willcox if she wants us to send a subpoena to Wellington Hall for the doctor's credentials file."

"What?"

"When Willcox applied for privileges at Friday Harbor General Hospital, he told them he was from Southern California, but we have reason to believe that he came from Arizona. Just ask her. I think that may break the impasse."

"Whatever you say." Frank closed the door solidly behind himself.

The women sat silently.

Frank returned with a flourish. "I don't know how you did it, but they just increased their offer to two hundred thousand dollars. I think you should seriously consider taking it. That's more money than you'll ever get from a jury."

Camille smiled. "No, Frank. We're just getting started. This time, ask Mrs. Willcox if she'd like us to subpoena records from Rebekkah's Manor."

"Rebekkah's Manor?"

"Yup. And it's R-E-B-E-K-K-A-H."

"I'm on my way."

Frank was hardly gone five minutes when he returned. "Three hundred thousand, and Winnie is steaming. Now what?"

"Is the hospital pitching in much?"

"You know I can't tell you that. It's all confidential, but if you have any zingers for them, this would be a good time to put 'em on the table."

Camille looked out the window at the Olympic Mountains towering over Puget Sound. She stood up very straight and tall and said, without turning around, "Tell the hospital that we will be calling the family of August Gianelli."

"You want to make a counteroffer?"

She looked slowly at Frank. "Two point seven."

"All right." Frank stood with his hand on the doorknob and took a deep breath and opened it.

Frank was gone almost an hour this time. "They had a bit of difficulty getting ahold of the hospital administrator. But he authorized them to increase their offer to four hundred thousand. I don't know what's going on here, but if I were you, I'd look in my bag of tricks and see what else I could pull out. It seems you've got them on the ropes."

"Okay, try this: tell Mrs. Willcox I've been toying with the idea of contacting the family of Rosa Antonio."

Gloria looked curiously at Camille.

"I'll explain later," she whispered.

Frank pushed his hair back with his hand. "Okay. Any counter?"

"I don't think so." Camille smiled mischievously.

Frank returned almost immediately and sat down. "Mrs. Willcox had to make a quick call on this one." He had a release in his hand. "I don't believe this. They've offered you one and a half million dollars."

Gloria and Robin looked at each other and smiled widely.

"I'll take the two million policy limit from Willcox and half a million from the hospital," Camille responded.

"Are you sure you want to push your luck?"

"Yep." She nodded.

"Okay, it's your nickel. Any more pearls for the hospital?"

"Just that it's a violation of the Consumer Protection Act for the hospital administrator and a credentialed doctor to falsely advertise a service to innocent consumers on a Facebook Live feed. And if I win on a consumer protection claim, they pay treble damages and all of my attorney fees. And give them this." Camille slid a thumb drive across the table. "Explain to them that this is a recording of Willcox and Dahlquist illegally guaranteeing the result of a surgical procedure. We're going to get something to eat. We'll be back in a half hour." Camille stood and ushered Gloria and Robin out of the room.

"What was that?" Robin whispered as they walked to the reception area.

"A recording of Willcox and Dahlquist mouthing off about his success rate on a Facebook Live. We have a strong argument that it's a violation of the Consumer Protection Act. The hospital won't want to risk paying us triple damages and attorney's fees. Pretty sure Cleo will make them come up with some serious money once she hears the tape."

———

The women sat in a booth at Cutters, the upscale restaurant on the building's first floor. They were just finishing their lunch when they spotted Frank surveying the crowded restaurant, looking for Camille and her client. Camille signaled for him to come over and sit down.

"Congratulations, ladies. I have an agreement and a release in the amount of two point five million dollars. Let me buy you a drink."

Frank beckoned the waiter and ordered a bottle of champagne. "So, you gotta tell me. What the hell went on back there?"

"Can't, Frank. Confidentiality, you know. Now, open that bottle." Camille looked out the window and caught Lorrey Lincoln's eye as he schlepped down the sidewalk with Winnie Douglas nipping closely at his heels. As soon as he noticed Camille, he straightened up and tried to look nonchalant. Camille held up her champagne glass to him and smiled.

CHAPTER THIRTY-ONE

The hospital administrator jumped up and closed the door behind Willcox and Burton before they even had a chance to sit down. "We've got trouble. Big trouble."

"Slow down. What's going on?" Willcox always dealt with Dahlquist. Burton didn't have the patience, or the charm.

"The disciplinary board is all over the Jackson matter. And now they're asking for the charts of"—he glanced at the note on his desk—"a Gianelli and a Read." Dahlquist turned and paced nervously back and forth across the bright-green carpet. "Who's Read?"

"A woman who died of a complication during a hysterectomy," Willcox answered.

Dahlquist nodded. "I remember. She lived alone, no family, not many friends. Sad case."

Willcox ignored the rambling little shit. He grabbed the phone. "Hang on. I'll just call Rex Maple down in Olympia. He's the investigator on those files. There's no way he'll let this investigation heat up. Believe me, he has a very nice condo in Tarrington waiting for him as soon as he retires."

"What's Tarrington?"

"Uh . . ." Willcox looked sheepishly at Burton, who glared at him with daggers in his eyes. "Premier retirement community in the desert, east of Phoenix," Willcox stammered. "He was telling us all about his upcoming retirement plans when we had our preliminary interview with him a few weeks ago."

"Well, I just got a call from"—Dahlquist picked up another note from his desk—"a Ms. Lois Birmingham, from the state disciplinary board. Says she's taking over the file, and she'll be here first thing Monday morning to go over the records."

Willcox's face was flaming. "What do you mean she's taking over the file? That was Rex Maple's file. She can't take it over!"

Burton tugged at Willcox's sleeve. "Well, apparently she has. Let's go, Andy. We'll get back to you, Tom."

The twosome strode out of the administrator's office, with Willcox leading the way.

"Where are we going?" Burton ran to catch up with his partner.

"The medical records office. We need to log on to the computer and get rid of those charts before the disciplinary board gets ahold of them, but first we need paper copies so I can edit them off-line. That way when we crash the computer system, I'll have the records I need and can go online and do it quickly once they get it back up." Willcox explained as he took off down the hall.

"Computer system is going down?" Burton asked.

Willcox ignored the question and directed Burton to follow. He crashed through the doorway to the medical records department. "I need you to print out hard copies of the Gianelli file, the Jackson file, and the Read file, please." He looked at the name tag on the hospital volunteer behind the desk. "Ruby."

Ruby's smile was more curious than genuine. "Of course, Dr. Willcox." She paused and scrambled to find a piece of scratch paper. "Could you spell those names for me, please?" She wrote the names down as Willcox spelled them at her.

Ruby scrambled to input the names into the system. "This is going to take a while, Doctor. Can I have them delivered to your office?"

"No," Willcox almost shouted. Then he calmed himself. "I need to review them tonight for an upcoming surgical case."

"Well," Ruby suggested as she hit Print and went over to grab the paper spitting out of the high-speed printer, "you could just log on to the system from home."

Willcox could feel his blood pressure rising, but he didn't want to raise any suspicions, so he responded gently. "Under normal circumstances, you're absolutely right . . . Ruby. But after that big storm the other night, our home internet went out, and if you can believe it, we're still waiting for a fix."

"Oh, I hear you, Doctor. It's one of the trade-offs of living up here in the Islands," Ruby responded, noting to herself that the recent storm had only knocked down a few trees, and when there was an internet outage, it was usually all over the local Facebook page.

"But to be honest, I'm an old-school guy. I like actual paper charts." Willcox tried to be nonchalant so the old lady wouldn't think it was odd for him to want a paper chart.

Ruby smiled at the doctor. "Me too. I can't believe all the people reading on Kindles and iPads. Give me a good old-fashioned book any day."

Willcox gave Ruby a forced smile as she gathered up the three stacks of documents and secured each chart with a rubber band. "Here you go, Doctor."

"Thank you." He looked at her condescendingly. "And God bless you, Ruby."

Willcox and Burton hustled down to Burton's lab, where Willcox closed the door and leaned up against it. "Shit!" Willcox shouted. "I'm gonna call Maple and wish him happy retirement . . . in his little trailer park in the dark, dingy woods near Olympia. He can kiss his condo goodbye."

"Let it go, dude. All we need at this point is some drone from the disciplinary board saying we tried to bribe him. Call him up and see what's going on. It's probably some kind of mistake. I'm sure he has more seniority than anyone down there, and he can just take those files right back from Ms. Birmingham. But we need to be ready in case she really does show up Monday."

Willcox wiped the perspiration from his forehead. "You're right."

"What's next?"

"Well, first we need to make sure the charts aren't available for her to review, at least not until we have a chance to go through and sterilize them. Then we get the protoplasm we need for the patients over on

Brigantine. Then we need to go dormant for a while." Willcox was all business.

"What about the records?" Burton directed them back to the crisis at hand.

"Anyone who wants those records is gonna get them from the goddamn computer before we can get in there and fix them!" Willcox paused. "I don't think the computers will be working properly on Monday morning. C'mon. Let's go." He took off down the hall. "Have a nice weekend Ruby." Willcox smiled automatically as they ran past her.

"Why, thank you, Dr. Willcox. You too." Ruby turned back to the copy machine.

Willcox bounded down the stairs to the basement computer department, Burton close at his heels.

"What the hell do you know about computers?" Burton asked breathlessly.

"Not a fucking thing." Willcox answered as he lit a match and threw it into the big recycling bin right next to the server bank.

"What are you doing?" Burton yelled.

"Disabling the computer system so the chick from the disciplinary board can't get any of the records." Willcox looked on as the fire licked at the wires behind the bank of servers. "That should take care of it."

"Jesus Christ! You're out of your mind! They have everything backed up on the cloud, you know." Burton took the stairs two at a time as smoke began to build up behind him.

"All we need to do is distract them for a few days. This'll do the trick." Willcox pushed past Burton at the top of the stairwell. "We don't both leave at once." Willcox eyed the empty hallway. "I'm gonna head out and drop these off at the house before the St. Patrick's Day choir practice. I have a solo, you know." Willcox hugged the stack of records to his chest as the twosome hurried past Ruby's desk on their way out the main hospital entrance.

Willcox looked at his watch and took off, speeding past the arriving fire department brigade.

———

Trish arrived for her rendezvous with Ruby to find the place surrounded by fire trucks, their lights flashing. Ruby was huddled on the
edge of a group of hospital admin staff, several of whom were furiously
dialing their phones, obviously trying to deal with a potential patient
evacuation.

"What's going on?" Trish asked as she tried to size up the situation.

"Well, at first I assumed it was just a fire drill, but this one is the
real thing," Ruby responded. "And wait till I tell y'all what happened
today," Ruby whispered as she and Trish mingled away from the small
crowd. "Dr. Willcox and Dr. Burton came down to medical records
and asked for paper copies of the charts of Dallas and Gianelli and
someone named Read. Well, Lord knows, I know Dallas, and I remembered the name Gianelli from when y'all called me from Arizona. And
I don't know who Read is, but I have a hunch that she's another one of
Willcox's victims."

The two women followed the instructions of the firefighters and
talked as they moved farther from the yellow tape that was being
unfurled around the small hospital.

"I knew something was up when they asked for those charts, so
I decided to make copies for you girls too, but that's when the entire
computer system crashed and the fire alarm went off, so I didn't get
more than a couple of pages of the Read file printed before we had to
evacuate."

"So, where were Willcox and Burton while all this was going on?"
Trish asked.

"They took off like a couple of bats out of hell. First they ran to the
left, then before I knew it, they were running in the opposite direction.
That's when I heard Dr. Willcox telling Dr. Burton something about
heading out to drop the records off at his house before choir practice.
They just about flew past me on their way out to the main hospital
entrance."

"Are you sure they had the charts when you saw them running out
the door?"

"Oh yes. Willcox was clutching the records to his chest—each chart
was about three inches thick, so they were bulky and hard to carry."

"Okay. I need to figure out how to get into Willcox's place to get
those records."

"Can't you just wait until the computer comes back online?"

"Yeah, but I have a hunch they'll be editing the charts and deleting stuff. Those paper copies are probably the only ones with the original notes and reports."

"Well, getting into the Willcox place isn't going to be that easy," Ruby noted. "We had a church luncheon there a few months ago, and you have to go through a big security gate to even get onto the property."

"Good to know." Trish paused. "I'll drive by and check it out."

CHAPTER THIRTY-TWO

Oversized floral bouquets with huge green shamrocks framed the door to the sanctuary of the Friday Harbor New Faith Christian church where Trish stood on the steps, planning her strategy for getting onto the Willcox property. Ruby had been right. The security there was tight.

Just then, someone put their hands over Trish's eyes. "Hey, gorgeous. Guess who?"

Trish turned to Mike and smiled. "I wondered where you were. I didn't see you in church."

"Latecomers get seated in the back," he teased. "Hey, I hear your sabbatical is about up." He cleared his throat. "I, uh, I was wondering if you'd like to go on a picnic with me this afternoon. Mrs. Willcox suggested I bring you over to the pagoda at their place."

Willcox's house? Trish perked up. "That sounds lovely."

Trish wasn't sure which one of them was more excited. Mike was beaming with the victory of a possible romantic rendezvous turning out better than expected, and Trish was giving herself an inner high five for getting such easy access to Willcox's estate. She began plotting where in the house the records might be. Trish looked at the hopeful mechanic and wished for him that he'd soon find himself a nice heterosexual girl.

—

"Mrs. Willcox?" Mike hollered softly as he opened the door to the Willcox's kitchen.

"Ah, Mike! And Patsy, how nice to have you back. I have your picnic all ready, right here in this basket," BJ gushed.

"Oh my gosh. Mike didn't tell me you were making lunch for us. I'd have been happy to bring sandwiches if I'd have known." Trish looked at the festive picnic basket sitting on the kitchen countertop.

"Don't be silly. It's my pleasure. We like to keep our employees happy, don't we, Mike?" BJ grinned knowingly.

Trish detected a snippet of flirtation between BJ and the young mechanic. *Don't even go there.* She held back a smile. She watched BJ brush up against Mike as she handed him the basket. "Here you go. What a lovely day for a picnic. I'm going back to church to help with the children's shamrock face-painting party, and Dr. Willcox is on call this afternoon, so you two lovebirds have the grounds to yourselves. You be good, now." She turned to go.

"Thanks, Mrs. Willcox," the twosome said in unison.

—

Within minutes, Trish and Mike were settled into the pagoda on the Willcox's expansive front lawn overlooking the San Juan Channel.

Trish took a crystal wineglass from Mike's outstretched hand. He pulled out the cork and poured her a glass of white burgundy, spilling more than a little on the wooden pagoda deck.

"Be careful. That's expensive French wine!"

"No sweat. Willcox has a ridiculous wine cellar. You can have as much as you want. They'll never miss it."

"Aren't you having any?" she asked.

"Nah, I got me a beer. Black Butte Porter, my favorite."

Trish peered into the gingham-lined picnic basket. "So, you hungry?"

"You bet. Mrs. Willcox says there's a special vegetarian sandwich for you."

"Gee, how nice. Thanks."

"You want some chips? I saw some up in the kitchen."

Perfect opportunity to get inside the house alone. Trish started to get up. "I'll get them."

"No, you sit still. You girls are always waiting on us menfolk. I've seen you scurrying around at church. You just sit still and enjoy your sandwich. Is it okay?"

"It's actually really good," Trish answered, her mouth full of grilled eggplant and roasted peppers. She wondered what the slightly acidic taste was. Probably one of those new gourmet mustards.

Mike nearly skipped across the pavers toward the huge house. "I'll be right back with the chips."

Trish looked across the water to Shaw Island. She'd been planning a trip over to Parks Bay with Gigi this summer. With any luck, this investigation would be over soon, and the two of them could actually enjoy some Island time. It was hard not to drain the glass of wine—it was unbelievably good. She took out her phone and snapped a picture of the label. *One of the perks of the job.* She smiled.

Mike's amorous mood progressed as the afternoon wore on. Trish fended him off by suggesting they play a game of cards. She couldn't wait to get inside the house to look for the mysterious records.

No time like the present. She stood up and slung her backpack over her shoulder. "I need to use the restroom, and I saw a deck of cards on the kitchen counter. I'll grab them and bring them out."

Mike smiled drunkenly. "The bathroom is to the left of the kitchen, first door."

"Thanks." She hurried up the path and closed the kitchen door behind her. Looking around, she didn't see any obvious cameras, so she quickly surveyed the first floor. It took a matter of minutes to locate what was obviously Willcox's office, where the stack of records had been haphazardly thrown on the desk. *This guy never even considered that he'd get caught.* Trish grabbed her backpack and shoved the records inside. As she stood up, a wave of dizziness overtook her, and she grabbed the desk to steady herself. *It must be the wine.* She wasn't much of an afternoon drinker. Or maybe it was just a little touch of the flu. A couple of her fellow choir members had come down with something over the past week. She quickly made it back outside, squinting at the suddenly glaring sun just before it went behind a big gray cloud bank. The waves out on the strait were picking up. Maybe looking out over the stormy water was making her dizzy. She tried to focus on the pagoda several hundred yards away. Her skin began to prickle.

Mike was almost asleep in the last of the midday sun when Trish finally reached the picnic site. Maybe she'd get through this day without the inevitable discussion of the importance of maintaining her virginity until her wedding night. It should fly with this guy. After all, they'd met at church. Man, she felt queasy. She lay down on the floor and took some deep breaths. What on earth was wrong? Her heart began to race.

Mike rolled over and sat up. "You okay, Patsy? It's getting a little chilly out here. Maybe we should go back up to the house."

"I think I may be coming down with something." She tried to stand but was too weak. Something was definitely wrong. Her vision blurred. She judged the distance to the front of the house where she'd parked her car. But since she could hardly get up, it was unlikely that she could get herself into her car and back to Gigi, who'd know what to do. Her mouth went dry.

"Patsy, you're not looking too good."

"Yeah, I feel pretty lousy all of a sudden."

"Here, let me help you to the house." Mike picked her up and carried her across the lawn and into the family room, where he placed her gently on the couch.

Trish panicked. Maybe Mike wasn't as innocent as he appeared. Maybe he was another of Willcox's pawns. And no one knew where she was. "I need to use the bathroom again, if you don't mind." She tried to sit up again, with no luck. "I'm so hot. Can you help me get out of this sweatshirt?"

Mike complied, pulling the shirt slowly off her head. "You're drenched with sweat, Patsy. Your T-shirt's soaked. I think we should get you home."

"Good idea," Trish responded weakly. The room spun around her. She itched all over. She scratched the skin on her arms, where large welts and an unusual rash were beginning to appear.

Trish looked at the triple image of the Hugh Jackman look-alike hovering over her and dropped her head back on the couch. She began to have trouble breathing.

"I'll go get my truck."

The vibration of the front door slamming sent waves of pain through every fiber of Trish's body. "Hurry," she barely whispered. Her mouth was parched. She tried to focus on the horizon outside the french doors when everything suddenly went dark.

The next thing she knew, she was on a gurney, drifting in and out of consciousness. The short, bespectacled ambulance attendant leaned over. "Don't you worry, miss. We have some of the finest doctors in the Pacific Northwest here in Friday Harbor. Everything's going to be fine."

———

Dr. Hennesey closed the chart he'd been dictating and stuffed his tuna sandwich in his mouth. The attendant wheeled the gurney into the ER. Probably a ruptured appy.

"White female, approximately midthirties." The medic talked as he pushed the gurney. "Sudden onset of nausea and chills while at a picnic this afternoon. BP one hundred over forty, pulse one fifty, respirations forty-six. Temp one hundred two point six. Skin extremely diaphoretic. Patient in and out of consciousness."

"Name?" Mary-Alice, the nurse, scribbled notes frantically on the clipboard she had poised in her hand.

"Patsy. Patsy . . . something," Mike answered nervously. "Is she going to be okay?"

"Allergies?"

"Don't know."

Dr. Hennesey helped the medics transfer the patient to the table. He noted the grimace that spread across the young woman's face when he palpated her abdomen. "Who's on for surgery?"

"Dr. Willcox," Mary-Alice responded while removing Trish's clothes and covering her with a hospital gown.

"Shit," Hennesey said under his breath. "Better get him in here. She's got rebound tenderness. Probably an appendix."

"Did I hear my name?" Willcox dramatically threw open the privacy curtain. "I was just passing through on my way to afternoon rounds, and I couldn't help but overhear."

"Wanna take a look at her abdomen?"

Willcox pushed Trish's gown up, running his hands over her breasts as he did so. He pushed so hard that Trish opened her eyes, saw Willcox, and let out a blood-curdling "No!"

"Looks like you called this one right on the nose, Hank. I can't remember the last time I saw this bad a case of rebound tenderness. Let's get her to the OR. Call me when the blood arrives. I'll be in the doctors' lounge."

Mary-Alice flipped the call button and yelled into the speaker on the wall. "Sally, can you call the blood bank for me and get some blood sent up? This gal's going to the OR . . . And can you bring me a consent?" She slid the long needle into the patient's vein and hooked it to the clear tube running from the IV. "Hey, Dr. Hennesey?"

The doctor answered without looking up from the note he was writing. "Yes?"

Mary-Alice held the patient's arm, underside up to the light. "Can you come here for a minute?"

"What is it?"

"Look at this." Mary-Alice held the patient's arm up to the light so the doctor could see the streaky red rash covering the inside of her entire arm up to her armpit.

Dr. Hennesey gently took the arm and examined it. "Huh." He pulled open the top drawer of the exam table and took out a magnifying glass. "Jeez . . . I haven't seen anything like this since I was in the peace corps. Give me the loupes, would you?" The doctor held his hand outstretched, palm up, without taking his eyes off the patient's arm.

The nurse handed Dr. Hennesey a headset with built-in magnifying glasses hanging under a strong light. "Well, I'll be . . ."

Trish came to consciousness for a moment and groaned.

"It's okay, hon. You're gonna be just fine." Mary-Alice stroked the patient's hair. "What is it?" she whispered into the doctor's ear as she hovered over his shoulder anxiously. Trish's eyes rolled back in her head.

"Get me the ID hotline at the university. I think we may have us a case of Coral Fever, although I have no idea where or how this young lady may have contracted it . . . Miss . . . Miss . . . I'm Dr. Hennesey . . . Can you hear me?" He spoke loudly, as if yelling would somehow bring the patient out of her fog. "What's her name?"

"Patsy," prompted the nurse. "What's the ID hotline?"

"It's the infectious disease hotline at the University of Washington. The number's on the wall next to the dictation desk. They have a doctor available to answer questions twenty-four-seven. Have the ward clerk get them on the line immediately."

"Patsy, I'm Dr. Hennesey. You have a rather unusual rash. Have you been out of the country recently? Have you been to the tropics?"

Trish groaned in response.

"Patsy, can you hear me? Have you been on vacation lately?" Dr. Hennesey yelled.

Sally came into the room and handed the chart to her colleague. "What's all the fuss about?"

Mary-Alice held up Trish's arm. "Take a look at this rash."

"That's weird." Sally held Trish's arm and turned it over. As she put the arm down, she glanced at Trish's face, which was beginning to swell up. "Hey! I know this woman!"

Dr. Hennesey perked up. "You do?"

"Yeah, she's a friend of Tony Quarton's."

"Get Tony on the line and see if you can find out if she's been in the tropics lately," Hennesey said.

A voice came over the intercom. "University ID hotline on line three, Dr. Hennesey."

"I'll be right there." He turned to Sally. "Hurry up and call Tony. If this young lady has Coral Fever, time is of the essence."

"I'll see if I can track him down." She ran down the hall to get her purse and find Tony's cell phone number.

"This is Dr. Hank Hennesey calling from Friday Harbor General Hospital."

"This is Sam Taylor, department of epidemiology."

"I have a patient here. Young woman, mid to late thirties. She has a rash that's reminiscent of Coral Fever. And her symptoms are consistent. Rapid onset of nausea, dizziness, extremely diaphoretic, intermittent loss of consciousness. BP one hundred over forty and falling, pulse one fifty and rising. Temp one hundred two point four. Rapid respirations."

"Any history of international travel?"

"Don't know, but she has a tan, so I wouldn't be surprised."

"Jeez, I haven't seen a case of Coral Fever in the US in twenty years. It's typically seen only on a couple of isolated island chains in the Caribbean."

"Do you have any treatment recommendations?"

"Oh . . . oh, of course. Run the IV full bore. The virus causes a rapid depletion of interstitial fluids, and renal failure is a distinct possibility, although it doesn't make its way to the internal organs immediately. You need to run a battery of virology tests. Does the patient have abdominal pain yet?"

"Yep. It's pretty severe . . . the surgeon wants to get her to the OR, and I initially agreed, but when I saw the rash, I got to wondering."

"Nice call. And remember the virus attacks the nerves first. But it only takes eight hours for it to move to the other organs. Once the patient goes into renal failure, it's over."

"She's clearly in the early stages now. I've got her loaded up with morphine. The surgeon will just have to back off."

"Not too much morphine. You don't want to suppress her respirations. She needs to blow off that extra CO_2."

"Oh, you're right. Good point."

"Listen, why don't you start the viral studies. If the prelim looks like Coral Fever, I'll have some antitoxin flown up right away. I'd send it now, but it costs a fortune, and the department wants us to confirm diagnoses before we sign any of the tropical antitoxins out. Call me right back as soon as you know anything."

"Okay. Thanks, Sam."

"No problem. I'll be standing by."

—

Ruby looked up at the gathering clouds and hurried up the steps to the hospital on her way to the patients' St. Patrick's Day dinner. She waved at Sally, who was pacing back and forth at the nurses' desk. "At least the weather held for the children's face-painting party," Ruby hollered gaily as she pointed at the shimmering green shamrock on her left cheek.

"Hey, Ruby, can you stick around down here for a little while? We have an emergency, and we may need some stat labs run," Sally shouted.

"That's what I'm here for, darlin' . . . I'll take over the phones. You girls go tend to your patient now." Ruby took off her coat, dropped her purse in the bottom drawer of the desk, and took the phone from the young nurse.

"Thanks. I'm waiting for Tony Quarton to answer. I need to talk to him about a friend of his. She just came in. She's critical, and it's very important I speak to him."

"Okay, dear. You run along. I'll call you as soon as he comes on the line." Ruby shooed Sally back to her patient, wondering what Tony had to do with the situation in the ER.

"Thanks. Willcox wants to operate, but Dr. Hennesey has been on the phone with some bigwig at the university. They think she may have some weird virus."

"Lord-a-mercy, never a dull moment."

The line was full of static. "This is Tony Quarton."

"Hi, Tony. This is Ruby. Sally wants to talk to you."

Ruby held the phone to her ample bosom and spoke loudly into the intercom. "Tony's on line three."

"Tell him his friend, the one whose sailboat we visited, is in the hospital—I could have sworn her name is Trish, but her ID bracelet says Patsy, which might mean her real name is Patricia," Sally noted thoughtfully. "At any rate, she's in critical condition, and Dr. Hennesey wants to know if she's been out of the country. He thinks she has some rare tropical virus."

"Did you say Trish?"

"Yeah, I thought that was her name, but I must have remembered it wrong."

Ruby tried to calm her shaking hands. "Tony, Trish's here in the hospital. Dr. Hennesey thinks she may have some kind of tropical disease. Where are you, Tony?"

"I'm heading over to Bellingham to pick up some blood for a case in Friday Harbor. I'll be back as soon as I can. Don't let anybody touch her! Especially Willcox. You'd better call Camille. And hurry."

CHAPTER THIRTY-THREE

Camille finished clearing off the table covered with the registration forms the runners filled out for the St. Patrick's Day Dash. Grace waited impatiently as her mother filed the forms in a portable plastic file tote while Libby sat on the picnic table, talking on Camille's cell phone. Camille could overhear her comparing her race time with her friends from school.

"C'mon, you guys. Let's go!" Camille hollered.

"Mom, Casey's going to be here soon. Can we wait, please? And how about a Ben and Jerry's?"

Sam was on call. *No need to hurry home to an empty house.* "Okay, we can walk over there when Casey gets here." Camille sat on the deep grass in the park next to Green Lake, soaking up the early spring sunshine. "There's no telling how long this weather will last this time of year. We might as well enjoy it."

—

Willcox leaned over the counter, where Ruby sat dialing and redialing the phone. "Where the hell is the blood for the gal in room two?"

"I don't know, Dr. Willcox. It should be here any minute. They're flying it in from Bellingham."

Willcox turned to Sally. "Nurse! Is my patient prepped for surgery?"

"Not yet, Dr. Willcox . . . Uh, you might want to discuss her status with Dr. Hennesey."

"Where is he?"

"I think he's in the doctors' lounge on the computer, looking something up."

"What the hell is he doing in the lounge when we have a critically ill patient here who needs to get to the OR stat!" Willcox stormed off down the hall.

Burton and Vic waited anxiously outside the door to Trish's room.

"Get in here!" Burton hissed through clenched teeth. "And calm down!" He pulled Willcox into the room.

Vic sidled up to Trish's gurney and pulled up the covers. "Jesus Christ! What a waste!"

"Get away from her! What if one of the nurses come in while you're getting your jollies?" Willcox snapped.

The blonde opened her eyes ever so slightly and tried to talk. Nothing came out. She groped along the side rail and grabbed the nurse's call bell, which Willcox promptly removed from her grasp.

"She can still hear, can't she?" Vic asked.

"What difference does it make? She's not going anywhere." Willcox pulled Trish's gown up, pretending to examine her abdomen. "BJ's right. I'd say she's worth at least a few million. Maybe more. Look at the great shape she's in."

Dr. Hennesey rushed into the room with a color printout of a deep-purple rash. "Hey, take a look at the medial side of her arms, Andy. See the rash?" He glanced at Burton. "Hi, Carl." Hennesey walked over and gently turned Trish's arm to the light. "Look here." He held the image up to her arm. "I saw something like this when I was in the peace corps. It's called Coral Fever. I'll bet you a million bucks she's been in the tropics recently."

"Nonsense! This woman has a textbook case of appendicitis."

"I don't think so, Andy. I called the ID hotline at the U and talked to the guy on call. He says it's definitely Coral Fever."

"What the hell are you talking about?" Willcox spit.

"It's a tropical disease that's typically only seen in a handful of islands in the Caribbean."

Willcox glared at Hennesey. "We are not going to waste another minute discussing some ridiculous Caribbean disease. I'm taking her to surgery immediately. Let's go." He unhooked Trish from the wall oxygen and began pushing the gurney toward the door.

Hennesey held her chart to his chest and stood in the doorway. "Not so fast. She's not going to the OR unless she needs surgery."

Willcox roughly pushed the gurney into Dr. Hennesey. "I'm the surgeon, and I say she's going to the OR!"

Hennesey stood his ground. "No. We're going to wait for the tests to come back. I sent preliminary virology screens to the lab fifteen minutes ago."

Willcox glanced at Burton knowingly. "Carl, why don't you go down to the lab and see what's taking so long?"

"I'm on my way." Burton intentionally bumped into Hennesey as he left the room. "Vic, can I see you in the hall for a minute?"

———

Burton pushed Vic into an empty examining room. "Pull up your sleeve." Burton busied himself gathering the necessary equipment to draw Vic's blood.

"What the hell are you doing!" Vic clutched his arm to his side.

"I need some virus-free blood. Sit down."

Vic backed up until he ran into the wall. "Oh no you don't!"

"Give me your arm."

"I . . . I really hate needles."

"Hurry up, sit down, and give me your arm. That's an order."

Vic slumped into the chair and held his arm out and twisted his neck to look away. "Jesus Christ! What are you using? A shovel?"

"Sorry. I haven't drawn blood since I was an intern. Hold still. I almost have it." Burton dug the needle around as Vic squirmed. "Ha! Thar she blows!"

Vic held the gauze tightly against his skin in a futile attempt to stop the gushing blood. "Holy shit. I look like a goddamn junkie—look at this bruise."

Burton threw Vic a Snoopy Band-Aid and hurried out of the room, the tubes of warm blood tucked safely in the pocket of his lab coat.

—

Grace sat on Camille's lap, eating her ice-cream cone. "Can we feed the ducks now, before we leave? I don't need to eat the cone," she suggested.

"We can feed the ducks, but not a sugary cone. We need to go get some grapes. I just read that we should feed ducks grapes instead of bread."

Camille looked across the lawn at Libby still chattering away on Camille's cell phone, which she had on speaker between her and her friend Casey. "Enough, Libby! Let's go! I just told Gracie we can go get some grapes to feed the ducks, then we need to head home."

"Just a couple more minutes. We're trying to figure out who all's going to opening day of the Mariners. Dad can get tickets, can't he?"

"I think so, but I don't know how many." Camille grabbed her purse and took Grace by the hand, with Libby and Casey following closely, still talking intently into Camille's phone.

—

Ruby picked up the phone and crossed her fingers. "Friday Harbor General."

"Hi, Ruby. It's Tony. Any luck reaching Camille?"

"She's not answering her phone."

"Okay. Let's get ahold of Sam."

"How do we do that?" Ruby asked.

"Try the university."

"Gee, that's a big place, sugar. I don't know where to start."

"Just call the main switchboard."

"I'll try."

"And you keep trying Camille, right?"

"Every two minutes . . . Hey, Tony?"

"Yeah?"

"I don't think you should hurry back here too fast, hon. You've got the blood for Trish's surgery. As long as there's no blood, Willcox can't operate."

"Shit. This blood is for Trish?"

"Yep. Take your time."

"Roger. It looks like you're on your own, Ruby. Call me if you need anything."

"Okay, but what should I tell them about why you're taking so long?"

"Tell 'em I'm having engine trouble. Tell Sally I'm in that plane I told her about at dinner the other night. The one with the temperamental engine."

—

Willcox tried to reason with the pudgy doctor covering the ER. "We need to get the patient ready for surgery. Let me get her to the OR," he pleaded. "I won't start till I have the lab results . . . I promise."

"There's no reason to take her down there now. She can wait here."

Vic entered the room, casually rolling down his sleeve. "Uh, I'd be happy to get busy prepping her." He held up the surgical prep tray.

"Good idea, Vic. Go ahead." Willcox looked disapprovingly at Vic as he ripped the chick's gown off and began scrubbing her abdomen with Betadine solution. "Hey, dig these tan lines."

The patient groaned.

"I think she wants to say something." Dr. Hennesey bent forward close to listen.

—

Camille held her hand out. "Give me the phone. I need to call Dad."

Libby held up her forefinger at her mother. "I gotta go . . . Okay . . . You call Suzy. I'll call Darcy."

"Now, Libby."

"I really gotta go. My mom's getting mad." Libby hung up and answered the phone as it immediately rang.

"It's for you, Mom."

"Oh, thank God you're there, Camille. I've been trying to reach you all day. It's Ruby. I . . . I . . . Trish's in the hospital, darlin'. Doc Hennesey says she's in critical condition. I don't know what on earth to do, Camille."

Camille felt like a wave of fire was sweeping across her skin. "What hospital?" Camille braced herself for the answer she dreaded.

"Friday Harbor General, in the emergency room. They think she has some rare tropical virus. Either that or appendicitis."

Camille tried to slow her panicky breathing. "I'm on my way. Ruby?"

"Yes?"

"Whatever you do, don't let them know anything about Trish, especially her name. She's undercover, remember?"

Camille clicked off her phone, relieved that Willcox's calendar had him out on vacation until the next day. "C'mon, you guys! We gotta go. I've got to get up to Friday Harbor right now."

Camille dialed her cell phone while she waited for the girls to pile into the car.

"What's up?" Sam asked. He always sounded hurried when he was at work.

"We've got a big problem," Camille announced.

"What do you mean?"

"Trish's in the hospital up in Friday Harbor. I gotta go get her outta there."

"Was she in some kind of accident?"

"No." Camille raced past the historic Ivar's restaurant on her right. "They think she's got some weird virus. What an ER doc in Friday Harbor knows about tropical viruses, I'll never know, but—"

"Oh shit. I just got off the phone with a guy at Friday Harbor about a potential case of Coral Fever. The symptoms he reported to me were classic."

Camille felt her breathing become shallow. "What the hell is Coral Fever?"

"Some Caribbean virus that specifically attacks the brain and nervous system."

"Oh my God! I think that's the name of the virus that Irving told us Burton discovered the antitoxin for when he was at Harvard." She barely stopped at the five-way stop as she headed for the University Bridge.

"Now that you mention it, I do remember there being a big deal about some huge pharmaceutical grant having to do with Coral Fever when I was a med student."

The vibration of the grate on the drawbridge sent a shock up Camille's spine. She gripped the wheel. "Sam! They've poisoned Trish!"

"Calm down. If she's really got CF, it's curable. It only affects the nervous system at first, and it's reversible. I've got some antitoxin in my lab. But it needs to be given within eight hours of the onset of symptoms. I'll call Tony and get you a ride up."

She looked across Portage Bay, where she had lived with Dallas and Robin back in her nursing school days. UW Medical Center loomed on the northern shore. Sam was up in the research tower as they spoke. "Aren't you coming with me?"

"Can't. I'm on call, remember?"

"Can you meet me at the dock with the antitoxin, then?"

"Yep, I'll meet you in ten minutes."

"Hurry. I'll see you at Tony's."

Camille dropped the girls off at the top of the houseboat dock and sped off down the narrow street where the houseboaters parked their cars. She squealed into the parking lot on the southern shore of the lake and nearly ran over Sam, who was sitting on a weathered old bench in front of the tiny floatplane service.

"More trouble," he said as Camille slammed the car door.

"What now?"

"When I went to find the antitoxin, there was a vial of CF virus missing from the fridge."

"Don't you keep that stuff under pretty tight security?"

"Yeah. The shit's gonna hit the fan when I report this so soon on the heels of my key being missing."

"But you have the antitoxin, don't you?"

He held out a small wooden box.

"Thank God." Camille looked around. "Where's my pilot?"

"That's the other bad news."

Camille whipped her head back toward Sam. "What do you mean other bad news?"

"Apparently, Tony's stuck in Bellingham, waiting for blood for surgery at the hospital. He can't get away."

"So, where's Steve or Bart?"

"Not around. Steve is off on some kind of family thing, and Bart has the stomach flu."

Camille dropped her purse on the ground and burst into tears. "So, now what?"

Sam held up a set of keys. "Now, you get back in the saddle and ride the horse."

"What do you mean?"

"I mean that you can fly that plane down at the end of the dock as well as anyone. Tony told me it's the exact same kind of plane you used to fly before your accident. I suggest you get busy with the preflight checklist."

CHAPTER THIRTY-FOUR

Camille reluctantly took the keys from Sam's outstretched hand and slowly approached the red-and-white Cessna 206 floatplane. She shakily put a hand on the fuselage, as if she were trying to calm a skittish horse. She closed her eyes and focused.

"You can do it. You have to." Sam's voice sounded like he was talking down a long metallic tunnel.

Camille froze. If Dallas were here, he would tell her to face her fear head-on. She recalled the pep talk he had given her shortly after she had crashed the ostensibly out-of-gas floatplane into the icy Strait of Juan de Fuca twenty years earlier.

Camille felt as though she were looking down on herself from ten feet above as she climbed onto the float. The pilot's step up to the wing was exactly where she remembered. She put her left foot on it and climbed up so she could see into the fuel tank, located inside the wing. She would never trust a fuel gauge again. She looked in and sighed with relief at the sight of the shimmering fuel sloshing up close to the top of the tank. The pungent smell burned her nostrils.

She was back in the freezing water of the Strait of Juan de Fuca, struggling to put on a life vest as she spit out the mixture of salt water and slippery airplane fuel. A visual fuel check was a basic part of the preflight inspection. She had cursed herself for having been in such a hurry that day as she bobbed wildly in the whitecaps. Her eyes smarted so much, she never even saw the fisherman who had pulled up beside the turtled plane and rescued her from certain hypothermia.

She brought herself back to the present and waited for the smell of fuel to dissipate into the breezy afternoon, then screwed the top back onto the tank and double-checked it, just to be sure it was tight.

"You're doing great, hon."

Camille ignored her husband. She grabbed the safety handle firmly and climbed back down onto the float. The black numbers on the rear of the plane seemed bigger than life to Camille as she walked slowly around the plane, carefully checking the fuselage, floats, and rudders. She opened a cowling hatch, then pulled the oil and fuel drain to release a small amount of fuel to look for any sign of water or contamination. Maybe she could do this after all. She looked up at the sky, trying to gather her courage and slow her pulse down to somewhere below two hundred.

Sam looked like he was a million miles away, standing on the dock, his hands on his hips. "You okay, babe?"

Camille nodded, expressionless. Her dry mouth made it impossible for her to speak.

He walked over and opened the tiny door. "It's just like riding a bike. It'll come back to you. Go ahead. Get in." He strapped the box containing the antitoxin onto the passenger's seat.

As soon as Sam stepped out of the plane, Camille took a deep breath and climbed into the cockpit. The familiar dashboard brought back memories of lazy afternoon flights up through the San Juans. Her heart began to slow. Slightly.

"You'll be fine. Trish's lucky to have a friend like you." Sam closed the door. He kissed his fingers and pressed them against the window.

Trish. Camille looked at the box on the seat beside her. She closed her eyes and counted to ten. *Relax.* She put on the thick black headset and rolled her shoulders. It was all coming back to her. She gave Sam a thumbs-up and started the engine.

The grinding propeller shook the plane as Camille taxied away from the dock. *Don't look back,* she admonished herself and focused on her preflight routine. She shoved the throttle all the way in until the tachometer registered 1,700 rpm, then she pulled the pitch modulator all the way out. The engine whined in return. *So far, so good.* She ran through the entire cycle of preflight checks and then remembered she needed to announce her intended takeoff on the local radio frequency.

Camille clicked on the radio and rummaged around in the pouch located in the door. *Where the hell was the list of radio frequencies?* She searched her memory, trying to remember the frequency for Lake Union. The clock on the dash read 15:21. Time was of the essence. *Never mind.*

The engine temperature edged up toward green as Camille finished her run-up. *That's good enough for me,* she thought. *No time to baby the engine. It's now or never.* She scanned the sky, looking for air traffic. *I'll find the radio cheat sheet once I'm up,* she thought.

Camille held her breath, shoved the throttle straight in, and pulled up on the yoke as the plane bounced across the water, gaining speed. The propeller sprayed water across the salt-stained windshield as the houseboats lining the lake melted into one another. She shook her head and ordered herself to concentrate. Her skin tingled, and her breathing stopped. Suddenly, the water dropped out from under her. She was up. Butterflies dancing in her stomach dodged the sledgehammer that was erupting in her chest. She exhaled loudly and tried to grab her sanity back from the far reaches of her mind.

A man's voice came over the airwaves. "Aircraft on the water! Aircraft on the water!"

Camille slammed back into full consciousness when she heard a panicked voice yelling on the radio. "This is floatplane three-one-one Yankee Zulu. I'm on final approach for Lake Union. Do you acknowledge? Do you acknowledge?"

Camille's hands were frozen onto the yoke. Her eyes darted to the radio stack in the center of the control panel.

"Aircraft on the water, announce your intention!"

She tore her attention away from the jumble of lights and knobs that surrounded the radio and pulled back from full power to stabilize the plane, then flipped the lever to retract the flaps. If she stayed low, he could cruise right over her. He'd figure out what she was up to if she made it clear by adjusting her heading. She banked sharply to the left. As she looked up to locate him, she realized she was aiming straight for the Aurora Bridge.

"Aircraft departing Lake Union, this is November three-one-one Yankee Zulu. I am approaching for landing on Lake Union to the south. I am directly west of the Aurora Bridge! Acknowledge your intentions!"

No time to chat. Camille frantically pulled on the yoke to climb steeply up over the bridge. Not too fast. She knew if she climbed too steeply, she'd stall and drop like a rock. She could see the faces of people in cars staring out their windows in horror as she headed directly at the bridge. She looked at her altimeter. Shit.

Most people committed suicide by jumping *off* the 180-foot-high Aurora Bridge, not flying under it. Camille shoved the yoke in hard and reflexively ducked as she dove for a spot twenty feet below the center of the bridge. She held her breath, half expecting to hear the scraping of the plane's metal wings against the bridge struts. She exhaled.

Suddenly, the air exploded with angry black and gray forms as a flock of startled pigeons flushed down from under the spectacularly high bridge. There was a loud crack as one hit the windshield. She jumped. Another went through the prop, spraying a fine pink film across her line of sight. She cringed.

"Aircraft departing Lake Union, announce your intentions!"

"Shut the hell up!" she screamed and recoiled without taking her hands off the yoke. She turned off the radio and pulled up on the yoke to regain the altitude she'd lost during her dive, narrowly missing the blue-and-orange tower of the Fremont drawbridge directly below and to the west of the Aurora Bridge. She began a steady climb.

Camille tried to swallow away the feeling of nausea rapidly spreading from her stomach to her chest and down her arms and legs. The front of the plane was a mess. Feathers still clung to the spot of the bird strike. And blood mingled with the green and turquoise of bird innards streaked across the windshield.

She attempted to calm herself by focusing through the obfuscation to locate the canal that led from Lake Union to Puget Sound. As the wind wiped the gunk from the windshield, she could see a tugboat pushing a barge into the locks while a cadre of pleasure boats stood by, waiting for the green light to beckon them into the 780-foot-long lock. *Think of anything! The weather.* "Nice day for a sail," she said hoarsely, looking up at the clear sky.

Camille banked to the right and passed Shilshole Marina. The two thousand masts below her looked like a collection of silver toothpicks sparkling in the afternoon sun. She felt her heartbeat begin to slow. Out on the Sound, sailboats cut across the deep-blue water in the crisp wind. She modulated her breathing. Another beautiful Seattle spring day. She tried to swallow, but her mouth was still too dry.

A wisp of clouds hung over the snowcapped Olympic Mountains to the west. Camille held the yoke tightly to steady the plane as it buffeted around in the gradually increasing wind. She passed over a green-and-white ferry heading into the dock at the charming waterfront suburb of Edmonds.

Whidbey Island, the longest saltwater island in the contiguous United States, loomed up ahead. Was there a weather front moving in, or was it just a bit of afternoon haze accumulating over the large expanse of water to the west of Whidbey? Camille reached up and turned the radio back on, scanning for the ATIS channel at Paine Field, which could provide local weather conditions. No luck.

It's just a thin, gauzy haze, Camille reassured herself as she flew directly over the high clay cliffs on Whidbey Island. She noted with dismay the sailboats heeling deeply through the mounting whitecaps and stiffened as she considered the very real possibility that a weather front was moving in. She carefully reviewed the gauges and dials in front of her and concentrated on her compass heading.

To get to the San Juans, she had to go through the navy practice bombing range on the northwest side of Whidbey Island. *Where the hell was the radio cheat sheet?* She ran her hand underneath the pilot's seat and tried to remember the frequency to request permission to enter into naval airspace. She tried 118.1. "Whidbey Naval Air Station, this is November nine-two-seven Whiskey Juliet."

No response.

Shit. She flipped to 118.5. "This is November nine-two-seven Whiskey Juliet. Come in, Whidbey Naval Air Station."

Nothing. There was no way she was going to enter the restricted area without permission; jets flew through there at five hundred knots. She looked to her left. Port Townsend should be out there, across Admiralty Inlet. She squinted to see. "I must be farther south than I thought," she said out loud.

A serious female voice interrupted the silence.

"Aircraft calling Whidbey tower, this is Whidbey Naval Air Station."

Camille shouted "Yes!" and hit the button to transmit. "Whidbey Naval Air Station, this is November nine-two-seven Whiskey Juliet. I'm about five miles southeast of Port Townsend. Request status of restricted zone."

"Restricted areas are cold until sixteen hundred. Go ahead, Whiskey Juliet."

Camille looked at the clock. It was three forty-five. She had fifteen minutes: plenty of time.

She glanced to her right and to her left, then headed over Point Partridge, the jumping-off point for the twenty-mile crossing of the Strait of Juan de Fuca. The restricted zone was just ahead. Her compass heading was 350 degrees. She looked across the strait for Cattle Point, at the south end of San Juan Island, but all she could see was an opaque fog rolling in over the water.

You'll be fine. You've been through this a hundred times, she tried to convince herself, knowing full well that a late-afternoon fog was a fairly common but potentially deadly weather condition that should signal a prudent pilot to turn back or at least to follow the outline of the land below. She glanced at the clock and did some mental calculations. If she followed sight of land, rather than heading directly across the strait, it'd take her almost an hour to get there. She visualized Trish, lying on a cold hospital gurney. She had to make a run for it. She thought she could see the outline of San Juan Island through the scuzz. Maybe.

Camille narrowed her gaze and took a compass heading of 310 degrees. She headed directly for where Cattle Point should be and looked below as the rapidly increasing fog first hid, then revealed the surface of the water. "Where the hell is Smith Island?" she yelled. She knew it was smack-dab in the middle of the strait and directly in line with Cattle Point and that it should be visible by now. She also knew that if the fog completely covered the water, she would be unable to land.

Camille pushed the yoke in and dropped altitude to look for the tiny rock island. Feeling a bit dizzy, she tried to orient herself in the thin fog. Whitecaps kicked up on the water below. Camille shuddered as she remembered that this was almost exactly where she had tried to land that damn floatplane she thought had run out of fuel. She pulled the small plane back up. *If I don't see Smith Island soon, I'm outta here.* She hesitated as she looked back at the box on the seat beside her. A chill traveled through her body, and she gripped the yoke harder. She began to cry. "Goddamn it, where the hell are you?" she screamed toward where the island should be far below.

A dark form came into sight. She choked. *Now what?* She banked over lonely Smith Island sitting in the midst of the burgeoning storm and looked back into the nothingness behind her. She looked forward. Whiteness. That's it. She tried to loop back around and avoid vertigo, knowing that once she got dizzy, it was over. It was all she could do to focus on the artificial horizon indicator on her dash, trying to keep the airplane straight and level. She cried harder and wiped the hot tears from her face. Off in the distance, she heard the throaty roar of the navy jets. The clock read 16:07. There was no turning back. The walls of the tiny cockpit seemed to be physically closing in on her. Her chest tightened.

"Just steer three ten," she ordered herself out loud. *This shit's usually thickest over the widest expanse of water. It will clear as soon as I approach the Islands.* On the other hand, a mile of thin stuff looked exactly like a thick fog. If she flew into thick stuff, she was toast. Out of the corner of her eye, she noticed the pigeon blood wedging into the base of the windshield.

She reached down and turned on the radio, which seemed to be glowing, dreamlike, from its perch in the console. "San Juan Unicom, this is November nine-two-seven Whiskey Juliet."

Silence.

She concentrated, trying to squelch her rapidly rising nausea and locked her eyes onto the artificial horizon. "Don't let the fog fool you. Trust your instruments," she said aloud.

"San Juan Unicom, this is November nine-two-seven Whiskey Juliet."

Her head was spinning. *Don't look out the window.* She was completely disoriented.

"This is November nine-two-seven Whiskey Juliet calling for any San Juan traffic!"

She pulled up on the yoke. *Maybe it's clearer up above.* Was she really gaining altitude? She began to second-guess the altimeter. *You can never really trust your instruments,* she reminded herself as she remembered the faulty fuel gauge that had landed her in the icy strait.

"Whiskey Juliet, this is Alpha four-four-five Romeo Charlie at Lopez Airport."

A voice!

Camille took a deep breath. "Do you have weather for Cattle Point? Over."

"I've been trying to take off from Lopez for over an hour. It's pea soup up here. Suggest you head back to the mainland. Over."

"I just passed Smith Island. I think it'd be easier to continue on up. Do you know what it's like at Friday Harbor? Over."

"I came from there earlier, and I think it's still spotty. Why don't you try radio frequency 128.25? Someone up there can probably give you more current information. Over."

"Thanks. Over."

"Good luck, captain. Out."

Camille flipped to channel 128.25. "This is November nine-two-seven Whiskey Juliet calling San Juan Unicom." She swallowed hard and stared through the fog. Was it her imagination, or was there land down below her? Her hands were aching from gripping the yoke so tightly. She descended, just a little bit to see what was down there.

"This is November nine-two-seven Whiskey Juliet calling San Juan Unicom. Please help me!" she cried.

The water was coming at her fast. She pulled up on the yoke and screamed at the whiteness.

CHAPTER THIRTY-FIVE

The Colonel poured himself a shot of Wild Turkey and switched on the spare radio he kept in his "cockpit," the corner of his office where he retreated to regain his senses and exorcise the demons from his past.

"This is November nine-two-seven Whiskey Juliet calling San Juan Unicom. Please help me!" a woman's voice screamed.

He put down his drink and picked up his headset. "Whiskey Juliet, this is nine-eight-seven Delta Bravo. I read you."

"Oh, thank God!"

Women. What the hell were they doing flying airplanes anyway?

"What can I do for you, Whiskey Juliet? Over."

"Request weather for Friday Harbor." She was obviously trying to sound brave.

The Colonel looked out the window of his office that hovered over the socked-in marina. "Fog. Thick fog. Where are you, Whiskey Juliet? Over."

"I . . . I'm not sure. The fog came in pretty fast. Over."

"Are you instrument rated? Over."

"No."

Holy shit. This babe's in a world of hurt. "Okay. Stay calm, Whiskey Juliet. Keep your attention on your artificial horizon. Trust your instruments. No matter what."

"Okay." Her voice sounded weak.

"Now, turn on your transponder and flip to channel 850. That'll get you to Seattle Approach. They'll get a location on you, then they can vector you in. I'll stand by if you need me. Over."

"Thanks. Over and out."

The Colonel grabbed his tattered chart and drained his Wild Turkey, then poured himself another. He waited, knowing all too well what was going on up there in the cockpit of November nine-two-seven Whiskey Juliet. As always, the jungle hovered at the fringes of his consciousness.

———

Camille turned to channel 850. "Seattle Approach, this is November nine-two-seven Whiskey Juliet." God, she was dizzy.

"Seattle Approach. What can we do for you, Whiskey Juliet? Over."

"Request my location. It's pretty foggy up here. Over." She tried to sound professional.

"November nine-two-seven Whiskey Juliet. Are you declaring an emergency?"

Camille hesitated. An emergency declaration would guarantee her a greeting by a cadre of bureaucrats trailing reams of red tape. It'd take her an hour to complete the paperwork, if she was lucky. "No. No emergency. But I'd appreciate a vector to Friday Harbor."

"Squawk 4507 and ident. Stand by one. Over."

Camille dialed 4507 on her transponder and pushed Transmit, then focused her entire being onto the artificial horizon and waited.

"You're twelve miles southwest of San Juan Island, on a heading of 291 for Vancouver Island. Over."

Camille forgot to answer. She flipped back to 128.25. "This is November nine-two-seven Whiskey Juliet calling Delta Bravo. Are you there?"

"Okay, Whiskey Juliet. This is Delta Bravo. I heard your location. Are you trying to make Friday Harbor?"

"That's affirmative."

"What's your altitude?"

"Four hundred fifty feet." She cringed.

"Can you see water below you?"

"I think so."

"Good."

She squeezed her eyes opened and closed. "I'm getting lightheaded."

"Take a deep breath. You're gonna be just fine. Are you familiar with the area around here, Whiskey Juliet?"

"Yes, somewhat."

"Okay. You're heading for the Coastal Mountain Range on Vancouver Island. You need to turn about ninety degrees to make Friday Harbor. Are you on floats?"

"Affirmative."

"Good. Then make a slow turn to a heading of 010, and stay level."

"I'm going to climb to two thousand feet. I need to avoid the mountains."

"No, no. You're fine. Don't climb. You'll just get more disoriented. Take a heading of 010. And keep the water in sight. You'll cross over land at the south end of San Juan Island. There's nothing in that area that's all that high. If you stay at four hundred feet, you'll be okay."

Camille turned her full attention to her compass and banked slowly to the right. "Okay. I'm at 010. Over."

"Good. Now what's your altitude? Over."

"Four hundred twenty feet, but I'm losing the water."

"Hold your course. Descend to three hundred feet. You've got a ways to go. You're pretty far off course. Over."

"Oh God. I'm in a huge hurry. Please help me."

———

The Colonel stood up straight. At attention. He shook his head to clear out the images of the tropical jungle bombarding him. It had been monsoon season. He was flying blind in the sideways rain. Back in Nam, there had been no one to talk *him* in. He cringed as he relived the fiery plane crash that had precipitated his stay at the Hanoi Hilton.

His breaths came fast and furious. He opened the cupboard, took out a brown prescription bottle, and shook out twice the recommended dose of light-blue Valiums. He washed them down with a swig of Wild Turkey and waited for the familiar floating rush. He closed his eyes and envisioned the lost pilot hovering above Haro Strait in the murky fog. He'd get her down. He had to. Anything for a fellow pilot. Even if she was a woman.

Get her talking. Keep her mind off her troubles.

"Whiskey Juliet, you should see land in about five minutes. Why don't you land on False Bay and wait out the fog?"

"I can't. My friend's in the hospital. I have her medicine with me."

The Colonel grabbed the navigation dividers and placed them on his chart to measure how far the woman was from the west coast of San Juan Island. "Must be quite a friend," he said.

"The best."

He heard a muffled sob. *Change the subject.* "What's your name? Over." He spoke slowly, in an effort to calm her down.

"C-Camille. Over."

The Colonel put his feet up on the desk. "Camille. Nice name." *Camille?* He sat up, almost knocking his shot glass off the edge of the desk. "Camille what?"

"Delaney. Camille Delaney. Over."

Holy shit. He cradled his floating head in his hands. If someone had been there for him in Nam . . .

"How 'bout you? Over." Her voice went up a pitch.

Honor. Stand by your fellow pilot at all costs.

"Hello?"

He'd made himself a promise all those years in the camps. Loyalty.

"Delta Bravo?" She sounded forlorn. Her voice trailed off. "Come in?"

Honor. No amount of money could buy his loyalty. *Willcox could go fuck himself.* He clicked on his microphone. "My name's Ben. They called me Benny," he said softly.

———

Camille looked up and mouthed *thank you.* A long pause.

"Can you see anything down there yet? Over."

Camille scanned the whiteness below. "No."

"Hang tight, Whiskey Juliet. You should be coming over San Juan Island anytime now. Over."

"It's really mucky up here. And I'm so dizzy."

"Hold your heading. Shake it off. You can do it, Camille. Over."

"I can't."

"You can. You're almost here."

Camille squeezed the tears from her eyes.

"Keep on coming. You're doing great."

She began to hover outside herself.

"Camille? Camille? Are you there?"

"Yeah. I'm here . . . somewhere."

"Take a deep breath."

A form edged out of the fog below. "I see land!"

"Good."

He sounded so strong.

"What exactly do you see? Over."

"A house with . . . with a blue roof, on a bay. Over."

"Okay, that's the Blanchard place on False Bay. You need to take a heading of 085 and bank over Griffin Bay, then around Turn Island. Are you familiar with the landing pattern for Friday Harbor? Over."

"Yeah, but help me out. I'm really scared," Camille pleaded.

"It's okay. You're fine. I'm gonna stay with you. You just tell me what you see out there. What's your altitude? Over."

"Two hundred feet. I'm passing a farm with a yellow house and a red barn."

"You need to get a bit of altitude. You're too low. Go to three hundred fifty feet. Over."

"I'm afraid I can't see from three hundred fifty feet."

"You have to. You don't want to run into Mount Finlayson. Over."

"Okay. I'm climbing to three fifty. And I can barely make out Griffin Bay campground. Over."

"Stay on course until you are well over the water, then come to three thirty. Over."

"Okay."

"Now, do you see Turn Island? It'd be on your left. Over."

"I see it!"

"Okay, you're here. Come around Brown Island, and you'll have a straight shot at the harbor. Over."

"Thanks. Over."

"Remember, when you're at Turn Island, start notching your flaps down, ten degrees at a time. And slow to seventy knots. Over."

"I got it." Camille hesitantly hit the lever to notch down her flaps. The plane bounced toward the choppy harbor.

"Don't forget to announce your landing. Over."

"Thank you, Delta Bravo . . . Uh, I mean, Benny," she sobbed.

"It's my honor. Now announce your landing. And good luck with your friend in the hospital. This is Delta Bravo, over and out."

"Right. Friday Harbor traffic, this is November nine-two-seven Whiskey Juliet at Turn Island for a straight-in landing in Friday Harbor, on the water."

No response from traffic this time. Good. She held her breath and notched her flaps down another ten degrees. Then another. She half expected the plane to hit a wayward wave and flip. The wind caught her left wing and caused her right wing to dip dangerously close to the water. The right float skidded on the choppy sea. She increased power to stabilize the plane and fought with the yoke, trying to keep the airplane in a landing attitude.

Try again. She glared intently at the water directly in front of her as a blanket of spray mingled with the crusted pigeon blood on the windshield completely obliterated her vision. The little plane bounced violently across the water. She closed her eyes. The yoke shuddered in her hands. She bit her tongue as the plane hit a big wave, and her mouth filled with the metallic taste of blood. The searing pain jolted her back to reality. As the plane taxied across the harbor toward the dock, she fumbled with the latch on the tiny door. *Come on!*

She thrust her weight against the door and caught herself as she nearly fell out of the plane. She pulled herself back into the cramped cockpit and looked up to see the Friday Harbor Marina welcoming her through the mist. Her tears mingled with the salty air whipping across her face.

CHAPTER THIRTY-SIX

Burton burst into the hospital lab and shouted at the technician.

"I have another stat lab for you to run. I'll take over that one." Burton handed the tech the warm tube of blood. "What kind of test are you running here?"

The tech looked at Burton quizzically. "Uh, it's a viral prelim for some tropical virus. I'd like to keep an eye on it, if you don't mind. I've never done one of these before."

"It's just like every other viral. There's nothing of interest here." Burton nearly pushed the young man off his lab stool. "Here. This is a stat CBC." He handed the tech a tube of blood.

The tech took the tube and said, "Dr. Burton, you can't stop the machine in the middle of the run. It'll skew the results."

"Oh, right. Don't worry. I've got it under control, my boy. Now you get busy on that CBC."

Burton watched anxiously as the tech turned his attention to Vic's blood sample. As soon as the tech looked away, Burton quickly replaced Trish's blood with the second tube of Vic's. He waited a moment, pulled out his cell phone and stealthily dialed his own pager number. In thirty seconds, his pager went off. "Shit. I'm needed in the OR. Gotta go. You better take over here." He left the confused tech standing in the middle of the lab, watching him as he slammed the door on his way out.

—

Camille couldn't remember ever seeing the Colonel anywhere but in his office. And he never ever went out on the dock to help anyone tie up. Even in a storm. But for some reason, there he was, standing at the end of the dock, waving at her to throw him the line. Her cheeks were burning from having the cold salt water beating in her face as he pulled her in and cleated the line stretching from the plane to the dock.

"I've got it. You hurry along," he said in an almost friendly tone.

This was no time to psychoanalyze the Colonel. She handed him the stern line and took off, carefully throwing the bag containing the antitoxin over her shoulder as she ran. She looked back to see the Colonel standing at attention saluting her. *What on earth? Never mind! Hurry!*

Camille could barely make out Gigi paddling her kayak in the creeping mist. Camille yelled as she ran down the ramp to the decrepit wooden dock where the dinghies were stored upside down for the winter. "Gigi! Gigi!"

Gigi playfully waved the paddle back and forth in the air, nearly losing her balance in the choppy water. "Camille! Hi!" She paddled over to the dock.

Camille held her hand to Gigi to help steady the boat so she could disembark. "Gigi, I . . . um . . . there's . . ."

"Camille! What's wrong? You're drenched with sweat. Is everything okay?"

"Not exactly." Camille took Gigi's arm and looked her in the eye. "Trish's in the hospital."

"What do you mean the hospital? What hospital?"

"Friday Harbor. They think she has a tropical virus of some kind. It's called Coral Fever."

"That's absurd. Coral Fever is only found in the . . . Oh shit, that's the virus Burton worked on at Harvard, isn't it?"

"Yep." Camille helped Gigi pull the kayak up onto the dock. "Let's go! Sam gave me the antitoxin. It's in my bag."

Gigi took off for the parking lot. "We're gonna have to hitch a ride, you know."

"I was quite a hitchhiker in my day." Camille tried to lighten the moment with a half-hearted joke. "There's a cab, right over there!" She grabbed Gigi by the arm. "C'mon. I've never seen a cab parked up here." Camille opened the car door for her friend and slid in next to her.

The cabdriver turned around and said, "I understand you ladies need to get to the hospital right away."

Camille looked at Gigi, raised her eyebrows, and shrugged. She turned to the driver. "Please hurry!"

—

Willcox screamed at Mary-Alice for the umpteenth time that afternoon. "What the hell do you mean the plane carrying the blood has engine trouble?"

"Sally just got off the phone with him, and he's going as fast as he can."

"Get this patient to the OR *now*! I mean it. Any more stalling and I'll have your job!"

Mary-Alice disconnected Trish from the wall oxygen again. "Have it your way." She reconnected the tubing to the oxygen canister under the gurney and pushed Trish toward the orderly who had been watching *Wheel of Fortune* in the waiting room.

Ruby's voice came over the intercom. "The lab results are back on your patient, Mary-Alice."

"I'll be right there." She turned around to see Willcox hurling himself at the reception desk.

"Ah-ha! I told you so. The tests are all negative!" Willcox shouted at Hennesey, who had been pacing up and down in front of Trish's door. "There's no crazy Caribbean virus!"

Hennesey glared at Willcox. "That's impossible. There must have been some kind of lab error."

Willcox turned to the orderly. "We're going to the OR stat!" He pulled the gurney as the orderly ran to catch up with him.

"Let's go, Vic! Is anesthesia ready for us?"

"He will be by the time we get down there," Vic answered as they pushed through the heavy doors to the operating room.

"Get her set up. I'm going to go scrub!" Willcox directed.

Nurse Nancy Jo Williams stood behind the two doctors at the scrub sink. "Oh no, you don't. Hospital policy: no case goes forward until we have blood on the premises."

"Well, I'm overruling hospital policy. This is a life-or-death emergency."

Nurse Williams ignored him. "Dr. Willcox, this is not a life-threatening case. It's a routine appy. You'll wait for the blood."

"Try and stop me." Willcox pushed past her, his hands held up in front of him. "Let's go. Put her to sleep," he directed the anesthesiologist.

Nurse Williams held up her finger to the man standing next to the scrub sink, looking through the observation window into the OR. "I'll be just a minute," she hollered to him.

"We gotta talk," Vic whispered as soon as the nurse was out of earshot.

"Go scrub. We're getting started here." Willcox threw the surgical drape over the patient.

Nurse Williams stood across the table from the patient and moved the surgical instrument tray away from the table protectively. She repeated firmly, "You can't start the procedure without the blood."

Vic sidled up close to Willcox, who was shrieking, "Give me that tray! Now!"

"I happen to know that gentleman standing at the nurses' station out there. Name's Kimball, Dave Kimball. I knew him from the agency. The guy does only unusual homicides, euthanasia, stuff like that," Vic explained.

"What do you mean?"

"I mean that the nice redheaded gentleman standing at the window is an FBI agent," Vic whispered.

Willcox's face flushed. "Holy shit. An FBI agent here? In the hospital?"

"Try here, in the OR suite. I don't know about you, but I don't think it's a coincidence that he'd show up here just now."

"Get us a flight out. Immediately. We'll meet you at the dock."

Vic threw his surgical attire into the hamper next to the sink. "I'm on my way."

—

Camille and Gigi ran up the limestone steps to the little square hospital. "Where is she?" Gigi shouted at Ruby, who stood behind the ER triage desk, hopping from one foot to the other.

"You just missed her. She's in the OR. The lab results came back negative for that virus. Hurry!" Ruby pointed down the hallway.

"Let's go!" Gigi turned and took off running. "Which way to the OR?" she asked the bald man with the silver earring, who was hurrying out the door to the parking lot. "To your left."

Camille caught up with Gigi and pulled her to the right. "This way!"

They crashed through the double doors to the OR suite.

Nancy Jo Williams chased Camille, Gigi, and the FBI agent into the OR suite, where the patient lay asleep on the operating table. Willcox and Burton had disappeared. "You can't go in there!"

Gigi ignored the nurse and pushed past her as she reached into her pocket and pulled out a university badge with her picture prominently displayed on it. "UW Medical Center!" she announced authoritatively. "This patient is under quarantine."

Special Agent Kimball automatically grabbed his own badge and flashed it at the confused nurse and followed Gigi and Camille. "Special Agent Kimball, FBI."

Nurse Williams put her hands on her hips and shook her head.

Gigi pushed the surgical drapes off Trish and stroked her face. "Trish?"

The anesthesiologist stood up. "What the hell?"

Gigi flipped her badge at the confused doctor. "Dr. Georgia Roberts! University of Washington. This patient is in quarantine!"

"Special Agent Kimball, FBI." He stood, bewildered, in the middle of the OR. "Did you say *Trish*?" He hurried over to take a closer look at the anesthetized woman.

"You know her?" Camille asked as she undid the restraints and held Trish's hand.

He nodded. "We were at the Seattle Police Department together for a few years."

"Camille, get me the antitoxin, now." Gigi's strong voice reverberated around the operating room.

The agent stepped back out of the way.

"FBI?" Camille asked as she pulled the vial out of its carrying container and handed it to Gigi, who grabbed a syringe off the anesthesia cart, pulled the cap off with her teeth, and administered the serum through Trish's IV.

"Yeah. We've been investigating a doc up here. And the agency got a call from some infectious disease doctor at the U about a potential problem at the hospital, so I decided to show up and see if I could help." He turned to Nurse Williams. "Where's Willcox?"

"Beats me. I thought he was in here."

—

Vic banged on the door to the vacant floatplane service. He cupped his hands and looked through the glass window, then hit the wall in frustration. "Shit!" He turned to walk up the dock when his eye caught a red-and-white floatplane bobbing loosely on a long line at the end of the dock. He ran over to check it out. Other than a bunch of goop covering the windshield and the front of the plane, it looked pretty much flight ready. He looked down the dock expectantly.

The door of the plane was slightly ajar, and the keys were in the ignition. Vic jumped in and started the engine just as BJ Willcox ran up to the plane, her Louis Vuitton backpack thrown over her shoulder.

"Jump in." Vic reached out and grabbed her hand. She was more athletic than she looked. He smiled.

Ignoring the fog, he taxied out to the middle of the bay and grabbed the microphone. "This is"—he glanced up at the call letters—"November nine-two-seven Whiskey Juliet announcing takeoff from Friday Harbor to the east."

Without waiting for a reply, he hit the throttle and pulled up on the yoke.

As he floated up off the water, Vic looked down and smiled at Willcox and Burton standing alone on the end of the dock, watching the small plane disappear into the gray evening haze. He handed BJ a headset so they could talk over the sound of the engine.

"Did you transfer the money?" he asked as he stroked her hair.

"Yep. I had him refinance everything so he'd have enough liquidity for some property that doesn't even exist out in Tarrington and for a resort up here that exists only in his imagination. And I made him put everything else in my name. I told him we needed to be sure no one would know who was buying up all the land."

Vic shook his head and smiled.

"Then I emptied out all of the accounts when you called me from the OR."

"Including the funds he got from the big refi in Arizona?"

BJ raised an eyebrow. "All of it. Every last dollar. He's totally leveraged. I even took the pittance of equity out of Brigantine. Without the cash, he's dead-ass broke."

"By the way, it was brilliant of you not to submit the plans for the resort up here."

BJ smiled. "No reason to submit nonexistent plans."

"What? Are you shitting me?"

"Well, why waste my time drafting plans for something we knew we'd never build?"

"So, you kept those two and their crazy Caribbean medical pals running around doing transplants to raise money for land and projects that don't even exist?"

BJ shot him a big grin. "Pretty much. No need for retirement communities to provide them with organs when I had no intention of continuing this operation. It was getting way too risky. Time to take the money and run."

Vic let out a huge guffaw.

"They're idiots." BJ's disdain was palpable.

"I guess."

"You have no idea how stupid they are. They sent me to the mediation to settle the case. Delaney threatened to expose the Manor, and she knew about Gianelli."

Vic looked at her in astonishment. "And they still decided to go through with the blond chick? Wasn't that kind of asking for trouble?"

"All kinds of trouble." BJ grinned widely. "That's why I didn't bother to tell them what the lawyer knows. We would win either way—either they finished the harvest, in which case we get the money for the actual transplant, or they get shut down and arrested."

"How'd you know they'd get arrested?"

"Maybe because I called the Feds this morning to let them know what was going down. I had no idea there was already an agent on the case."

"So, what's going to happen to the surgical team? They're over on Brigantine, waiting for a bunch of organs that aren't ever going to show up."

"Actually, I called the red alert. Then I transferred money to them so they could take off before the house of cards falls apart."

"Red alert?"

"Yeah, we always knew that it would be possible for this plan to fall apart without much notice, so we practiced evacuating—from here to Canada, and from Arizona to Mexico."

"Why'd you give them money to relocate? Why not just let them go down for the crime?"

"I didn't want to give our two losers anyone else to blame in an effort to reduce their culpability. So, I wanted to be sure to get the team out of the country."

Vic looked at BJ with honest admiration. "I could totally see those two trying to pin the blame on a bunch of foreign docs."

BJ continued. "Or on us for that matter. It seemed the cleanest way to close this scheme out was to wire each team member half a million bucks to go get a new start. By now they should be cruising over the Canadian border. Then, from there, they can scatter wherever they want."

"Did anyone ever tell you you're a fucking genius?" Vic banked the plane to the north.

BJ threw back her head and laughed. "By the way, where in the hell are we going?"

"I got us a permit to land in Haida Gwaii. I thought we'd have to borrow a friend's plane, but as luck would have it, this one was just there for the taking. I'll let him know we're good."

"Haida Gwaii?"

"Yeah, there are something like four hundred islands up there. It's almost to Alaska. My buddy is a leader in the Haida Nation, kind of like the Native Americans of the Canadian coast."

BJ nodded approvingly. "Maybe we'll run into our friends from Grenada up there." She smiled.

"I doubt it. No one will ever find us. This is kinda my own special red-alert plan. We can hang out for a month or two. Then . . ."

"And then, the world is our oyster." BJ picked up Vic's hand and kissed it.

CHAPTER THIRTY-SEVEN

The open house at the Jackson Center for Women was in full swing. Balloons were tied to the fence surrounding the meadow, and there were two huge tables overflowing with tacos, taquitos, chimichangas, burritos, and nachos smothered with guacamole and sour cream. Fredrick and Randy, the owners of The Islander B&B, tended the tables while several women lounged on the grass and others sat at picnic tables, watching their children enthusiastically playing in the meadow. The Bloomfields, the young biotech entrepreneurs who had sold the property to Gloria, were perched on the porch swing, holding their newborn daughter.

Not surprisingly, Pella had shown up magically to help celebrate. Camille smiled lovingly at her mom, who was directing a cadre of screaming children as they took turns swinging at a colorful pinata at the end of a pole being held by Pella. Maybe this time she could talk her mom into coming back to Seattle and hanging out with the family for at least a weekend.

Around one of the long teak picnic tables, Sam, Gigi, Trish, Robin, Ruby, Tony, and his nurse friend, Sally, sat laughing and enjoying the picture-perfect day. Three scruffy rescue dogs chased the children as they careened between the pinata and the softball game that the Taylor girls and Kaitlin were officiating. Gloria was radiant.

A government-issue Chevy Tahoe pulled into the parking lot, and Special Agent Dave Kimball got out and waved.

Camille stood up and hollered, "Welcome to the Jackson Center! Grab a plate and c'mon over." She climbed up from the picnic table and went over to greet Dave and introduce him to Gloria. "Gloria, meet Dave Kimball, the friend of Trish's we told you about."

Gloria held out her hand to Special Agent Kimball. "It's an honor to meet you, Dave. And thank you for all you did for Trish. It sounds like it was a rather close call."

Dave was clearly charmed by the pixie-like woman. "Thank you, but Camille and Gigi actually had the situation entirely in hand. I just stumbled in at the last minute and provided another badge just to scare everyone." He smiled warmly.

Camille looked up at Dave. "Well, it never hurts to have an FBI badge to back up Gigi's UW Medical Center cafeteria pass."

"Cafeteria pass? You're kidding!" Dave laughed. "Nicely played."

Gloria looked at Dave, then Camille. "What does a cafeteria pass have to do with anything?"

"I gotta say I was mighty proud of my friend Doc Roberts standing in the middle of the operating room, flashing her cafeteria pass and ordering a quarantine." Camille laughed.

"Well, I'm telling ya, I thought we were all gonna be sent to some sanitarium and hermetically sealed in our rooms for life," Dave added.

Pella turned her pinata job over to Robin and joined Camille and Dave as he surveyed the buffet.

"So, any word on Willcox's whereabouts?" Pella asked.

"Oh yeah. We're all over him. He's toast. But not so much the wife and their sidekick." He shook his head.

"What about the medical team over on Brigantine?" Camille inquired.

"They took off without a trace. Willcox and Burton are going to take the fall alone on this one."

Pella smiled. "Ha! They can't plead out by offering testimony against their coconspirators if no one can find them."

"You sound like some kind of criminal lawyer." Dave was clearly impressed.

"My mom's an international asylum lawyer," Camille offered proudly, and then she looked at her mom. "But when you were teaching at law school, didn't you teach criminal law?"

"I did," Pella reminisced. "I hated having to teach about the conspiracy theory."

The whole table was silent as she began to lecture to no one in particular.

"Look around you." She pointed at the formerly incarcerated mothers sitting on picnic tables and blankets around the lawn. "I bet a fair percentage of these women ended up in prison because their significant others turned them in, in exchange for a lighter sentence."

"What?" Camille nearly shouted.

Dave nodded. "Happens all the time."

"Exactly." Pella nodded. "And not that I want a bunch of guilty folks to get away with murder, but I kinda like that Willcox and Burton can't finger someone else so they can avoid, or at least reduce, their prison time."

"Well, I'm not sure they would be so successful at a plea on this one," Dave explained. "The prosecutor just added an arson felony to the attempted murder charge. Those two just about burned down a hospital full of patients."

Camille caught her breath. "It's a miracle they didn't get caught sooner. I wonder who really masterminded their operation. They seem too stupid to have cooked up this scheme on their own. Who starts a fire in a computer room at a hospital and thinks they'll get away with it?"

"Someone panicking, most likely," Dave mused.

Trish came up and playfully stole a nacho from the agent's plate. "So, were we right about their plan to build retirement places in remote areas where they could import healthy older folks who would be potential organ donors?"

"As far as we can tell, that looked to be their plan. And what set their operation apart from others who sell organs on the red market was that they actually built transplant centers so they got the money on both ends of the deal."

"Red market?" Camille asked.

"Yeah, that's what we call the illegal organ trade."

"I had no idea that selling organs was actually a thing," Camille said slowly.

"Unfortunately, it's definitely a thing. But it's usually done by kidnapping people and harvesting their organs." Dave shook his head. "This operation was pretty damn bold."

"Is it common in the US?" Trish asked. "I always thought of this as a third-world back-alley type of thing."

"Not particularly common here but worldwide something like ten to twenty percent of all organs transplanted are illegally purchased."

Trish and Camille looked at each other and made a face.

"I've asked around, and none of my colleagues, even in other countries, have ever heard of the same guy removing the organs during surgery and then transplanting them in his own surgicenter. This guy got paid for the original surgery, the organs, and then the transplant surgery and recovery fees."

"Have you been over to Brigantine Island yet?"

"Oh yeah. They had quite an operation over there, designed and built by his architect wife. State-of-the-art transplant setup—they did hearts, livers, lungs, kidneys. No eyes or skin but most everything else."

Camille looked at Trish. "Looks like your pals from Grenada were pretty good docs. Pity they didn't use their skills for legal surgery."

"Well, keep us posted on when you arrest them."

"Will do—and check this out. The insurance company that paid the Jackson claim filed a civil suit against Willcox himself to recover all the money they paid to you guys."

"And?" Camille asked.

Dave smiled. "Well, it seems Willcox had just closed on a refi of his Arizona property and on his property next door here, and Brigantine Island was totally leveraged. He was trying to buy this place and build it out." Dave swept his arm to encompass the area where they all stood. "And he'd gotten prepaid for the next round of organ transplants." He winced, looking at Trish. "Which thankfully never panned out. So, he had around thirty million cash in the bank." He laughed. "Turns out his wife transferred all of the money to an offshore account and took off with Willcox's assistant." He laughed again. "You can't make this shit up."

"Oh my God. What d'ya bet the wife was the brains of the operation? She set them up and took off with all the money."

"Women." Pella nodded. "They get the job done."

"And," Dave added, "I seriously doubt the insurance company will ever get back a dime. And they declined to pay the defense lawyer, Lincoln. Said he should have discovered that Willcox was a criminal risk."

"Perfect." Camille smiled and took her mother by the arm. She always felt safe when her mom was around. They walked toward the rocky lookout over Haro Strait.

"So . . ." Pella squeezed Camille's hand. "You did it."

Camille nodded.

"How do you feel?"

"I feel like I did the right thing."

"And the system? Did it work?"

Camille turned and looked at all the women scattered across the lawn. Several were holding young children, and the older kids were hungrily pounding down platefuls of Mexican fiesta food. Gloria was flitting around, pouring lemonade from a huge clay pitcher while Robin followed behind with a bag of home-baked cookies.

"Actually, things really couldn't have turned out any better, given the circumstances." Camille kissed her mother on the cheek. "You gonna say you told me so?"

Pella shook her head. "Nope, I'm going to say you'd better enjoy yourself today because there are more families out there like Gloria and Robin who need you."

Camille and her mother locked eyes.

—

It was late August in the tiny resort town of Ogunquit on the coast of Maine, and there was just a touch of fall in the air. The pastor of the New Life Christian Church stood on the left side of the doorway to the picturesque steepled white chapel overlooking the rugged shoreline. His well-worn black overcoat barely protected him from the chilly breeze.

"Brother Donahue, my warmest wishes for you and yours to have a blessed and fulfilling week." The pastor shook hands with the wizened old fisherman and his wife.

"And to you, Pastor." The wife smiled and moved along to make way for the next parishioner.

A hearty barrel-chested man patted the pastor on the back. "Hey, you'll never guess what happened!"

"Try me." The pastor's eyes twinkled.

"The city council just got a zoning request from some outfit that builds retirement communities. They've made an offer on the dilapidated old Paulson place out on Rocky Bluff. Seems the only contingency is whether we'll grant them a permit to build a facility to house two hundred residents. We could really use a large-scale employer like that around here. And Harvey over at the bank has already approved their loan application—they don't have much in the way of collateral, but the borrower is a surgeon. He just got admitting privileges, so they'll be good for the money."

"They almost gave away the property—it's been for sale for over four years," the fisherman said.

"It's like the answer to a prayer."

"*Like* an answer to a prayer?" the pastor said.

"Okay, Rev. Ya got me there."

"Well, I don't imagine they'll have to wait too long to hear back from the council, will they?"

"Nope. I've called a special meeting for Tuesday night."

"God bless, Brother Goodman."

On the right side of the doorway stood a tall, handsome man looking oddly out of place in an elegant cashmere overcoat. He opened his arms to accept the embrace of the boyish-looking man who had clearly sought him out.

The young man laughed and shook his head. "I can't thank you enough, Dr. Woodward. I know you were hoping to have some peace and quiet up here on the coast, but I'm convinced you were divinely guided here to help us out. I don't know what we would have done without your generous offer to help out over at the hospital."

"Well, how could I resist the not-so-gentle arm-twisting of the youngest and brightest hospital administrator in New England?"

The last parishioner in line was a small man with mousy-brown hair combed over his bald head from his right ear to his left. "Aaron?

Aaron!" His deep voice boomed across the foyer, and everyone turned to look. "Aaron Woodward? I don't believe it!"

The tall man with gray-and-blond-streaked hair looked at the skinny man with the unusually deep voice winding his way noisily through the crowd to the front of the line. "Connor? Connor Benson? What on earth are you doing here?"

"The missus and I just bought a retirement place a mile up the coast. Out on Kingswood Point. I can't believe it. I haven't seen you since, what, 1980?"

Dr. Woodward looked at the young hospital administrator standing next to him and shook his head in mock disbelief. "I don't believe it, Timothy. This must be your lucky day. I'm proud to introduce you to Dr. Connor Benson, Harvard class of 1993. And, I might add, the best pathologist in New York City." He leaned closer and whispered to the ambitious administrator, "I don't think Benson is any more cut out for retirement than I am. I'll bet you can get him up and running before you even break ground for the new wing."

—

The young administrator breathed in the chilly marine air and smiled as he followed the last of the parishioners to the parking lot, leaving the pastor alone on the church steps, deep in conversation with the two doctors. None of them noticed the three black Chevy Tahoes pulling up and the cadre of agents in the unmistakable FBI windbreakers bounding up the church steps two at a time.

ABOUT THE AUTHOR

Amanda DuBois started her career as a registered nurse before becoming a lawyer. She has practiced in the areas of medical malpractice and family law. She is the founder and managing partner of the DuBois Cary Law Group in Seattle, Washington, where she is actively engaged in litigation. She also founded Civil Survival Project, an organization that teaches advocacy skills to formerly incarcerated individuals. Amanda serves on several boards that support social justice and women's issues. Her most recent passion is funding her Full Circle Scholarship, which provides tuition assistance at her alma mater, Seattle University School of Law. This scholarship is specifically granted to students whose lives have been impacted by the criminal legal system. All of the author's profits from your book purchase will be donated to the Full Circle Scholarship and social justice organizations. Amanda's goal as an author is twofold: to introduce readers to her lead character, Camille Delaney, and Camille's quest for justice, while at the same time inviting readers to take an interest in how we define justice in our legal system.

Amanda and her husband split their time between the San Juan Islands in Washington State and Todos Santos, Mexico. They have two adult daughters and two beautiful grandchildren. This is the first novel in the Camille Delaney Mystery series.